3 8043 27090592 6

D1344606

STIGMATA

COLIN FALCONER

CORVUS

Published in trade paperback in Great Britain in 2012 by Corvus,
an imprint of Atlantic Books Ltd.

10 9 8 7 6 5 4 3 2 1

A CIP catalogue record for this book is available from
the British Library.

Trade paperback ISBN: 978 0 85789 112 9
E-book ISBN: 978 0 85789 118 1

Printed in Great Britain by the MPG Books Group

Corvus
An imprint of Atlantic Books Ltd
Ormond House
26–27 Boswell Street
London
WC1N 3JZ

www.corvus-books.co.uk

This book is for Norman and Janet. Who always had a bed and a whisky for their wayward brother after his missteps. Thank you.

PROLOGUE

Five leagues west of Acre,
year of Our Lord, 1205

HOPE.

A man cannot live without hope, Philip thought. It is the one thing that makes death appear unattractive. My wife is my hope now, God and honour have played me for a fool.

They sailed with the tide on Sunday, the Lord's Day. It would be his last glimpse of Acre and the Holy Land where Jesus had walked, and his eyes did not linger. He was leaving his best friend in a shallow grave on the hillside just outside the castle walls; the other liegemen who had travelled with him had no Christian burial at all, except that offered by the vultures and desert hyenas.

Mist clung to the water, which was flat and sluggish as oil.

He could still picture her face. *Alezaïs, my sweet, my darling.*

One of the sailors was looking at him. 'What was that you said?'

Philip glared at him. 'Were you addressing me?'

The man touched his forelock. 'Sorry, seigneur. You took me by surprise. You said a woman's name.'

'Yes, my wife,' he said. 'I imagined her here.'

It was an insolence, of course, for a common sailor to ask such a question of someone of his birth. But he wanted to talk, and telling this man what was on his mind seemed better than wandering around the deck, muttering to himself. 'My uncle arranged the match. I was his ward. My father had died in a joust when I was ten years old. When I was eighteen he gave me land and a fortified manor and a wife. She was fifteen years old and she wore her veil right through the churching. My cousins told me she had a wart on the end of her nose the size of a walnut, so when she drew back the veil I could not believe the sweet face that looked back at me. I have been smitten ever since. Some think me unmanly but she is the only woman I have ever known.'

'My lord, I should not think you unmanly, I should think you fortunate. Not many men would attest to loving their wives. It is a rare conjunction of a man's stars.'

'I swear, if you saw her, you would despise me for leaving her to come to this wasteland.'

The man crossed himself and turned away at this blasphemy.

Some friars gathered on the deck under a banner of the holy cross and began to sing a hymn. They believed that through prayer and piety they could banish the Mohammedan from the Holy Land. He supposed he had believed it too, once, but he did not believe in miracles any more.

He leaned on the wooden rail, and when he closed his eyes it was the stone parapet of his castle at Troyes. The women were down at the river for the great wash, the bed linens spread out on rocks to bleach them in the sun. The gate to the castle was open and the masons were repairing broken corbels and attending to crumbling mortar. Below him the courtyard was full of servants and horses, the groomsmen were mucking out the stables with buckets and black streams of water poured across the courtyard carrying bits of black straw. Chickens clucked and ranged on the cobblestones and the air smelled of horse and wet manure and spring.

Not long now. It waited just beyond the bright horizon, and he had the breeze at his back. Soon he would be returned to his wife and his land, where he could rest and repair the wounds to his soul.

The mist burned away and it was as if he was roasting under a brazier. He sought shade on the deck under a narrow sail. His face had turned nut-brown after twelve months in Outremer, but there were patches of livid pink where the skin had peeled in strips. He longed for rain and dew-wet mornings.

He closed his eyes, and in his reverie he stepped over a serving boy slumped asleep against the wall near the hearth as a scullion staggered towards him struggling with a massive half-barrel of water he had drawn from the well. He plunged his face into it and drank deep, then breathed in the morning smell of the castle: burned wax, sweat, cold food, old ale.

There was a fire in the great hearth. He ducked behind a stone pillar to observe his wife at supper, unseen. She was accompanied by her ladies and her chaplain, and pages hurried in carrying finger bowls so she might wash the grease from her fingers. At her signal her minstrels came to the table to finish the remains of the supper, then grace was sung and the trestles were set aside.

She withdrew to take her ease by the window, her ladies around her on benches or seated on cushions on the floor. He watched a small crease form between her eyebrows as she stared from the window to the uncoiled river and the grey-slated roofs of the manor. She wore a close-fitting gown of blue velvet, the colour of her eyes. Her ladies teased her to join in their game of knucklebones, and she squealed like a child each time she won.

He had tormented himself each day in Outremer: *I wonder if she has taken a lover, some troubadour, some envious duke. Has she thought of me as often as I have thought of her?*

*

No sooner were they out of sight of land than they were becalmed. They spent four days and nights baking under the sun and shivering with cold at night. Another of God's little jokes. He wondered now if he would ever get home.

As their ship wallowed in the calm, five hundred men sweated and cursed and moaned. The stench of animals and soldiers in the dead air was suffocating. Sailors whistled for the wind, a low moaning sound that he thought would send him mad. He crouched miserably on the deck and thought about his wife and what he would say to her when finally he saw her again.

It had only been a year but it felt like a hundred. He had been spurred to display his fidelity to God, give Him the duty of his service. He was such a different man then; he thought he would be fighting to restore Jerusalem. Instead he was hostage to endless bitter disputes between barons and Templars over who runs what, sent to fight a few lonely skirmishes in the desert that achieved nothing except the death of a few good men.

He could taste the salt on his cracked lips. Every time he tried to moisten them with his tongue they cracked and bled. It was worse than being back in the desert. The sun was relentless. There was shade below decks but he would not venture down there because of the heat and the stench and the rats.

Wait for me, my heart. I am coming home.

PART ONE

I

Toulouse, 1205

GOD CHOSE FABRICIA BÉRENGER in the middle of Toulouse during a lightning storm. With one thunderous touch of his finger, he sent her reeling.

The day had been mild, unseasonably so. The storm appeared suddenly, ink-black clouds broiling up the sky in the north, just as the bells of Saint-Étienne were ringing for vespers. A blast of icy wind hit her like a slap as she ran across the marketplace, a blow so violent and unexpected that it almost knocked her off her feet.

The rain exploded on the cobbles like a barrage of copper nails and in moments her skirts were soaked through. She had no warning of the jagged spark that arced from the heavens. There was a moment of blinding illumination and then nothing.

The lightning strike, someone later said, sounded as if the sky itself had rent in two pieces. But Fabricia did not hear it; she was already lying senseless on the ground.

Even her father, on the other side of the square, tumbled on to his haunches from the shock of it as the cobblestones trembled underneath him. They said every dog in Toulouse went mad that day.

Anselm Bérenger waited for either God or the Devil himself to appear in the sky. But neither of these things happened. After a few moments, when his wits returned, he reached for the support of a stone pillar and pulled himself to his feet. It was then he saw his only daughter lying in the middle of the flooded square and thought she must be dead.

He let out a wail, stumbled across the cobblestones and rolled her over on to her back, screaming her name. She was white. Her eyes were half-lidded, and rolled back in her head, giving her the look of a demon. He scooped her up in his arms and ran blindly with her through the streets, cursing aloud the name of God as he ran, for there was no doubt in his mind who had murdered her. The sky shimmered and flashed and the sound of the thunder drowned out his agony and his blasphemies.

*

When Fabricia opened her eyes, there were three people in the room, and only one of them was smiling. Her mother and father crowded above her, Anselm's face twisted in a rictus of dread.

'She's alive!' he gasped.

'I told you she would be all right,' her mother said.

'She was dead, Elionor! It's a miracle. God has spared us! He has given my little girl back to me.'

Fabricia shuddered with cold. 'Fetch another blanket,' she heard her mother say. 'She's frozen. How long did you leave her lying there in the rain, you old goat?'

Fabricia rolled on to her side, wrapping her arms around herself and curling her knees up to her chest. Her skin felt as cold as marble. She was naked. How did that happen? She tried to remember. She was more puzzled by the woman standing in the corner. She wore a long blue gown, with a hood, and her skin was made luminous by the guttering candles. She knew she had seen her before, somewhere.

'*Mon petit chou.* Are you all right? Say something.'

'Who's that?' Fabricia said.

'She can speak,' Anselm said. 'Thank God!'

Elionor wiped tears from her face. She clambered on to the bed and spooned her daughter into her breasts. Fabricia felt her warm breath on her neck.

'Who are you?' Fabricia said to the emptiness in the corner of the room.

Anselm looked around. For the second time that day he was very, very afraid. 'Fabricia?' he said, 'who are you talking to?'

'What happened, Papa?'

'Don't you remember? A thunderbolt struck you as you were crossing the square before Saint-Étienne.'

'I should never have sent her,' Elionor sobbed. 'I should have brought your supper myself.'

14

'I don't remember,' Fabricia said.

'I thought we had lost you!'

'You are chosen,' the woman in blue told her.

'But why choose me?'

Her mother sat up and shook her. 'Fabricia? Who are you talking to?'

'There's no one,' Anselm said. He took her face in both his hands, forcing her to look at him. 'Fabricia? What is it? Who is here, who are you talking to?' His eyes went wide. 'Something has happened to her,' he said to his wife. 'She has gone mad.'

Elionor eased her daughter's head back on to the pillow and covered her to the chin with bearskins. She smoothed back her hair and kissed her forehead. 'Just rest now,' she whispered. Then she cuffed her husband smartly around the head. 'She's not mad! What are you talking about? She just needs to sleep. Can't you see that?'

There was a fire lit in the hearth and Fabricia watched them retreat there, huddling together on two stools. Anselm pulled off his wet smock and hung it to dry, steaming, in front of the flames. He and Elionor whispered to each other, but she could not make out what they were saying.

The woman in blue had vanished. 'Now I remember who you are,' she said aloud. The remembrance made her wonder if she really was still living. She placed a hand between her breasts and felt for her own heartbeat; it was different, somehow, every now and then it gave a little kick, like a baby in a womb.

The woman was not real, she decided. It was just the shock of having death brush past so close, a fever of the brain. She would sleep now and in the morning it would all be forgotten.

II

Pèire de Fargon was a stoop-shouldered giant just a year or two older than Fabricia. He reminded her of one of the sculptures her father made for the capitals in the church, fashioned over-large for the sake of effect. He had chestnut hair that fell over his dark brown eyes, one wider and darker than the other. He could not see as well out of it, which made his skill with hammer and chisel the more remarkable.

He stood over her, his face creased with concern. Anselm stood at his shoulder.

'Pèire? What are you doing here?' she said.

He seemed stricken. Her father nudged him hard with his shoulder. 'Your father told me what happened,' he said. 'I was worried about you.'

'It was nothing. I'm all right.' She tried to get out of bed but she could not. Her legs felt too weak to support her. Her mother pushed the two men aside and made her lie down again. 'I told these two oafs not to disturb you.'

Fabricia remembered what had happened the last evening, how she had been crossing the square and then the next thing she had woken soaking wet here in her bed, with her mother and father standing over her. Not a dream then.

Elionor shooed the two men out of the door, scolding them for disturbing her daughter's rest. She brought her a hunk of bread and some broth from the stove for her breakfast. 'You have to rest today,' she said.

Fabricia discovered she was ravenously hungry and tore at the bread with her teeth. Her mother sat and watched her, as if she could not believe Fabricia was really there. 'What was Pèire doing here?' Fabricia asked her as she drank the broth.

'You know he likes you,' Elionor said. 'Your father wants to arrange the match for you.'

Fabricia managed a weak smile. At that moment marriage to Pèire seemed just as real to her as the lady in blue. The only thing to do right now was to forget about both of them, and pretend she had imagined them.

'There is a fair in the square tomorrow, for St Jude's day. If you are feeling stronger, Pèire is going to take you.'

'I should like that,' she said. She meant of course that she would like to go to the fair; how she felt about Pèire was a different matter.

III

THE BELLS OF Saint-Étienne rang for terce, muffled by the mist
that hung white and heavy on the river. The sun would be hot
today, and already the air was thick and damp. Steam rose from the
cobblestones. The big storm had clogged all the drains and left the
city stinking, the mud in the marketplace thick as porridge.

As on any feast day the streets and squares were full of people.
The toll gates were busy, and there was scarcely space in the market
square for all the ox and donkey carts that had been brought into the
town. She smelled dung and the hawkers' pies. The main square was
clamorous from the sounds of the bear-baiting, and the raucous
songs of the minstrels.

They stopped to listen to one of the jongleurs. He had taken out
his hurdy-gurdy from a sheath on his back and started to play.

Look on this rose, O Rose, and looking laugh on me,
And in thy laughter's ring the nightingale shall sing.
Take thou this rose, O Rose, since Love's own flower it is,
And by that rose, thy lover captive is.

The way the minstrel played it, with such a look of comical
suffering on his face, he soon drew a small crowd around him,
laughing and shouting. He started to play again, not a song this time
but a monologue that he accompanied with dramatic stanzas on his
hurdy-gurdy.

I shall teach gallants the true way to love.
If they follow my lessons they shall soon make numerous conquests.
If you want a woman who will be a credit to your name,
then at the first hint of rebellion, adopt a threatening tone.

If she dares answer back, then your reply should be a punch in the
    nose.
If she should be nasty to you, be even nastier back,
and soon she will obey you implicitly.

There was laughter from the audience all through this, and wild applause at the end. When he had finished he sent around a monkey holding a small cap and into this the crowd tossed their deniers to show their appreciation, Pèire as well.

'So, do you believe all that?' she asked him as they walked away.

'Of course not.'

'So when you have a wife, you don't intend to box her nose if she answers you back?'

'As if I would dare!' he laughed. 'Your father says you used to beat every boy from miles around if there was a rough and tumble in the street!'

'The boys were smaller then. Besides, how do you know that I shall be your wife?'

He looked at her, as if the question puzzled him. 'Your father has promised me,' he said.

A smudge of black cloud appeared on the northern sky, the promise of yet another storm later that afternoon. Pèire talks of marriage as if everything is settled. She tried to imagine a whole life-time in his company and could not. But what else might she do? She could not stay under her father's roof for ever. She heard the distant rumble of thunder. Perhaps it would not come to that; perhaps the fates had other plans. She realized they had stopped by the fountain where the lightning had struck her. There were fresh burn marks on the stone. Except for that, everything was as it always was. 'Three years now I have worked without a wage for your father so I could learn my craft,' he was saying to her. 'Next year will be my last as journeyman and the guild will make me a mason and I shall have my own mark. I shall go out on my own own building houses for rich burghers. You shall not regret making your marriage with me.' When she did not answer, he said: 'I have watched you right from the moment I saw you. It has never been anyone but you.'

This confession caught her off guard. She did not know what to say to him.

'You never knew?'

She shook her head.

'I near died too when I saw what had happened to you. I come out of the church and there was your father holding you in his arms like you were a babe, and you were white as plaster and your head and limbs all hanging down like you were dead.'

'I don't remember anything about it.'

'Did it not leave a mark? My mother says she once saw a man who was struck down in such a manner. There was a sort of bruise where it went in and another where it went out. But he was dead, mind.'

She knew about the man; just the previous summer another pilgrim from Gascony had been similarly chosen for God's attentions during a tempest and all that was left of that unfortunate were his sandals and a small pile of ashes.

'No, there was no mark.'

'Perhaps it struck next to you, then. I have heard that happens.' She saw by his expression that though he liked her well enough, he was also a little frightened of her. No doubt he had heard the stories. Some people thought her strange, always had. She even wondered that a straightforward lad like this would want her at all. 'He said you rambled, that you talked to fairies and phantoms.'

'If he says so, then I must have. I don't remember anything until the next morning.'

'Well I am glad you are well again for I don't know what I should have done if something had happened to you.' Well, she thought, he had made his declaration and now he waits for me to show that I am pleased by it. And why should I not be? He is a big strong boy and like my own father in many ways, hard-working and good-natured. What more should I hope for?

A preaching friar was about his business outside the church of Saint-Étienne, haranguing the good people of Toulouse for their infidelity to Rome, and describing for them the torments of hell. He wore the white gown of the Piedmont overlaid by the black cloak of the Augustinian canons. It marked him out as one of the disciples of Dominic Guzmán, the Spanish monk whose name her mother could not even mention without spitting in the fire. One of the town burghers halted his morning's errands to take issue with him, encouraged by cheers and the ribald comments of the small crowd gathered on the steps.

Pèire bent down and hurled a handful of mud in his direction. The crowd laughed.

'Pèire, what are you doing? The Lord will punish you for abusing a man of God!'

'He's the Pope's man, not God's,' he said. 'Why don't they leave us alone?'

Fabricia also wanted to be alone. All this talk of marriage had unsettled her. But she did not want to hurt him, so she told him she wanted to go inside the church and thank the Madonna for her deliverance. It was not quite a lie; how else might she have survived, if it were not a miracle?

'I shall come in with you,' he said.

'No, wait for me out here,' she told him. 'I shall not be long.'

*

The church was already crowded with pilgrims, the hawkers doing brisk business with their beef and raisin pies. It was like this every summer, the city crowded with pilgrims on their way to Santiago de Compostela, and there was not a priest or an innkeeper in the city who did not profit from them. She was accustomed to their raucous piety, parading through the streets singing hymns, the more enthusiastic of them barefoot, whipping themselves with chains as they went. Every day there were crowds of them, on their way to Notre-Dame de la Daurade to gape at the golden mosaics of Christ and the Virgin before coming here to pray over the bones of the saints.

She pushed through the mob crowded into the nave, wrinkling her nose at the stench. Most of the pilgrims carried long staves, like shepherd's crooks, and several wore lead badges sewed on to their robes to represent the holy places they had visited: a pair of crossed keys for Rome, a scallop shell for St James. These worthies were no doubt pilgrims by trade, paid in coin by some wealthy burgher to do his penance for him.

She knelt among the wreaths of flowers, face to face with the Virgin. She kissed the saint's feet, placing her forehead against the pedestal.

She lit a taper. 'Mother Mary, thank you for my deliverance, for taking pity on me, a poor sinner.'

The sun broke through the mist. It was already high enough in the sky so that it angled through the high clerestory windows, reaching into the cathedral vault like one of God's golden fingers. She was gladdened to see that His divine touch was gentler than the last occasion He had pointed towards her.

Suddenly there was a buzzing in her head like a swarm of bees descending and in that moment the lady in blue stepped from her pedestal and held a marble hand towards her. Fabricia gasped and blinked.

'You are chosen,' she said.

Fabricia rose halfway to her feet and looked around, thinking that others must have seen this miracle also, but no one stared, shouted, or pointed. It was as if the Virgin was still there, in her niche high up the wall. For a moment she was tempted to call out, so that she might have witnesses, but then she realized a more terrible truth: Papa was right. I have lost my reason.

Panicked, she lowered her head again, concentrated on her hands, still bunched in prayer.

Be calm, Fabricia. When she looked up again, Our Lady was returned to her imperious vigil above her and the saint's eyes were sightless once more, mere artifice carved and polished from stone. She must tell no one about this, she decided. It was a moment's madness; she would pretend it had never happened. Miracles and visions were for saints; not for the daughters of stonemasons. She stayed on her knees there a long time; not from piety, but because her knees were shaking so badly she could not stand. All that was real was slipping from her. The world and everything in it was as solid as mist.

When Pèire finally came in to look for her, she was still there on his knees, trembling, and as he told her father, 'she looked like she had seen a ghost'.

IV

'THERE WAS TROUBLE today, just down the street,' Elionor said. 'Old Reynard and his wife. Some of the Bishop's toughs broke down his door and went through his house tipping over kettles and threw everything the poor man has into the mud. All because he let two *bons òmes* stay at his house this last St John's Day.'

'Well, they should not harbour heretic priests!' Anselm said, but then added: 'They didn't hurt him, did they?'

'By grace of God, no. Rabble!' Elionor brought the pot of beans and mutton to the table. 'Here, eat.'

'There was almost a brawl today in the square, right outside the cathedral. Some of the people were mocking a friar.'

'These clerics deserve all they get. All they ever talk about is hell and saints' days and that we should all pay our tithes on time.'

'They threw muck at the poor man for preaching God's holy word! If Jesus himself came to Toulouse I swear they would jostle him and turn him out of the gates.'

'The good Lord would not come here if he saw how his priests behave! Fornicators and thieves, the lot of them.'

Fabricia saw the colour rise in her father's cheeks. What made her mother bait him like this? These days they argued over religion all the time. 'There are some who do not bring shame upon their calling.'

'Name two!' Elionor said, through a mouthful of food.

'The good preacher who was so badly used by the crowd in the market today. By all reports all he lives a chaste life and all he has are the clothes on his back.'

'That's only one.'

'Well then, the monk who is coming to see me tomorrow. Father Simon. His reputation is blameless. A good man and a faithful servant of the Church.'

Elionor smiled and her tone became gentler. 'Well, that's two, sure enough, husband. But two in one of Christendom's greatest cities is not overmuch. What business do you have with this priest?'

'He is the prior's secretary. He has commissioned me to make certain repairs to the cloister at Saint-Sernin. He has offered most generous payment for our services.'

'As he should.'

'The Church has many benefactors.'

'Indeed. The whole of Christendom, plus a percentage!'

Anselm ignored the jibe. 'Enough work for another two summers at least. By then perhaps Pèire will be ready to take over from me.'

They both looked at Fabricia, who felt her cheeks blush hot. She looked down at her bowl and tried to concentrate on her food. 'Did you tell her what you decided?' Elionor asked him.

'What we *both* decided.'

'I said only that I would not object. The *bons òmes* say that all procreation is a sin and that therefore marriage will lead to sinning. If marry she must then I will not stand in the way of it.'

'You would not welcome a stout son-in-law with skilful hands who can give us grandchildren and look after us when we are old? A man who will take good care of our daughter when we are gone?'

'I know you want only what is best for us all,' Elionor said, more gently. 'But as I get older, I worry more for my soul than this worn-out body.'

Fabricia thought her father would burst. 'These heretic priests have turned your head!' he said. He turned to Fabricia, looking for her to support him in his case. She knew he wanted only to do the best thing by her. How could she tell him she did not wish to marry Pèire when she had no good reason?

'Perhaps you do not see the stares you attract in the market,' he said to her. 'I will sleep easier knowing that you are wedded and churched, so that every young buck in Toulouse does not watch you like a wolf after his dinner.'

'Anselm!'

'It is true. She is comely and she needs a husband like Pèire to protect her from such insolence.' He reached across the table and took her wrist. 'He's a good man, as good as any in Toulouse. He'll look after you and though he's big, he's gentle. Won't even swat at a fly that lands on his cheese at lunch.'

When she did not answer he added: 'I am making you a fine match, Fabricia. You will be churched in the proper way.'

It was true she was old enough to be wed, but she wondered why her father was suddenly so fervent about it. Perhaps it was seeing her struck down during the storm. Bad enough for him that he had no son; without a daughter he would have not even grandchildren to comfort him in his old age.

'Pèire will carry on the work one day, when I can no longer hold a hammer or climb so high. It is God's work and he is well suited to it. He has a carter's brawn and an angel's temperament. I should rest easy knowing that one day a grandson of mine would leave his mark on the cathedrals of Toulouse, and take my seat in the guild.'

Still she said nothing.

'What is it? Don't you like Pèire? Has he offended you in some way?'

'I want to take orders,' she said, but her throat closed and the words came out as barely a whisper. He did not say anything for a long time and she wondered if he had heard her.

When she looked up, he was staring at her, aghast. 'A pretty girl like you? You want to spend the rest of your life in a convent? Why would you wish such a thing?' When Fabricia did not answer, he turned to Elionor. 'Did you hear what she said?'

'I had no knowledge of this.'

'This is not your doing then?'

'Why would I wish more of *Rome* on her?'

Fabricia had expected his anger; this look of pain and profound disappointment was much worse. 'Those places are for widows and shamed women,' he said.

What could she tell him? *I have never felt I am a part of this world, Papa. All my life I have been afflicted with strange dreams and premonitions. Now I see statues move and talk like living people. I think I have a kind of madness. I don't want to infect anyone else.* 'I want to give my life to God,' she mumbled.

Anselm pushed his food away and slammed his hands on to the table. 'This is madness,' he said, and although it was not his exact meaning, the words still jarred with her.

'I cannot marry Pèire. He will die soon.'

'Pèire? But he's perfectly healthy. I have never known such a robust young man. He has never been a day sick in his life.'

'What your father says is true. What do you mean? Why do you think he will die?' Now Elionor was staring at her too, her face betraying bewilderment as well as fear.

'Forget this nonsense,' Anselm said softly. 'You will do as I say.' He got up and went to sit by the hearth, grumbling to himself. He stared into the embers of the cook fire until they grew cold and he was still there when his wife and his daughter took themselves to bed.

*

Fabricia could not sleep.

What was the matter with her? She thought about what had happened to her that day in the Saint-Étienne cathedral, when the statue of Our Lady had moved from her pedestal. She could see her in her memory as clearly as she could picture her own mother and father at dinner. That did not mean it was real. Did she really believe the Madonna had spoken to her?

Ever since she was a child she had seen things that no one else could see, heard sounds no one else could hear: half-glimpsed wraiths; the sudden beat of a crow's wings in a darkened chamber; the rustle of a cloak in an empty room; the sound of voices whispering from the shades when she was quite alone.

She was barely able to walk when she first laughed at the fairies in the garden and pointed; her animated conversations with the invisible at first made her father smile, then frown, then scold. By the time she was old enough to walk unaccompanied to the market she had learned to pretend she did not hear the wails from the deserted cottage by the eastern wall, or the dark spirits of the hanged under the walls of the Garonne.

It felt to her as if she had not slithered completely from the womb. A part of her still sensed the world from which she had come and longed to return to it.

To hide her secret, she clung desperately to what was hard and real; to the stone of her father's church, the hearth of her mother's kitchen. With practice, she might pass months when the only people she saw were those who were really there; no stars twinkled in the hearth light, no spectres moved in the corners. The world was solid and smelled of earth and damp and stone.

She decided she would forget about what happened today in the church and do what her father said. Marriage to Pèire would not be so bad. He was a good, strong boy and he would put bread on the table. So why did she see him sprawled on the floor of the church with his brains sprayed across the flagstones?

*

The next morning she asked Elionor about Pèire. Did she think he was the right choice for her?

'He's strong and he works hard and and you'll never go hungry.'

It was the answer she should have expected. What more should a woman want from a marriage, after all? 'What is it like to . . . lie with a man?'

'So that's what worrying you? Look child, your father's the only man I've ever known. For all his size, he's a gentle man and I've never shrunk from his embraces. You know that.'

'Did you love him from the first then?'

'From the first? The first for me was just like it is for you. My father arranged things and I am grateful for his wisdom. It was never like one of the minstrels' songs, I suppose, but we grew to like each other and I suppose now I love him as much as anything in the world, except for you.' She put her arms around her. 'Everything will be all right, you'll see. Now get yourself dressed, child, and be off to the market or the best of everything will be gone.'

V

S HE COULD HAVE found her way blindfold through the streets to
the Saint-Étienne gate, for every day for two years she had gone
by the same way to bring her father his dinner. She recognized the
tincture of roses from the apothecary; and she knew the inn by the
smell of sour wine and fish, for the innkeeper made salted herring
to feed his customers and they habitually spat the bones on to the
reeds that covered the earthen floor; next came the tapping of a
smithy at his furnace, and she felt the blast of heat as she hurried
past the smoke-blackened shop.

She flattened herself against the wall as a Templar knight came
along the lane on his great warhorse, the stench of him enough to
fell an ox, never a by-your-leave to anyone, a bearded giant with a
broadsword on his belt that was bigger than her. She tried to dodge
the mud thrown up by its hooves. The size of them! They could
pound a bone to splinters and dust.

Another storm overnight had left the square a sea of mud and
rubbish. The fug of the city was made worse by a sticky mist of rain
and tempers were short. A troupe of travelling tumblers who had
performed every day in the square had moved on, and now there
were just a few housewives haggling for eggs and salt with the shivering stallholders. A fight broke out at one: two women come to
blows over a short measure.

Just nearby a spice monger, already convicted of tampering with
his weights, stood miserably in the pillory. There were not even any
youths out to toss stones at him.

She ducked aside from an ox and cart, the mud from the wheels
spraying up her dress, and ran across the square towards the church.
Some men-at-arms, standing by their master's horse, called out to
her with lewd remarks and she hurried away.

Anselm called out to his daughter, and Father Simon Jorda
looked up from where he and the stonemason were mapping out the

walls of the priory in the mud. Fabricia Bérenger made her way through the market crowds, a wicker basket on her arm. He saw a blaze of red hair, like a torch carried among the drab and jostling humanity below the cathedral steps.

For a few heartbeats of time he was not aware of the din of the hawkers inside the Saint-Étienne gate, or the bargaining and the quarrelling in the markets, the barking of dogs, the stink of people. His eyes were drawn only towards the possessor of this mane; a young woman, slim as a reed, with startling green eyes. He realized, with a feeling of something close to dread, that she was heading straight for them.

'There is the question of cost,' he said, trying to once again concentrate his mind on the problem at hand. But by then the young woman with the red hair had reached them and her father enveloped her in a bear-like embrace. She wore a long tight-sleeved tunic of fine woollen cloth, over a high-necked linen chemise. There were soft calf's leather shoes on her feet.

Her startling hair was wild and untamed, and its highlights caught the sun. He detected the scent of lavender on her clothes; she was a delight for all the senses. He stared at her for longer than he should. When she saw the direction of his stare, she did not lower her eyes, but stared back at him in a way that was as inflammatory as it was immodest.

He tore his eyes from her as eagerly as a starving man might push away a heaped dinner. From that moment he pretended – though with little success – to ignore her. It was as if there were rocks piled on his chest. He was as surprised as he was dismayed. Lust – or love, as the Minnesingers called it – was an old enemy to a monk and Simon thought he had defeated it long ago..

He hurried through the rest of their business. As Anselm took his dinner from the girl he expanded on his plans for the priory. Simon pretended to listen, and then mumbled a question about the wages for Anselm and his labourers. He paid scant attention to the answer. He agreed on a contract and scurried off.

Mea culpa. Mea maxima culpa.

'Who was that?' Fabricia said.

'That's the priest I was telling your mother about. Father Simon Jorda. A good man, and though it pains me to say it, your mother is right: there are few enough of them in the Church these days.'

She followed her father into the nave. The Église de Saint-Antoine was just across the square from the great cathedral of Saint-Étienne; 'crumb to the bread', as Anselm called it, all but forgotten for almost a century. Anselm had been commissioned to repair it.

'What do you have for our lunch today?' he said. He looked inside the wicker basket. There was some bread and boiled bacon and a jug of wine. 'Is there enough for Pèire as well?' Pèire was working on the scaffold high above their heads. He waved to him and Pèire waved back. 'Pèire!' Anselm shouted. 'Come down! It's time to eat!'

Fabricia looked around. The work on the Église de Saint-Antoine proceeded slowly for Anselm had only a handful of labourers and carpenters to help him. It seemed the Bishop would rather spend his money on his own palace in the *bourg*. Today there was just a carpenter, a glazer, a painter and several serfs or freedmen as barrowmen and labourers. There was also a rough mason who laid and mortared the heavy stones that made up the new wall rising from the southern transept, which was still hidden behind a scaffolding of roped poles. A stone was being hoisted into position by a complex arrangement of ropes and pulleys. It was done in stages, for the men had to haul each goliath almost to the height of the tower.

Anselm was proud of the commission, for what had once been a dark limestone box was being transformed by his hand into something glorious. The paint on the vault timbers was faded with age, but now there was at least gold leaf on the capitals and new wooden stalls for the monks in the choir. He had enlarged the apse to contain a new chancel, and extended that part of the building sideways to form a transept, thus remaking the whole structure into the form of a cross.

She stared at the faded frescoes on the wooden ceiling. Anselm came to stand beside her. 'It's a poor thing, isn't it?'

'It would have been beautiful once.'

He shook his head. 'These flat ceilings depress the spirit. With the new architecture we can use buttresses and pointed arches to raise the ceilings higher and higher. This is what they are doing at Chartres and at Bourges. How I would love to build a cathedral!'

'But if you worked on a cathedral, you would never live to see it finished.'

'It would not matter to me. I would have my mark on the foundation stone. When I get to heaven I could point down and say, see there, that is what I built. And they would have to let me in!' He took her by the arm. 'A church is built to be a parable of our life. Did you know that?'

He was interrupted by the yapping of a dog that some yokel had brought in with him while he gaped at the tapestries. Nearby, two burghers argued heatedly with each other over the price of a wool bale. He frowned, and led her away from them, to the other end of the aisle.

Dust motes drifted in a shaft of sunlight. He pointed to the rows of pillars that crowded the nave. 'These pillars and arches, they are the darkness of the forest from which we have all fled. And up there, just above the altar; imagine one day a great rose window. It will be like the sun, showing us the way forward. And what is the way? He is!'

Jesus hung suffering on his cross, head bowed and bleeding. 'Our Lord suffers for each one of us, leading us towards the path of our redemption. The aisle here is the path of our life and he is there at the end of it, waiting to lead the faithful to resurrection.'

He pointed to the vault. 'And finally when we arrive here, at the end of our lives, we look up, we see the light of heaven pouring through the windows in the clerestory, and we are reminded of the great and heavenly Jerusalem that awaits us. This is what your father does for his daily bread, Fabricia. A humble stonemason, yet I show each person who comes here his purpose in life and God's mercy in it.'

She smiled. She had heard this tale before, of course, but she never grew tired of the passion in his face as he told it, for he seemed never to grow weary of telling it.

She looked up again, saw Pèire preparing to come down from the scaffold. She knew at once what was going to happen and looked to the lady in blue, there in her niche in the wall. *Please, no.*

Pèire screamed as he lost his grip on the wooden scaffold. His arms cartwheeled at the air in that piercing moment when he realized he was lost and he yelled out once more, this time a groan of despair. The sound he made as he hit the stone flagging sickened her. She thought she felt the floor shake but that was just her imagination, the horror of it.

Anselm did not see him fall. He turned around only at the last moment to see Pèire crumpled in the nave, his skull split like an over-ripe tomato, his limbs splayed at an unnatural angle from his body.

He ran over and cradled the young man in his arms; oblivious to the gore on his hands and in his lap. 'Pèire! Pèire, my son. What have you done?'

His brains were everywhere. She thought she might vomit. Anselm stared at her, his mouth open and she could read the question in his eyes.

I cannot marry Pèire. He will die soon.

'How did you know?'

Fabricia could not answer. She looked around at the lady in blue, who only smiled back at her, kindly as a mother. A form of madness it might be, but not one she could just wish away.

She sank to her knees beside her father, placed a white hand on the big, lifeless body in his arms, as if she was herself responsible for his death, just by foreseeing it.

'I'm so sorry,' she said.

VI

THERE WERE DAYS when Anselm did not utter a word. He started work in the church soon after the angelus bell at dawn, was still there long after vespers. He took both his dinner and supper there, and with the days growing shorter, often worked by candlelight. Without his journeyman apprentice, there was twice the workload, for now Anselm was the only mason to do the work.

But Fabricia knew that was not the reason he worked himself so; what was it that he cried out in the cathedral the day that Pèire died? *Pèire, my son.* His grief was hard for her to watch, and she felt herself somehow accountable.

One afternoon she brought him his supper in the church. Winter was drawing in, the feast of St Simon and St Jude had passed, and the mornings were cold. The new stone laid in the church was packed with straw so that the mortar did not crack from the frosts. The scaffolding on the new work made it appear like the decaying bones of some giant beast. Soon the barrowmen would be paid off and her father would withdraw to work in the chapter house. He would spend the winter cutting and ornamenting the stones for the niches and the windows.

Anselm wore a tunic and apron and the little round cap that distinguished him as the freemason, the one who carved the 'free' stone, the ornamentation in the vaultings and narthex and in the traceries of the clerestory windows. He was at work with hammer and chisel on a block that would take its place on the tympanum over the south portal.

She watched him work. His breath made little clouds of vapour in the air. It was gloomy and frigid inside the church, but he wore fingerless gloves, for he needed the nimbleness of his fingertips for this work. His hands were thickly calloused so that he might as well have been wearing leather gloves, and his forearms were thick as an executioner's; yet he could tease flowers and vine leaves from capitals as if they were moulded from clay.

He looked up and saw her and his face creased into a grin. 'Fabricia! Good. The cold has made me hungry. I hope you have some of your mother's warm bread there in that basket.' He tucked his hammer and bradawl into his apron.

'And some ewe's cheese I bought at the market and a flask of spiced wine to warm you.'

He took a knife from his apron and cut into the cheese. Then he upended the wine flask and poured the wine into his throat, his head tipped back.

She studied the work he had left on his bench. He was sculpting the stone to the shape of a devil, worked into a pattern of vine leaves. The work was so fine it did not look like a carving at all, but life wrought from raw stone. It was eerily lovely. Who would have thought such a gruff man kept visions in his soul?

'It's beautiful,' she said.

'It's just stone, Fabricia. Now you, you are beautiful. Your mother is beautiful. This is just imitation of it, for God's holy purpose.' He shook his head. 'Though I confess I do not always understand His purpose. Why did he take Pèire? All that boy ever wanted to do was build churches for His greater glory and now he is gone.'

Fabricia laid her hand on his. She could feel the warmth of him even through her glove. So much pent-up energy in him, he radiated heat like a furnace, even on the coldest days.

'How did you know?' He looked up at her and she saw fear in his face. 'You said he was going to die. How did you know?'

She shook her head.

'Why didn't you stop it?' he said.

'How, Papa? How do you tell someone something that has not happened and make them believe you? How could I stop Pèire climbing the scaffold and doing his work because I had a dream?'

'You still should have said something.'

'I did.'

Anselm closed his eyes, nodded. 'But who dreams such things?'

'A witch?'

'Be still! You are not a witch! It was that storm, wasn't it? The lightning? You have not been the same since.'

'No, Papa. I was never the same as everyone else, ever. There were things before that. After the storm, they just got worse, that's all.'

'What things?' She did not answer him. Anselm hung his head. 'My little rabbit,' he said. 'What are we going to do with you?'

She took a breath. She knew he would not want to hear this. 'Papa, please, help me. I wish to take orders.'

'No. I will not speak of this now.'

'It's the only way for me. We both know this.'

'Not now,' he said, and tore his hand from hers and went back to his work.

*

Instead of returning directly home Fabricia went to visit the shrine of Our Lady in Saint-Étienne. In the street by the side of the great church there was a locked door that led to the sacristy. Something made her turn as she passed the doorway; she saw a couple in there, the boy with his hose around his knees, the girl with her ankles around his hips. Fabricia stopped and stared.

She could not take her eyes from the woman's face. She had seen bawdiness in the street before, Toulouse was a crowded place and people took their vices where they could, but this was no penny whore. Her head was thrown back, her mouth open in a silent scream. This was passion, not street commerce. Could any physical experience be so intense? The woman clung to her lover so tightly her fingers were white. This is what joy looks like, Fabricia thought.

The woman's eyes blinked open and for a moment the two women stared at each other. Then Fabricia turned away and hurried inside the church, shaking.

She lit a taper by the feet of the Madonna and kissed the cold marble hem of her robe. She closed her eyes and tried, by force of will, to persuade her to speak, as she had before.

'Move for me,' she implored her. 'Talk to me! Tell me what to do!'

She pressed her hands hard, painfully, against her forehead and waited for the saint to speak. But there was only silence.

That night she lay on her straw pallet beside the fire, listening to the watchman in the square rattle his iron-shod staff and cry out the 'All's well!' But all is not well, she thought.

She had long feared a slow descent into madness, ending her days in the gutters, foam on her mouth, covered in ordure, bearing the stinging stones of jeering little boys. She had decided that if she were instead secluded in a monastery, her mother and father would be spared her shame, and would not be outcast along with her.

'Please, Blessed Mother, make this stop,' she murmured. Exhausted, she closed her eyes, dreading sleep for what dreams might come.

And what she dreamed was a knight with steel-blue eyes. She was riding a pony and he was walking beside her, leading it by its halter. He was smiling at her. Suddenly he fell, an arrow in the centre of his chest. He disappeared into a chasm that fell away from the mountain beside them. She woke in the night, screaming his name.

Philip.

VII

Vercy, fifteen leagues from Troyes
Burgundy, France

'ALEZAÏS, MY HEART.'
She was straddling him, hands behind her head, fixing the curls that fell loose about her shoulders. He cupped her breasts, like small fruit, dusky and ripe. Her eyes were like a cat's in the dark.

The blue night curtains were tied back on the wooden canopy. It was late summer and the soft copper wash of the sunset retreated through the window, and a scribble of smoke tumbled towards the draught. There was the aroma of freshly burned rosemary.

His wife, so delicate, so pale by daylight but with the snuffing of the candles she was transformed. *You get energy from the moon,* he said to her once.

She arched her back and her hips writhed, serpentine, each uncoiling drew another groan from his lips. She had all the skill of the King's tormenter, teasing him slowly to his little death.

She bit gently at the lobe of his ear: *Take me to the tilt, my warrior. Bury your lance as deep as it will go.*

He took her face in his hands. *Alezaïs, my sweet, my darling.* He felt her breath on his face, sour wine and strawberries, chased the golden shadow of her soul in the cloister of her eye. *You are my hope.*

*

He started awake, realized he had been dozing in the saddle. His sergeant-at-arms pointed: the castle loomed above the valley on a bend of the river. A smudge of smoke rose from the keep and stained a filthy sky; he saw the flare of a torch behind the arrow slits of the *donjon*. He looked for the window of their bedroom, high in the tower. He knew that beneath it there was an iron chest, ornamented with iron scrolls, in which she kept her treasures and rarities. It served her also as window seat and prie-dieu and he wondered if she was there now, if she could see him.

His wife, his home.

He felt many eyes watching their approach. He wanted to gallop the rest of the way but he could not. The mud was frozen hard with frost and rutted from the passage of cart wheels and his horse stumbled, exhausted. He had ridden her hard to arrive before nightfall.

A wolf howled somewhere on the mountain and he crossed himself.

They stopped outside the gates and his sergeant-at-arms called out the password. The wooden doors of the gatehouse rumbled open.

The torches were already lit; the servants tumbled from the *donjon* and the stables. He was home; for one fleeting moment he felt young again, and unscarred. But even as he clutched at the moment, he felt it slip from his grasp.

He looked for her among the servants and soldiers, but she was not there. He knew straight away there was something wrong. It was written on all their faces. They averted their eyes, none of them wanted to be the one to say.

He dropped from his horse. Renaut, his squire, pushed his way forward.

'Just tell me,' Philip said.

'She's dead; it's been half a year. It happened on the Eve of the Annunciation.'

'How?'

'It was a birthing.'

He remembered their last night together. *Take me to the tilt, my warrior. Bury your lance as deep as it will go.* So that was it then; he had sewn the seed of his own despair.

'I wish I might tell you otherwise,' Renaut said and fell to one knee. His entire household followed.

He wanted to sink to his knees in the mud with them but that would not do, for he was still master of this castle and these people. He felt them all watching him. It was a rare thing to feel pitied.

I do not want an audience for my grief, he thought, I would rather be alone, away from this stink of smoke and horses and mud. 'Look after my horse,' he said and limped inside.

*

The next day nothing would do but her gentlewomen must give him the account of how it happened. The pains began after mass; she had laboured with the child all through the next day and the next night before Renaut was sent to fetch a wise woman from the village. How she suffered and moaned! When at last the child was born there was a sudden onrushing of blood: not enough linen in the whole of the castle to stem the flow. Some women sent to the chapel to pray. I just want to sleep now, she said. Don't close your eyes, we all told her, didn't we? But we could not prevent it. She would not rouse. And her skin! Cold as mildewed stone.

He would have preferred their account brief, but they wished to tell him every detail. It had been their burden all these months and they needed to be free of its weight, hand it to him. It was his now.

It was not our fault. We did what we could.

'Did she say anything?' he said.

They shook their heads. One word from her deathbed might have made a difference. But there was nothing to report, it seemed.

The priest was called and she slipped away during the night. They all woke to slate roofs dusted with snow and a lady frozen in death.

He sent them all away, climbed the stairs to their bedchamber and perched uneasily on the edge of the bed where she died. A sour wind howled around the walls and the candles guttered and danced.

He tried to picture her face but already it was fading. Just that afternoon he could summon every curl and every glance, but she was alive to him then, though six months in her grave. He heard her voice from the dark passage. *You did not even ask about the child.*

'I cannot believe you have left me here alone,' he said.

What was it she had said before he left? *Promise me you will come home safe to me.* He had never thought to say: *Promise me you will still be here alive when I return.* Now she was gone, the sun was behind her and he could not stare into the light.

She had tried to make him stay.

'I cannot,' he had told her. 'I am a knight, and I am foresworn to make one pilgrimage to the Holy Land in my lifetime and fight for the Lord. I have to do my duty.'

'I am afraid that if you go, we will be parted for ever.'

'That is for God to decide.'

'No, it is for you to decide, husband.'

'It is not goodbye,' he had said. 'I will come back to you, I promise.'

She turned away from him.

'You have to understand, *mon coeur*. God demands this of me.'

'Oh, I don't think so,' she said and would have left it at that. He pressed her on it. 'It's the Pope in Rome that wants it, husband. Can you not serve God just as well by staying here and serving the people whose lives depend on your presence?'

The next day he put on his surcoat. Her ladies had stitched a red cross on to the fabric and he strode into the great hall to show it off. 'What would you say if you were a Saracen and saw me come at you with my sword raised?'

Her eyes were clouded. 'I would say, go home to your wife and leave us here in peace.'

What is wrong with me? he thought. I had been happy then. Any other man would have squeezed every measure from every day and not tested God's patience and the Devil's sense of mischief.

And now she was gone. You wasted your brief time with her in that infernal country, looking for God's favour, when He had already given you more than you ever deserved. And now look what has happened.

*

When he woke, his mouth was foul and parched, his head splitting from too much wine. Renaut was sitting at the foot of the bed. 'I should have fetched the wise woman sooner,' he said. 'Else she might still be alive.'

'You are not to blame, Renaut. No one is to blame but me. I should have been here.'

It was raining outside. Last night he had thought that if he slept he would wake up and find her lying beside him in the bed, smell the musty warmth of her, spoon his body into hers. But instead he woke cold and aching. He went to sit by the fire, drew close to the meagre warmth of some green logs. He called for more wine.

VIII

THE BLACK-ROBED friar was again about his work in front of the cathedral. He seemed a mild sort of man for a preacher, Anselm thought, his shoulders bowed like a scribe and pouches under his sad grey eyes the size of pigeon's eggs.

But when he started to harangue the crowd those same eyes were of an instant lit from within by a messianic fire and his voice thundered even over the braying of the mules and the shouts of the hawkers.

'It is only through Christ and his Church that you will be saved! If you listen to your heretic priests you will be consigned to the terrors of purgatory, for such is reserved for those of you who turn your back *on God's holy word!*'

From the folds of his cloak he produced a human skull and brandished it in the face of a housewife on her way home from the market. She yelped in shock and spilled the eggs she was carrying on the cobblestones. A yellow-backed cur pounced on this unexpected windfall and began to lap at the spilled yolks.

'This is what awaits you! Every man and woman here owes God a death and you do not know when it will come. Are you ready to meet your Judge? Are you ready for the Last Trumpet?'

The moment these words left his mouth there was a loud blast on a horn and several of the women who had paused to listen screamed and jumped back. A small child started to cry.

Anselm was not quite so startled, for the trick was not new to him. He had seen one of the friar's accomplices slip inside the nave of the cathedral some moments before, a trumpet concealed in his robe. This elegant piece of theatre had a great effect on some but produced only rage in others.

An apprentice retrieved some fresh horse dung from the cobblestones and hurled it at the friar. It hit him about the midriff, leaving a large yellow-brown stain, much to the mirth of the crowd.

At this some young toughs appeared from behind the pillars and threw the dung-thrower into one of the pie stalls. Some others of the hecklers came to his aid and a brawl began.

Anselm Bérenger shook his head and turned to Father Jorda. 'What a world, where men should so disrespect a man of God.'

'It is the times we live in.'

'Indeed, Father.'

Father Simon Jorda tucked his hands inside the loose sleeves of his cassock to warm them a little. He was struggling to conclude their business. It was difficult, Anselm appreciated, to express both sympathy and self-interest at the same time. He felt sorry for the friar; he did not doubt that it was the prior who insisted on pressing him on business matters so soon after Pèire's accident.

He thanked the priest once more for his condolences, and agreed that such a fine young man must at that very moment be enjoying the fruits of his virtue in heaven. He then assured him that but for a slight delay while the guild found for him a journeyman of equal abilities, his work would proceed apace. By Anselm's calculation they would be finished by the following autumn, and could then continue as planned with the new work on Saint-Sernin.

Simon was about to return to his duties. He hesitated, sensing from the stonemason's manner that there was something further on his mind.

'Is something wrong, mason?' he said.

Anselm wondered how to begin. He possessed a deft hand with stone; but when he was with his wife or a clergyman, he felt like a piece of marble himself.

What a sight he makes, Simon thought. Yet this giant contrived somehow to look like a child about to be upbraided by his father for some mischief.

'Father,' Anselm muttered into his beard, 'there is something . . . I wonder if you might do me a service.'

'If it is within my power,' Simon answered, thinking he might wish a special dispensation for some sin. Some unscrupulous priests refused absolution for those sins that weighed heaviest on the penitent's mind, in order to extract payment for their pardon. A priest might ask for two or three *sols* from a peasant for an adultery; twenty or thirty from a man like Anselm, who could afford it.

He despised such practices. He would refuse no man the grace of God, if he were truly penitent.

'It is about my daughter,' he said, and Simon's heart froze.

'Your daughter?'

'Her name is Fabricia. She is a good daughter, and virtuous, and loves the Church.'

'That all men should be so blessed. What is it with her that you wish to discuss with me?'

'She loves the Church a little too much, I believe.'

Simon strained to hear him over the noise of chisel on stone from the men working around them. 'How can we love our Church too much, Anselm?'

'Father, you know me, I am a simple man, I have no under-standing of such things. The skills God has seen fit to give me, I use in the service of the Church, when I can. But there are some things . . .'

'What is it you require of me, Anselm?'

'She has expressed a desire to take vows, and live under the Rule, as a nun. Although I know it is a great virtue to serve God in this way, she is my only daughter, and I wish to dissuade her of it. I believe she may serve God better as a good wife and a good mother. Will you speak with her, Father?'

'You wish me to persuade her against this?'

'I do.'

'That is quite impossible,' Simon said, and turned away, lest Anselm see the blood colour his cheeks. But he could not hasten because of the litter of stone blocks around his feet, and Anselm would not give up so easily.

'Father, though she is only a daughter, I love her with all my soul!'

'Your soul is for loving God.'

'She is the only child I have. God has not seen fit to bless our union with more. Someday I hoped for a grandson to whom I could pass on these few humble skills that I have . . . if you would only talk to her, Father.'

'There is no better purpose to life than to commend it to God.'

'But, Father, she is just a girl, and has good prospects to marry . . .'

Simon rounded on him, meaning to upbraid him for his

importunate manners. The sight of this goliath reduced to hand-wringing stayed him. If only this wretch knew what was in my heart! The ways of the Dark One are truly insidious, he thought. Or perhaps God has sent this as a test for me. He intends this as my moment to overcome the Devil's power, to defeat him as surely as the Lord defeated his temptations in the wilderness.

'Please, talk with her, Father. If I had a son, it would be a gift I could give to God, knowing it was of some value. But a daughter . . . really, the sacrifice is hers alone, and I do not believe she understands the gravity of it. Will you prevail on her, for me?'

Simon could not find his voice. He retrieved the hem of his cassock, stepped over a large block of marble, and hurried away.

Why did he choose me? Simon wondered. Was it just because he knew me and had cause to converse with me often? There were some clerics who would not even speak to a woman, saying their gender was responsible for the sins of Eve and thus the suffering of all men. He himself believed it was because such priests did not trust themselves, were afraid that the charms that the Devil lent women could lead them from a sinless life.

I never before counted myself among them.

It was admitted that virtuous men were not easily found within the Church. There were many clerics who knew fornication better than they knew the words of the mass, and monks who, if they did not have a reputation for scandal, should have no reputation at all.

He always thought himself exceptional; had convinced himself that on the Day of Judgement God would find no blemish on his pure heart. This was a test of his virtue, that was all. And he would prove finally to himself, and to his Lord, that the Devil held no play over him whatever.

IX

THE BÉRENGER FAMILY lived in the narrow streets on the Garonne side, close to the sweatshops and the bleachers and tanners around the church of Saint-Pèire-des-Cuisines. To get there Simon passed through several mean alleys, with workshops and stalls on every side. The imprecations of the whores and the shrieks of snot-nosed children were a vexation. Gangs of adolescents roamed there, mocking the old and the lame and getting into fist-fights outside the ale-houses.

As in Paris, the population of the town had no other means of disposing of waste than by throwing everything into the street. The rickety upper storeys jutted at angles over the narrow lanes and Simon had once experienced the unrelieved joy of having the contents of a night jar emptied on his head. On one famous occasion even the Bishop had been so anointed. The most hideous filth was piled up outside every door, where dogs and pigs squabbled over the fare. Simon held a scented handkerchief to his nose while being forced into a doorway to make way for a shepherd and a flock of mud-spattered sheep.

He reached a small square with a stone cross at its centre, the junction of three streets. It was here that the mason had his house. Shops faced on to the square, the wrought-iron signs hanging above their lintels creaking and swaying in the wind.

Despite the weather, a crowd gathered around a bear sward, and voices rose as the betting and cursing began. He heard the yelping of the dogs and the desperate and enraged cries of the bear as it fought for its life. The world was steeped in sin, he thought. Only the eternal has worth.

Remember that, Simon, before you go inside. Remember that.

*

Anselm Bérenger lived well, for as a master mason he received twenty-four silver *sols* every week, which sum afforded him a good stone house and meat on his table for most suppers. Simon was greeted in the parlour. In the middle of the room there was a fireplace, a welcome log crackling in the grate. Mushrooms, garlic and onions hung on strings to dry above the hearth.

He looked around. There were three small windows covered with oiled linen, which allowed a creamy light into the room. To relieve the austerity, the oaken roof timbers were painted in bright colours, wine-red and moss-green.

Anselm brought him to stand by the fire to warm himself. Steam rose from his damp cloak. Anselm's wife brought him a cup of mulled wine. Simon noted that the mother much resembled her daughter, though Elionor's red curls were now flecked with grey.

As his eyes grew accustomed to the dim light inside the house, he noticed Fabricia waiting patiently in the corner. She wore a soft grey tunic, a linen chemise visible at her neck and wrists, decorated with lace. He imagined he could detect the faint smell of saffron from its last washing. She was practising her needlepoint and her brow was knit in a frown of concentration.

After some desultory conversation, Anselm and his wife left him by the fire with their daughter, who had to this point remained silent. They went upstairs to their private chamber.

He knew he should put her at her ease with some casual conversation – the weather perhaps, or an enquiry after the manner of the embroidery she was making – but he found to his horror that his throat was dry and his hands were trembling. Such was his panic that he launched instead straight to the business.

'Your father tells me that it is your wish to give yourself over to the service of God.'

'He has sent you here to dissuade me, has he not, Father?'

'He wishes me to ascertain if you have the temperament for it.'

Simon settled himself on his stool and sipped his wine. Now the conversation had begun, he felt a little more certain of himself. Many young women had been moved by the stories of virgins suffering for Our Lord; it was for such hysterical notions that their sex was famed. He knew that a man of his training and intellect should be able to disabuse her of such thoughts without too much difficulty.

'I cannot say whether I have the temperament for it, Father. I just believe that it is what God wishes me to do.'

'How might a girl such as yourself know the mind of God? Only the Holy Father in Rome is truly allowed to understand the divine, and even His Holiness professes puzzlement on occasion.'

Fabricia did not answer him. She stared at the rushes on the floor. Such insolence!

'Speak up, child,' he said, though he ought not to have called her child, perhaps, for he was only a few years her elder. 'Why should you think such a thing?'

She raised her eyes from the floor and the blazing look she gave him took his breath away and set stirring in his loins an ache he thought years of prayer and diligence had banished. She bit her lip; his first thought was that it was a device to entrap him but then he allowed that it might simply be an effort to stop herself from speaking about certain private things in his presence.

At last she said: 'Do you think it is wrong then for a humble woman such as myself to wish to dedicate my life to His service?'

There was an easy riposte to this; but her earnest expression disconcerted him. When he finally found his voice he reminded her that it was not enough to love God, that a chosen servant must also have a disposition sufficiently robust to serve him properly.

'You mean like the Bishop?' This caught him off balance, for the Bishop's worldliness was well known, if not much discussed, by the town in general.

At least he had wit enough for a rejoinder. 'But you do not intend to become bishop, surely?'

'I do not think I should have the strength for it. After a week I should be exhausted from drink and fornication.'

Simon did not know what to say. Already the direction of the interview was slipping from his control. She might be merely the daughter of a stonemason but her tongue was as sharp as an executioner's knife.

She dropped her gaze again to the floor. 'I am sorry, Father. Sometimes my tongue is a little too free.'

'Indeed. It is quite plain to me already that you have none of the attributes necessary for the monastic life. Obedience and humility are the foundation stones of the Rule. If you are unable to hold your tongue, I fail to see what service you might be able to render to God.'

Feeling that he was once again in control of the situation, he warmed his legs before the hearth and told her stories of Augustine and of Benedict of Norcia, to illustrate to her what a true love of God entailed. He was approaching the topic of St Agnes's martyrdom when she suddenly looked directly into his face, and said: 'I have visions, Father. I see things I should not.'

It was as if she had dashed a pail of cold water in his face. She was not listening to him at all.

'What manner of visions?'

She shook her head. 'I cannot tell you that.'

'Why not?'

'You will take it as a blasphemy.'

'I shall be the judge of that.'

She stared at the floor. Outside the tinkers clattered past in their wooden shoes and a priest, with his hand bell, was summoning all to pray for the souls of the dead. Finally, she said: 'I have seen a woman, very much like Our Lady. Only I do not think she can be real.'

He watched the firelight play in her hair. 'Because you see things, Fabricia, it does not mean they are there. Young girls of your age before they are . . . wed . . . are famed for such notions.'

'So a monk or a priest or even a nun might see God and know it is real but if it is a young girl then it is a kind of madness? Is that what you are saying, Father?'

'Where did you see such things?'

'Once, in Saint-Étienne, while I prayed at her shrine. She descended from her pedestal.'

'She moved?'

'Yes, Father.'

Simon sighed and affected forbearance. This was the source of her supposed devotion to God? 'You give too much weight to mere flights of fancy, Fabricia Bérenger .'

'You think so, Father?' she said, and then looked at him with such directness that he averted his own eyes. He wanted desperately to touch her.

'You must confess,' he said.

'Confess? Have I sinned?'

'Of course you have sinned!'

'But I have no control over such things.'

'That does not matter. In this . . . fancy . . . did she speak to you?'

'She did.' She lifted her right hand and laid it on her breast. 'I felt the words here, in my heart.' His eyes followed the ecstatic passage of her fingers from her shoulder to her bosom. He imagined the porcelain softness of her breast beneath the crisp linen, the pale vein that succoured the swollen bud of her nipple.

Her skin would smell like lavender and musk, and there would be a sprinkling of the finest red-gold hair below the dimple of her navel, visible only in the golden splash of sunlight that fell across her bed in the late afternoon.

Her back was sinuous and slender, like the wriggling of a snake as she slid between his thighs . . .

He jumped to his feet, spilling both his stool and his mead on to the floor. The Devil threw back his head and roared with laughter. Fabricia stared up at him, startled.

'There is nothing to be done with you!' he shouted and fled the house without another word.

X

SIMON KNEW HE must never again return to the stonecutter's house, for that was utter folly and would invite disaster. But he had to know what Fabricia had told Anselm about his visit with her and he approached him on some pretext one day in the Église de Saint-Antoine. As he was leaving he said, as if an afterthought: 'Has your daughter spoken to you more about this notion to take up the Rule?' He feigned no more than a casual interest.

'No, Father, she has not, though she has been greatly preoccupied. She is not herself at all. She hardly speaks.'

There was something in him that found this news deeply gratifying. 'I believe I made some progress with her,' he heard himself say. 'But I shall need to speak to her again.'

'Of course, Father. When?'

'This Sunday,' he said, and left the mason to his work.

He walked away, both astonished and appalled at what he had done. I do not do this for personal profit, he persuaded himself, I do not seek to gain advantage over her. I have set myself a test, that is all, as God has designed, and I shall prove my mettle this time. I shall triumph over my own carnality and lead this girl to proper understanding of herself, as her father wishes.

That was all.

*

Simon accepted Anselm's mumbled obeisance and a sullen greeting from the wife. Then he and the girl were again left alone by the fire, so that he might continue his instruction of her.

'So, Fabricia, have you given consideration to our last conversation?'

'Indeed, Father, I have thought of nothing else.'

'And you have prayed?'

'With all my heart.'

'As have I, for the right way to instruct you in this matter. Have you experienced any more of these visions?'

'No, Father.'

'That is well. Such visions as you describe may be many things: a shadow moving on the wall perhaps, or a flash of sunlight reflected for a moment on a stained glass window. An imagination fuelled by a great love of God, which I am sure you possess, is prone to such fancies. But a lifetime's service to the Holy Church, this is about dedication and discipline, not bewilderment or ecstasy. Living by the Rule is not the simple thing you may imagine. And you have a duty also to your father.'

'But does the Church not teach that we should honour God above even our own parents?'

'There are many ways to honour God. You do not have to enter an abbey to do it. And your vows, should you submit to them, bind you to a life of discipline unimaginable to you now. Easily foresworn, harder kept.'

'You mean the vow of chastity?'

He blushed then, and stared into the fire, discomfited by her directness. 'You are young. I do not think you fully understand what chastity means.'

'You are young too.'

Simon got up and paced the floor. 'We all struggle with our humanity.'

'You have overcome your demons, Father. Could I not overcome mine?'

'It is harder for Woman. She is more wanton than Man.'

'If you heard what is said behind my back in the markets you would not say so.'

Simon embarked on a long speech, drawing inspiration from the works of Jerome and Paul, and quoting also from the lives of the virgin martyrs. He explained to her how love of the divine was so much greater than the love of mortals for each other.

She quickly grew weary of it, but he did not seem to notice.

*

'You seem agitated, Father,' she said, interrupting him as he attempted a discourse on the nature of love from St Augustine.

He gaped at her; that the daughter of a stonecutter – or any woman – should pass comment on a monk's behaviour showed a breath-taking presumption.

'You are not an easy pupil to instruct.'

'And you are surely young to have attained such a position in the Church. My father says you are spoken of as a future bishop.'

'I shall serve God in any capacity I am best able.'

'So you have already considered this possibility?'

This one remark disarmed him utterly. He was a Cistercian monk, a man of God, and she should show him absolute deference. Instead, she now claimed to read his thoughts.

'I think you would make a good bishop,' she said, but before he could summon a proper reply, she posed her next impertinent question. 'Why does a man such as yourself come to live in a monastery? Were you found at the gate?'

A man such as myself?

'Is that what you think?' It was true that several of his brother monks had been abandoned at the monastery steps as infants. Why did she think he was one of them?

'Were you, Father?'

His pride got the better of him. He looked at her down the length of his nose. 'My father is a burgher of no little reputation. I was the youngest of his sons and he rightly saw an opportunity for me in the ranks of the Church.'

'You have never regretted his choice?'

This was the moment, Simon thought later, when he made his great mistake. He should have scolded her for asking such scandalous questions and reminded her of her station. But he did not. He allowed himself a moment's intimacy with a woman and what followed later issued inevitably from the decision to share his heart.

Why did I do it? His daily communion with God should have been sufficient balm for his heart's bruises. His real betrayal of the divine was that in succumbing to her questioning he allowed that a life with only the divine for solace was not enough.

'Yes,' he said, 'there are times when I have wondered what man I might have been in other circumstances.'

'What kind of man is that?'

A flutter of a smile, a childhood habit awkwardly retrieved from his memory. 'I would doubtless have been a sinner.'

'We are all sinners, are we not?'

'Some of us hope for redemption.'

Their eyes locked and he felt his loneliness as he never had before. He longed in that instant to be keeper of her heart as well as her body. He knew he must retreat or be lost. 'I do not regret those choices made for me, Fabricia. When I look at the world, at its false-hoods and futilities, at the evil I see every day around us, I know that seeking only God's goodness is the right path.'

'Did you never love a woman before you became a monk, then?'

She grew more impudent by the minute. Yet he was overcome by a desperate need to unburden himself, even though he knew where this ache in his treacherous heart might lead him. He sat down again. 'Fabricia, you must understand. I was just a boy when my father offered me to the Church. My father had five sons, and I was the youngest. He was – is – a wool merchant in Carcassonne, a man of some wealth, but not enough to secure an income for so many sons, so he used his influence to gain a place for me in the abbey.'

'You look sad,' Fabricia said.

'I am not sad.'

'You miss your brothers.'

Such a hard truth and so frankly spoken. He remembered his first few months as a novice, how he cried himself to sleep every night on his hard wooden pallet. 'My father gave me an opportunity to prosper. It was difficult at first but I am grateful to him now for what he did, for it led me to God and a blessed life.'

'And yet you long for a life not quite so blessed. Is that not true?'

She might as well have hit him with the soup kettle; it would have shocked him less. He felt suddenly naked in her presence. She had disarmed him utterly.

She had astonished even herself by speaking in such a way. She thought he would upbraid her for it but instead his shoulders seemed to sag under the weight of some great burden.

His hands shook. Such beautiful hands! They were smooth and soft and white, so unlike her father's, which were calloused and criss-crossed with scores of small cuts that evidenced his daily travails; but these, these were hands that turned the pages of books, delicate hands that came together for prayer.

When he finally spoke, his voice was so low she could scarce hear him. 'I took a vow of constancy to God, yet I am still a man. It is an oath of no small consequence for I struggle with it every day.'

His frankness disarmed her. She was sorry now she had been so blunt.

'This vow may seem trifling to you now,' he went on, 'but with each year it grows heavier on the shoulders. You should think of this before you take up the veil.'

'But you are a man of God. Do you think it is wrong for me to dedicate my life to His service, simply because I might find the life difficult?'

He was just a young man who wanted to be good, she thought, and to listen to her mother talk, there were few enough of those in Toulouse. She found him both endearing and sad and for a moment she felt an unexpected stirring in her heart.

It was growing dark in the square; the grey light that seeped through the oiled linen on the windows was almost gone. The fire leaped and danced in his eyes. He said suddenly and without preamble: 'You are so very beautiful, Fabricia.'

Perhaps he did not mean to speak this thought aloud. He seemed as shocked as she.

He got to his feet. 'I must go,' he said.

After he left her mother and father crept back down the stairs holding a smoking tallow candle. They seemed puzzled, but said nothing. Her mother seemed to have divined what had happened.

All churchmen were alike. She said it often enough.

*

SIMON HURRIED ALONG an alleyway of wine shops, bawdy houses and tinker's stalls. Evening was drawing on, the Devil's hour. An ox cart creaked past and he shrank into a doorway. The whores took this as an invitation to mistake him for the Bishop and one of them bared her breasts at him and offered him congress against the wall for three deniers.

He pushed away from her with an angry shout. She had foul

breath and bad teeth like a demon. I have made of myself a common joke; a monk transfixed by a woman, he thought wildly. I have dedicated my life to contemplation of the divine; instead I am fixed on cunny like a bawd.

What was it that St Augustine said of woman? *The gate by which the Devil enters.* She is a temptress set by Lucifer to lure a man from his perfect state. Fabricia was then a perfect demon: fire-haired, slender and ripe as bruised fruit.

He passed a man lying in the street who had been blinded as punishment for some crime. His empty sockets were horrible to look at, and he sat in the filth of the gutter, with his arm outstretched, begging for coins. Some small boys were tormenting him for their own amusement; they pinched him and slapped him while he raged at them and tried in vain to catch hold of them, which of course only made the game even better.

Simon saw himself there: blind, grovelling, wretched, tormented by the Evil One for jest. *I must stop this.*

He caught one of the wretch's tormentors by the ear and reproved the lad in the name of the Church. He found a few coins in his purse and gave them to the beggar. He was no doubt a thief – or had once been – but had paid his terrible price, and Simon had no stomach to see him suffer more. He would not survive much longer in the street anyway.

He returned late to the monastery, as the bells rang for vespers. He was tardy and received the reproving glances of his brothers.

The Devil remained his companion all that night both in the chapel and in his bed. He weaved moist dreams of Fabricia and unclothed her in his sleep. He felt her breath on his face, sweet as strawberry wine; her hair smelled of summer, and his arm was around her waist, which was soft and yielding. Finally, in some ragged scrap of dream, he saw her lying naked in a cornflower field, and tried to go to her. But someone pulled him away. A man's voice called his name.

It was Brother Griffus shaking him awake to attend matins and lauds. His hand went guiltily to his groin. He pulled on his robe in the darkness, desperate and aching and ashamed.

The candles wavered in the draughts of the dark choir, illuminating the sacristan's bible, throwing long shadows of his cowled brother monks and the carved saints above their heads. The ranks of the holy stood against him in the gloom.

His lips moved with the words of the psalms and responses while he felt her warm breath even in that cold, dark chapel, tasted the salt of the sweat at the nape of her neck. It was just a dream but his memories of it were as vivid as if it were real; so real that he believed that at that very moment she, too, was sitting upright on her pallet bed, seeing his face as clearly as he saw hers. Impossible to imagine that he could conjure such an intimate moment and that she had not felt it also.

After the service he returned eagerly to his cell, hoping a swift return to his moist and salty dream, and to Fabricia Bérenger. But a dream is not a place; he could not go back. Instead, he lay awake through the long night and begged God to take away his temptation, then reminded himself that every soul is forged in the fire. How could he be spared what every man must endure if he is to save himself?

What was he to do? If he did not go back, it would signify that the Devil had won. If he did, his soul would be in mortal danger. Might he yet prove himself worthy to his God? He tossed and turned until the first greasy light of dawn inched across the floor of his cell. A new day was never so welcome.

XI

THE PRIOR WAS a good man, in Simon's estimation. He was stern in his discipline and strict in his habits and brooked no lewd behaviour at the monastery. He decided to go back to him. The next morning he went to his cell, fell on his knees and asked him to hear his confession.

The prior sat on the stool behind his writing desk, and his grey and moist eyes regarded Simon with the weariness of age; near fifty years of listening to men's tiresome complaints of the Devil.

'Forgive me, Father, for I have sinned.'

Father Hugues laid a cool hand on his tonsured head. 'What is your confession, Brother?'

The words choked him. How could he tell him the truth? Just a portion of it then; he had seen a woman in the square and entertained lustful thoughts. That was enough of it, for now.

'You have prayed?'

'I do nothing else.'

The prior sighed. 'You are a young man, Brother Simon. The vow of chastity is not easy. Even the blessed founder of our Rule, St Benedict himself, was not immune to such pollution. There are many ways that the Devil finds to a man's soul, but a woman is the most powerful of his agents. This is why men must cloister themselves in monasteries, for all women are lascivious creatures.'

'What am I to do?'

'When St Benedict was a young man he secluded himself from the world in the desert, so that he might free himself from its temptations. But even there he was haunted night and day by the memory of a woman he once saw, like you, in the marketplace of his town. The more he fought against this image of her, the stronger her picture became in his mind, until he could think of nothing else. He was about to succumb and return to the city and surrender to its worldly pleasures, when he saw a thorn bush close by. He threw off his clothes and flung himself into the bush and wallowed there. His flesh was torn into strips and there was not a place on his body that did not bleed or did not cause him to suffer. But these sacred wounds cured the ungodly desires of his flesh and his soul.'

Simon felt the blood drain from his face. He had himself considered harsh medicine for his ills, harsher than even the saint had imagined. Perhaps that was truly the only way.

That night he prayed with his brother monks in the darkened chapel at the office of compline. He shivered with cold. In the high gloom of the choir, the cowled prior led them in their nightly hymn.

From all ill dreams defend our eyes,
From nightly fears and fantasies;
Tread underfcot our ghostly foe,
That no pollution we may know.

He longed for faultless perfection. Instead he heard only the discomfiting laughter of God's fallen angel. He must drive himself harder; he must do better than this.

XII

EVEN THROUGH HIS childhood Simon had contemplated his own death. He lived in terror of what would happen on the dread day he gave up his final breath for the walls of every church bore lurid depictions of Judgement and hell.

And yet, with Fabricia Bérenger he had acted as if there were no Devil and no damnation. He followed the prior's advice, pulled down his robe and attempted to quench the unholy fires that burned in him with a whip. The thongs of the scourge were embedded with iron tips.

The first strokes were timid, his hands shaking so badly he dropped the scourge several times. But he persevered, and as the whip tore the first stripe on his shoulders he cried out as if racked. He took a deep breath to steady himself.

His hands were slick with sweat and he wiped them on his robe. He was determined that this should be done. He would give to God his pain and like Benedict he would prevail. He beat himself over several hours; he beat himself until the blood flowed freely down his back and dripped on to the floor.

But when he finally collapsed exhausted on the stone, all he could think of was Fabricia Bérenger; he imagined the soft touch of her lips on his, the warmth of her breath on his face, whispering consolation to him through his agony. He was no longer a monk. He was just a man.

*

His distraction became cause for comment in the priory. There were protests to the prior about his laxity at chapter; his students complained that his lectures were rambling and ill prepared.

Whenever he could he slipped secretly away to observe the mason and his family; he soon came to know their habits as well as he knew his own. It was not a difficult task for they were only three, and Anselm had no servants. He learned that the mason left the house each day at first light, while each morning, just after terce, his wife went to the market. From then until sext Fabricia was at home, and unattended.

*

A change in the air, unexpected, a brief return to warmth, the last before winter. Today he did not need his cloak. A warm wind blew from the south rolling in from the salt pans and the sea. Everywhere in the streets people remarked on it. An aberration; the autumn turned on its head.

When he reached her house he did not knock, but went straight in. Fabricia was at her loom, spinning wool into twine. She looked up in surprise.

'My father is not at home,' she said.

Simon had rehearsed a speech but now could not think of a single thing to say to her. He just stood there, one hand opening and closing into a fist at his side.

'You are welcome to wait here by the fire, if you wish,' she said.

He sat down on a little stool, his mind blank with panic. He feared that he might not do what he came to do, and also that he would. He suddenly had no idea how to proceed.

How was this done? With a whore you paid your penny and she lifted her skirts, or so he had been told. A wife arranged herself dutifully in the marriage bed and awaited her master. Was there another way? He overheard certain students at the university talking of the women of the town, when they thought he was not within hearing, discussing what some would allow and others would not. It seemed that although it depended on the nature of the girl, it also depended much on the nature of the man, and his boldness with words and action.

He knew nothing of such stratagems. He could hardly believe his own ears when he heard himself say: 'Fabricia Bérenger, I think of you day and night. I can think of nothing else. I am on fire.'

He grabbed her arm and pulled her to her feet. There was no tenderness in him at that moment; he was just bent on getting the thing done, taking what he so desperately wanted. Like a common thief.

He dragged her down on to the hard floor and lifted her skirts. She did not resist him, and he was insensible to her pain when he possessed her, nor did he hear her protests. It was over quickly; there was a sudden gasping moment, which he tried to slow or stop, and then it was done.

It came too quickly, this boiling moment of ecstasy and despair; he cried out as he slipped to a moment's heaven and was at once thrown out again. His body barely ceased its spasm when he was overtaken utterly by the blackest shame. He heard the blood rushing in his ears, and he wished only to be anywhere but where he was. He caught his breath and held it. *I will be damned by this moment for ever.*

He felt physically sick with revulsion at what he had done. He leaped to his feet, pulled down his robe and ran from the house without looking back.

XIII

Vercy.

FOR DAYS, WHENEVER he looked up, Renaut was there, trailing him around like a lost dog, scampering away when he threw his wine flask at him, always trotting back when he had exhausted his rage.

Renaut's father, Gauthier, had been sergeant-at-arms to his own father; they had fought side by side in Outremer and it had made a bond between them. As a boy he remembered them sitting together at the table in the great hall like brothers and getting drunk and leaning on each other and laughing too loudly. It was the only time Philip had ever seen his father bawdy.

Gauthier had had lost an eye at Acre fighting the Saracen and the cicatrice traced from hairline to jaw, so that one side of his face looked as if it had once been wax and left too near a fire. It made him fearsome. When he had had too much wine it was his pleasure to chase the children and serving women around the hall growling like a bear. Philip himself only ever remembered a good-tempered man with a fondness for candied fruit.

Gauthier and Philip's father fell out just before his father died and Renaut's father found employment elsewhere and Gauthier died before they could reconcile. It was his father's only regret and on his deathbed he made Philip promise that he would make amends. He has a bastard son somewhere, he said.

So when Philip was invested at Vercy, he sent for him, to the astonishment and relief of all.

He arrived on All Souls' Day, on the wettest day Philip could remember, the rain falling straight down from a sky the colour of pewter, no wind, mud up to the ankles. Renaut sat on a piebald pony, its flanks shivering with cold and misery, escorted either side by two squires barely older than he was.

They had rung the chapel bells for nones but already the light was seeping out of the day. The porter and the stable boys went out with Philip to meet him, all of them in a hurry to get back to the fire in the great hall and a warm cup of spiced wine. Renaut was not a robust lad, even then; he had baby curls and a face like a stricken angel. But it was his eyes that signified most; they were of the most startling blue.

'Are you cold?' Philip asked him.

'I've been colder.'

Really? He had only a leather cloak over a thin tunic. Philip had seen drowned dogs with better aspect.

'All right, young man,' he had said. 'How about a warm fire and some hot beef? What do you say, young sir?'

The boy hesitated, his face solemn. 'I should first tend to my horse.'

'Did your grandfather teach you that? Well, we have stable boys to attend to that here.' He would have scooped him from the horse's back as he would a child but instead Renaut slid from the saddle and followed Philip back into the castle, hands clasped behind his back.

He'll do, Philip thought.

Steam rose from him as he stood by the fire. Even his lips were blue. The men laughed and the women fussed. 'My name is Renaut,' he said.

'I know who you are.'

The women rubbed him with linen towels and were about to strip him there in the hall but he intervened. 'We gentleman shall retire to dress in private,' he said and led the boy upstairs to the bedroom.

That had been ten years ago. In the intervening years he had taught him to tilt a lance at the quintain, how to fight with sword, mace and dagger, and how to ride straight-backed in the saddle. He had also showed him how to use a longbow and the boy had the steadiest hand and best eye of any man he had ever seen. He had planned to purchase a palfrey, armour and a sword for him in the new year, and have him dubbed a knight at the Easter festival.

He had grown in the year he had been gone; just a twig before he left, now there was meat on him and he answered back. He had blue eyes and sandy hair like his father, stubborn as he was, and loyal to a fault.

'Seigneur, you should eat,' he said.

'I'm not hungry,' Philip growled.

But he let Renaut help him to his feet and he staggered downstairs. Dogs picked at the gnawed meat bones on the floor, sniffed at a litter of half-eaten brown pears. Mud all through the hall and no one had thought to sweep the rushes. There was the sound of snoring from the straw by the cold fire and laughter from the stables. He went to the window, saw the stable boys playing knucklebones in the yard. They should be feeding the horses and mucking out the stalls.

He dragged the nearest of the servants to his feet and took him by the ear. 'Your master's home, and is done with his grieving now. Today it is just a scolding; tomorrow I shall come down with the whip. Be sure to be about your business.'

He rolled the rest of them out of the straw with his boot. They ran off: he would not need the whip. He would not have used it anyway, but they did not need to know that.

He went down to the scullery, stepped over a kitchen boy asleep on the stairs. There were weevils in the flour, mouse droppings in the larder. Grain crunched under his boot. Rats had chewed through every one of the grain sacks and a pheasant lay unplucked on the bench. It seemed that no one had thought to salt the pork and it had turned rotten.

'I tried to tell them,' Renaut said. 'They wouldn't listen to me. There was even talk that perhaps you were not coming back.'

'There's mildew in the pot, for the love of God.'

What did I expect? he thought. When I put on the cross, it had fallen to her to pay the soldiers, scold the servants, have the hides tanned and the grain milled and keep count of the spice boxes and the candles. Perhaps she was right, God's cause was better served here in Vercy than in Jerusalem.

'When the lady Alezaïs died . . .'

'I understand. The fault lies with me, no one else.' The boy was awake now, standing by the cold hearth, wide-eyed with fright. 'Get the servants here now,' he said to him. 'There's work to be done.'

The boy ran off.

He turned to Renaut. 'The sun is out. I want all the bed and table linen washed. Have we enough firewood for the winter? Get it done. Now that I am home I think you will find they listen to you better. Tomorrow we go hunting. Let us pray we find a stag or two and fat boars or it's going to be a lean winter.'

Somewhere in the castle a child was crying.

'In God's name, what is that?'

'He does not have a name yet,' Renaut said. 'Do you want to see him?'

'Not now.' He turned for the stair. 'I'm going to see to the stable boys, throw their dice in the moat. Then they can saddle my horse.'

'Where are you going?'

'I need to talk to my wife.'

XIV

Toulouse

FABRICIA GROANED AND rolled on to her side. She put her hand between her legs and stared at the slimy, watery mess of blood. She imagined this might be what it was like to be a young man knocked down in a fight, robbed and beaten by the companion with whom you were so taken a few minutes before.

And she had thought him so sad and so gentle.

She must get up off this floor; her mother would soon be home from the market. Would she tell her? But then her mother would tell her father and he would act upon that knowledge. Her family would be brought to ruin.

If I am to go to the nunnery then my maidenhead is no longer of concern to any future husband, so no harm done there, she thought. Unless he has got me with child. But there is an old woman who lives just outside the city walls who they say can give a girl a potion of herbs that will flush away a babe before it has a chance to grow.

All this decided and I have not yet pulled down my skirts.

She dragged herself to her feet, brushed the rushes from her clothes, smoothed down her hair. No bruises, then, no marks.

I feel as if I have been ripped and I want to spend the day weeping but I shan't, and yes, aside from this, no harm done.

Silence then, and the old woman at the wall.

*

The city glared back at him. He shared conspiracy with the meanest cutpurse; the lowest beggar glanced up at him from the filthy alleys and knew his sin to its core.

He avoided a leper who passed him on the street, shaking a rattle to warn of his approach; but who shall taint whom? he thought. He went down a street of butchers, the blood from their slaughter-houses running through the sea of mud and rubbish. Flies swarmed around the banquet. *There lies my soul.*

He wandered blindly for hours before returning to the priory, where he went direct to his cell and fell to his prayers. He knew that he must now confess what he had done to the prior.

If only he might have the morning again, to undo what had been irrevocably done. He wanted to weep and could not. Each time he closed his eyes he saw again his loathsome sin.

But he did confess to the prior and within a day a curious thing happened. He began to want her again.

His desire began as a perverse whisper inside his head, at first scarcely heard among the screams of self-loathing. But before the second day was out she had already begun her haunting of him, even as he tried to exorcize her. As he prayed abjectly for forgiveness, a part of him wished to sin again.

He kept to his cell, feigning sickness. The prior, concerned, sent the infirmarian, who prescribed a potion of herbs and, of course, a bleeding. Simon accepted his medicines without complaint and with not a little disdain. He knew he must take action against his importunate desires if he was to save his soul, and when the way and means of it finally suggested itself, he was so low in spirit and in mind that there was in him no resistance to the terrible cure.

XV

THE BRIEF SUMMER must be paid for. The weather passed from June to midwinter in just a day, the wind turned to the north and now there was ice in its breath and the sky was the colour of a dead man's shroud.

Simon turned up the hood on his cloak as a flurry of rain soaked him. Outside the common round of the Toulousains were crowded in the streets before the monastery of Saint-Sernin, in all their stinking ardour for commerce and congress, no matter what the weather. Life must go on. Simon's pony shied from an ox-cart, skittish on the frost-hard cobbles. He was hemmed in by the water-carriers and onion-sellers.

A hand caught the reins. Blessed Jesus, save us; he must have been waiting outside the gates all morning. Should he feign impatience or outrage?

'Anselm! What is the meaning of this? I have business to attend to. Release the halter, if you please.'

'Father, a moment of your time.'

'I have pressing affairs this morning. Should you not be at your work?'

'I am told my services are no longer required. Another mason is to be contracted to finish the work.'

'What business is this of mine?'

'I thought I might begin my work at the monastery all the sooner.'

'Impossible. The prior has changed his mind. He has asked me to contract another man for the work.'

Simon tried to jerk the reins away from him but they were bunched in the stonemason's fist and it would take a troop of the Count's yeomanry to release them. 'What is it that I have done to offend the Church?'

'I do not take your meaning.'

'Father, please, tell me what it is that I have done so that I might make amends.'

'I do as my prior commands me. You should ask him these questions. Now please, remove yourself.' He jerked at the reins but Anselm held fast, and his right hand closed on Simon's wrist. Simon cried out in pain and Anselm stepped back, as if he had put a hand in a fire.

'I am sorry, Father.'

'You would assault me in the street?'

'A thousand pardons. It's just that . . . I felt sure you could aid me with this. I am at a loss.'

Above them, on the corbels of the Porte des Comptes, devils were devouring the private members of the damned. My repudiation from heaven, he thought, in God's eloquent calligraphy. But I am too far gone in this now to turn back.

'I am sorry for your misfortune, Anselm. But I know nothing of this business. Now good day to you.'

Anselm gaped at him, but then his confusion changed to outrage. Ah, he understands now, Simon thought. What was it that betrayed me? My own intransigence perhaps? My indifference to his plight? For the mason had lauded me as a good man and it had not, until this moment, occurred to him that he might be wrong. He worked with the hard certainties of stone and a man like that could never truly appreciate the ever-pliable, ever-shifting nature of the soul.

What would Anselm do now?

But he never had to find out; he slapped at his pony's rump with his stick and urged it in the direction of the Capitole. Anselm went after him but was hemmed in by the passing of a mounted knight and his retinue, on their way to the castle. He looked back just once, saw Anselm standing outside the *porte*, a figure of despair as Toulouse jostled and shouted and laughed about him. He turned a full circle as if he was lost, put his head in his hands and then struck his knees with his fists. People stared at him, thinking him mad, stepping warily around this big man with the fingerless gloves and fists like hams.

Simon passed a beggar in the street, crumpled in the gutter with bandages on his bleeding sores. Not all these supplicants suffered, some only feigned their wounds, applying rags stained with mulberry juice to healthy limbs in order to beg alms and make their way through deceit. By day they cried out like the lost but at night they waited in alleyways to slit an honest man's throat for his silver coins.

Look at his broken teeth, his lying eyes. It was like looking in a mirror.

*

When Anselm arrived home the first thing he did was put his fist through the door, splintering the wood and sending a spray of blood over his knuckles. Elionor gasped and ran to him, but he pushed her away. He turned to his daughter.

'What did he do to you?'

Fabricia backed against the wall, terrified.

Elionor stepped between them. She had never seen her husband this way. 'What is wrong with you, husband? Speak up. You're scaring us.'

His eyes were wild. 'I have been dismissed from my employment by the Bishop's order. No reason was given. When I spoke to the priest from Saint-Sernin he said that the prior had hired someone else for the commission that he had promised to me.'

'What has this to do with Fabricia?' Elionor said, but even as the words were out of her mouth, she knew. 'The priest!' She slapped her fists against her husband's great barrel chest. 'What did I tell you? Why didn't you listen to me?'

Anselm caught her hands and looked at Fabricia. 'Is it true? Did he violate you, then?'

She could not find her voice; Elionor had no such impediment. 'You said he was a good man! There are no good men, not in the Church!'

Anselm picked up his bradawl and headed for the door. 'I'll kill this bastard,' he said, but immediately the two women were on him, one at each arm.

'No!' Elionor screamed at him. 'Think about us! What will we do without our breadwinner? Have you thought of that? Kill a priest and they will show us no mercy!'

Anselm hesitated, let them pull him back into the house. He knew Elionor was right. There was nothing they could do, not against the Church.

They made up their minds that very day. He discussed it through the long afternoon with his wife and they concluded there was no other choice. Simon must have persuaded the prior who had persuaded the Bishop and with the Bishop against him he would find no employment on any church in Toulouse.

'We'll head south, into the Albigeois,' he told his wife. 'They haven't any time for the Bishop down there. We'll start again.' He looked at Fabricia and fought back rage and pity. He would have liked to have crushed the priest's skull like a nut. 'Why didn't she tell us?' he asked his wife.

'She was trying to protect you,' she said and he knew straight away that she was right.

'We'll leave at the end of the week,' he said. 'This stinking city. Perhaps if we go south far enough we can find a little peace. I hope that bastard rots in hell.'

XVI

Vercy.

THE BELLS CHIMED for nones and he had still not returned, so Renaut rode down to the village to look for him. He found the seigneur's horse cropping the grass outside the church.

He went in. A light burned in the sacristy. He took a moment to accustom his eyes to the dark and then went down the narrow steps to the vault, his boots echoing on the stone flags.

Philip had lit a candle beside her resting place, and he was curled on top of her tomb, his rabbit's fur cloak wrapped around him. His breath froze on the air. It was crowded with death down here, every member of the baron's family had been buried in this cellar for five generations, and there was little enough space now for more.

'What are you doing here?' Renaut said.

'Saying goodbye.'

'You will freeze to death.'

'I do not mind that.'

'Death is a false friend, my lord. It makes you forget your duty to the ones who are still alive and rely on you.'

Philip rubbed the rough stone of the tomb with a gloved finger. 'She must have suffered before she died. I never understood why death must take so long about his work. Especially to those who themselves are not cruel. She deserved better.'

'Yes. She did.'

'I had a friend in Outremer. He was a southerner, from the Languedoc. A good man. Once I saw him knock some ruffian down for abusing a horse. And twice he saved my life. He was devout in his faith, went regularly to communion and would never do any man harm. But the manner of his death was beyond imagining. He took a wound to the belly in a skirmish and died a week later, still howling. He deserved a sweeter fate. Yet other men, they wore the cross even while they raped women, took greatest pleasure in torturing their prisoners, and these men survived our wars in good humour and good health. I confess, I do not understand the workings of God or the life He has put us in.'

'Yet we are here, and we must make the best of it.'

Philip laughed. More a bark really, of surprise, or perhaps he was just abashed at having spoken so plainly with his own squire. He sat up. 'Yes, you are right. We must to our duty. And yet . . .' He traced the carving of her name on the stone. 'Sometimes, if you take a single man or woman from the world, it is suddenly empty.'

'She left you something to remember her by.'

'This runt of mine took her life from me.'

'I am sure he did not wish to be without his mother. He is as wronged as you in this grief. And what of your good wife in heaven now, pray God? Would she want you to abandon him?'

Philip sat up slowly, reluctantly, and clapped him on the shoulder. 'How did you come to be so wise when you only have eighteen summers? You are right. Enough now. Show me my son.'

*

The wet nurse who held him had a kind face and seemed reluctant to let him go. He was almost half a year old now, a milksop who kicked and grinned and chewed like a hungry woodsman on his fist. When he saw Philip he offered a toothless grin.

Philip had entered the chamber prepared to meet the enemy who had murdered his wife but with this one stroke he was naked and disarmed. 'But he's perfect,' he said to Renaut, as if the child had been handed to him by accident.

'He is a fine boy. He has black curls like you.'

'But he has his mother's eyes. See, Renaut, they are just the same. It is as if she is staring at me.'

'He thrives. Look at him. He will be a giant like you one day.'

'I feel her in him.'

'He needs a name, my lord.'

Philip turned to the wet nurse. 'By what name do you call him now?'

She ducked her head. 'Just *petit m'sieur*, my lord.'

'Has he not been blessed by a priest?'

'When he was born. The priest called him Philip, after you.'

'No, I don't want him to be like me. The Philips of this world make war when they should be making peace. We will call him Renaut and hope that he will grow up as fine a young man as my young squire here.' Renaut's cheeks flushed bronze, overwhelmed by this honour. Philip handed the child back to the nurse. 'I let them down, both of them. I left when I should have stayed. I will never let it happen again.'

PART TWO

PART TWO

XVII

Saint-Ybars, in the Pays d'Oc
spring, 1209

THERE WAS IN the hour before the sun disappeared behind the mountains a time when the light was at its most perfect. Fabricia felt as if she could reach out a hand to touch each stunted thyme, each lavender bush and dwarf oak of the *garrigue*. In the valley below the wheat fields and pastures, the *faratjals*, looked like a giant's chessboard.

There were buds on the almond trees in the valley and, though the sun was still pale and the fire in the hearth had no warmth at all unless you sat right by it, a slow thaw had begun. Melted snow trickled down the lanes, the ice that hung from the roofs and lintels dripped steadily during the day, and the snow that yet clung to the shadowed alleys had turned to a dun-coloured slush. The air was so clear she could make out the grey branches of birch and ash on the far side of the valley.

Soon there would be no good excuse to wear her woollen gloves each day.

She watched the hunchback Bernart make his slow and difficult way out of the east *portal,* back to his *ostal* on the other side of the valley. Over his shoulder he carried the few meagre onions he'd brought to the market to sell. Some small boys were following behind, mocking him and throwing rocks. One of the stones caught him a glancing blow on the side of the head and he toppled into a ditch.

She set down her pannier and ran after them. They scattered into the lanes. 'I know who you are!' she shouted after them. 'Your mothers will know about this!'

Bernart was lying on his face in the ditch. At first she thought he was dead but when she shook him he opened his eyes and sat up. He did not seem to know where he was, and started to scramble for the onions that were scattered over the path. 'Are you hurt?' she said.

'No, not hurt,' he said. He was accustomed to such usage, she thought. Like a dog, you kick it, and it still licks your hand.

'You're bleeding,' she said. The stone had knocked off his cap and now she laid her hand on his head to examine the wound. It was an old head, and twisted, shaped like a bean; they said he was born that way, deformed when he came out of his mother's womb.

Bernart closed his eyes at her touch. 'Are you all right?' she said.'

He swayed on his knees, then reached up and took hold of her wrist. She drew back. He had frightened her.

'I'm sorry. It just felt so good. Like a cool river running through me.'

She felt immediately ashamed of her fear. Old Bernart would not hurt anyone. She helped him back to his feet, gave him his cap, gathered the rest of the onions from the ground and put them back in the sack. '*Dieu vos benesiga*,' she said.

'God bless you too, Fabricia,' he said and limped away.

Fabricia hurried back to the village. The *bayle* closed the gates at sunset and she got there just in time. It was late in the year for wolves but Catalan brigands roamed here from time to time. A muddy lane snaked between the houses huddled side by side up the hill. Chickens scattered fussing out of her way.

She saw a man in a brown cassock making his way towards her and she stopped, looked for another way, hoping to avoid him. But it was too late.

'Fabricia,' the priest said.

'Father Marty.'

'Have you been in the fields?' He stopped in front of her, blocking the way. A big man – he might have made a fine stonemason, her father had said. Instead of a lousy priest, her mother answered. He had a broad smile and greedy eyes, a glance quick to calculate a tithe or a dispensation. He once carried off the bedclothes of a dying man to whom he had just administered extreme unction and who was otherwise unable to pay. Or so they said.

His brother was the *bayle* so you watched yourself around him.

Half the unmarried women in the village, and a good portion of the wives, had been his mistress at one time or another.

'I've been collecting herbs for my mother.'

He took her pannier from her to see what was in it. *He doesn't want the thyme or the belladonna but he'll still take some, just to show that he can.* 'Is it true she's a wise woman?'

'Are you sick, Father?'

He didn't reply, just gave her back the pannier, lighter than when he took it.

'It is almost dark. I must get home,' she said.

He grabbed the sleeve of her dress and pulled her into a doorway. 'I heard you had a lover in Toulouse, a priest like me.'

'Hardly a lover. He raped me.'

'You women, you always say it's rape afterwards.'

It was dark in the lane, no one to see. She could scream, but then what might he do? *Better to try and talk my way out of this,* she thought.

'Are you worried about sin, little Fabricia? For I tell you, a lady who sleeps with a true lover is purified of all sin. The joy of love makes the act innocent for it proceeds from a pure heart. If you are happy to do it, you will not displease God.'

'Unless you do it with a husband, you go to hell.'

'Who told you that?' he said and tried to kiss her.

'Please, Father, I am afraid for my soul.' *But mostly it is because you repulse me,* she thought. *But if I say it, you and the bayle will make life miserable for my father, and haven't I done enough to him?*

'Then confess to me on Sunday and I will absolve you.' He put his hand on her breast and pressed hard against her. She thought about Simon and the bright, watery blood on the rushes after he was done with her and instinctively she brought up her knee, hard, and Father Marty crumpled to his knees. Fabricia twisted away and ran. She did not stop until she reached their *domus*, high up the hill, near the *bayle*'s château.

*

In Toulouse they had lived in a stone house with solid doors fitted with locks and there were fine hangings on the walls. Each time she came home to their new *ostal* in the village, Fabricia experienced a stab of shame for how they were reduced. Draughts whistled under the door, and just a single ham hung from the rafters by the hearth, instead of the flitches of bacon, black puddings and rillettes they had before. They were rich compared to the other villagers, they had a stone fireplace and even a *solier*, a room above the *foganha*, where her parents slept. Most of the other houses were just wood and daub. But it was still nothing compared to Toulouse.

Her mother was chopping herbs and onions and throwing them into the *payrola* that bubbled in the hearth in the centre of the room. Anselm was toasting his toes before the fire. His hair was almost completely grey now, for he was getting to be an old man, almost fifty.

Her mother could sense straight away that something was wrong.

'Are you all right, girl? You're white as a sheet.'

'I saw old Bernart as I was coming back from the fields. The baker's sons were tormenting him again. They hit him in the head with a rock. I get so angry. Why don't they leave the poor man alone?'

'They say he is possessed,' Anselm said.

'Because he has a hump on his back?'

'A sign of the Devil.'

'He is not possessed! He is utterly harmless. He has a crooked back, but the sweetest nature of any man in the village!'

'Don't talk to your father that way!' Elionor said.

'Even the priest says it,' he mumbled.

'Father Marty is from the Devil if anyone is.'

'You see? I'm not the only one in this family who hates those vultures,' her mother said.

'Did God not make all things, Papa?'

'He did.'

'And did He not make Bernart also?'

Anselm looked sulky, as he always did when trapped in argument.

'Why did God make such a creature as Bernart unless He meant him to be that way? How can a God that is truly good make something that is evil?'

'Because God did not make the world!' her mother said. 'It is like the *bons òmes* say, the world belongs to the Devil. That is why!'

'*Basta!*' her father shouted. 'Enough! I won't listen to heresy in my own house! And Fabricia, what have you done to yourself? You're bleeding.'

She stared at her glove. Some blood had seeped through. 'It's from Bernart,' she said. 'It must be from where the boys hit him with the stone.' She stared at him, daring him to challenge her in the lie. But he just shook his head and returned his gaze to the fire. Even her mother did not demand to see the wound and clean it. So: this is what you have come to, Fabricia Bérenger. You shout at your father, make him cross with your mother and then you lie to both of them. If there is a purgatory, then the devils will be warming the forks for you. You deserve it.

Later that night, after her parents had climbed the ladder to the *solier* and gone to bed, Fabricia crept to the fire and examined her hands in the dim light of the embers. As if she did not have enough to worry about already without these strange marks on her hands! A girl did not bruise the tender pride of the second most powerful man in Saint-Ybars and not think that tomorrow, when the sun rose again, there would not be trouble for it.

Help me, My Lady, she whispered into the crumbling ashes. Take these wounds away and save me, again, from one of your priests.

*

'Why was she so late getting home from the fields?' Anselm whispered.

'She was in the church again, I dare say. She spends all her time in there praying to the Madonna. After what that priest did to her, you'd think she'd never go in one of those places again.'

'She's never been the same since the storm. It turned her head a little, I do believe. Do you think she's all right?'

'If only she'd married Pèire, perhaps none of this would have happened.'

'She knew about it, do you remember? She said it would happen. "He will die soon," she said. And a few days later he falls from the scaffold.'

Elionor was silent. Anselm put an arm around her shoulder and felt her settle in. Where to find a good husband for her here? You didn't give a pearl to a swine. But he would have to do something, and soon.

XVIII

THERE WERE GREEN buds on the vines. Some of the vineyards were a thousand years old, Elionor had told her. They had been brought from Palestine by the Jews who fled to the Pays d'Oc when the Caesars were lords of Rome. Gauls and Jews lived side by side then, she said, there were cities and towns in the land of our language long before there was a king in Paris and a Pope in Rome.

Many different vines have been grafted here, she said. *Don't listen to your father. He's a good man but he's from the north, what would he know about the real story of the world? Your blood is rich, you yourself are a grafting of many vines. In the north they marry their sisters and count with their fingers. Here in the Pays d'Oc we have known the whole world: the Jews with their cabbalas, the Moors with their al-jabr and knowledge of the stars, the Templars who brought home muslin cloth and exotic fruits.*

You are a grafted vine. When your father spouts his nonsense about his saints and his Resurrection, don't forget that.

*

'Why are you wearing gloves today? Winter is over. You could roast a goose on the cobbles today.'

'I'm cold,' Fabricia said.

'You can't be cold, you silly girl.'

'It can't be summer. We haven't had the feast for St Mary yet.'

'The sun doesn't care about feasts. If it's hot, it's hot. You're limping. What's wrong, girl? You've been acting strange since last night. Where are you going?'

'To the market.'

'Show me your hands!'

Fabricia stared at her. *Why do I even try to lie to her? She always knows.*

Fabricia started to take off her gloves. *Now there will be trouble. Perhaps they will listen to me now, let me take orders.* Someone hammered at the door. Elionor hesitated. 'Who on earth is that?'

'Madame Bérenger!' a man's voice shouted. 'Quickly!'

'I'll see who it is but then I want to know what it is you're hiding!' she said to Fabricia and threw open the door. She was shoved aside as four of Anselm's labourers pushed their way in, grunting and sweating, holding Anselm by his legs, his arms, his belt, his shirt. There was blood everywhere. They hefted him on to the bench in the kitchen.

'*Paire Sant!*' Elionor shouted and pushed the men aside, wailing in grief. 'Is he dead?' Fabricia shouted.

But Anselm was not dead. He coughed, spitting blood on the table and down his shirt. Alive, then; but just. Elionor cradled his head in her hands. 'What have you done to yourself, husband?' She looked round at the men. 'Did he fall?'

'The carter's dray,' one of the men said, wiping the blood off his hands on to his smock. 'We'd just finished unloading some stone and it took fright and bolted. He missed the hooves but not the wheels.'

'Was it laden?'

'We'd taken off most of the stone but I saw the wheel go over his chest. I heard his ribs break.'

'What shall we do?' the youngest said. 'There's not one doctor in the village knows physick.'

'We don't need a quack, just a priest,' another said, and the others glared at him and he fell silent.

Fabricia touched her mother's shoulder. Elionor put her fist in her mouth to stifle a scream. Fabricia could hardly bear to look; there was blood bubbling from his mouth in a pink froth. It sounded like he was drowning.

The men crowded back against the wall, terrified. 'They're right,' Elionor whispered. 'We need Father Marty.'

'You hate the priest.'

'Yes, but it's his religion. I won't let him die without it. It's the one thing that ever scared him, dying without the unction.'

'He's not going to die.'

'Of course he is, look at him!' She picked up his hand, held it to her lips. 'Didn't I tell you to be careful?' She wailed at him and put her head on the bench and sobbed. 'Why didn't one of you help him!' she shouted, and the men shrank further back against the wall, and for all their size they looked like little children hiding from their father's belt.

Fabricia felt sorry for them. It wasn't their fault. 'One of you fetch the priest,' she said. They almost fought each other to be first out of the door. They had to push their way through the crowd that had gathered there. News of the accident had travelled through the village already.

Anselm tried to raise his arm. His eyelids flickered. 'Eli . . . onor . . .'

'Don't talk, husband. Save your strength.'

'. . . *t'aime . . . mon co . . . eur . . .*' I love you, my darling.

'I told you to be careful!' Elionor wailed again.

Fabricia fetched a pail of water and a cloth and washed the blood out of Anselm's beard. His forehead was cold and damp and his breath rattled in his chest. What are we going to do without you? she thought. We've taken you for granted for so long.

The carter's wheel had left an imprint on his chest. There was a bloody weal on his skin, and an ugly purple bruise had spread over the whole left side of his chest. Instinctively she put out a gloved hand and laid it there, where he had been hurt. Her mother stared at the blood that had seeped through the wool, staining it the colours of rust.

'What are you doing?' she whispered.

'It is just comfort,' Fabricia said.

'What is wrong with your hands?'

'It's nothing.'

Anselm gave a great sigh, as if the cart had been sitting on his chest and they had just hefted it off. Elionor dropped her head on to her arms in despair and waited for Father Marty. She knew her husband would not die until his damned priest had given him the rites.

'Do you smell that?' she said, dreamily. 'How curious. Lavender.'

*

'They told me he was dying,' Father Marty said.

'You sound disappointed,' Elionor said.

'The fee is the same whether he lives or dies.' His eyes followed Fabricia. Anselm murmured a few words of confession and Father Marty put his ears to her father's lips to listen. He repeated the words of the holy rite. 'Two *sols*. How will you pay me?'

'Get your eyes off her, you dog! I have the money right here. Get out.'

Father Marty took the coins and with a final leer at Fabricia he left. Elionor stared after him. 'Devils. The lot of them.'

Anselm was too heavy to move to the bed so they surrounded him with blankets and bolsters on the bench to make him comfortable. His colour was better and it did not seem to hurt him so much to breathe. Fabricia allowed herself a prayer that he might yet live, but dared not say the words aloud. They said that if the Devil heard you hope, he would come and make it his business to put an end to it.

They stood either side of the bench and watched him breathe. Elionor stroked his hair. 'Don't you stop fighting, my big man. You won't leave me in this world alone.' She looked across him, at Fabricia. 'Show me your hands. You thought I had forgotten? Come on, show me.'

Fabricia took off her gloves. Elionor drew in a breath. '*Paire Sant*! What is that?'

'I burned it on the fire, taking the pot from the hearth. It is nothing.'

'This is like no burn I ever saw! Did someone do this to you?'

'No one did it to me.'

'Are you in pain?'

'Yes.'

'Does anyone else know?'

She shook her head.

Elionor dared to touch the edge of the wound, but quickly snatched her hand away, as if she had been scalded. 'What does it mean?'

'I don't know, Mama.'

Elionor walked around the bench and stood behind her. She put her arms around her waist and held her.

She watched the laboured rise and fall of her father's chest; he coughed again and another froth of blood trickled down his cheek. She felt suddenly faint and started to fall, but Elionor held her in her strong arms. 'Be strong, *filha*,' she whispered. 'We will get through this.'

XIX

Anselm's eyes blinked open. A log jumped in the grate. Fabricia had kept the fire stoked through the night. Elionor, dozing on a chair next to the bench, sat up as soon as she heard him stir.

'Anselm, don't get up! You're hurt.'

'I did not mean to sleep so long,' he said. 'What hour is it? Is the sun risen?' He swung his legs over the side of the bench. Elionor tried to stop him getting up but he pushed her hand away. 'What are you doing? I must be up and to work.'

'No, you can't, not today. You were hurt yesterday. By the carter's dray. Look.' She showed him the bruises. 'The priest has been here, he gave you the blessed sacrament. We all thought you were dead.'

Anselm seemed confused. He looked at the bloodstains on his tunic, gouts of it dried black into the gaps of wood on the bench. He put a hand to his ribs and winced. 'They are a little sore.'

'*Paire Sant!*' Elionor breathed and sat down. 'This cannot be. Thanks be to Jesus, but it cannot be.'

Anselm stood up, rocking on the balls of his feet, and steadied himself against the bench. 'How long have I been asleep?'

'Since yesterday morning when the men carried you in,' she said.

'Look, it's a scratch, nothing more,' he said. 'I must have bumped my head a little, that's all. I feel like I've been drinking all night.' Elionor started to weep. He ruffled her hair. 'Don't take on so, *mon coeur*. I'm all right.'

'I thought you were dead!'

'Not me,' he said, as if he were indestructible.

Fabricia had been watching from the other side of the room. She ran over, put her arms around her papa's neck and breathed in the smell of him; the sweat and stale blood stank, but it was sweet as life to her. He patted her shoulders, embarrassed by the fuss.

'I really scared you two, eh?'

'You have to rest today,' Fabricia said, and he let her ease him back on to the bench; but later that morning as the two women slept, exhausted, he gathered together some bread and cheese and a new tunic and slipped out of the door and went down the hill to the church, to make sure those lazy good-for-nothings he employed to carry his stone were not idling on the job.

XX

THE NEXT MORNING as Fabricia made her way down the lane to the *portal* there were no hands raised in greeting and no familiar smiles, just fearful looks and neighbours scuttling into doorways to whisper. Perhaps it is these gloves, she thought. Has anyone seen the blood dripping? No, I have bound them as well as I am able, but I cannot disguise how I walk, the pain I am in. Perhaps it's that.

Then she saw Father Marty. He grinned at her. Well, there was no point in running away, so she stopped and let him come to her. Let us be done with it; he would have his revenge somehow, for the bruises to his pride, inside and out.

He stopped, his hands on his hips. 'Last time you took me by surprise,' he said. 'The next time I shall not be so careless.'

Her feet were agony and she had to take the weight off them. She leaned against the wall of a house, trying not to let her distress show on her face.

'What did you do to your hands?'

'Nothing. I am cold this morning.'

'And the rest of the village sweating!' He grabbed her hand and peeled back her glove. 'Bandages! I saw them the other night when I gave your father the rites for the dying. What did you do to yourself?'

She snatched back her hand.

'What are we poor villagers to make of the Bérenger family? You bandaged for no reason, your father dead and now living. I saw him this morning up a scaffold, repairing the nave to my church instead of lying under it. How can this be?'

'A miracle, *paire.*'

'But how?'

'*Deus lo volt.*'

'God wanted it, yes, perhaps. Others think it was the Devil's craft and that you had a hand in it.'

'Who says so?'

Father Marty just smiled and she thought: So this is how he is going to take his revenge. He is going to make me into a witch.

'There are rumours about you and Bernart.'

'I don't understand.'

'They say some children knocked him down with stones, that he was dead before you laid your hands on him and brought him back to life. The way you did to your father.'

'I had nothing to do with it. My mother is a healer. She gave him opium and belladonna.'

He smiled but his eyes were hard. 'There is not a soul in the village who does not think you had a hand in it. A bandaged hand!' He laughed at his little jest. 'What is your secret, Fabricia Bérenger?'

She picked up her pannier and limped past him. This time he did not try to stop her. 'You walk like Bernart,' he said.

She winced with each step. Soon everyone would know her secret; she could not hide it much longer. Blessed Mary, why have you done this? she thought. My heart is overcome with gratitude that my blessed Papa is still alive when we should this day be putting him in the ground. And yet, now Father Marty wants everyone to think I am a witch and I can bring the dead back to life.

Why can't they all just leave me alone? Why did this happen to me?

XXI

MOSTARDA BURNED HIS feet on the hearth trying to reach the ham hanging from the rafter. Now he sat mewling and licking his paws in the corner. 'You don't eat the ham, you eat the mice,' Fabricia scolded him.

She sat alone at the bench chopping vegetables for the pot; Anselm was at work in the church, her mother had gone to the market. Fabricia was better at bartering than her mother, knew how to smile and when to wink and when to toss her hair at the butcher's boy and the widowed farmer from the next village, but today was a bad day, she could hardly walk with her feet in such a state, and so Elionor had gone in her stead. She heard another shower of rain whip against the oilskins on the window and she didn't mind being here by the warm hearth.

It was the pig snuffling in the mud in the yard that warned her; better than a dog he was, his high-pitched squeal letting her know a stranger was in the yard. She heard someone come in through the back door. She caught her breath and her fingers tightened around the bone-handled knife in her fist. Not that it would help her, a knife wasn't much use unless you were prepared to use it.

'Don't be afraid,' he said, smiling.

She remembered the last time a churchman appeared unannounced at her *domus*. 'I'm not afraid of you,' she lied.

He took off his cloak and set it on a chair by the hearth and sat down, toasting his toes as if this were his own *ostal*. He twisted the large amber ring on his finger. 'You should be afraid. Most people in this village are afraid of me.'

'No, they despise you. There's a difference.'

His smile fell away. Why can't I keep my thoughts to myself? she thought. Mocking him will only make it worse. I am here alone and I know he has come here for only one purpose, two if he intends to hurt me as well. Bite your lip, girl, get this over with.

He leaned forward. 'Who do you think you are, talking to me that way? Put the knife down.'

'Why, do you think I might stick you with it? Maybe I would.'

'Put it down,' he repeated.

She put the knife on the table.

'I could destroy you. You and all your family.'

'In God's name?'

'In any name I choose.'

'What do you want?'

'You know what I want,' he said.

'And then? If you get it, will you leave me in peace?'

'It depends.' He stood up and walked around the bench, trapping her in the corner. His cassock was wet and the wool stank. He raised the hem of his robe, all the time keeping his eyes on her face. Fabricia flinched.

'Look,' he said. The tumour on his thigh was gross, a great swollen piece of flesh, livid in its centre like a bruise. Fabricia felt her gorge rise. She looked away.

'Heal me,' he said.

'What?'

'Put your hands on me like you did to Bernart.'

'I didn't do anything to Bernart. There was nothing wrong with him. I just helped him get up.'

'Everyone knows what you did. Your father too. His men swear he was near dead when they brought him here. What did you do? Is it some prayer you have? Do you see devils?'

'I don't do anything,' she said again. She dared another glance at his diseased leg. It was so grotesque, she almost felt sorry for him. 'Does it hurt you?'

'Not yet,' he said but she could tell that he feared it soon would.

She held out her hand, hesitated. Even when she was wearing woollen mittens she shrank from touching such a thing.

'What, am I too filthy for you to touch? Do for me what you did for Bernart! Well? You touched a cripple and you won't touch me?'

Fabricia encircled the extrusion of flesh with her palm. His skin was pale with coarse hairs, and the mass growing out of it reminded her of the jelly on pork fat after it had been boiled. 'How long have you had this?' she asked him.

'I saw it first just before the Feast of the Epiphany. It was then a lump the size of a walnut, no more. But every day it grows more, right in front of my eyes.' There was a tremor in his voice. 'I have tried salves and a wise woman in Carcassonne gave me a poultice of herbs but it has done no good.'

She placed her hand on it, closed her eyes and said a prayer to the lady.

'I can feel something,' he said. 'What do you have under those gloves? Show me.' He grabbed her wrist.

'Do you want me to heal you or not? Then let me go.' *Why did I say that to him? Have I started to believe these stories too?*

He let go of her arm and then looked around the room, as if he was searching for something. 'Do you smell that?' he said. 'It's like lavender. Have you been chopping herbs?'

Fabricia had noticed it also, at the very moment she put her hand on the priest. She looked into the corner to see if the lady in blue was there.

'What are you looking at?' he said.

'Nothing. You should go now.'

'You thought you saw something!' he said, as if he had caught her out in a lie.

'No.' He lowered his cassock. What was the expression on his face, was it fear, loathing or hope? Perhaps all three of them, mixed together. With one snake-like movement he snatched up the knife and buried the point of the blade into the wooden bench between her hands. 'If this doesn't work, I'll be back. Don't make a fool of me a second time. The Martys never forget an insult.'

'Just don't tell anyone about this,' she said.

'Just our little secret, òc?' He picked up his cloak from the fire and pulled it on. 'Pray that I get well. For your sake, if not for mine.'

XXII

THE *BONS ÒMES* made their way up the hill through the narrow lanes of Saint-Ybars. People came out of their houses to kneel down as they passed. Everyone knew days ago that they were coming. The *bayle*'s mother and old Gaston were dying and both had asked to be baptized with the *consolamentum* so that they would pass to the next world better prepared. The two priests would stay that night at the house of Pons the weaver, an honour he had keenly contested with three other villagers.

No heretic priest might go unnoticed anywhere, least of all Guilhèm Vital. He was tall and angular, and the way he strode along, it suggested a man marching fearlessly to his doom. He was clean-shaven and his long black hair hung about his shoulders. She imagined it might be how Jesus would have looked if he had Spanish blood in him. His companion – his *socius* – was a head shorter and hurried to keep up with his long loping strides.

They both wore long black hooded robes, the colour of mourning, to display their grief at finding themselves in the Devil's world. They carried with them on a roll of cord about their necks, the Gospel of John, the only text sacred to them. They leaned on long staffs as they made their way up the hill.

They were priests, as Father Marty was a priest, but there she supposed the resemblance ended. The *bons òmes* never threatened any who did not believe in their teaching, and they did not charge a fee for naming children or burying the dead. Nor did they live by tax or by tithe, only by the goodwill of the *crezens* – even the Catholics – who held them to be good men.

The heretics believed in Jesus and the Gospel of John but not the cross; the mass, they said, was a sacrilege; the entire Roman Church was the work of Satan and the seat of all damnation. In their preaching they pointed out that there was nothing in the testaments that allowed bishops to live more sumptuously than princes and wear furs and jewels. They themselves lived as itinerant preachers, owned nothing and were paid nothing, refused even to carry a weapon in case they harmed someone by accident.

Their creed was this: all that was not spirit was doomed to destruction and merited no respect. Yet though they were hard with themselves, they were gentle with others; they allowed that not everyone could live lives of such harsh discipline, and so all that was necessary to save the soul was to believe in their preaching – to be a *crezen* – to offer them respect, and take the final right of baptism into the faith just before death.

Which was why so many villagers came out of their houses to prostrate themselves at their feet and ask their blessing as they passed. It was the first time heretics had come here since they had lived in Saint-Ybars and Fabricia had not realized how many *crezens* there were, just in her village alone.

She watched, curious about them, and it was only at the last that she realized they were headed for her own *ostal*. Elionor, standing beside her, did not seem at all surprised at this honour. Fabricia realized rather that her mother was expecting it and when she understood the reason her cheeks burned with humiliation.

Guilhèm Vital stopped at their door. Elionor sank to her knees. 'Bless me, Father, and pray that I come to a good end.'

Guilhèm gave her his blessing and then looked at Fabricia, offering her the opportunity for the same. Fabricia pulled back her hood and lowered her head but did not ask for his benediction. Like Anselm, she still thought of herself as a good Catholic, no matter what anyone said.

Elionor led the two priests inside and sat them down by the fire. She brought them water and a little bread. They ate little else, Fabricia had been told, never meat or wine, and they did not fast just at Lent but all year round. You could tell that by the look of them.

It was strange to her to see someone break bread without first making the sign of the cross. Afterwards they knelt to pray the Our Father and when Elionor joined in, Fabricia fell to her knees also. No harm in that, she thought, even though Papa wouldn't like to see her do it.

'So, you are the famous Fabricia?' Guilhèm said at last. He held out his hand for her to come closer. His bony wrists were covered in a mat of dark hair. She had heard a lot about him since they came to the mountains: his preaching, his prodigious energy, his skill as a healer. Physically, he was no more than a pale skeleton with piercing black eyes, though his demeanour was at odds with his appearance for he had the manner of a kindly uncle. 'Show me these wounds.'

Fabricia looked at her mother. 'You have told people about this?'

'Why do I need to tell anyone? They all talk enough already.'

'Is this why they have come here?'

'What was I to do? You won't talk to me about it. Paire Guilhèm is the best doctor in the mountains. Everyone knows it.'

'Give me your hands,' Guilhèm said. 'Come on, I won't hurt you.'

Fabricia peeled off her gloves. Guilhèm unwound the scraps of cloth that Fabricia had used to bind them, taking great care. As he peeled back the bandage she heard his *socius* take a sharp breath and look away.

Guilhèm frowned. 'You must be in great pain.'

'Sometimes.'

'But these wounds, they have pierced the palms almost through. How long have they been like this?'

When Fabricia did not answer he turned to Elionor.

'When the weather grew warmer and she would not take off her gloves I was suspicious. That's when I first knew. I don't know how long before that.'

He brought her hand to his nose and breathed in. He seemed deeply puzzled. 'But there is no rotting, no foul humours or excretions.' He looked up at Fabricia. 'How have you kept this wound so clean?'

Fabricia tried to draw her hand away from him but he gripped her tight. For such a thin man he was very strong. 'I don't. I just keep some cloth bound on them to stop the blood seeping.'

Guilhèm shook his head. 'Your mother says you have an injury to both your feet as well. Show me.'

Fabricia sat on the bench and removed her boots. One of the cloths was bloodied. 'This is impossible,' the *socius* said.

Guilhèm seemed less perturbed. He placed one of her feet on to his lap and peered closely at it. 'How do you walk?'

'Sometimes it is difficult.'

'Difficult? You should be crippled. How did you come by such injuries? Has someone abused you? Your father perhaps?'

'Papa would never hurt me!'

'Then who has done this?'

'No one did it.'

'Was it you?'

'I don't understand.'

Guilhèm looked at Elionor. 'She has made these wounds herself.'

Fabricia twisted away and quickly rebound her feet. She felt her mother's eyes burning into her.

'This is what I believe also,' Elionor said.

'Believe what you want.'

'There is no other explanation,' Guilhèm said.

'But why does she not have the rot and the fever?'

'You are a healer?' he said to Elionor, pointing to the herbs drying in bunches above the hearth and on the windows.

'I make potions and restoratives when I am asked. I learned it from my mother and she learned from her mother before her.'

'You have taught Fabricia?'

Elionor shook her head.

'Then she must have watched you. She uses potions to clean the wounds. Yet I confess she must be very skilled, for they are deep. Her will is extraordinary for she must suffer a great deal every day.'

'My husband says these are the wounds of Jesus on the cross,' Elionor said.

Guilhèm looked sad at this suggestion. 'The cross. This terrible torture that the Whore of Babylon seeks to glorify. Your daughter has taken their lies too much to heart.' Fabricia blanched. She had never grown accustomed to hearing these gentle men refer to the Pope as a whore.

He turned back to her. 'The cross is not something you should revere.'

'You think I want this, that I would do this to myself? Do you think I want everyone staring at me like I am a devil? Our Lady wanted this, not me!'

'What lady?' Guilhèm asked her. Such a gentle voice, such compelling eyes, it would be easy to confess everything to him, have him tell her it was all a young girl's fantasy. But she was almost nine-teen years old now and she was not a girl any more.

Anyway, how could he possibly understand? For all their gentleness and piety the *bons òmes* were as convinced of their opinions as the priests.

She put on her boots and ran out of the house, down to the fields, to be alone.

XXIII

ELIONOR SHOVED THE door to get it open; the rain had made the wood swell. Fabricia heard her climb the ladder to the *solier*. Earlier, she had gone to Pons's *ostal* to hear Guilhèm preach.

She heard her father's voice: 'How many were there?'

'Half the village.'

The fire was down to just embers, and it was the only light. The darkness seemed somehow to magnify every sound. She heard mice scuttle in the corners, and then her father whispered: 'I fear for your soul.'

'They are good men, husband. You should listen to them.'

'I have never doubted that they are good men.'

'Good men and good priests. You could never say that about these other devils in cassocks. They don't bleed us dry in tithes, they don't keep prostitutes. In his own church Guilhèm is like a bishop and he doesn't live in a palace like that dog in Toulouse.'

'Because they live good lives does not mean I must agree with all they say.'

'They live as they preach. How else would you judge a man's religion other than by what he does? Have you seen how that Father Marty makes eyes at Fabricia? He bleeds everyone dry, him and his family. And you still want to call yourself a Catholic?'

There was a long silence, then: 'Did you hear what happened in Toulouse? Someone murdered Peter of Castelnau.'

'Who's he?'

'The Pope's man, sent here from Rome. Someone stopped him on the road and butchered him.'

'As if that would be a loss!'

'Except that it is, for now the Pope blames Count Raymond for it. They say he will send a crusade against him, to punish him for harbouring men like Guilhèm. This is not a good time to pronounce yourself a heretic, *mon coeur*.'

'A crusade against Christians!'

'Guilhèm may call himself a Christian but that is not what they say in Rome.'

'Those whores!'

'*Basta!* I won't have you talk like this in my own house!'

'Who's going to harm us here in the mountains? Perhaps in Toulouse or Carcassonne. No one worries about those things up here. If they killed every heretic in Foix there would be no one left.'

They fell silent. The wind whistled through the cracks in the door. Fabricia huddled deeper under the furs. She thought they had left off their arguing to sleep, but then a little while later it started again.

'Why did you have them here today? I told you I did not want those men in my house.'

'I wanted them to look at Fabricia's hands. He's a healer, isn't he, the best in the whole of Foix.'

'What did he say?'

'He thinks she made the wounds herself.'

'What? Why would she do such a thing?'

'How else do you explain it?'

'He thinks she would torture herself? Your holy man is mad.'

'He made her uncover her hands and feet. I almost fainted. It's getting worse. I swear one of the wounds goes right through the flesh of her hand.'

'You don't think she is possessed? Mengarda was possessed. She had the falling sickness, frothed at the mouth when the Devil was in her.'

'There is all this talk about Bernart in the village. He says he saw great bolts of lightning shoot out of her hands when she touched him.'

Lightning? Fabricia thought. Had he really said that or had people made it up? All she did was help the old man to his feet. She pulled the furs over her head, opened her mouth and screamed silently into the dark. She didn't want to hear any more.

'. . . they say I would have died too if she had not laid her hands on me. Is it true? Did you see her do something to me?'

'She prayed for you and held you, just like I did. That was all.'

'You know, these wounds she has, they are the same as the wounds Our Lord bore on the cross.'

There was a long silence and Fabricia held her breath. Then her mother's voice: 'Guilhèm says that God cannot die and that Jesus was just a good man come to help us. He says the cross is the Devil's sign because it is about the power of Rome, not the power of God and –'

'I don't want to hear any more of your blasphemy in this house!'

The wind sent the linen curtain flapping and a full moon swept from behind the clouds. Fabricia held her hands towards the light. She wore gloves now, even to bed. 'Let this pass,' she murmured. 'If I truly have the power to heal wounds, let me heal my own. Oh Lady, Saint of Sinners, have some pity.'

'What are we going to do?' she heard her mother say.

'I don't know, *mon coeur*. When we were in Toulouse she said that she wanted to take orders. I was against it then, but perhaps it is the only answer. It is the only place she might be safe.'

You see? Fabricia thought. There only ever was one choice. I don't know why I was chosen for this, but when God points his finger at you, you cannot slink away into a corner and hide. Perhaps he died on the cross, perhaps he didn't; all I know is he sent the lady in blue to set me apart, and now all I can do is try and bear it.

XXIV

ALL THOSE WHO had gone to Pons's house to listen to Guilhèm Vital preach now huddled into the little church outside the *portal* to attend the mass, alongside all of those who had not. On Sunday everyone was a Christian. Some of them, she heard her father say, fished from both banks; they bowed to the *bons òmes* and asked for their blessing but confessed to the priest as well in case there was a Judgement and Jesus really did drag their mouldy bones from the grave to answer for themselves.

It was raining for the third day in succession and freedmen and the poor were all crowded in, shivering in their thin woollen cloaks and wooden clogs. The stink of bodies and wet wool was overpowering. The fog of incense only made it worse, making a sweet church stink that made Fabricia's head ache and her eyes smart.

Father Marty droned an incomprehensible babble of Latin. No one paid him much attention. Some barrowmen at the back had brought their dogs, and the miller's wife was gossiping to her neighbour as if they were in the marketplace. The young men of the village wandered in and out, flirting with Pons's daughters and making remarks among themselves.

Elionor made the sign of the cross as Father Marty held up the host. 'Here's my forehead, here's my chin, here's my ear, here's the other one.' Her neighbour snickered. Anselm glared at them both.

After they shared the body of Christ they sang a prayer of thanksgiving, and then filed out of the church, escaping into a bitter morning. The wind blew and water poured down the gullies in the lanes, turning them into sticky mud that dragged at your boots and sucked them off your feet if you did not take care. Outside the *portal* a dead crow lay drowned in the ditch. A bad omen.

They joined the rest of the village in the ragged procession back up the hill. They pulled their hoods over their faces to keep out the cold.

A woman trudged after them. It was Mengarda, Father Marty's latest mistress. Fabricia knew from the look on her face that she meant trouble. She was a sulky creature with swollen, over-ripe lips. She walks upside down, she had heard her mother say to her father once when she thought she could not hear. She never smiled at anyone, just stared with those hooded eyes as if everyone was talking about her. Which she supposed they were. The village liked to talk and Father Marty's latest mistress was as good a subject of conversation as any.

'*Es vertat?*' she said, falling into step beside them. Is it true?

'Is what true?'Anselm growled.

'Paire Marty says you healed his leg.'

Anselm stopped walking and stared at her, then at Fabricia. 'What is this?' he said to Elionor.

She shrugged. 'I don't know anything about it.'

'He said she put her hand on his thigh,' Mengarda said. 'There was a canker there, it had been there for months, growing larger every day. But the next morning it was gone.'

Fabricia wondered whether to believe her. Was it just another of Father Marty's rumours, designed to bring her down? What about their pact? *Just our little secret,* òc? Could it be true, did she have some special magic? No, this was surely just some game he was playing with her still.

Fabricia looked at Anselm and Elionor. 'I'm sorry.'

'What is it you're sorry for exactly? Is it true what she is saying?' Anselm said.

She did not know how to answer. She had not told them about his visit because she did not want her father to be drawn into a conflict with Marty, to be run out of another town because of her. And besides, what was there to tell?

'I didn't do anything,' she said.

'That's not what he says,' Mengarda crowed. 'It's not what he's telling everyone!' It was a vicious thing to say – it was meant to be. Was Mengarda really that jealous of him, did she really think Fabricia would lay her hand on that devil's thigh because she wanted it there?

Mengarda turned and ran back down the hill through the mud. Anselm pulled the hood around his face. Another man, she thought, another father, might have beaten her until she was blue. She had shamed him yet again. Only Jesus made miracles, not a stone-mason's daughter.

Another of the villagers approached. It was Bernart. He fell down on his knees in front of her. Poor simpleton, he really believed what they had told him, that she had brought him back to life. 'Please don't,' she murmured, but he could not hear her and even if he had, it was too late.

'God bless you,' he said and laid at her feet two skinned rabbits and three larks.

'What's this?' Anselm said. 'We need no one's charity.'

'It is my thanks to your daughter for bringing me back to life,' Bernart said, and he, too, hurried away; no boys to chase him now, or to taunt him about his crook-back or his limp. He was their miracle and they owned him as sacred.

Elionor picked up the basket and trudged back up the hill. Fabricia and Anselm followed. Elionor did not say a word until they reached their *ostal* and then all she said was: 'Will you feed the pig for me?' She went inside. Usually feeding the pig was something they did together. But Fabricia was an exile now, so she had best get used to doing things alone.

XXV

ANOTHER FILTHY MORNING: the false spring of a few weeks before had given way to drenching rain. The clouds lowered from the mountains and for days at a time they could not see the sky above or the valley below.

It rained as if the world was about to end and the crowded lanes of Saint-Ybars turned into a brown porridge of mud. The pig huddled miserably under the eaves and rainwater toppled in rivulets from the walls of the châtelet. Mostarda did not move from the fire.

Fabricia heard Anselm descend the ladder from the *solier,* put on his boots and a heavy leather cloak to keep off the worst of the rain. He pulled open the door and she waited for the slam as he shut it behind him, for on these wet mornings the wood swelled and made it difficult to close.

Time for her to get up and light the fire. A flurry of wind flapped at the oilcloth across the window and moaned under the door. She huddled under the furs, delaying just a little longer under the warm bearskins.

Anselm walked back into the house, stamped across the floor and drew aside the heavy curtain that separated her bed from the kitchen.

It was still dark and hard to see his face, but she knew from his voice that something was very wrong. 'Get dressed,' he said. 'You had better come and see this.'

Fabricia dressed quickly. Anselm lit an oil lamp and went to the door. Elionor was awake now, too; she heard her moving about in the *solier.*

'What is it, Papa?'

'See for yourself,' he said.

He swung open the door.

It seemed as if half the village was out there in the lane. Some carried oil lamps, and these ones she recognized: the tailor's mother, the one who was blind, leaning on her son's arm; a man from the next village she knew only as Pèire, with his family on the back of a donkey cart; Pons's son, with his wasted leg; a shoemaker called Simon, the one with the mulberry birthmark that covered half his face.

When they saw her, there was a murmur of anticipation. Several of them called out to her. They started to surge forward and Anselm slammed the door.

'What are you going to do?' he said.

Elionor came down the ladder and gripped Anselm's arm. 'What's happening?'

'Our daughter is famous.'

'What are you talking about?'

'Every invalid and unfortunate in the whole of Foix is camped outside our door. They think Fabricia here can do miracles.'

The oil lamp threw crazy shadows on the walls.

'What should I do?' Fabricia said.

Anselm made the sign of the cross. He looked at his wife. 'Well?'

'Please, Mama, I can't help them. Look, I can't even heal my own sores!' She held out her hands.

'You have started something here,' he said, 'and I do not know where it will end.'

'Lay hands on them if that is what they wish,' Elionor said, more gently. 'What else can you do? If we send them away they will only follow you around the village.'

'Just tell me one thing,' Anselm said. 'What happened between you and Father Marty?'

'He came here one morning, to our *domus* while Mama was at the market. I thought he wanted – you know what I am going to say. Instead he showed me the canker on his leg and told me I must heal him.'

'Now the devil has told everyone in the county,' Elionor said. 'There's gratitude.'

'I do not pretend to know how that bastard's mind works,' Anselm said. He turned back to his daughter. 'What magic have you learned here?'

'There is no magic. I prayed for him, but silently, that is all. Just the words of the Our Father. I did not feel anything for his condition, not as I did for poor Bernart, and I did not plead with God as I did when you were there on the bench, and I thought you would die. I did not heal the hunchback and I did not heal you. And I do not believe I healed Father Marty either.'

'Maybe you did heal him, maybe you didn't,' Elionor said. 'The secrets of his groin are vouchsafed only to Mengarda. For now, anyway.'

Anselm peered through a crack in the door. 'I don't know what we should do. Look at them! The sick, the lame, the bald – they will all be outside our door soon. Then the Bishop of Toulouse will hear of it and who knows where it will end. Here, child, don't look so miserable!' He dragged her into his arms and held her. She buried her face in the rough wet leather of his cloak. She wished she could stay there for ever.

'Let me take orders, Papa. It is the only thing for it now.'

He nodded. All the fight had gone out of him. 'You remember that day in Toulouse, the thunderstorm? That was when this all started. Something happened. What is it that God wants with my daughter? Why you?' But it was a question he did not expect an answer to. 'Shall I fetch them inside?'

*

In they came, all through the morning. She did not believe it would make any difference to any of them. Her mother sat by the fire watching, her face pale with dread, as Fabricia laid her gloved hands on filmy eyes, on withered arms, on swollen and crippled knees, on thin, wheezing children. One old man complained he could no longer satisfy his wife, but she would not put her hand *there*. She made him kneel and placed her hands on his head instead.

More arrived through the morning, as word spread of what was happening, and it was dinner before she was done. Afterwards, she felt utterly exhausted, as if she had spent the whole day working in the fields in the hot sun. Finally alone, Fabricia lay down on her bed and slept. It was dark when she woke and her father was standing over her, staring at her hands. Her gloves were soaked in blood.

XXVI

Cathédrale de Saint-Gilles
Toulouse, 18 June 1209

To THE GREATER glory of God: the saints in the tympana and the portals of the great cathedral, vivid in polychrome, watched the humiliation of their prince and were vindicated in their unwavering belief.

Simon could not see him through the crowd but he knew that at this moment he knelt on the steps between the two gilt lions, where the reliquaries had been laid. Those old bones now had more power than him.

To the greater glory of God: he passed beneath the frescoes in the nave, painted the colours of dark blood and bright blue, under silk banners threaded with jade and ochre and royal gold.

This was how he imagined heaven on the Day of Judgement. Incense hung in the air like a fog, mingled with the taint of the mildewed vestments and the press of people. The cathedral was lit by a thousand candles, each one reflected a thousand times in the gilt of the grails on the altar and the saints in the transepts. But there was no choir, not today; Raymond entered in silence, save for murmurs of astonishment or satisfaction.

To the greater glory of God: nothing will be the same after this.

Count Raymond VI of Toulouse, once brother in law to the King of England himself, entered by the western portal. He wore no jewels, and there were no knights to guard his person; he was stripped to the waist like a penitent, just a frightened old man with a beard carrying a candle. All of Toulouse had seen it now; they said almost the entire city had tried to pack into the square outside.

A tepid sun was refracted through the high windows of the clerestory, touching fire to the gold of the vestments and mitres of the three archbishops who had come to accept his obeisance. Simon took his place at the shoulder of the Bishop of Toulouse, himself just one of a score of bishops crowded on to the altar to witness this moment.

The crowd parted and he caught his first glimpse of the most powerful man in Toulouse, in all of the Albigeois: he was scrawny, with pale flesh and a nest of grey hair on his breastbone. He wore a cord around his neck to signify his contrition.

The crowd spilled into the church behind him like a human tide, craning their heads and pushing for a view of this astonishing moment. The Archbishop himself followed him up the aisle, wielding a scourge made from birch twigs. There were livid red weals on the old man's back. It was not merely a ritual flogging; he had made the blood run.

The punishment was completed there on the altar. So much for the worldly power of a prince when confronted with the infinite majesty of God, Simon thought. Through the mitres and tonsured heads he glimpsed Lord Raymond's silver hair hanging lank around his face. His eyes were empty, his skin grey. He felt sorry for him. The press of people inside the church made it impossible for Raymond to return the way he had come. The Archbishop hastily conferred with his attendants and Raymond was ushered down into the crypt, to make a shabby departure through the underground vaults. He would have to pass the tomb of the papal legate whose murder had brought him to this pass. As soon as he was gone everyone started to whisper at once; a murmur of astonishment spread out, from altar to nave, nave to narthex, then like a wave through the great west doors to the square, from the centre of Toulouse to the whole of Christendom.

Raymond had been protector and champion to heretics, and because of it the Pope had brought this once proud prince to his knees. There was no doubting the primacy of Jesus Christ now. Innocent had put God's enemies on notice, Simon thought. We will not tolerate heresy any longer, we have been patient long enough.

From the moment some hothead skewered the legate Peter of Castelnau this was inevitable. Raymond might think tolerance a virtue, but this Pope did not, God be praised. The sheep must be brought back to the fold.

He felt a thrill of anticipation. He was on the razor's edge of history, at the vanguard of God's legions. The angels were watching him. He would yet prove himself to heaven and obliterate his past sins. He was sure of that.

XXVII

A FEW DAYS later, Simon was summoned to the scriptorium. He expected to be confronted by the prior, and wondered what infraction of the Rule he might have committed that would bring reprimand. But when he went in, the man sitting in the prior's chair was a complete stranger. He wore the white woollen robes of a canon and the black travelling capes of a Spanish priest. It identified him as a friar preacher, a follower of Guzmán. He was tonsured and around his neck he wore a large silver cross. His neat beard was flecked with silver. The prior himself stood by the window, looking down into the garden. When Simon entered he said: 'I shall leave you to your conversations,' and went out.

Simon was taken aback. The preacher did not rush to explain himself; he had the air of a man rather careworn and tired, a bookkeeper overwhelmed with figures in a ledger. Simon was not fooled by his mild demeanour. He had seen him at work.

'My name is Father Diego Ortiz. I am a brother at the Cistercian monastery at Fontfroide,' the friar said.

'I know, I have seen you before.'

The friar raised an eyebrow.

'Here in Toulouse. You were preaching outside the church of Saint-Étienne.'

'That was a long time ago.'

'Four years.'

A suspicion of a smile. 'You remember?'

How could I forget? he thought. It was the summer I met Fabricia Bérenger. 'It left an impression on me.'

'Good,' the friar said. 'Come and sit.'

There was a single wooden chair opposite the simple trestle

table where the friar sat. Simon settled himself.

'I know a little about you, also,' the friar said. 'Your father is a wool merchant in Carcassonne. You have four brothers, older, and they are all merchants like your father, and they attend mass regularly. Your father showed his gratitude to God for his bounty by offering his youngest son and his services to the Church. Are you sorry for that?'

'Never,' Simon said, and hoped he sounded convincing.

'A man can do worse than dedicate his life to the salvation of men's souls.'

'Of all my brothers I consider myself the most fortunate.'

'You have been satisfied with the education the Church has afforded you?'

'I mastered the trivium of grammar, rhetoric and logic and the quadrivium of arithmetic, geometry, music and astronomy. I have studied Ovid and Horace, Euclid and Cicero, and the *Organon* of Aristotle. At twenty-one I was invited to teach philosophy at the University of Toulouse. I am now the Master of Students. I am also personal assistant to the prior, overseeing the administration of all buildings and finances here in Toulouse.'

'I see you occasionally allow yourself the sin of pride.'

Simon lowered his eyes. He should be more careful of his tongue with this one in future.

'What do you know of Dominic Guzmán?'

'I know that he enjoys a very great reputation for sanctity. I understand he has spent the last four years living off alms and preaching the Word of God with nothing but a Book of Hours and his own considerable faith to sustain him. I also believe that at times he has slept by the roadside and been forced to endure the taunts and abuse of the godless.'

'I see you have followed his ministry closely. What else do you know?'

'That he has entered into countless public debates with the heretic priests called Cathars to try and bring them back to the true faith. I heard that he once called the Abbot of Cîteaux a wolf in sheep's clothing and told him, to his face, that if he wanted to win converts he would not do it from the back of his horse with his jewels and his women following in the carriage behind. I understand that he wishes for us priests to lead by example, and lead lives of chastity and obedience once more.'

The preacher nodded. 'You admire his work?'

'Very much. If I were in his place, I should allow myself the sin of pride.'

A flicker of a smile. 'There are a number of us who share your good opinion of him, who have, in fact, become his disciples, if you like. I myself met him six years ago, in Montpellier. I have been devoted to his cause ever since.' He stood up and went to the window. 'Before you came in, the prior was sharing this view with me. He told me that the garden down there is a perfect symbol of God's perfection. The rectangle of paving around it represents the created world; the cross formed by the paving stones that dissect it are the four branches of the cross; the fountain at its centre, the water reflecting the sky, is how the earth should reflect the peace of heaven.' Simon saw the fire return to his eyes, that same passion he had witnessed in the marketplace four years before. 'Thy will be done, on earth as it is in heaven. This is the task we are charged with, Brother Simon Jorda.'

'It is what I believe also, with all my heart.'

'Have you ever seen the Devil?'

The question shocked him. 'No, and I pray I never shall.'

'But you must, Brother Jorda, for he is all around us! If you wish to serve God then you must be equally well acquainted with His adversary.' He leaned on the table. 'Do you have the courage to face the Devil, in whatever form he chooses to take?'

'I think so.'

'I have been talking to your prior about you. It seems God has seen fit to give you a quick mind and a profound understanding of His Word. We need men like you.'

'What would you have me do?'

'A great cataclysm is about to take place and it will start in the Albigeois. The Church here has grown fat and lazy, and a cancer has taken hold. We are the laughing stock of the laity; there are monks and canons who have taken wives and live by usury. Some have even set up as minstrels. They eat swans for breakfast and give their mistresses rubies the size of pigeon eggs. They have turned the Church here into a scandal. Men are dying with their sins still upon them while the Archbishop of Narbonne counts his money.

'Meanwhile these southern lands have been infected with every kind of damnable heresy. The Count of Toulouse and his kind have allowed these *bons òmes*, as they call themselves, licence to go about the country preaching their filth and none to stop them. Do you know what was reported to me the other day? There is a village deep in the mountains in Foix where these heretics chased out the priest, scrubbed the murals of the crucifixion from the walls of the chapel and now hold their monstrous services there. In God's own holy place!'

Simon nodded. 'I have heard these things too.'

'What else have you heard?'

'I have heard they disdain sexual congress, even in marriage.'

'That is because they are all notorious sodomites!'

'This may be so,' Simon said, 'though if I may speak plainly, the same thing is said of our Bishop.'

'No one will dispute you on that point, Brother Simon. The Church must be cleansed from within as well as without.

'Jesus admonished us for our sins and asked that we set them aside and trust in him. I do not understand why this is so hard a thing for some men to comprehend.' He sat down again. 'Brother Jorda, as you know, for several years I have tried to speak peace to the people here, besought them with my tears to return to the Holy Church, but to no avail. Now the Holy Father's patience is at an end. Force will prevail where gentle persuasion has failed.

'Rome has called for a great crusade against the heretics of the south to stop the abominable heresies that have taken place here. But this will not be a war of siege and sword. We must not only destroy the church of the heretics, but remake our own.'

He leaned forward. 'I have been directed to join the crusade and provide spiritual direction to the brave knights who have joined us in our holy quest. I need a good men to join me, well grounded in philosophy, theosophy and debate.' His eyes were fierce. 'A man of good virtue, who can teach others to walk in the footsteps of our Lord Jesus Christ.'

Simon pressed his hands together in a prayer of fierce gratitude. It was the sign he had waited for. 'Look no further,' he said. 'You have found your man.'

XXVIII

Château Vercy, Burgundy

L ITTLE RENAUT OPENED his eyes. He looked anxiously around the
room. Philip leaned forward. 'I am right here, son,' he said. The
boy looked so frail that the pile of furs on top of him might crush the
life from him. *All that was left of her.* He stroked a stray lock of hair
from the boy's face.

Satisfied that he was not alone, Renaut went back to sleep.

Philip heard larks outside the window and knew that it was
morning. He went to the window, opened the shutter a fraction to
peer out. The morning was foggy and cold. Even the palisades of the
château had vanished into a cloying white mist. No sun yet to burn
it away. A hunting horn, muffled by the fog, echoed along the valley.
His squire, Renaut, would be leading a pack of russet and white
hounds across the ford below the castle, waiting for the mist to clear,
hoping to find a boar or a stag before they returned to the deep
forest.

These days he often wondered what might have happened to him
if he had not taken up the cross. Alezaïs would have died just the
same, he supposed. But it was the injustice of it that tormented him.
He had gone to Outremer in God's name; wasn't he deserving of a
greater reward than this?

What did he achieve, what had any of them won for their sacrifice? That's what people here didn't understand about the Holy
Land: the great waste of it all. The Templars were all mad, and did
as they liked in the name of the Pope, doing deals with the Muslims
and even living like them; no one there wanted to fight the Saracen
any more, they did not have the energy after they had finished
fighting each other over what remained of the ever dwindling
kingdom of Jersualem. The Christian princes charged with the
defence of God's land were neither very adroit nor very fervent and

they would rather be drinking sherbets with their whores than guarding pilgrims and fighting Saracens. But he had stayed on and given his full year of service.

It had all been futile. He wished now he had stayed in France with his wife.

Renaut sat up suddenly, and vomited on to the floor. When he was done he looked contrite, as if dying like this was some mischief that required reprimand.

'It's all right,' Philip said. 'I'll clean it up.'

Renaut tried to say something but instead dropped back exhausted on to the bed.

Philip fetched a rag and a water pail from the corner and knelt to mop up the mess, then went down to the scullery to get warm water from the hearth. He could have a servant girl do all this but he told himself that if God saw his dedication He would give him a miracle and give him back his son.

As soon as he got back, Renaut started retching again. Philip held a bowl under his son's chin, then wiped his face with a linen towel. There was nothing much left in him but bile.

It was cold. He relit the fire in the hearth and flung on a handful of dried herbs. The air was stale and foul, but he could not open the shutters; they said that Death crept in through windows and doors and perhaps it was true.

Renaut fell asleep again. Philip called one of the servant girls, told her to watch his son and then went down to the chapel.

A century of incense clung to the dark stones. Greasy black smoke from a branched candlestick rose to the vault, a dark prayer on its way to heaven for blessing, while the wax dripped on the flagstones. Two of his wife's ladies whispered novenas to a statue of Our Lady. He had ordered that all the ladies of the castle should take turns to say litanies there for his son day and night.

He dismissed them, told them to return after nones. When they were gone, he slumped to his knees on the prie-dieu. The bronze crucifix above the altar appeared to tremble in the aura of the candles. He sent his entreaty to his savage God.

Help me.

Why do you keep me alive, just to suffer like this? And there is no doubt, you have blessed me with more luck in battle than most.

Three times I nearly died in Outremer and here I still am. So what is it you want from me? Don't keep me alive just so that I can suffer more. Show me some meaning to all of this.

Please God, do not let him die. I will do anything. Leave me one thing of her, one thing that I love. If you're really there in your heaven, listen to me now, and make him well again.

Look, he's just a boy. If you like, take me instead. He has a whole life to live and I have had mine, at least enough of it that I have loved and warred and had my chance. He has had none of that. Take me in his place. I am ready to die; this sadness I feel has stricken me to my very bones. There it is, my bargain. Take me and leave the boy.

The candles flickered in a draught and the cold stone beneath his knees seeped into his bones. But he stayed and prayed. When the ladies returned at nones, his joints were so stiff he could not properly stand. But he did not find an answer and God did not speak.

XXIX

HE HAD NOT wished to remarry. There was no one to replace Alezaïs in his bed or in his heart. But a man, of noble blood or not, did not marry for love. Marriage was for the forging of alliances and the making of sons. There must be someone to run the household and scold the servants when he was not there. He had a duty to his name and to those who called him lord.

There was no doubt that his new wife was capable as well as beautiful. The carved escutcheons on the walls were freshly painted, and there was white napery on the tables. Giselle had insisted they make some effort to abandon the drab existence to which present circumstances had brought them for the visit of his cousin, Étienne. He had been given the place of honour at the high end of the table, at Philip's right hand. Giselle sat at his left, affecting gaiety in a long gown of raspberry silk, the sleeves so long they dragged on the ground. Two of her maidservants held them for her when she ate.

A fine wife. He just couldn't stand the sight of her, and none of it was her fault.

Étienne selected a morsel from the stew and brought it to his trencher, dripping gravy on the polished oak table. 'You will not join the Pope's crusade against the Count of Toulouse?'

'I have earned my ease in heaven, Étienne. I spent a year in Outremer for God and for Jerusalem. Besides I do not see how one Christian lord can go against another Christian lord and call it holy. Though I am sure a churchman could explain it to me.'

'The Pope says that the Count has been harbouring heresy.'

'If Count Raymond burns every heretic in the south lands he will not have any subjects left. If the Church thought more of men's souls and less of tithes and taxes she might find herself better thought of in Provence. What about you, will you take up the battle cry again?'

'I thought I might show my devotion another way. A pilgrimage at this moment might be a wise step.'

'Bare feet and a hair shirt?'

'I was thinking more of a good horse and good whores. They say the women in León bear looking at.' The servitors brought wine, the boy splashing more of the good Rhenish on the table than he did in their cups. Étienne leaned forward and said, in a whisper, so that Giselle might not hear over the general hubbub: 'Talking of such matters, cousin, who warms your bed these days? Not your wife, if rumour is correct.'

'I care for her as well as I can.'

'What is wrong? She's beautiful enough. Do you have a mistress?' Philip shook his head. 'You never used to be so gloomy, Philip. When we were squires, you were lusty enough.'

'A man can change.'

'You cannot mourn Alezaïs for ever. She may have been an agreeable wife, but a woman is just a woman. They are making more of them all the time.'

Philip envied and pitied his cousin. A joust, a roll in the hay with a serving girl and a good dinner and he was happy. Perhaps it is me. I think too much, I feel too much. Alezaïs used to tease me about it, and then said it was what she loved most about me. Giselle broke in. 'What are you two plotting over here?'

'I was asking your husband how little Renaut fares.'

'I am afraid he grows weaker every day.' she said.

'I am sorry to hear it. Children are too mortal. That is why we need a lot of them.'

Étienne had himself lost two sons before they were weaned. But he had heeded his own advice and bred two more. It was the sensible thing. He knew his duty to his family, to his lands.

Giselle was distracted by a minstrel and clapped and cheered with the others as he started to sing.

'Why did you marry her?' Étienne whispered.

'She looks like her,' he said.

'You married your second wife to remind you of your first? As poor a reason to marry as ever I heard.' Philip's stewards brought a roast swan from the kitchen. It had been artfully attached to the hindquarters of a pig. It brought shouts of amusement and a round of applause from his guests. Philip selected the choicest cuts from it with his fingers and placed them on Étienne's trencher.

Étienne leaned in. 'It is not my place to intrude on your affairs, but I hope you are wary of Giselle's kin. Her brothers are poor and grasping. Her father had too many sons and not enough land. They do not wish you well.'

'What are you saying?'

'I am saying that they would be only too glad if you were to die without an heir. So you should see to it that they are disappointed.'

After dinner was finished and all his guests were drunk or snoring, the tables were pushed back to the wall and the trouvères and minstrels brought in so that the ladies and the young squires might dance. Philip left his squire Renaut to be the master of the festivities and when Étienne slipped away with one of Giselle's ladies he went upstairs to sit with his son and hold his hand.

XXX

A ND SO: THE doctor, in his hood and biretta, standing in a corner of the room examining his patient's urine, which he swirled around a wooden bowl. He sniffed at it and then placed a finger into it to taste it.

'It is slightly astringent and the colour is dark. I shall bleed him again tomorrow.'

'Why not do it now?' Philip asked.

'He was born under Capricorn and by my calculations today is not a lucky day for either bleeding or purging.'

'You have bled and you have purged and still he sickens. Is this all the medicine that you have?'

'I trained in Paris. You will not find better than me.'

'But I think it is time that I tried. Get out of here. Don't come back.'

'It is God's punishment,' Giselle said. 'You refused the Pope's call to arms. Now you are paying the price.'

'For pity's sake,' he murmured. He asked for a little more hot water for his bath but she would not permit the servant girl to do it; didn't trust her apparently. It might have been more pleasant, he supposed, if she had poured the scalding water into the bath instead of tossing the whole bucket over his back. Hearing him roar in pain only seemed to make her more angry. 'What sort of man refuses to fight for God?'

'Warring for Rome is not always the same thing as fighting for God.'

'That's a blasphemy!'

'They are pitting Christian against Christian.'

'The Albigensians are not Christians! Heretics, all of them. If you wore the cross, you would earn remission of all your sins and, by my counting, they are plenty. And an assured place in heaven! Is that not worth fighting for? Instead your son is sick, and all because you will not fight.'

'I have never shirked a fight if there is just cause in it. And I wore the cross in the Holy Land for the Pope for one full year, so it baffles me to hear you talk this way. Why would God seek to punish me now?'

'What if one of your servants expected you to feed him for his entire life because he once saddled your horse? You ride every day.'

'The promise of heaven was for one crusade against the Saracen, not to fight all Christendom for the rest of my life!'

He eased his head against the edge of the wooden tub and took a calming breath. The scent of the dried rose petals that perfumed the water eased his frayed nerves. But not for long. The second bucket of water went over his head. Praise God, this one was cold and not scalding.

'God's blood, woman!'

'If you don't care for your soul or for the Pope you might at least give thought to bringing back some silver to pay off your debts.'

'Debts that were accrued fighting for the Pope the last time! Heresy is the Church's business, not mine. Raymond of Toulouse may be an inveterate liar but he does not worship the Devil and he is brother-in-law to the King of England. How can a war against such a man be a holy war?' He swung his legs out of the bath. There was no ease to be found here. Giselle took her time handing him a cloth to dry himself.

'What are you staring at?'

'Reminding myself what it looked like.'

Philip dressed quickly. A quilted tunic instead of a woollen one, a fashion he had brought back with him from the Orient. He put on rich hose of royal blue velvet; he could not afford them but was damned if he would advertise his penury.

'He was sickening before the Pope called this crusade.'

'God knew what you would do.'

'You have an answer for everything.'

Giselle stood, hands on hips, by the window. He closed his eyes, imagined Alezaïs with him, tried to conjure the comfort she once gave him when he was troubled.

'Every day he gets sicker,' he murmured. 'I have watched him waste to a skeleton in front of my eyes. At Epiphany he was a normal boy chasing the dogs around the hall and eating more than the

Bishop. Now . . . if it were not for the bearskin rugs on him I swear he would float away. He cannot keep anything down. I beat every day at the gates of heaven for a miracle but I get no answer.'

'He's dying, husband. Everyone but you knows it.'

'He is not going to die!'

'It is God's will.'

'Then God will have to think again, because I am not going to let him die!'

Giselle folded her arms. 'There is nothing you can do about it.' What was this? Gloating?

'He is not going to die!' he repeated and stormed out. They had heard the yelling in the great hall below and when he came down the stairs all the servants ran to get out of his way.

XXXI

PHILIP STORMED ACROSS the courtyard, shouting for someone to bring his horse. When he reached the stables, a boy leaped from the straw where he had been dozing, only for Philip to push him back down again. 'Don't bother, lad, I'll do it myself.'

Leyla, his six-year-old Arab, pricked up her ears at his approach. She was a handsome high-stepper, a chestnut with white tail and white mane, with white spots on her forefeet. He fetched an undercloth from the rail and a bridle and riding saddle.

The stable boy hovered.

'Just stay out of my way,' Philip told him.

He galloped out of the gate, rode her hard for over a league at full tilt. Instead of crossing the ford he headed blindly into the forest, splashing through the shallows and up on to the bank into a meadow of buttercups. Leyla's flanks heaved; sweat foamed around her bridle.

He released the reins and dropped from the saddle. He raised his face to the sky and shook his fist at heaven. 'Damn you, God! Damn you!'

He closed his eyes and waited for God to strike him. Nothing. An eel splashed in the river shallows; a mosquito, drawn by his sweat, buzzed around his face. He heard Leyla cropping the grass, then walking slowly to the water's edge.

The starlings and linnets in the pines, stunned to silence, returned to the bushes to fuss and chatter.

And then, something else, the snap of a twig, a rustling of fern. Leyla gave a little whinny of alarm. Philip looked around. A squirrel darted across the meadow with a hazelnut in its jaws.

Leyla laid back her ears. Her flanks twitched, and she stamped a hoof.

Then he smelled it. Wild boar had a rank smell of their own, unmistakable to any man that had hunted them. Good game from the saddle when you had a pack of *raches* at your command, enough meat to feed the entire household.

But this was different. Here he was, rash and unarmed, and a good thirty paces from his horse. He clicked his tongue and Leyla's ears pricked again and she started to walk towards him, wary, the stink of the hog making her nervous.

Too late. The boar burst out of the thicket fifty paces to his left, a hideous brute with slitted eyes and tusks that could disembowel a horse. Hadn't he seen it happen enough times?

It stopped, watching him, trying to understand what he was, what threat he posed.

If I stand quite still, he thought, it will perhaps move on. It can't put me on a spit and eat me, as I would do to him. And he isn't sure of the danger. The presence of the horse has confused him.

If I stand quite still . . .

He yelled and ran towards it. The boar put its head down and charged.

*

The arrow struck the animal in the neck and sent it reeling away, squealing in pain. Its blood steamed as it made contact with the air. It staggered sideways, then dropped.

'Renaut,' he said.

His squire stepped his horse out of the shallows. One arrow, through the jugular at forty paces. He had taught him well.

'How did you find me?'

'I didn't. I followed you. You almost lost me though; your Arab is too fast for my little mare. I almost kept going at the ford but then I heard a man shouting. I thought you were dead.'

'And so I would have been if you had not spent so much time at the archery butts.'

He got down from his horse. 'You left the château so fast, I thought the Devil himself was after you.'

'Worse. Giselle.'

They walked over to the boar. It had bled out and the huge mountain of flesh still twitched even though it was dead. Renaut pulled out his arrow and then ran his hand over the tusk to the razor tip. 'I'm glad I found you. I should not like to die this way. Nor should you.'

Did he see me rise and run towards my death? Philip wondered. What was I thinking? He was right. Not a good way to die.

'What did the lady Giselle say to you that you preferred the company of this razor-tooth?'

'She wishes me to join the Pope's crusade against the Midi. She thinks that is why my boy is sick.'

'He sickened before the crusade was called.'

Philip shrugged. 'God's ways are mysterious, they say.'

'I still do not understand why you took another wife.'

'Renaut, ours is a normal marriage. I have her rather modest dowry, which I needed to pay off some of my debts. She has a husband with a château and a fief and her family has a useful political alliance. It was what I had with Alezaïs that was not . . . usual. We loved each other. It is something that a man more often only finds with his mistress or another man's wife. For a while I was fortunate. Now . . . not so much.'

'How is your son?'

Philip tested the pig's belly with his boot. 'Some good meat there.' He walked back to his horse.

'You know, there is a crone in Poissy, just ten leagues from here. Her name is Marguerite.'

'Yes, I have heard of her. She makes love spells and delivers babies.'

'More than that, she can make a poultice to draw the poisons from wounds and brews potions that cure the ague and the flux and ward off the pestilence. She collects every kind of herb and bark and plant to make her salves.'

'A sorceress and a heretic. She makes incantations to the moon.'

'Does it matter what she is if she can heal your son?'

Philip picked up Leyla's reins from the grass. 'If you stand guard here on your kill, I will fetch some men and horses to drag the carcass back to the château.'

'You have tried everything else. These butchers who call themselves doctors have bled him and purged him and done every foul thing and still he sickens.'

'Thank you for saving my life. Come the next Easter, you will be more than a squire.'

'Marguerite. At Poissy. Think about it.'

'The woman is unholy.'

'God has not been faithful to you in this. Do what you need to do, seigneur.'

'You're a good man, Renaut,' Philip said and turned Leyla's head and headed back down the stream through the shallows to the ford.

XXXII

MARGUERITE LIVED HALF a league from Poissy, in a wild place where no trees grew and rushes disputed the marshy ground with ferns and young willows. The forest they passed through was dank, with impenetrable thickets of bracken and old trees with tortured branches. His men were sullen and quiet. Philip felt eyes on them, perhaps animals, perhaps sprites. All knew that in woods like this fairies slept in the leaf bowers and strange dwarves scurried through the shadowed gloaming. Any man who died here without the holy sacraments would be damned to be a will-o'-the-wisp for all eternity.

A skein of white smoke drifted up through the trees, and guided them to her cottage. The crone was in her garden, collecting herbs. She had wild grey hair to her waist, and possessed the chilling stare of a cat. She watched their approach, one hand on her hip, the other shielding the sun from her eyes.

'You're Marguerite, the wise woman?' Philip said.

'I am. And you're Philip of Vercy. What is such a fine seigneur as yourself doing out here in the wood?'

'Do you not know?' he said, testing her.

She bent down and snapped a sprig from a rosemary bush. 'I have heard your boy has been sick. I dare say you have had him bled and purged and prayed over and now you have come to see me as a last resort.' She smiled at his confusion. 'I cannot read minds, my lord. I am just not as mad as I look.'

Philip handed the reins of his horse to his sergeant-at-arms and slid from the saddle. There was a plank path that sank into the mud with every step. 'They say you heal all manner of sickness with your potions and salves.'

'I am equally famous for those I don't cure. You'd best come inside.'

Philip followed her, knocking his head on the low door. It was very dark. With a quick glance he made out some herbs and dusty sprigs of dried flowers hanging from the ceiling, others drying over the hearth fire. A rusted pot sat crooked over a pile of ash and charred wood.

Marguerite pulled aside a tattered curtain at the back of house; behind it there was a table with two chairs, and a few narrow shelves crowded with jars. He recognized some petrified sprigs of fleabane and another of blackberry leaves. Most of the others he did not know. There was a pestle and mortar sitting in the middle of the table.

'Sit,' she said to him.

Well, this is novel, he thought. Not often I have been ordered about like this. Not even by my wife. But he sat, without complaint.

'I'll have the servants bring spiced wine in a moment,' she said.

'Just some figs and sherbets will do.'

She teased a sprig of rosemary between her fingers, split it, held it to her nose and breathed in the aroma. 'God makes fine things,' she said. Her hands were brown and gnarled with age, all crooked joints and swollen veins. But she had a young woman's eyes, bright and quick and intelligent. 'But then He unmakes them. It is a mystery and sometimes a very painful one. Tell me about your son.'

'It started just after the Feast of the Epiphany. He was slow to rise in the mornings, seemed listless, and then could not keep down his food. We had the doctor look at him; he applied leeches and such. But by Easter he was barely out of his bed and all he can take in now is water and a little broth. He is skin and bone, no more.'

'Does he suffer?'

'The doctor prescribed belladonna. For a time it helped but now he moans and tosses night and day. I hardly leave his side; I am afraid to fall asleep, thinking that when I wake up he will be gone. As you say, we have prayed and prayed, have fetched doctors from as far away as Bayeux, sold much of my wife's dowry to pay for them. Still no good.'

'Is there fever?'

Philip shook his head.

'Does he pass blood?'

'If he did not moan and occasionally call out for his mother, who is now in her grave these four years, he would no longer do anything that a living creature does.'

Marguerite reached across the table and took his hands in hers. He was surprised at her strength and the heat coming off her. He was also surprised that she might presume to lay hands on her seigneur without bidding.

She took a piece of hessian cloth and some jars from the shelf; she poured a little from one, more from another. Other herbs she crushed in the mortar before adding them to the little pile of leaves and powder on the cloth. She deliberated long over each bottle before she was finally satisfied. Then she took needle and thread, tied it into a bundle and handed it to him.

'What is this?' he said. It smelled foul.

'Hawkwood, sorrel, marigold, purslane. Also some hellebore, spikenard and nightshade. Angelica for purifying the blood. Many things. You must make an infusion with this, and have him drink it, as much as he can stand.'

'This will cure him?'

'Perhaps.'

'I will not let him die.'

'Even a prince cannot argue with Death.'

He took the bag from her and handed her some silver coins. She passed them back. 'I'm not a quack, or a priest, thank God. Only pay me when he is well.'

'That is just for your time. Make him well and there will be ten times that.'

As he was leaving she called him back. 'I wasn't always a hag,' she said. 'I once had a son, and a husband too. They both died. And I could not help them, though to others I give my herbs and they rise from their beds like Lazarus. I am not a witch, seigneur. I cannot do magic for you. I wish I could.'

'My son is not going to die,' he said.

She watched him ride away. A good man, they said.

But too proud by half.

XXXIII

PHILIP WENT DOWN to the scullery to prepare the infusion himself. He poured warm water into a kettle and hung it over the fire.

As he was bent there he felt his wife's hand on his shoulder, the warmth of it; he was so startled that he turned his head to look for her. But the dead do not come back to life.

Alezaïs, my heart, help me. I am doing all I can.

When the water on the herbs had boiled down, he swung out the crane and filled a pewter mug with the bubbling mess. The smell was sickening. He wrapped the handle in a towel and went back to his son's bedchamber.

He tried to make Renaut drink some of the witch's magic tea but he could not keep it down. Again and again he vomited, retching with such violence that he thought he must tear his stomach out. The vomit was streaked with bright red blood. Finally he pushed the mug away. When Philip persisted Renaut struck out violently and sent the mug and the precious contents crashing on to the flagstones. Philip yelled in frustration and kicked the mug across the floor. It landed in the fire.

Renaut twitched and kicked, muttering words he could not understand. Philip wrung a cloth in cold water and laid it across his forehead. 'I will not let you die,' he promised him.

A few chinks of light found a way through the shutters, fading as the afternoon wore on. He lit a taper and continued his vigil.

He had found Alezaïs's comb, silver and tortoiseshell. He had taken to carrying it with him everywhere, inside his tunic. He rolled it over and over in his hands like a puzzle. It still had her hairs in it. He unravelled one, held the fine strand towards the light. He put the comb back inside his shirt. She is gone, he reminded himself. She is gone and she is not coming back.

There was a tapestry on the wall, above his son's bed, of a battle between a Christian knight and a Saracen. Once it had hung above his own bed, when he was a child. He had dreamed of being that knight, of the glory he would win himself, capturing Jerusalem from the infidel single-handed, hailed as Christendom's greatest-ever warrior. The reality had been so different. *What should I put in my tapestry now?*

He heard the bell in the chapel strike for compline. He felt tired to his very bones. He called for a servant girl. *Watch him, fetch me if he wakes, even if he just cries out. Do you understand?*

His men-at-arms were drinking ale by the dying fire in the great hall; some dogs were sniffing around the rushes, looking for scraps left over from supper. Some of the other men were already on the floor, asleep. He stopped for a moment to stare at one of the stable boys, curled up under his cloak with one of the laundry maids, his head on her breast. *I will exchange your place there for my warm bed and cold love, if you like.*

He went up the narrow stone steps to his bedroom at the top of the *donjon*. He imagined he was greatly envied, for the seigneur and his wife had the one thing denied everyone else; they could sleep and love and bathe without being seen or heard.

Tonight he just wanted to sleep.

Moonlight angled across the bed from the window. By the sound of her breathing Giselle was asleep, thanks be to God. He groped towards the bed. His bed! One of the greatest luxuries of privilege: a feather mattress, a bolster filled with down. For the last three nights he had dozed fitfully in a hard wooden chair beside his son's bed.

There was a curtain to keep out the draughts. He pulled it aside and felt for the wooden pole that kept their clothes from the rats and mice, hung his breeches and tunic on it, then folded his shirt and placed it under the bolster. A long time now since he had come to bed without his clothes. He pulled back the linen sheet.

Suddenly she sat up. 'Well. A strange man in my bed.'

'Expect little. I am too exhausted even to speak.'

As he reclined on to the bolster she swung her leg across him, so that her breasts were level with his face. Fine breasts, too, pert, ivory in the silver moonlight. If he had loved her it would not have mattered if he had just walked a hundred miles across the desert.

'Let me comfort you,' she said, and reached down and cupped him in her hand.

'I am beyond comfort.'

'I can make you another son.'

Did she really say that? He was tired; perhaps he had only imagined she said it. But wasn't that the reason for marriage? Children, politics, money; especially children. For a man of noble birth it was just good husbandry to have a wife and produce heirs, it should have nothing to do with love. An heir to lands is never his own master, his father had told him.

Yet something in him rebelled. Lose a son, make another; lose a wife, marry another. He had made all the necessary compromises with life and now he despised himself for them.

'My son is dying, woman,' he whispered and pushed her away. After a while he felt her crying, though she was too proud to weep out loud. What did you think, Philip, that you could reject her and she would not mind it? Married a year and you have bedded her just twice. Is she really such a vixen or did you make her into one? He got out of bed, left the feather mattress and the bolster filled with down, and dressed. Then he went back downstairs to sleep in a wooden chair and listen to his son whimper in his sleep.

*

Old Marguerite sat on the palfrey as if perched on the edge of a cliff. The servants watched from the windows; the stable hands stood around, staring. Well, he knew this would excite talk. Enough that they gossiped about his relations with his wife, or lack of them, now here he was bringing a sorceress to the castle.

Where would it end?

'Thank you for coming,' he said.

'I did not have a choice when these ruffians showed up,' she said, indicating Renaut and his sergeant-at-arms.

'These men would not hurt you. They look terrifying but you would slay them both in a fair fight.'

The men lounging by the gate laughed. For all that he was half-mad at least the seigneur had not lost his sense of humour.

He helped her down from the horse and led her inside the *donjon*. His son's bedroom was just below the great hall. He was awake, the great blue eyes sunken yet further into his head, the blue veins livid against his skin, which had turned a ghastly grey colour. No flesh on his skull. This is how he will look when he is dead, Philip thought. Except he will no longer blink.

The old woman knelt beside his bed and put a hand to his forehead, but tenderly as a mother would do. He guessed his son wanted to ask her name and who she was but did not have the strength.

'Poor child,' Marguerite said.

'Please,' Philip said. 'Do something.'

'Did you give him the infusion?'

'I did. But he could not keep it down.'

'Something is eating him from the inside. I told you, for everyone that I cure, another dies. I can heal what might be healed. I cannot do magic.'

'There must be something. I will give everything I have to save him, just tell me what to do.'

The old woman hesitated. 'Do you mean this?'

'I never say anything I do not mean.'

'Well, then, there is one way. I have heard travellers talk of a woman in the south who does miracles. It may be just rumour for I have never seen this woman myself. And the chances that you will find her, that you might even bring her here . . .'

'Where does she live? I will find her.'

'She lives in the Albigeois. In the village of Saint-Ybars in the Comté de Foix. People say of her that she can even raise the dead. She is your only hope, for nothing apart from a miracle will save your son, seigneur.'

'Tell me her name,' Philip said.

'Her name is Fabricia Bérenger. She is the daughter of a stonemason.'

'Thank you,' Philip said.

XXXIV

THE AIR IN the great hall was acrid, for there was too much green wood on the fire. Trestle tables were piled against the wall, ready to be brought out for dinner. Several of his sergeants lounged, playing dice; the hunting dogs whined and grizzled in the straw, dozing, stretching, playing. He glanced at the heraldic shields above the great doors, symbols of his proud Burgundian ancestry and the source of his privilege and his chains.

Ah, his chains. There she stood, in the midst of his private domain, in her robe of raspberry velvet, lined with fur, looking sumptuous, anxious and furious at once.

'Are you quite mad?' she shouted, startling the dogs. The men looked up from their dice game, thinking there was sport to be had.

'Leave us,' he said, and waited until their audience had left before he responded. 'You heard what the old woman said then?'

'Some old witch tells you to go to the Pays d'Oc and you saddle your horse? You would not go at the Pope's command but you would listen to some crone?'

'I am going for my own purposes, not for Rome's.'

'And what do you hope to find there? You think some woman will put her hands on your son and he will be cured? Is that what you think?'

'I won't let him die.'

'Children die all the time.'

'So we will just toss him away with no more thought than hurling a chicken bone to the dogs at dinner? Is that all a life is worth to you?'

'You cannot sacrifice everything you have for one sickly boy.'

'He was never sickly before this.'

'He is going to die no matter what you do or how much you love him. This is God's will.'

Philip shook his head. 'I am leaving in the morning. My squire

Renaut is coming with me. I shall take my men-at-arms and be back within one moon.'

'Who will protect us here?'

'Protect you? You need a porter for the gate and another to stop the stable boys stealing the chickens. If you feel threatened you have three brothers within ten leagues of here who will ride to your aid, but I cannot see the eventuality. You are quite as capable of running affairs as I. I shall be returned by Midsummer Eve.'

It was at that moment that Renaut strode in, come to rescue him no doubt, as he did that day in the forest. He wore a blue tunic over leathers, ready for the morning's hunt. He had delegated to a sergeant the duty of escorting Marguerite home.

Giselle decided to enlist him to her side. 'Can you talk some sense into the seigneur?' she said. 'You have heard what he plans to do?'

Renaut hesitated, his eyes moving between them as if he were assessing two enemy combatants before a fight. But it is to me he owes his allegiance, so he must be politic, no matter what he thinks. I imagine now he regrets sending the sergeant to Poissy in his stead.

'The seigneur must do what he thinks best,' he said carefully.

'Don't toady to him! Do you actually want me to believe that what he proposes makes any sense to you, or to anyone here in the château but him?'

'It is not for me to say.'

'You are both mad!' Giselle screamed. She picked up her skirts and fled up the stairs to her bedchamber.

Renaut let out a breath. Poor lad. Only eighteen years old and this is his first combat. He acquitted himself rather well.

'Thank you, Renaut. That was bravely done. Now you may speak openly.'

'With respect, seigneur – are you quite mad?'

'With respect, Squire Renaut, you were the one who told me to visit the old woman.'

'She lives in Poissy, not the Pays d'Oc.'

'I am not going to wait and let him die. You heard what the crone said. She says there is a woman there who can heal with her hands.'

'Even if it's true, we would be riding into the middle of a war. The northern army is headed towards Béziers and has laid waste to much of the Midi already. There are brigands on the road and the

Count of Toulouse's soldiers ambush any northerners without proper escort. And if we do not wear the crusader cross we would be in danger from both sides.'

'I have been to war before. I will get us there and back.'

'I should never doubt either your courage or your skill, just the reason you would put them to such a test. And you know, even if we find this woman, even if everything the crone says about her is true, which cannot be proven, even then . . . how would we persuade her to return with us here to Vercy?'

'I will pay her. And if that is not sufficient persuasion, then we might kidnap her with all gentleness, as you did this morning with the witch. There is always a way to do things.'

'And what of your duties here?'

'You think Lady Giselle cannot manage the day-to-day running of this château and the estate? She is easily bored with music and her weaving. She will enjoy assuming the mantle of justice for Vercy; in a few weeks there will not be a vagabond within five leagues who is not in the stocks. She will be stricter with the servants than I, the cooks and the serving girls will soon be in terror of their lives.'

Renaut took off his riding gauntlets and slapped them against the andirons before the fire. 'May I speak freely?'

'I thought you were.'

'It is just that . . . I think you go too far. Death is certain for each of us. This is beyond all reason.'

'You're eighteen, are you not, Renaut?'

'Yes, seigneur.'

'Young, to know so much of life. And do you have children?'

'You know I do not.'

'Then you cannot understand what it is to face losing one. Should you ever have a son, then you can pronounce judgement on my reason. But as you do not, I ask you to prepare the men and the horses. Tomorrow we are riding south. We are going to find this Fabricia Bérenger and bring her back here to lay these magical hands on my boy. That's my final word.'

XXXV

IT OCCURRED TO him on the day of his departure that he might never see his son again. He brushed the thought aside. *I will not fail again.* He bent down and left a kiss on the boy's cheek. He barely stirred. 'He must be alive when I return, do you understand?' he said to the startled servant girl as he left the chamber, as if she had the power to do anything about it.

Outside, the dawn had raised an ochre rim to a cold sky; light seeped into the day like a stain. Torches still burned in the sconces at the gatehouse. Feathery wisps of vapour rose from the horses as they snorted and pranced. They would bring palfreys for resilience and stamina, the strongest geldings and mares for speed.

The stable hands brought out Philip's chestnut Arab, a piebald mare for Renaut, and then a few cobs loaded with their modest baggage.

Renaut appeared, a cloak flung over a short coat of mail, helmet under his arm.

'Where is the lady Giselle?' he asked.

'She will not leave her bedroom.'

'You have said your farewells?'

'She threw a chamber pot at my head as I ducked behind the door. If you call that a goodbye then yes, we have made our parting.'

There was the clink of scabbards and armour; the flash of a lance caught the first rays of sun. Whether going to war or to the chase Philip was stirred by the jangle of bridles and trappings, the smell of the horses, and leather.

'Why so glum, Renaut?'

'Seigneur, I believe this to be a most grave mistake. But I shall follow you anywhere.'

'Very well then, let us go. The sooner we depart the sooner we shall find this lady of miracles.'

XXXVI

The Abbaye de Montmercy
in the Montagne Noir, Pays d'Oc

A DEAD CHILD thrust into her face, small and grey. A withered arm. A young woman, tongue lolling, hoist in the arms of two burly young men, perhaps her sons; another man covered with sores. *Help me, help me.* A whole world in need.

A man with wild eyes thrust her against the wall. *My wife died. You said you would heal her!* The crowd surged forward. *You said you would heal her!* Sòrre Bernadette used a staff to drive them back. 'Go back inside!' she shouted at Fabricia.

'But they need me,' she said.

'Go back inside!'

The porteress, Sòrre Marie, pulled her behind the gate. Sòrre Bernadette followed, and she and the porteress slammed it shut and barred it.

Bernadette leaned against the wall to catch her breath. She had lost her wimple in the struggle and her hair, dark brown but riven with streaks of grey, lay matted about her face. She replaced the wimple and smoothed her habit. 'Ruffian,' she murmured.

'I never said I could heal anyone,' Fabricia said. 'I have never promised anyone anything.'

'Pay him no heed.'

'I will wait here a while; they won't go until I have put my hands on them.'

Bernadette took her by the arm. 'No, Fabricia, you cannot go back out there today. Let them wait. Even the sick should learn to mind their manners.' The sub-prioress was a long, thin woman with a soft voice and firm resolve.

'Did they hurt you?' Sòrre Marie asked her.

Fabricia shook her head, no.

She followed Sòrre Bernadette back to the refectory, two steps to every one of hers. They went past the orchard, plum and pear trees bowing under the weight of fruit, two of the sisters trying to scare birds with long rakes. Flies were frantic for the windfalls in the long grass, the air sonorous with them.

In Saint-Ybars it would soon be Midsummer Eve. Her mother would be collecting mugwort, elder, sage and wormwood to make into garlands to hang about the *ostal* as fragrance or to smudge out any dark spirits. Last year's garlands she would throw on the great bonfire outside the walls. The whole village would be there. Except her.

Still, if this life was not what she wanted, it was at least the one she chose. There was no help for it.

*

She went back to her work in the kitchen, scrubbing the floors, helping the other sisters scour the pots. Some of them smiled and bobbed their heads, as if she were the abbess. From others she received only dark looks. *About time. So you've decided to join us, at last? They're finally on to your little game, huh?*

The small copper bell that hung from the rafters in the oratory summoned them to morning mass and chapter. Fabricia tossed the pot she was scrubbing back into the trough, grateful for the rest. She joined the other sisters as they made their way across the cloister to the chapel.

The statue of Our Lady, in her blue robe, watched over them from a niche high in the south wall.

As the office began, Fabricia spoke the litany but her attention was focused inwards on her own private entreaties. When she closed her eyes she saw the dead child that had been thrust at her that morning outside the gates. She supposed she should be accustomed to such horrors, she had seen enough of them since that day she had so thoughtlessly touched Bernart outside the *portal* of Saint-Ybars.

Please, My Lady, make this stop. Give this burden to someone worthier, a saint, a monk accustomed to meditation, to the selfless life.

There was suddenly a strange taste in her mouth, as if she had been eating chalk. She heard a buzzing, the familiar bee-swarm aura that accompanied her madness, and Mary stepped from her pedestal, as she had that first time in Saint-Étienne. The stone flags moved beneath Fabricia's knees, and she let out a small gasp, thinking the chapel was about to topple. A greasy sweat erupted on her skin and her stomach rebelled. She steadied herself on the wooden prie-dieu.

She stared up, into the vault. A demon in a black robe grappled there with an angel. As they struggled, the demon lost his footing and they tumbled together to the floor of the chapel. The demon's head split open on the flagstones like one of the ripe plums in the orchard. His head lolled towards her; she made out a trim beard, grizzled with grey. He had the tonsure of a monk. *I am coming for you*, he said and then the angel's wings closed over him and he died.

Fabricia stood up and screamed.

The vision disappeared. She almost lost her balance, put out a hand to try and keep herself from falling. Bernadette was there to catch her. She was only vaguely aware of the shouts of the other novices around her in the choir stall and the cold stare of the sacristan before she fainted.

*

She lay on her pallet in her cell, Sòrre Bernadette leaning over her. 'Fabricia,' she whispered. She tried to sit up, but Bernadette eased her back on to the bed. 'You must rest now.'

'Did you see the angel fall?'

'What angel, Fabricia?'

Then she remembered: just a dream.

'What angel?' Bernadette repeated.

Fabricia closed her eyes. Bernadette left her to rest.

The pain behind her eyes began then. After a short time even moving her head was a torture. Half the world was taken away; she could see only one side of the door, one side of the tiny window, one side of her own body. When it was like this, lying in her cell with the shutters closed was the only cure for the pain.

*

The next morning Sòrre Bernadette came to fetch her. 'Are you feeling better?'

'A little.'

'The abbess wants to see you.'

It was difficult to stand. She staggered against the wall. The chapel, the dorter where they slept, the kitchen and the refectory were all grouped around an open courtyard of beaten earth. Bernadette took her arm and helped her down the stairs and across the quadrangle to the chapter house.

The abbess was a short, stout woman, peasant stock, with brute, angry eyes. Fabricia always sensed that what the abbess loved most about God was His wrath. The wooden cross at her breast swung with the force of her pent-up energy, like a diviner's rod.

'You did not attend offices yesterday or last night.'

'I was unwell, Reverend Mother.'

'Well, so you say. Are you feeling better this morning?'

'A little.'

'I noticed you are limping. And you are still wearing your woollen mittens though it is no longer cold, even at prime. Show me your hands.'

Fabricia removed her gloves. She was shocked at what she saw. The palms and the backs of her hands were caked with blood. As she opened her fist, it dripped on to her habit. Sòrre Bernadette's hand went to her mouth. 'Oh, Fabricia!'

The abbess shook her head, unimpressed. 'Look at this. What have you done to yourself now?'

'I did not do this.'

'Then who did? The Devil?' She reached across the trestle table between them and yanked her hand closer. Fabricia let out a whimper of pain. 'No wonder you feel faint. Prisoners are tortured with more restraint. How do you stand it?'

'Sometimes it is worse than others.'

The abbess looked up at Bernadette. 'Do you know how she does this? Is she stealing knives from the kitchen?'

'I searched her cell, as you ordered me to do. We found nothing. She is a gentle soul, Reverend Mother, I think you misjudge her.'

'I have been abbess here for twenty years, I have not been wrong about a novice yet. She has hidden a knife somewhere.' She sighed.

'One of the nuns told me there was a riot at the gate yesterday morning.'

Fabricia shook her head. 'It was not a riot, Reverend Mother, just some poor people looking for healing.'

'It's true what she says,' Sòrre Bernadette said. 'A few shepherds and their wives, a little too eager. That's all. These poor people come every day for healing.'

'Do you really think you can do miracles, Fabricia. Do you?'

'Other people say these things about me. For myself, I don't know what to think.'

'That's a blasphemy!'

'I make no claim to anything.'

'Can you tell me what happened in the chapel yesterday morning?'

Fabricia shook her head. She looked down at her hands. Look at these wounds! Now she was aware of them, they had begun to hurt her, and badly. She gritted her teeth and tried to concentrate on what the abbess was saying.

'You have the whole abbey in continual uproar. Are you mocking us?'

'Why would you think that?'

'Why would I not think it? Sòrre Bernadette, this girl's wounds are deep. They need dressing. You must take her to the infirmarian.'

Fabricia stood up to go.

'Wait. I haven't finished with you yet.'

She sat down again.

'What am I to do with you? I knew, when you came here, that you were causing trouble in your village. But then a lot of the young women who enter our holy refuge do not have pasts of which anyone is proud. Not every novice is drawn by a fierce devotion to the divine, we know that. But you go too far. Bad enough that you try and draw attention to yourself continually in this . . . this bizarre manner. But now you are upsetting the other novices. You distract them from their duties and their prayers. After yesterday morning's spectacle some of them even think that you have a devil in you. Did you know that?'

Fabricia watched a droplet of watery blood track down her hand. It hung suspended, on the tip of her little finger, and then dripped on to the flagstone.

'I suspect that you are a malingerer, at heart.'

Sòrre Bernadette started to protest but the abbess silenced her with a glance.

'I have tamed many young women in my time here; the lazy, the stubborn, the disobedient, the wilful. It has been done patiently and with serenity, over many years. But I have never known anyone like you. What is doubly intolerable is that you attract all these unfortunates to our doors . . . that you make us . . . *famous*. This is not to be borne. Yesterday there were a score of cripples at our gate. Tomorrow there may be a hundred. How many more will come?'

'I don't ask them to come.'

'Who do you think you are? This laying on of hands is to stop forthwith. Do you understand me?'

'But she helps so many people, Reverend Mother!'

'Sòrre Bernadette, you are far too gullible. She is making a fool of you and you cannot see it.' She turned back to Fabricia. 'It is to stop. Now. Do you understand?'

'Yes, Reverend Mother.'

'Good. Now get out of my sight. Both of you.'

XXXVII

THE ABBESS ENFORCED a strict Rule. Instead of the soft bed and bearskin rugs she had had in Saint-Ybars, they had given her a hard plank bed with a thin covering of straw.

The bell woke them in the middle of the night for the service of matins. She had already come to hate the sound of that bell. Still groggy with sleep, she pulled her black habit over her chemise and got out of bed, her feet freezing on the cold stone as she searched in the dark for her wooden clogs. Then she went down the stairs and across the icy cloister to mumble through the psalms in the gloomy choir stall with the other novices. When she first arrived her breath formed white clouds on the air even as she sang the offertory, and she could not even feel her fingers touch together when she prayed. She had to break a skin of ice on the trough in the cloister just to wash. What would it be like here in winter?

A few hours' sleep. Then the bell again, for prime. They broke their fast with dry rye bread and water, mixed with a little wine. Nothing more, as most of what they produced – the fruit from the orchard, the grapes from the vineyard, the milk and butter from the cow – was sold in the village or bartered for milled grain and firewood.

They had all been assigned their chores. Fabricia had been made cellaress, a lonely occupation, but she supposed that from the beginning the abbess had wanted to keep her separate from the other novices. The cellar was in the undercroft below the dorter. It was a gloomy cavern, but now that summer had finally come to the mountains the air inside was scented with hops and old apples and cheese.

She would spend the mornings counting the garlic and jarring the honey, only breaking off when the bell summoned them yet again to the chapel for more prayer. They went back to their cells after compline, a few hours' sleep, the bell again, and then it all began once more. There was little time or opportunity for friendship, or even for conversation. Besides, some of the other novices had taken vows of silence.

She remembered what Simon had told her once, in that other life she had had, in Toulouse. *It is not enough just to love God. If you will bear the vows you must have a disposition sufficiently robust to serve him for all your years, not just one or two.*

Fabricia felt hungry and exhausted all the time and there was no prospect that she would ever feel anything else. I don't know if I can live this way the rest of my life, she thought. I miss the life I had, and I miss the life I dreamed of having. But there's no choice. I suppose I'll get used to it.

The morning after her interview with the abbess, instead of going to the gate after prime and working her way through the line of pilgrims come to ask her to lay hands, she went straight to the cellar to start her chores. Flies circled slowly above a long table; fat blue-bottles crawled frustrated over the linen cloth that had been placed over a bowl of warm goat's milk. A wasp danced frantically around the lid of a honey pot. Where to start? There were olives in sacks in the corner that should be put in jars for preserving.

By now they will be calling out my name at the gate, she thought. It seems cruel to deny them their hopes. But what can I do? The abbess rules my life now. In a way, she was relieved it was forbidden her, for it drained her of the little energy she had, though she felt ashamed that she should feel so.

Her hands ached; her feet hurt her too much to stand. She sat down heavily on a stool and removed her gloves. She should wash the wounds and put on a fresh linen bandage before she started work. She made her way painfully back up the stairs and along the cloister to the water trough.

She filled a wooden bucket and set it on the ground. The sun bounced off the surface of the water, quicksilver, and she blinked and closed her eyes. When she opened them again, the water swirled and dipped and in the depths she saw dead-eyed men running through the dorter, their daggers drawn. Sòrre Bernadette was sprawled on the floor, naked and half dead, with blood on her thighs. A handsome man with green eyes and gore on his shirt stood over her with a knife.

She threw off her wimple and stuck her head into the trough. The shock of the cold water banished the vision. She looked around. Just a pleasant Midi morning with mare's tails chasing a blue sky. Where did such nightmares come from? She was going mad, she was sure of it. 'Please, My Lady, make this stop,' she murmured.

What was happening to her? When would this end?

XXXVIII

IT HAPPENED ON the feast of Mary Magdalene. They were at compline; Fabricia was half-dozing in the choir, longing for the liturgy to end so she might snatch a few hours of sleep before the next office. The abbess collapsed suddenly, her face the colour of beet, froth forming at her lips. Sòrre Bernadette and several others carried her from the chapel, the sacristan running after them.

Afterwards Fabricia went back to her cell with the other novices, fell instantly into a black and dreamless sleep. She was woken by the subprioress, pulling her to her feet even before she had opened her eyes.

'You must come,' she said, and led her through the dorter in her shift.

The abbess's cell was little different to her own: bare stone walls, straw on the floor, a hard pallet for sleeping. The room was lit by a single taper. A large wooden crucifix hung on the wall above the abbess's bed, and the Lord Jesus seemed to writhe with every flicker of the candle in the draught.

The old lady wore only her shift. Her hair was grey and shorn close to the skull, her face swollen and purple as if she had been choked. Someone had placed a rosary between her fingers. She was making a wet, gasping noise as if she were drowning. The sacristan and the infirmarian knelt beside the bed, praying.

As Sòrre Bernadette walked in, the sacristan said: 'We have sent the porteress to find the priest.'

Bernadette turned to Fabricia. 'Can you help her? At least keep her alive until the priest gets here?'

'I have been forbidden.'

'She forbade you. Not me.' And then to Fabricia's astonishment, Bernadette took her hand and went down on one knee. 'Please, Fabricia. You have a special gift, from God. You have no cause to love her, I know, but I have known the abbess from when I was a novice and I believe her a good woman at heart. Help her.'

The infirmarian and the sacristan moved aside for her. Fabricia fell to her knees. She placed both her hands on the old woman's chest and closed her eyes in prayer. The Our Father, ten Hail Marys. When she was finished she got back to her feet.

'Is that all?' the sacristan said.

'What else do you want me to do?'

'But . . .' She turned to Bernadette. 'I expected more.'

'Do you smell that?'

The other two nuns frowned. One of them said: 'It smells like flowers.'

'Lavender,' Sòrre Bernadette said.

They all looked at the abbess. There seemed to be little change in her condition. Fabricia turned to Bernadette. 'May I return to my bed now, sister?'

'Of course. Thank you, Fabricia.'

She went back to bed. In moments she was asleep.

XXXIX

TWO DAYS AFTER the feast of the Magdalene, the abbess was sitting up in bed, sipping broth. She did not look as formidable to Fabricia without her wimple and habit. She appeared smaller somehow, though no less stern. Fabricia hoped for reconciliation with her.

The porteress had fetched the priest from Montclair and he had given her the extreme unction. The next morning she had rallied. Now look at her, Sòrre Bernadette said. She will outlive all of us.

'I am glad to see you recovered,' Fabricia said.

'It was just a fainting spell,' the abbess said. 'There was nothing much wrong with me in the first place.' Fabricia saw the infirmarian exchange glances with Sòrre Bernadette.

'You wished to see me, Reverend Mother?'

'Indeed I do. I have disturbing news.'

'My parents are well?' Fabricia said, alarmed.

'This is of much greater consequence than the health of your family. You have heard that the Pope has sent a crusade against the heretics the Count of Toulouse has fostered here in the Albigeois all these years?'

'It will not affect us here, surely?'

'The Pope's holy Host have taken Béziers. Everyone inside the walls has been slaughtered, praise be to God, the city burned, even the cathedral.' Bernadette put a hand to her mouth. 'They have tasted God's vengeance for their sinfulness, to the last man, woman and child.'

'What about the priests?' Bernadette said.

'They had the chance to leave and they chose to stay. They are as guilty of harbouring heretics as the Count himself. They will answer to God now.'

Fabricia crossed herself. 'I thought they came to make war only on the heretics, and on the Count's soldiers.'

'Anyone who gives shelter to heresy spits in God's eye.'

My mother is a heretic, Fabricia thought, and my father loves her. As do I. Does that make us heretics, too? Does this mean we will burn, no matter how many masses we partake, how many confessions we make?

'That is ghastly news,' Bernadette said.

'It is God's holy wrath, retribution against sinners. We should celebrate the return of holy law to the Albigeois.'

'But what has this to do with me, Reverend Mother?'

'The infamy you bring us with your so-called healing and other hysterical nonsense was never welcome here. But in times such as these, it could be calamitous. You are to leave here, today.'

Fabricia turned to Bernadette for support, but she seemed as shocked as she. 'But she laid hands on you,' Bernadette protested to the abbess.

'You should not have allowed her to do such a thing! You think she raised me from the dead, is that it?' She pointed an accusing finger. 'Even to consider it is a blasphemy. Only Our Lord has the power to heal. Will you give her the credit every time any one of us wakes from a faint?' The blood rose to her cheeks. The effort of shouting had exhausted her. 'She is to leave here immediately.'

'But where shall I go?' Fabricia said.

'It is no longer my concern. I have judged you unsuitable for this life. Now go. Leave me in peace.'

*

Fabricia waited for the porteress to open the gate. She no longer wore her habit, just the simple brown tunic of a village girl. Her few belongings were tied in a bundle. Sòrre Bernadette ran across the cloister with several other nuns and threw herself on her knees. 'I cannot believe she would do this to you. What are you going to do?'

Fabricia was shocked and embarrassed to see the sub-prioress crying at her feet so she dropped down to her knees beside her. 'I'll be all right. I shall go back to Saint-Ybars and to my family.'

'I pray that He will keep you safe.' She pushed a bundle with bread and cheese into her hands. Sòrre Marie, the porteress, was crying now, too. The other nuns watched from the other side of the cloister, their faces hard.

Fabricia stood up and went out through the gate. What am I going to do now? she thought. It seems nowhere I go is safe.

X L

The Minervois, Pays d'Oc

WHAT A MISERABLE place.

Godless, Father Ortiz had said. 'If the Devil had a birthplace, it is here; the very air is tainted with heresy. Turn over a rock and a heretic comes crawling out.'

They followed the old Roman road, straight as an arrow, mile after tedious mile of it. There were stagnant land-locked pools on either side, some yellow scrub and salt pans. The heat was dashed at them by the fierce winds that blew off the Golfe du Lion.

The horses twitched and switched their tails, tormented by countless midges, while the cicadas rattled and hummed. No birdsong here; the local people had eaten them all. Simon felt something sting his neck and slapped at it. He felt light-headed. His body itched and stank under the black woollen habit. He glanced over at Father Ortiz. His face was blotchy red and shining with sweat and he barely had strength to swat at the flies. His mouth was open, panting in the heat.

We suffer for God. It is the way we show our love.

He squinted against the glare. There was a long line of horsemen ahead of him, two by two, each with a red cross on their white tunics. They rode upright, as they had been trained to do. Their discipline was faultless. And such horses they rode! Huge spirited animals, swinging their crupper cloths and tossing their heads, made more fearsome by their canvas hoods.

The squires rode behind, their masters' long shields slung on the sides of their own horses, three azure eagles on a sable background, the device of the house of Soissons. Each of the baron's knights had brought with them a small troop of foot soldiers and some cavalry, their vassals, friends and relations, their squires and sergeants. A dozen knights; perhaps three hundred men-at-arms, by Simon's calculation. Not a large army, but not a small one either.

Simon and Father Ortiz rode at the rear on their poorer mounts, alongside the supply carts. The armour was packed in there; the coats of chain mail were only for the knights, because of its expense, though a squire might have a mail hauberk that reached to his knees if his master was generous. A sergeant might have a *broigne*, a jerkin sewn with strips of leather. The common soldiery made do with a shield and a prayer for luck.

They had been assured that Béziers was only two leagues more, three at most, and it was there that they would finally join the Host. Their plan had been to link up with the crusader army in Nîmes, but they had been delayed on the way from Toulouse when Father Ortiz caught a fever, had lost almost a week while he recovered in a monastery outside Millau. By the time they arrived the great Host had already started its advance to the south. They prayed for better fortune and God had granted it; the next day Baron Gilles de Soissons arrived from the north with his army, on their way to join the crusader force, and he had offered them escort.

Simon sagged in the saddle, sore and thirsty and faint with heat. Father Ortiz threw up a hand to halt and he supposed that he needed to rest. Simon and the two *servientes* with which the Bishop had furnished them stopped also. The soldiers rode on, except the two at the rearguard some twenty paces back.

There was a woman by the side of the road, rocking gently back and forward on her heels, clutching a bundle of rags to her breast. What made Father Ortiz stop? Simon wondered. Nothing unusual to this. The road was full of pilgrims and the poor.

One of the servants got down from his horse and went over to her. 'What has happened?' Father Ortiz asked.

He spoke to her in the *langue d'oc*. 'She says her child is sick, Father,' he said.

'Bring her here.'

Leaning from his horse, he uncovered the filthy bundle she was holding in her arms. It was an infant, newly born, its head of a gross size and misshapen. 'The child is dead,' he said.

She shrieked and drew away.

'What is your name?' he asked her. 'Where are you going?'

She didn't answer. Father Ortiz got down from his horse. 'Give me the child,' he said. There was some quality to his voice that made her obey, half mad as she appeared to be. 'The child is dead,' he repeated, 'and we must now look to his soul. Do you believe in Jesus your Saviour and his Holy Apostolic Church?'

The woman's eyes were huge, like a child's. She nodded. She had no strength to resist Father Ortiz's charity.

'Has he had water poured on his head by a priest?'

She shook her head.

'Then we shall baptize him here and he will have a Christian burial so that his soul might be saved in heaven. Do you go often to church?'

Another barely discernible nod of the head.

Father Ortiz turned to his servants. 'We must bury the child,' he said and ignored their looks of complete astonishment. The ground was baked hard and it seemed to Simon the poor men were as near fainting as he was. But they did as they had been ordered, scraping a shallow grave from the pale dirt.

Father Ortiz performed a hurried baptism using a little water from the leather bottle at his waist, and then he took the stole from a satchel on his saddle and spoke the words of committal. All the while the two soldiers of the rearguard, who were now their only protection on the lonely road, grumbled and shook their heads, disgusted that he should have inconvenienced them so for the sake of a peasant woman.

The infant was placed into the shallow grave and covered over. It will surely be dug up again by foxes or dogs as soon as we are gone, Simon thought.

They remounted their horses.

'What about the woman?' Simon asked Father Ortiz.

'We shall take her with us.' He led her to his horse and told her to get up into saddle.

'Father Ortiz?' Simon asked. 'Is this wise?' He supposed what he meant was: is this dignified?

'I shall walk.'

'Then you must have my horse.'

'No, it is my decision. It is what Jesus would have done.'

And that is why Father Ortiz walked the rest of the way to Béziers. For, as he said, that was what Jesus would have done and he could do no less.

Béziers

When they arrived, the crusader Host had already been and departed. Fifteen thousand souls had lived in the town once. They were still there, but they lived no longer. Simon did not trouble himself to see them, but he could smell them. They were mostly charred, he was told; what was left of them anyway.

The afternoon heat lay ponderous on the burned stones, the citadel exhaling the stink of butchery. Fragments of grey ash still floated in the air. Here and there black smudges drifted upwards. A wall of the cathedral shimmered and fell as he watched. The air was heavy with the drone of meat flies. Vultures and crows dozed on the walls, replete. Dogs yelped and fought over scraps, though there was plenty to be had. No human sound.

'A miracle,' Father Ortiz said and fell on his knees and gave thanks to God.

XLI

Saint-Ybars

THE VILLAGE SLUMBERED under the hot sun. The grey stone houses were different to the north; they all had curved pink tiles on their roofs and each tile rested on a companion that was exactly the same but inverted. The eaves were weighted with large stones to prevent the mistral lifting the tiles from their position. The Romans had built their houses this way, they said.

The air was rich and somnolent, spiced with wild thyme. Dragonflies hovered among the cornflowers. The mountains of Castile had disappeared into the haze.

There were ripe figs lying under the trees and Gilles de Soissons got down from his horse and opened one, sucking at the soft grainy fruit inside. They all huddled under a hastily erected silk canopy, seeking shelter from the enervating heat. Over their heads, a banner with a cross, surmounted by the fleur-de-lis of the King of France, stirred and then was still.

'Well,' he said, 'they refuse to open the gates to us. They are Trencavel's men inside. They insult us and call us invaders and godless.'

Roger-Raymond Trencavel was the local viscount. He had been warring with Count Raymond of Toulouse for years and was accustomed to being invaded. His soldiers knew a siege like a summer's day.

'We have supplies enough to continue,' Simon said.

'I do not care about supplies, I care about their insolence. Do we leave a nest of heretics behind us, unharmed, when I have sworn on the holy cross to come here and eradicate them?'

The baron's voice was high-pitched and grated on the nerves. A curious one, Simon thought. He walks like a nobleman; nothing could disguise the gait of a man who had spent most of his life in the saddle. He just didn't look like one, in Simon's opinion. He was from the north, from Normandy, but not dark, as most of them were. His hair was white, even his eyelashes, and he had no beard. His eyes were pale, almost pink.

His boots were thick with the pale dust of the Midi, he had heavy spurs strapped to them and blood upon the spikes. So he is cruel to his horse, Simon thought. That tells you something.

It had been a surprise to find one of these *castra*, as they called these fortified towns in the Albigeois, still defiant. Every other town they had passed since Béziers had been deserted. Simon was not sure that massacre should become a Christian principle, but as a tactic of war it had succeeded in spectacular fashion.

'We should capture the town,' Gilles said.

'It is three hundred souls. Why bother? We have no siege engines.'

'We don't need siege engines. It is not a proper fortress. The walls are not high; most form part of the houses on the perimeter. They cannot be properly guarded and even if they could, by my estimate the garrison is not large enough to do it. There are a score of Trencavel's men in there, two score at most. A handful of my men can scale the walls during the night and at first light they can rush the gate and throw it open to us.'

'You do not have enough men for this,' Simon said.

'Correct me, Father, but you and Father Ortiz are here to lend spiritual direction to the crusade, not advise professional soldiers on tactics. Am I right?'

Simon turned to Father Ortiz for support, but he looked away.

'We should join the siege at Carcassonne. They were our instructions.'

'We do better service ensuring the army's rear.'

'If they had wanted this village they would have taken it.'

'Perhaps they were in a hurry to reach Carcassonne. For them this would be like swatting at a fly. It is better left to smaller armies, such as mine.'

Simon understood the baron's eagerness to start his war. It required only forty days of active campaigning under the cross to earn the remission of all his sins, so the sooner he began, the sooner he could mark his place in heaven and go home.

He rubbed at the skin of his back through the woollen cassock, feeling the raised cicatrices of his scars. They itched him when he sweated, hard as bone and inflamed in this heat. *Did I really do that?*

'If the people won't come out, then we will go in after them. Their defiance can only mean that they are harbouring heretics in there. If they will not bow down to Jesus they will bend their knee to the fire. I came here to do God's work and I am ready to begin.'

'It is the soldiers who defy you,' Simon said. 'Not the towns-people. They have no choice.'

'Very well, Father Jorda. Tomorrow morning I shall invite any who believe in the Holy Church to leave the village so we shall know there are only the godless left inside.'

'This is futile! Even if you capture it, you have not the men to garrison it.'

'There will be nothing left to garrison. I shall do as the Host did at Béziers. We will burn it to the ground and any heretics we find will scorch with it.'

Simon looked at Father Ortiz. 'Do you agree with his plan?'

'In Spain we have a proverb. "Where a blessing fails, a good thick stick will suffice."'

Simon looked up the hill towards the *castrum*. The watch lamps were already shining from the corner of the ramparts. 'Father, I do not think a big stick is a weapon that Jesus favoured. I thought we were here to save souls.'

'We are here to drive the Devil from his lair by any means at our disposal. Those that will be saved, we shall save. But our first duty is to defend Jesus Christ.'

'Tomorrow I will offer the good Catholics of the town their freedom,' Gilles said. 'If they do not choose to accept our mercy, then they shall reap the consequences.' It was late in the afternoon and his men had started to build their cook fires. 'Two nights hence we shall be warming our toes by a larger fire than any of these. The fire will have a name. We shall call it Saint-Ybars.'

XLII

ONE OF THE younger soldiers was retching with nerves somewhere in the darkness and his more experienced comrades,
ordered to silence, were kicking him with their boots to shut him
up. No moon, only the light at the watchtowers to show them the
way.

Diego and Simon stood at the front of the column beside Gilles's
white destrier, a massive beast with red eyes. It jerked on the reins,
stamping its hoof, excited by the press of soldiers around it. Two
squires struggled to hold it.

A scream startled him. The fight had started at the *portal*. Half a
dozen of Gilles's men had scaled the walls during the night and were
now attacking the soldiers at the gate.

Gilles had told Father Ortiz he must wait for his signal before he
gave the men his benediction. Now there was no further need for
silence, Gilles twisted around in his saddle and pointed at the friar.
'Say what you have to and be quick about it!'

'Men of Normandy,' Father Ortiz shouted, 'God is with you
today! Your enemy is Christ's enemy! Your crusade is greater than
even those who fight in the Holy Land, for the men you go against
are not mere heathens, who sin only from ignorance, but men
inspired by the Devil himself, Christians once saved by the blood of
Christ who in their wretchedness have now turned against him!
They have massacred priests and profaned churches and spat on the
cross! They kiss the anus of a black cat and call it Jesus! You can give
such people no quarter!'

There were warning shouts and the sound of death from the
portal. Gilles pulled on the reins of the destrier so that it rose into
the air and the great iron hooves crashed down inches from Simon's
face. The gates of Saint-Ybars swung open. Someone was swinging
a torch to give the signal.

Gilles did not wait for Diego to finish his valediction. He spurred his horse forward and shouted the command to attack. His chevaliers – his mounted troops – and foot soldiers surged behind him.

The Norman army converged on the gate. Simon watched, horrified and afraid.

'Are you all right?' Father Ortiz said.

'I'm all right.'

'Will you join me in song then?' He raised the cross above their heads, just as the sun rose over the mountain. It touched the very tip and flashed gold. He started to sing: '*Veni Sancte Spiritus* . . .'.

There was an explosion of flame at the *portal*, then another. They finished the hymn. Diego shuffled under the weight of the gold-plated cross. 'They are taking a long time to pass the gate,' he said.

Simon heard the panicked shriek of a horse. Soldiers ran from the *portal*, on fire. Something was wrong. They should have been inside by now.

'Shall we sing the hymn again, Brother Simon?'

They sang the *Veni Sancte Spiritus* twice more. As the sun rose higher in the sky, two thick plumes of black smoke spiralled into the sky.

'What you said to them,' Simon murmured. 'That business about the black cat.'

'What of it?'

'I have lived here in the southern lands all my life. I never heard of such a thing.'

'I have it on good authority.'

'These *bons òmes* are misguided on many things, it is true. But I do not believe any of them would do such a thing to a cat.'

'Does this matter so much to you at this moment, Brother Simon?'

'I believe that God made us guardians of a great truth. We do not need to embellish it with falsehoods.'

One of Gilles's foot soldiers ran back down the hill, his leather tunic smouldering. He ripped it off, howling in pain. Another followed. Soon there were dozens of them, stumbling, bleeding, cursing.

Now the chevaliers came, all Gilles's little army in ragged retreat.

'What has happened?' Father Ortiz shouted.

One of the soldiers came over. He had lost his helmet and

clutched at his arm, which hung useless at his side. Blood dripped steadily from his fingers. 'It wasn't just Trencavel's men on the walls! The whole village was waiting for us. Filthy Devil-fuckers!'

The last to return was Gilles himself. He looked like a hedgehog, his coat of mail bristling with arrows. Simon had heard it was hard to kill any knight, even at close quarters, as their armour was mostly impenetrable. It was only ever the foot soldiers that died, for they only had a piece of leather or a shield to protect them. Now he could see for himself that everything he had been told was true.

Perhaps that was why men like Gilles loved war so much.

The Norman removed his helmet and flung it into the dirt. His boy's face was flushed with sweat, his thin white hair plastered to his skull. More arrows quivered in his destrier's armour, though one had penetrated, near the shoulder, and dark blood streamed down its foreleg. It jittered and circled in pain and agitation.

'What happened, my lord?' Father Ortiz shouted.

'The townspeople are fighting alongside the soldiers. They had chains ready across the street to bring down our horses and even the burghers were on the roof hurling rocks down at us. Then they set fire to two hay carts and pushed them down the street. I lost two of my knights and God Himself knows how many men!'

'I told him we were not prepared for this,' Simon said to Father Ortiz.

'You said we were only fighting soldiers!' Gilles shouted at them. 'You said the people were good Catholics and it was only Trencavel's soldiers that would fight us! Show mercy, you said! Well, now see you where mercy has got us! There's not one of them in there that is not a Devil-kissing bastard!'

He drove his sword hard into the dirt, point down.

'This will not stand!' he said, pointing at them both as if they were responsible for his defeat. 'They will rue the day they stood against Gilles de Soissons!'

XLIII

ANOTHER LONG DAY on the road. It seemed the whole world was on their way to Lyons. It was pilgrim season, and they had passed thousands of them, all on their way to the southern lands. Holy wars are good for business, or so the innkeepers said.

They made their way alone or in groups, singing hymns, following monks and priests, and carrying banners. Everyone was walking: beggars, minstrels, serfs out of bond, students. Only rarely did Philip and his men encounter other horsemen: a baron or a bishop, or an ox-cart carrying timber or lead for a church roof. It was hard going nevertheless, for every league or so a flock of sheep or cattle slowed their progress and fouled the road.

Late one afternoon, just out of Lyons, they stopped to rest. The *écuyers* unsaddled the horses, cooling their coats with willow leaves they had dipped in the river. Philip's body was numb from exhaustion after a week of hard riding and chafed by the heavy coat of mail. He removed a heavy gauntlet to wipe the sweat and dirt from his eyes. Renaut helped him out of his travelling armour; he groaned with relief as he shook himself free of it, then he followed the other chevaliers down to the water's edge to scoop handfuls of cool water over his head and neck, drinking till his stomach felt stretched to burst.

As soon as the horses were watered they made camp; their tents, heavy baggage carts and cook fires extended a hundred paces along the bank. Night fell quickly. Philip had Renaut post sentries, then wrapped himself in his travelling cloak and tried to sleep, listening to the crackle of dead twigs in the fire, the low murmur of the men gathered around it. The salted pork they ate for their dinner had left him thirsty and restless. *Please God, let me be on time. Don't let my boy die.* A screech owl cried in the wood. Werewolves and goblins walked abroad on moonless nights like this. He touched the cross at his throat for protection.

Don't let my little boy die.

*

He woke to Renaut shaking him roughly by the shoulder.

'Seigneur, with your pardon, wake up.'

A soldier's instinct: he was instantly awake. 'What is it?'

Two of his men-at-arms stood there with flaming torches, a small boy between them. They were holding him by the arms, with some difficulty, for he was twisting and struggling and trying to kick them. One of the men got tired of this and hit him with the hilt of his sword. The boy's eyes rolled back in his head and he sank to his knees.

'Enough!' Philip shouted. He jumped to his feet and turned to Renaut. 'What's going on?'

'The sentries found him sneaking into the camp. He was trying to steal our food.'

Philip crouched down. The lad was tousle-haired and filthy, and scrawny as a tent pole. He lifted the boy's head. 'Who are you?'

But the boy was still senseless from the blow and couldn't answer. So they dragged him down to the river and ducked his head into the water to revive him. The child came round, shaking his head like a dog.

'Who are you?' Philip asked him again.

The boy's eyes focused, took in Philip's clothes, his velvet tunic and garnet ring. 'Well, here's a fine one,' he said. 'You look like the King of France.'

'Hit him again,' Renaut said to the sentry.

Philip shook his head. 'Leave him.' He took the boy by the shoulders. 'What is your name?'

'Loup, sir.'

'How did you come by such a name?'

'My mother gave it to me. Who are you?'

'You insolent little dog,' Renaut said and would have slapped him with his gauntlet but Philip held him off.

'My name is Philip, Baron of Vercy. I am the man you were trying to steal from.'

'I'm starving. Have you got anything to eat?'

Philip looked at Renaut. 'What shall we do with him?'

'If it were up to me, I should cut his ear off to teach him respect and then throw him in the river.'

'Have mercy, Renaut. He is not much older than you were when they brought you to me.'

'I'm just hungry, seigneur. I never meant any harm.'

'You're a thief.'

'Well, perhaps, seigneur. But either I'm a thief with one ear or I'm a stiff lying by the side of the road and I know which I'd rather be.'

Philip grinned despite himself. He hauled the boy up on to the bank and shoved him towards Renaut. 'Give the wretch something to eat.'

'Seigneur, this is not a good idea.'

'A bit of salted pork and some bread if he is so desperate. If he can keep it down then he's a better man than I am and he should have it. For mercy's sake, Renaut. I am asking God for His good graces, should I not answer someone else's prayer if it is in my power?'

Renaut shrugged. He grabbed the lad's arm and dragged him up the bank to the camp. Philip smiled. Loup. *Wolf.* A good name for a scavenger. He would feed the urchin and in the morning he would see him on his way.

The men were snoring and the fire was down to ashes. Loup huddled beside it, tearing at the salted pork with his teeth and scarcely bothering to chew. Renaut stood over him with a lighted brand. Philip studied him: a runt with a hawk face and limbs too long for his body. He had that beaten-dog look about him, eyes that watched for any unexpected movement, head constantly twisting and turning, ready to flinch, ready to flee.

'Where are you from?'

'Nowhere.'

'Don't you have a home?'

'I did, when my father lived. But he died and so we were headed for Paris where my mother has a cousin. She said he would look after us but she died on the road. Took a fever, she did.'

'Where is she?'

'Over there,' he said. 'Under a tree.'

Philip nodded to Renaut and the two men-at-arms. 'Leave us. I commend you for your duty. You did well. Thank you, Renaut.' He squatted down beside the boy, his back warmed by the dying embers of the fire.

'Where are you going?' Loup asked him.

'The Albigeois. A place called Saint-Ybars.'

'Why are you going there? There's a war. Are you joining the crusade?'

'No, we're not crusaders. I was a crusader once in Outremer and I shall never be one again.'

'Why then?'

'I have a son in Burgundy. He is dying.'

'So why aren't you there with him?'

'Do you believe in miracles, Loup?'

'I've heard of them, from the priests. But I've never seen one.'

'I believe in miracles. I believe that if I pray to God hard enough He will hear me and answer my prayer for my son. That is why I am going to the Albigeois. There is a woman there who can heal with her hands. I am going to ask her to come back with me to Burgundy and heal my son.'

'You're mad.'

'Yes, you're probably right.'

'Can I sleep here tonight? By the fire? I promise I won't steal anything.'

'Very well. But I shall give you fair warning. If you do try and thieve anything my squire Renaut really will cut your ear off. For all his youth he is as protective of me as a bear with its cub.'

The boy licked his hands for the taste of the pork grease and then lay down between two of the soldiers for the extra warmth. Philip sat for a time watching the breeze stir the ashes in the fire, then he took off his cloak and threw it over the boy. Then he went back to sleep, wondering why he had chosen to tell his troubles to an orphan and a thief. In the morning he was sure the little scoundrel would be gone, along with some bread and someone else's ring.

*

Philip was awake with the first seeping of the light. He shook the dew off, buckled on his belt and sword. To his surprise, Loup was still asleep where he had left him. He shook the boy awake and called for Renaut. They had the boy show them his mother's body. He had wondered if it was a lie to engage his sympathy, but a hundred paces from the camp they found her, just as the lad had said, stiff and cold under a chestnut tree.

The body was already foul and the foxes and crows had been at her. He told Renaut to have the men dig her a grave. No priest to see her vouchsafed to heaven, but Philip said a prayer over her when it was done and hoped that would be enough.

When Philip mounted Leyla, Loup stood in front of him, blocking the way. 'Take me with you,' he said.

Philip laughed. 'Why would I do that?'

'You see,' Renaut said. 'He's like any cur in the street. You've given him scraps and he thinks he deserves more.'

'Don't leave me here, seigneur.'

'You're no good to us boy. And I have my own business to attend to.'

'I speak the *langue d'oc*. I won't slow you down and I might be a blessing when you get among those fops and heretics.'

'I think thirty armed men shall not be more stoutly preserved by the addition of a runt barely old enough for leggings. And I speak a little of the language. I learned it in Outremer from southern knights.'

Loup caught the reins. 'Then as a mercy, sir, take me with you as far as Lyons.' Renaut shook his head, exasperated.

On an impulse, Philip reached down, grabbed Loup under the shoulders and lifted him up on to the saddle. 'Very well, my little lord Wolf. You're a beggar and a thief so you should earn your living there well enough.'

'Thank you, seigneur. I shan't be any trouble.'

'No good can come of this,' Renaut said.

LIV

JUST THEIR LUCK to reach Lyons on a market day, Philip thought. They could lose half a day's ride just getting from one side of this damned city to the other.

The streets were clogged, the toll gates chaos, and there was scarcely space in the main square for all the ox and donkey carts. The market was a grey sea of sheep's backs and the noise was an assault after the quiet of the road: water-carriers ringing bells, apprentices bumping their barrels over the cobblestones, honking geese, the scream of a bear from a bear-baiting pit and the single deafening braying of a mule. Over it all Philip heard the sound of a jongleur's lute, and the ripple of laughter from his audience.

The King's fleur-de-lis was everywhere, the city in a rage of patriotic fervour for the war, as if the Pays d'Oc were an infidel invader.

A priest was already at work outside the church, holding a golden cross aloft, enthusiastic crowds pressing around him. '. . . they desecrate the churches and use them for foul orgies of the flesh . . . they worship the Devil openly. They are no longer human but servants of Satan! Even these so-called noblemen, these lords of Trencavel and Foix and Toulouse! We have tolerated these devils too long in our midst. For you do not have to bow down to Satan to crucify Our Lord all over again! Just to harbour such people, to give succour to them, is enough. If you are not for God then you must be against him! But if you join with us in our holy pilgrimage against these devils then you will earn a place in heaven and all sins will be remitted for you have proved your love for God!'

Renaut and Philip stopped their horses to listen. 'They said the same to us before we went to Outremer,' Philip said.

'There are plenty of new converts here, seigneur.'

'They said the world would come to an end if we did not do something against the Mohammedan, but the only world that ended was mine. I find I do not care so much for heaven now.'

'Seigneur, you should not speak that way!'

Philip twisted in the saddle and looked at the boy. 'Did you hear what I said? Do you think me a heretic?'

'My father – when he was alive, God keep him – would say to me that if a man could be left his peace by making the sign of the cross, then he should do it. And he said if tomorrow someone else came along and said that it should be not a cross but a circle then a circle it was. Is that a heretic, sir?'

Philip laughed. 'Your father was a practical man.'

'He was a tinker, sir, and could turn his hand to anything.'

'And to any religion, too. But this is Lyons, young sir. I have kept my bargain with you. Now be on your way and good luck to you.'

Loup clambered down from the back of the great warhorse, but still clung to one stirrup. 'Won't you take me with you, seigneur? I could be useful.'

'What for?' Renaut said. 'As somewhere to store the lice? Be gone with you. My master has shown you kindness enough.'

Philip spurred his horse away and the boy was soon lost to the jostling crowds.

*

While his men-at-arms availed themselves of some watered-down beer in one of the inns near the main square, Philip found a church and went inside. For all his supposed lack of religion, he was not at all godless, for all his bluster. Wasn't the point of his journey to beg a mercy from God?

Massive iron candlesticks lit the gloom of the church like daylight. The saints painted on the pillars looked almost cheerful.

He found a statue of the Virgin, fell to his knees and whispered: '*Ave Maria, gratia plena . . .*' Then he said a prayer, as he always did, for his son. Perhaps he did not believe in popes or crusades any more. But he still believed in miracles and he hoped that belief alone might be enough.

There were ragged lines to the confessional, so many people

crammed into the church there was hardly time for each to whisper a *confiteor* and slip their mite into the priest's hand before it was time for the next furtive sinner. Holy wars were indeed good for business, just as the innkeepers said.

There was a commotion as he left the church. Some burgher, in his fur jacket and silks, was waving his scented handkerchief in the air and looked set to faint. Two of his retainers held a little ruffian between them, and one of them held aloft a velvet purse.

'It's here, sire!' he shouted. 'We have him fast!'

Philip ran down the steps and put himself between the burgher and his men. Their surprise changed quickly to alarm. It was immediately apparent to them that Philip was a knight and not a man to tangle with.

'Let him go,' Philip said, and he grabbed a handful of Loup's hair to lay proprietory claim.

'But, seigneur, he is a thief. He stole our master's –'

Philip rounded on him. 'If you are going to address a baron and a knight you will do so on your knees with your voice lowered.' His hand went to his sword. The man backed away.

Pulling a squealing Loup behind him Philip approached the burgher, and tossed a silver coin in his direction. 'For your inconvenience, sir. He will cause you no further trouble.'

He dragged Loup away. 'You seem determined to lose your ears, boy. I should have let them put you in the stocks as a lesson.'

'Owww, you're hurting me!'

'I should hurt you more. The art of being a thief is not to get caught. Did no one ever tell you that?'

'Where are you taking me? Owww . . .'

Philip was almost at the tavern when he let the boy go. Loup made a show of smoothing down his hair and then tried to kick him. Philip shook his head. 'Very well, you can come with us. At least until you learn to look after yourself better than you do now.'

Loup grinned. 'You mean that, seigneur?'

'I never say anything I do not mean.' He looked up and saw Renaut standing outside the inn, watching. His squire shook his head. You're going to regret this, the look seemed to say.

XLV

Saint-Ybars

TWO DAYS SPENT stitching gashes in horses and men, counting
their losses and exploring the geography of humiliation. Gilles
stayed in his tent and did not come out. Father Ortiz spent the
days singing psalms under a tree. The heat was oppressive; the
sound of the crickets maddening. Saint-Ybars, this feeble fortress
town, had shaken their faith. Normandy had thought it would go
easier than this.

On the second evening Gilles called a counsel, and Father Ortiz
and Simon were summoned to his silk pavilion along with his
knights and squires. There was one other in attendance, whom
Simon did not recognize, a slight man with a neat black beard. He
sat in the corner, on the only other chair, wearing along with the
colours of the house of Trencavel a look of utter terror.

The night drew a ragged breath; the air stuck to the skin and the
biting insects made everyone irritable. Gilles sat in a chair before a
trestle table on which was a large map, held down at the corners by
small rocks.

'Gentlemen, may I present M'sieur Robèrt Marty, lately *bayle* of
Saint-Ybars. During the night, knowing his duty lay to God and not
to his heretic lord, he stole away from the town and made himself
known to our sentries, and they brought him here to me. He wishes
to show us the way inside the *castrum*.'

'Praise be to God,' Father Oritz said.

'Can we trust him?' someone said, a midnight devil with one eye
and a red beard. His name was Hugues de Breton and he was the
Norman's most trusted lieutenant. He cracked his knuckles, playing
up to the air of menace lent him by his disfigurement.

Gilles turned to Robèrt. 'Can we trust you?'

'I have put myself in your hands. You think I would be sitting here if I planned to play you false? I know where my duty as a good Catholic lies.'

'Truth is he saw what we did at Béziers,' Hugues de Breton said. 'He's shitting his breeches.'

'He is one of us now,' Gilles said like an indulgent father. He stood up and indicated the chart that was laid out on the table. 'He has brought us this, a map of Saint-Ybars. What he wishes us to know is that there is another gate, right here.' He tapped the paper with his forefinger. 'There is a secret passage behind it that leads under the *castrum* and up to the *donjon*. Robèrt is going to lead us there. Hugues will take half our troops in by this way so that this time we can secure the gate from the *inside*. But we must do it tonight before Robèrt is missed. If they realize they have been betrayed they will flood the passage.'

'What is this passage used for?'

'It is an escape tunnel they have used in the past when they have been besieged by the Count of Toulouse's men. Most of the villagers left this way after our first attack. Only a few soldiers now remain inside. They plan to wait a further day and then flee also.'

'Why is he telling us this?' Hugues said.

Gilles tossed Robèrt a purse. 'He knows which master is better served.'

'A man who will betray once, will betray twice.'

'Once he leads us to the gate he will remain hostage here at the camp. He knows what will happen if he plays us false.'

'Our prayers have been answered,' Father Ortiz said. 'It is a miracle.'

'Greed is not a miracle,' Hugues said. 'Just an inevitability.'

'Get the men ready. Once Hugues and his men have secured the gates I will take my knights and claim Saint-Ybars for God.'

Am I the only man in this room who does not see the futility of this? Simon wondered. 'What of the men inside?' he said. 'What of their souls?'

Gilles looked at him in astonishment. 'Their souls? That is God's concern, not ours.'

'So we are to slaughter a few men who have remained loyal to their liege lord and reward this Judas?'

There was a heavy-breathing silence. Father Ortiz stared at him in astonishment. 'These men stood against God's army,' Gilles said.

'God's army is at Carcassonne,' Simon said. 'This has served us nothing.'

Gilles kicked the trestle over. 'We are ridding the land of heresy as your Church asked us to do! I thought you were here to guide us on matters of religion, Father Jorda? It seems we must now instruct *you*.' There was bitter laughter. Then he and his soldiers left the tent to fetch their armour and their arms.

Father Ortiz grabbed Simon by the arm. 'Never speak again unless I give you leave! Do not forget who is master here and who is the pupil.'

Simon knew it was pointless to argue further. He still could not get the stench of Béziers out of his nostrils: burned and rotting flesh mixed with horse dung and the drone of meat flies. He wondered if he ever would.

XLVI

IN TOULOUSE, IN Carcassonne, in Lyons, in any city in France, the butchers slaughtered sheep and cattle at their shopfronts and let the blood and offal run into the gutters; they would kill chickens in front of their customers so they might have the meat fresh and then throw the heads and feathers into the street. Simon was accustomed to hitching up the hem of his cassock when he walked through this mess, and even though he was a seasoned city dweller he would resort at times to holding a scented handkerchief to his nose on the hot summer days when the smell of bloodied meat and stinking guts made him gag.

But that was sheep; that was cows; and the blood was from domestic animals.

But this.

This . . .

He had never seen or imagined anything like it. One thing to kill a man; for a seasoned soldier such as these it might take one sword stroke, two at most. But why did they do this? They were not chopping the bodies up for meat, they did not have to spread the limbs and torsos through the street and decorate every doorway, every sewer, with them.

Black blood had dried in the gutters, gouts of it, puddles of it; its coppery stink as it dried in the hot sun made him retch and he tumbled from his horse and vomited into the street. Father Ortiz watched him, disgusted.

Simon wiped his mouth with the back of his hand. 'What have these men done here?' he said.

'I made a mistake with you, I fear.'

'What did you expect? I thought you wished for a theologian and a preacher on this crusade, not a butcher.'

'We cannot spend all our time with the hymnal. Was Our Saviour kind when he threw out the moneychangers from the Temple?'

'He turned over their tables; he did not chop them up like joints for the cook fire. Look at what these men have done!'

'Gentleness is what we bring to the weak and those in need of our charity. Should we extend it to the enemies of the Church also? Those who seek to bring it down? We are instruments of God and our duty is to save souls. What we do, we do from love, love of God.'

The market square was just dirt with a meagre fountain. There was a smoking ruin on the far side of it. Simon pointed, astonished. 'They have even burned down the church!'

'The church had been defiled.'

The limestone walls were charred and the roof had caved in. It was too hot to approach it, for the roof timbers were still burning on the floor of the chancel. But he recognized the taint of burned meat. 'What happened here?'

'They were heretics,' someone shouted behind him.

He turned around. Gilles de Soisson led a procession into the square: a handful of prisoners, Trencavel's men, chained by the wrists and each with a loop of rope around his neck, the end of which was tied to the saddle of his warhorse. His knights and a troop of foot soldiers followed.

'But they had sanctuary! They were inside a church!'

'It was no longer sacred. They were heretics in a place they had themselves defiled. So we burned it down.'

'You cannot know that these people you slaughtered were heretics!'

'They shielded heretics and that is the same thing.'

'Because a man has a heretic for a neighbour does not make him a bad Christian.'

Gilles turned to Father Ortiz. 'Father, instruct your *socius*, will you? He overreaches himself.' Gilles jumped down from his horse. 'God will know His own. When they are all in heaven let His greater wisdom divide them into the saved and the damned. You should understand, Father Jorda, that when we do this, it encourages others to be more diligent in their prayers. That's what you want in your flock, isn't it? Diligence?'

'The seigneur is right,' Father Ortiz said. 'Do you think a good Christian could live cheek by jowl with the Devil?'

Simon realized it was useless to argue further. He dropped to his knees and began a prayer for the souls of the dead.

'Oh, spare me the piety,' Gilles said. 'You want your Church saved for you but it distresses you to see it done. You are hypocrites, all of you.'

Simon looked at the huddle of prisoners, wretched men who had fought bravely and been betrayed at the last by their own *bayle*. 'What will you do with them?' he said.

'They have denied the cross. So I thought it might be instructive for them to find out at first hand what it is they think does not exist. Do you not think so, Father Ortiz?' He turned to the captain of the soldiers and started to interrogate him. One of his men, who spoke the Oc dialect better, relayed his questions. *Where are the rest of the townspeople? Which way did they go? Why did they leave?*

'They heard you were all butchers,' the captain said, 'and they begged us to let them leave. We planned to hold you off for two days more, then we would have done the same if that filthy dog the *bayle* had not betrayed us.'

'Where were they headed?'

'Into the mountains. Where you'll never find them.'

Gilles turned to Hugues. 'Go after them. They are on foot; so despite what this flea says you have a good chance of finding them and when you do, show them God's justice.' He remounted his destrier and wheeled away. 'Now show them what we do to heretics round here.'

A good summer for the meat flies. No excuse for any of them not to get fat and bloated and drowsy in the sun.

XLVII

THEY FOLLOWED THE old Roman road that led through the
Minervois, through smoke-blackened and deserted villages and
castra. The first man hanging by his neck from an olive tree was
remarked upon; after a dozen it was just a commonplace. With each
league Philip lost a little of his soul. How many abandoned babies
do you pretend not to see, because you cannot rescue even one of
them, and you might see a score of them every day?

And what of the soldier they had found lying by the side of the
road without feet or hands? Philip could still hear his cries and his
curses, as he begged them to put him out of his agony. Christian
soldiers had done this to him, not in the heat of combat, but as a
means of terror.

But if Christian soldiers had undertaken such an act, what should
his response be, sinner that he was? Did he leave the man to suffer
from thirst and let the carrion crows finish him while he yet lived?

He had jumped from his horse, sword drawn.

'Do it! For the love of God!' the man screamed at him. 'Why are
you waiting? Please, don't let me suffer like this! I beg you!'

One thing to kill a man in battle; another to murder in the name
of kindness. His men watched, but no one spoke.

The man screamed, rolled on to his side and tried to shuffle
closer. 'Please, m'sieur, I beg you! Do it! I will speak for you a thousand times in paradise, but please!'

How old was he? Philip wondered. His face was so covered in
blood and dirt it was impossible to tell. Pain had furrowed great
lines in him. He could have been twenty or eighty.

Philip raised his sword, but something made him hesitate. Not as
easy to kill a man you do not hate or fear. As he was about to bring
down the sword an arrow thudded into the man's chest. For a
moment he looked only surprised, and then the light went from his
eyes and he died with no fuss at all.

Philip knew who had shot the fatal bolt. 'Thank you, Renaut. But I did not need your assistance.'

'I am sorry, seigneur. I just couldn't stand to watch it any longer. I don't fear death as much as I fear that.'

Their eyes met. 'Then let us do what we came here to do and get out of this land of carrion crows,' Philip said, and got back on his horse.

*

The evening was windless, the shadows intensely black and the light as vivid as fresh paint. The land here reminded him a little of Outremer; olives and figs flourished in the thin, stony soil and drystone walls kept out the free-running goats and sheep.

Under the shadow of the walls, the terraced vineyards were laced with tendrils of mist. They said these vines were planted under the crack of the Roman overseer's whip in the time of Jesus. Now look at them. They had been torn up by the crusaders, the roots burned and twisted and dead.

The air smelled of thyme and of the charnel house.

The village had been burned recently, for last night's rain had not yet washed out the soot. Wisps of grey smoke still rose from the ruins. Foxes and wolves picked their way carefully through the scorched ground, lured into the open by the promise of fresh meat.

They followed the road up the narrow lane from the *portal*. Philip put a hand over his mouth and nose, heard several of his men gagging also. In the square there were seven crosses. Before this the only crucifixions he had ever seen had been carvings of the Lord, inside a church. He did not imagine that men might still torture one another this way.

A tree outside the church had been blackened and almost consumed by fire. Enough of it remained that they had been able to hang someone from it. The man's corpse twisted in the wind. A vulture flapped its wings to drive away the crows that were gathering around the carcass.

No one spoke.

Philip turned his horse's head and rode back out of the town. All this way, for nothing. The poor girl he had come to find was no doubt one, or several, of these pieces of raw and blackened flesh lying around the square.

God have mercy. She had been his last hope.

*

The crusaders had camped by the river to the south of Saint-Ybars; they found horse dung, flattened earth, and the warm ashes of their camp fires. There could not have been more than two or three hundred, Philip guessed.

Philip sat slumped under a fig tree with his head in his hands.

'What shall we do?' Renaut asked him.

'We can't do anything until the morning. Tell the men to make camp here tonight.'

He saw a shadow moving under the trees, a woman in a hooded tunic.

Renaut saw it too. 'What's that?' he said.

Philip was already on his feet and running. His quarry was hampered by her long dress and the treefall underfoot and he soon overtook her and wrestled her to the ground.

She lay where she fell, and did not try to fight him. He stood up. Her hands and feet were filthy and covered in cuts. She said something in the *langue d'oc* that he could not make out. And then she rolled on to her back and opened her legs.

Renaut ran up beside him. Loup had followed also.

The woman said something else to Philip. 'What did she say?' Renaut asked Loup.

'She said to do whatever you want but asks that you don't hurt her.'

Philip knelt down. 'I'm not going to hurt you,' he said. There was blood on her tunic. 'Did you live in Saint-Ybars?'

She shook her head. She was from Béziers, she said. She and her husband had fled before the crusaders arrived, but bandits had ambushed them on the road. They had killed her husband and her baby and then raped her. By some caprice, they had left her alive. 'What's your name?' he asked her.

'Guilhemeta.'

'Guilhemeta, we will help you if we can.'

'I don't want your help,' she said. 'I don't want anybody's help.'

'What are you doing here?' he said.

'The crusaders brought me. They had a priest with them and he was kind to me and helped me bury my baby and blessed him so he will go to heaven. But then their soldiers raped me and so I ran away.'

'What happened to the village?'

'The soldiers got angry when the people would not open the gates. They fought them and then they ran away. So they killed everyone left behind. Even the *bayle* who helped them. They hanged him.'

'Some of the people got away?'

'In the night. They escaped and went into the mountains.'

Philip turned to Renaut. 'It seems the witch might still be alive.'

Renaut shook his head, horrified at the turn this interrogation had taken. 'Please, seigneur. Let's leave the woman in peace and go. It's hopeless. This sorceress you're looking for could be anywhere in these mountains now. We would never find her.'

'If she's alive, trust me, I will find her.'

'But we don't know if she is still alive. We don't even know if she can do miracles. We could be just chasing a phantom.'

'I did not come this far to give up now, Renaut. Tell the men.' He stood up and held out a hand to Guilhemeta. 'Stand up. Come with me. No one's going to harm you here. We are men of honour. *Òmes de paratge,*' he said, using the Oc words.

Guilhemeta hesitated. She looked at the boy for reassurance. Loup nodded. Philip helped her to her feet and led her back to the camp.

XLVIII

NEXT MORNING, AS he rode, Philip thought about the mutilated soldier they had found on the way to Saint-Ybars.

He should have finished the wretch himself. Why did he hesitate? Renaut had had no such qualms. He could not forget the look on his young squire's face. It was neither pity nor terror; it had terrified him.

Philip had put Guilhemeta on a pony with Loup. Look how they clung to each other. Good for her to have another to care for, he thought, it might break her out of her despond. And Loup, he needed another mother perhaps.

Finally his mind ranged, as it always did, back to Alezaïs; she crept up to surprise him in death much as she did in life. *You're like a sprite,* he used to say to her, *I should put a bell on you so I know where you are.* Now he saw her in the dust spirals of midday, the clouds at evening. Four years in her grave and still she haunted him.

Let me go, my heart; if you cannot be here, let me go.

His throat was parched. Heat hummed in the rhythms of the cicadas, his own sweat tickled as it inched down his nose. A smudge of ink-black cloud appeared in the northern sky, the promise of a thunderstorm to cool the air. They saw no one, just stunted oak and beech.

And then a scream.

Not just one scream; many screams, from many people. Renaut pointed, and Philip saw them at the same moment that he did. The soldiers had caught their victims in the open, as they were crossing the neck of the valley. It was a well-executed ambush, three chevaliers sweeping in from the wooded spurs to chase the wretches into the path of their companions, who cut them down with slashes from their swords or trampled them under the hooves of their warhorses.

'These must be the refugees from Saint-Ybars,' Renaut said.

'They intend to massacre them.'

Renaut's palfrey smelled the blood in the air and shied on its back legs. He fought to calm her. 'What do we do?'

'We cannot just do nothing,' Philip said. He and his men were all wearing steel mail, had been travelling armed since Béziers, despite the heat. They had been expecting trouble and now they had found it.

Philip turned to his sergeant. 'Wait till they are all down from the spurs. Then we take them.'

The men seemed startled by his order. The knights and chevaliers down there wore the cross. Was it right to go against crusaders? But they were his liegemen and Philip knew they would do as he ordered them to.

He turned back to the skirmish and saw a woman trying to outrun a horse, splashing into the shallows of the ford, stumbling on the wet stones. The chevalier who pursued her did not even bother to raise his sword. He let his horse trample her and then went after a child who was running for the shelter of the trees.

Philip spurred his horse forward. It was a steep descent but Leyla went at the gallop, sure-footed as any mount he had ever had, and he gave her free rein. The crusader turned only at the last moment; he did not have the visor down on his helmet and the look on his face changed in a moment from surprise to terror. He had no time to evade the sword stroke that unseated him; then Philip was past him and after the next.

A blur of movement: a woman fleeing up the bank, a crusader with a fiery red beard pursuing her. Another of the villagers, a man, threw himself on top of her to protect her. The bearded knight was about to dismount to execute them both when he saw Philip. He tried to wheel his horse around to face him but before he could react Philip was on him. He slashed at him and the redbeard could only half-parry his blow and then his head snapped back and his helmet flew into the water and he fell.

Philip turned Leyla around and saw the rest of his men complete their charge. Shocked and outnumbered, the crusaders fled, escaping any way they could. The red-bearded knight remounted, shook his fist at Philip and followed his men into the hills.

Over in moments.

The ford was littered with bodies. Just four were crusaders, the rest were refugees. The river was stained with their blood. A child floated in the shallows face down, a sword slash on his back.

Renaut appeared beside him. 'Is this what the Pope had in mind when he ordered this crusade, do you think?' Philip said. 'Renaut, I will tell you this. I may never find my way into heaven, but sometimes I believe His Holiness himself will have some difficulty squeezing through the gate. Come, let's not linger. I wager Redbeard and his men will be back with their fellows soon enough to try and finish this business.'

*

A ragged lot, these benighted souls he had saved. A leper in a grey coat and scarlet hat, a ploughboy, a tinker, a stonemason. He had found them shelter in an abandoned shepherd's hovel, four walls with gaping holes in the mud and thatch. The mother of the murdered child was keening in the corner; others bathed their wounds as best they could with water from the ford. There was the smell of straw and goat and blood.

The refugees built a fire in the hearth with windfall twigs to cook up the little food they had with them. Philip gave them some of the salted pork. They seemed glad of it, but then they had not eaten for days.

Little children with huge dark eyes stared up at him from the straw. A woman put an infant to her breast. The woman still cradled the dead child in her arms, her shrill grief making him wince.

The sky was on fire somewhere near Carcassonne.

A man with shoulders as wide as his broadsword knelt at his feet. Philip recognized him as the man he had saved from the redbeard, the one who had thrown himself over the grey-haired woman to protect her. 'Whoever you are, seigneur, we thank you.'

Philip hauled him back to his feet. *God's blood, he's as big as me, this one.* 'Who are you?' Philip asked him.

'My name is Anselm,' the man said. 'I am a stonemason, from Saint-Ybars.'

'Where are you going?'

'To the Trencavel fortress at Montaillet. We hope to find protection there from the *crosats* – the crusaders.'

'How far is it? Those men will come back for you.'

'We can turn east, into the forest. It is a longer way but we will be harder to find.'

'Then you should do that. Rest here tonight if you must, but make sure you are gone before dawn.'

'May we know who has saved us? You talk like a northerner, like a *crosat*.'

'I *am* a northerner. My name is Philip of Vercy, I am from Burgundy.'

'Why don't you wear the cross? And why did you help us?'

'I am not a crusader. I am here looking for someone, a healing woman. You may know her, for Saint-Ybars was where I was told she lived.'

Anselm frowned and looked at his wife, then back to Philip. 'You came all the way from Burgundy for a healing woman?'

'Her name is Fabricia Bérenger. Did you know her? Is she here, with you? Is that her?' Philip pointed at the trembling waif in the corner of the hut. Aware of the attention, the girl ducked her head. 'Well, man? Speak up.'

'How do you know her name, seigneur?'

'Her reputation has travelled. I heard it first from a wise woman on my lands. She in turn heard it from a pilgrim who had just returned from Toulouse.'

'What do you want of her?'

'My son is dying. I came here to ask her to help me. I want her to come back with me and heal him for he is too sick to come here.' Philip saw the looks between the man and his wife. 'You know this woman?'

'You must have enormous faith to do such a thing.'

'He is all I have left. If I lose my son, I lose everything. Is it faith or is it desperation? I don't know. Please tell me what you know.'

Anselm sighed. 'This woman you are seeking – she is our daughter.'

'Your daughter?'

'Whether she can perform such miracles as you speak of, I don't know. If it's true, then it has brought her and us nothing but heartbreak. She left Saint-Ybars several months ago.'

'Where did she go?'

'To the monastery at Montmercy.'

'So she's alive?'

'Yes, she's alive, God be with her. She went there to try and find a little peace. In the village people called her witch or saint; either way they would not let her be, so she took orders. I don't know if it did any good.'

'Where is this monastery? How do I find her?'

'It's to the east, in the mountains near Montaillet, where we ourselves are headed. But the quickest way is back the way you came and then follow the Roman road. You will see the abbey four leagues on. There is a spur shaped like a horn and you will see it there, below a mountain they call Mont Maissac.' Anselm placed a hand on his arm. 'Seigneur, please, if you get there, tell her we are all right. She will have heard of the massacres. Tell her we still live and we send her our blessings and that there is not a day we do not say a prayer for her. Tell her we are headed for Montaillet.'

*

Night had fallen. Philip found Renaut sitting alone by the fire under the trees. He sat down next to him and shook him by the shoulder, unable to hide his excitement. 'I have found her!'

'Seigneur?'

'The healer! Her mother and father are here among these refugees! They say she is not far from here, at a monastery called Montmercy. Just a day's ride!'

'Seigneur, do you realize what we have done here today? We have killed men wearing the crusader cross. Even if they did not recognize us or our pennants, they will discover who we are soon enough. This makes us heretics. Although I do not doubt the rightness of what we did we are in great danger if we remain in the Pays d'Oc.'

'She's alive, Renaut! I will not give up on this now.'

Renaut shook his head.

'You have more to say on this subject?'

'I am your squire and liegeman. Where you say "follow", I will go.'

'Tomorrow we will find the girl, then we will leave this accursed place.'

Renaut did not answer; he just stared gloomily into the fire.

Philip left him there. One more piece of bad news to pass on, he thought, then I shall find myself a patch of soft ground and try to sleep. He found Loup tucked under Guilhemeta's arm, sucking his thumb, almost asleep. She was holding him against her breast and stroking his hair. He could have been hers, he thought, and she could be his. He crouched down in front of them. Loup opened one sleepy eye.

'A bad business today,' he said.

Loup sat up. 'No! I liked it! You smashed them! They ran away like Mohammedans!'

'Don't talk about things you know nothing about, boy. What happened here may have made you excited for the moment, but it will have bad consequences for us if they come back with the rest of their army. Now listen, these villagers are headed into the forest at first light. They are going to a place called Montaillet, a fortress where they say they will be protected. You are to go with them.'

'Go with them? But why? No, I want to stay with you.'

'That is impossible. This way you and the woman here will be safe, you may see out the summer in Montaillet. By winter this will be over. The Count of Toulouse and the King of Aragon will come with their armies and drive out these so-called crusaders.'

'You are abandoning us?'

'I am ensuring your safety. You cannot come with me. I have always made that clear to you.'

The boy's lip curled. 'I thought you were my friend.'

'I am your friend, I am just not your father.'

He walked away, found a grassy space beneath a stunted oak near the fire and wrapped himself inside his cloak. He tried to sleep.

But sleep would not come. He could not stop thinking about his adversary at the ford, the one with the red beard. Those men would not forget this skirmish and this insult. They would be back.

XLIX

S IMON JOINED FATHER Ortiz under the trees and together they knelt
in prayer. The rest of the soldiers joined them to sing the *Veni
Creator Spiritus* and ask for God's blessing on their holy endeavour.

The haze that would later disperse under the hot sunshine still
threaded between the pine and chestnut trees, hiding the distant
blue peaks of the Pyrenees.

They were less than a day's ride from Carcassonne. The Host had
left nothing in its wake; everything on the way was burned or
uprooted, and every hamlet and town was empty. They did not
know if it was the crusaders or the fleeing Trencavel soldiers who
had poisoned the wells and left animals to rot in the sun.

The siege of the city must be under way. The sky had turned red
the night before, and this morning a plume of black smoke smudged
the sky just beyond the horizon. Thunder rolled around a blue sky.
Simon had asked Father Ortiz what it was.

The siege engines, the friar had said.

He remembered his boyhood there, hours spent wrestling with
his brothers in the courtyard of their father's warehouse. It brought
an unexpected pang. Would he even recognize any of them now, or
his father? No, he decided, I wouldn't. The family I had is dead to
me now. The Church is all I have.

As they rose from their prayers they saw riders approach from
out of the rising sun. Simon put hand to his eyes and saw the three
blue eagles of Gilles's device. Even an untrained eye like his could
see straight away that there was something wrong; the formation
was ragged and several of the chevaliers were slumped in their
saddles, not upright in the stance customary to a knight or equerry.

Gilles de Soissons burst from his tent to greet them. Hugues de
Breton slid from the saddle, and took just one step forward before
he slumped to one knee. His hair and his beard were matted with
blood. As he lowered his head to the baron Simon saw there was a

gash from his temple to his crown. His helmet, which he held under one arm, had been half stove in. Whoever had struck him had all but taken his head off.

Gilles's hands closed into fists at his side. 'Sir Hugues. You met with some difficulty, it seems?'

'We found the heretics from Saint-Ybars easily enough, seigneur. We were applying God's holy justice when we were foully ambushed. They had superior numbers and slaughtered four of us before we knew that they were on us.'

'Trencavel's men?'

No, my lord. They were northerners, like us. Their shields had four red crowns.'

Gilles looked up to heaven, as if seeking explanation for this thwarting of his plans from God Himself, and then glared at Father Ortiz and Simon as if they also shared responsibility for this setback. 'How could this happen?' When they did not answer, he rounded again on Hugues. 'How many knights did they have?'

'Two score at the most.'

'You are sure this baron of theirs is a northerner?'

'I have no doubt.'

Only then did Gilles seem to notice the gash on his sergeant's scalp. 'You are wounded,' he said.

'Pay no heed to it, seigneur. Give me the men and I will go back and settle our account with these foul traitors.'

Father Ortiz stepped forward. 'Seigneur, enough of this. We have been distracted enough from our true aim. We should join the Host at Carcassonne.'

'Is that your spiritual direction? I do not follow your reasoning.'

'The Host needs us at the walls of Carcassonne.'

'Do they? To what purpose? We are here to rid the Pays d'Oc of the enemies of Christ, is that not so? It seems to me that it is easier to send a heretic to eternal flames when he has not the benefit of a stout wall to hide behind. The Devil-fuckers who attacked my soldiers have sided with the heretics so they must be heretics themselves and they shall reap the reward for their foul belief. This insult to our honour will not stand, gentlemen!' He turned back to Hugues. 'Wash your wounds and take the rest of my chevaliers and find these traitors to God.'

'But, seigneur, we cannot delay any longer!' Father Ortiz protested. 'There is nothing to eat here and the wells have all been poisoned. The army needs us elsewhere.'

'And the army shall have us all, in spirit and body, in due time. Sir Hugues will join us at Carcassonne after he has enacted God's vengeance.'

'It seems to me we are continually being diverted from God's holy purpose.'

'On the contrary, we pursue it relentlessly.'

'But if Hugues takes our knights and chevaliers we will be left with just foot soldiers and equerries!'

Gilles stamped his foot, petulant as a child. His face flushed to pink, livid against the whiteness of his hair and eyebrows. 'You will not harangue me, Father Ortiz! Neither shall you lecture me on my duty or my tactics!' They stood nose to nose. Simon held his breath.

Gilles turned to Simon. 'And you, do you have anything to add?'

'In this, I stand with Father Ortiz. We can only advise you on your spiritual duty, which I too would remind you lies at Carcassonne, with the Host.'

'Thank you for your counsel.' Gilles turned back to Hugues. 'Avenge our dead and then honour us with your presence at Carcassonne, as soon as you may. Three days. No more.'

Hugues grinned. 'Thank you, seigneur,' he said, dragged the wounded from their saddles and told the rest to be ready to ride again within the hour.

L

THEY SKIRTED SAINT-YBARS on the way back down the mountain. Black ravens and vultures circled high over the village. The war was going well at least for the carrion crows.

Philip pushed his men and the horses as hard as they would go.

As he rode he tried to calculate how many days since they had left Vercy, how long it might yet be before he saw its familiar *donjon* once more. Time was slipping through the hourglass. He prayed to a God who had so far proved faithless: *Give me enough hours to save him.* We are so close, let me find her and let her be the miracle I am owed.

But when they crossed the stream below the *castrum*, he saw a lone rider on the far bank, slumped beneath a tree. The man's horse cropped the meadow, exhausted; she had been ridden hard, and there were lines of white foam on her withers and round her jaws. He recognized the four red crowns embroidered on to the horse's underblanket, and as they drew closer he recognized the young man that stood up to meet them, an equerry from his household by the name of Jean-Pierre Gaignac.

His face and clothes were splashed with mud from his wild ride. This could mean only one thing. Philip held himself straighter in the saddle, tensed his shoulders ready to receive the blow.

Jean-Pierre fell to one knee.

'How did you find us?' Philip said.

'I rode to Narbonne, asked the watchmen at the gate the way to Saint-Ybars, for my mistress told me this was where you were headed. The man told me to follow the Roman road, that it would lead me here.'

'How long have you been here?'

'An hour, no more. I despaired of finding you, but was too exhausted to ride on until I had rested.'

'God has been watching over you. A rider alone in this godforsaken place . . .' He could think of no further questions and Jean-Pierre was not eager to impart his message, as if by delaying the moment it might help his son live a little longer.

'Was it your mistress who sent you then?'

'Indeed, seigneur. I have come at the express command of the lady Giselle.'

Renaut walked his horse alongside him and they exchanged glances. What was the look in his eyes? Sorrow, of course, but relief too perhaps. It was over; now they could go home.

'What is your news?'

Jean-Pierre stared at the ground. 'I bring words of solace and sympathy from the lady Giselle. Your son is dead. She asks that you return swiftly to Vercy to console her and your household in their shared grief.'

Philip slid from his horse. Jean-Pierre flinched, perhaps wondering how the seigneur might react to this news, if he might be disposed to punish the messenger for his message. But Philip merely handed Leyla's reins to Renaut and walked into the forest without another word.

He did not know where he was going, he knew only that he wished to walk and that he wished to be alone. He heard Renaut call after him but he ignored him.

He plunged off the path into the undergrowth. He startled a hart; the young deer was so close he might have reached out and stroked its hide. It stared back at him with bright black eyes before darting away into the undergrowth.

He came upon the ruins of an ancient wall. A few steps further on and there was another. The Visigoths had built their towns and cities here; this was an old land, with old ghosts. Who thought to find them still here, in the brambles? The old Merovingian kings had come this way too, and then the Saracen for a time; all these old bones lay underfoot, the bloodless dead who succoured the olives and the grapes and the figs.

I should join them, soon. Why not? Everything I held precious is gone.

He heard the caw of a black crow.

I should weep now. Why can I not weep? Where are the tears I have held dammed all these months?

He slumped to his haunches, his fingers exploring the cracks of the crumbling bricks under the forest mould.

What should I do now? There is nothing left but to go home.

But what was home, now? A cold and smoky castle in a dank forest, a wife he did not care for, the grave of a son beside his mother in a crypt. Ghosts slipped beyond the green shadows of the leaves.

Perhaps I shall sit here for ever. Perhaps I shall not have the strength to go home.

He reached into his tunic, pulled out the silver comb that he had carried with him all the way from Vercy. If he held it close to his nose he could still smell her hair.

What must I do to tease from my faithless gods some sliver of grace, some lapse in their glowering piety, so that I might find some chink of hope in the darkness of this blue morning?

He heard Renaut calling his name. He steeled himself to rise and then walked back to the clearing, leaving the ghosts who had built the wall to their ancient sleep. He found his way through the trees by following the sound of Renaut's voice, wished that there might be some other voice that would likewise summon his soul away from the air and the light, towards the green dreaming of the dead, if only they would show him the way.

L I

THERE WAS JUST one duty yet weighing on him, and that was to get his men safely back to Vercy. Nothing else mattered to him now. They were almost out of the foothills; he could even see the Roman road in the distance. Once they reached Narbonne, it would be a clear road north to Burgundy and home.

It was instinct that warned him first, a prickling of the small hairs on the back of his neck. He saw some rooks pecking at a heap of yellow dung on the grass, and when he got down from the saddle he found the droppings were still warm. Horses had recently passed this way. He knew then that they were in the jaws of a trap.

'Put your helmets on,' he shouted. 'Draw your swords.'

The words were barely out of his mouth when the first bolts hissed through the air, followed by the shrieks of men and of horses. Several of his soldiers fell and were trampled under the hooves as the horses panicked. Their riders circled, searching the hills for their hidden enemy.

Then they saw them well enough.

They swooped down from the trees above them, scores of them from either side in a pincer action. He looked for the pennants, saw three royal-blue eagles on their standards and livery. Redbeard had come back, as he knew he would.

There were too many of them to fight. They would have to ride or die. 'Follow me!' he shouted.

He spurred Leyla forward. It was what she had been born to do, and she bent her ears back and galloped, her neck muscles straining with every stride. Already the two arms of the pincer had begun to close and the first of their attackers appeared in front of them. His lance smashed into Philip's shield and splintered.

Another rider turned in front of him, Philip swung with his sword, felt the blow strike helmet or shield or armour, he did not know which, then he was past him as Leyla charged on. Suddenly he saw Redbeard beside him, his visor up, grinning. Philip swung back-handed with his sword.

Leyla reared, confronted by three more horsemen.

Men were screaming and shouting and cursing all around him, but Philip could no longer hear them. He was aware only of those closest to him, the next enemy, the next combat. He fought as he had been taught from a boy, striking at the nearest target, continually turning Leyla so that he could not be taken from behind. He saw Renaut beside him, then a hand grabbed at his squire's reins and he slashed down with his sword and severed the hand at the wrist.

For a single heartbeat he stopped, saw the severed limb spouting blood, a crusader reeling back in horror and pain. Then he felt a blow to the back of the helmet. A Norman on a dun horse raised his sword to strike again and he thrust with his own sword, found the gap in the man's hauberk just below the armpit and the man screamed and fell backwards off his horse.

He wheeled Leyla around again, searching for Renaut. He was gone.

Their charge had stalled. Three of his men lay on the meadow, spitted or clubbed; more of Redbeard's knights were rushing at him. He was dazed from the blow to his helmet. His vision was doubling; he could not focus. There was no way out of this, he realized. He was going to die.

It surprised him how dearly he yet wanted to live.

His sergeant, Godfroi, was suddenly beside him. He thrust his sword into the ribs of one of the less well-armoured chevaliers, then grunted to retrieve it, tugging and swearing. Another rider came at Godfroi with his lance. Philip turned Leyla's head and charged at him, knocking off his aim and then slashing with his sword. He thought he had missed his blow but then the man fell and blood sprayed in an arc across the grass.

He clutched at his horse's mane to keep from falling. Everything was blurred. He saw a path open in front of him and he galloped Leyla through it, towards the road.

Finally he stopped and looked back, felt something warm on the back of his neck; he tore off his gauntlet and reached behind. When he looked at his hand it was covered in blood. Someone rode towards him, his sword raised. 'Seigneur!' It was Godfroi, his sergeant. More of his men had broken away and were close behind.

'Where's Renaut?' Philip said. He started to slip from the saddle. Godfroi grabbed him and held him there. He heard him say: *We have to get him out of here,* and that was the last he remembered of the day.

LII

PHILIP OPENED HIS eyes, blinked twice, tried to remember where he was. He stared up at the sky, the light dappled through forest leaves. He heard the rushing of a stream, and sat up. Godfroi, his sergeant-at-arms, was sitting on a large rock soaking his feet in the water. When he saw that Philip was awake he got up and padded over in his bare feet.

'You're lucky he didn't take your head off, seigneur.'

'Who?'

'Redbeard. He swung at you with his battle axe.' He reached down and picked up Philip's helmet. 'See, the dent.' He knocked it against his thigh. 'Good Toledo steel, or else there wouldn't be much of you left.'

Philip took the helmet and tried to study the damage, but he still could not focus his eyes properly. He tossed it aside again. 'Where are the rest of the men?'

'This is it,' Godfroi said.

'Only five of us left?'

'We were lucky any of us got away.'

Philip stumbled to the river's edge and put his head into the water to rouse himself. He put a hand gingerly to the back of his head. Blood had caked into his hair, and there was a lump there the size of an apple.

'We are not safe here,' Godfroi said. 'They are still searching for us. They passed close by a little while ago while you were still passed out under the tree. They will not give this up easily.' Godfroi put a hand to his chest. He had bandaged it with a strip of linen but it was soaked in blood now and useless. He looked around at the rest of his men. Each of them nursed some kind of wound.

'They have Renaut?'

'Dare say he is dead, along with the others.'

'You saw him dead with your own eyes?'

'Yes.' Godfroi looked to the others for support. Philip wondered if they would try to lie to him as well. They hated him now; it was in their eyes.

'I have to see it for myself. I will not leave if there is a chance he is still alive.'

'But, seigneur, the crusaders are still hunting us and now we are only five men!'

'Honour is not a matter of numbers,' Philip said. He stood up, staggered. Redbeard had given his head a good rattling. Well, perhaps next time it would be his turn.

He remembered his squire on his piebald pony, in the rain, that very first time. '*Are you cold?*'

'*I've been colder.*'

If he were dead, he would not leave him to rot in the sun; a Christian burial at least. There was yet a chance he might be alive, hiding out in the woods.

They didn't like it, Godfroi and the others. But they didn't have to like it. It was their lot, and it was not much worse than his. He could hardly claim privilege now.

*

And he was right; they did find Renaut.

He was sitting near a well with a bloodied bandage over his eyes. Once a shepherd might have used it to water his sheep, for the place stank of animals. They had left him near the meagre trickle so that he would not die; at least, not straight away. Their horses' hooves had stirred up the mud around the well and trampled the grass.

Philip scrambled down from his horse and dropped to his knees. 'Oh God, Renaut, what have they done to you?'

'Seigneur, don't shout, it hurts when you shout.' The lad was shivering from head to foot, like a wounded animal. He remembered when Leyla had taken an arrow in her shoulder near Acre, how she had just stood motionless, just like this, her flanks quivering.

A gout of blood dropped from Renaut's nose. Philip turned to Godfroi, called for water, called for a comfort no one could give, called for the Devil to rise from the earth and take away to damnation whoever had done this to the boy.

There was not much he could do for him but wrap a clean linen bandage around the wound. Renaut's breathing was ragged, his hands rested on Philip's shoulders as he worked. Philip gave him fresh water, and all they had left of their red wine to replace the blood he had lost. He wished they had opium or belladonna.

When he had finished he had Renaut's blood all over him, his blood and his tears.

'I knew you'd come back,' Renaut said.

'I would not leave you.'

'They thought you might. They waited here for a while, I could hear them, in the trees. But then they gave up and left.'

'Are there are any others surviving?'

'Only me. I lost my sword in the fight and they overpowered me. Seigneur, I would rather these devils had killed me.'

'I will avenge you, Renaut, I swear it, I swear it on my father's tomb.'

'No, just take me home,' Renaut said. 'I don't want to die here.'

Philip got him to his feet and with Godfroi's help he put him on Leyla, hoisting him up into the saddle. The other men turned their heads as this was done, could not bear to look at what they had done to him. He must be in searing pain, Philip thought, yet he makes no sound.

'What a place you led us to,' Godfroi said.

Philip did not answer him. 'The sun is near to setting,' he said. 'Let's get away from here and find some shelter.' They heard the distant howling of a wolf. A vulture flapped lazily into the trees, replete.

LIII

Not a living soul between them and Avignon, at least none that would show their faces to armed men, as sorry a sight as they were. It was already twilight when they found a hamlet in the shadow of a defile. It had been freshly torched, and the rotten straw in the barn was still smoking. But the church and a few ragged huts had escaped the flames and these would at least provide some shelter.

Godfroi sniffed at the acrid smell of burned meat. 'We might even find something to eat, seigneur.'

'Nothing that isn't charcoal by now.'

'Then it looks like we'll be eating crow shit again,' another of the men said.

The grass was still on fire, the undergrowth crackling as it burned. Red smoke drifted along the valley, backlit by the dropping sun. Philip thought it remarkable how the aftermath of destruction and terror could appear so eerily beautiful.

'Look at that,' he said to Renaut before he could stop himself.

A sparse dinner: some wild figs, a handful of olives. They watched their shadows dance on the smoke-blackened walls of the hut, tried not to look at the young man sitting hunched and miserable and shivering in the corner. Renaut would not eat. One by one they drifted outside, preferring to sleep under the trees in between their watches than listen to his muffled sobs.

'I promise you,' Philip said when they were alone, 'I will find the man who did this to you.'

'Seigneur, this was not your fault. Don't blame yourself.'

'I led you here, Renaut. You warned me of the dangers.'

'You were trying to save your son. I spoke then from fear. Though I did not tell you this before, I so admired you for what you did. I would not have had the courage.'

'Yet you followed me here.'

'I had no choice. You are my liege lord.'

Philip jumped to his feet, put his mailed fist into the wall. The daub and wattle crumbled away under the blow. 'What kind of men would do this?'

Renaut let out a small cry. 'It hurts so much,' he said.

It outraged him to see such a beautiful young boy reduced to this huddled and shivering wretch. 'I will take good care of you, Renaut.'

'I don't want to live like this,' he said.

Philip did not know what to say to that. I should not want to live without my eyes either, he thought.

'Do you remember that soldier we found on the road? They had cut off his hands and feet. He begged you to kill him, remember?'

'It is not so easy to take a life when the blood is cold.'

'So you would not do it for me if I asked you?'

'Especially not for you. Do not ask it of me.'

A log cracked in the fire. Outside the humming of the cicadas rose to a crescendo. 'You are a good man, seigneur. A man of honour. I wanted to be like you one day. I am proud that I served with you. I always wanted to fight alongside you, and I did, didn't I, for that one time.'

I have lost two sons now, Philip thought. The son I had, and the son I could have made this boy into. It was black outside, black as God's heart. Inside himself he felt a cold ache, worse than hunger.

'Please my lord,' Renaut said. 'Do not pace like that. Come here and sleep by me.'

*

Philip did not remember falling asleep. He started awake to a filthy dawn, grey and treacherous. Where was Godfroi? They should have had the horses saddled by now. He got up and went outside.

His sergeant-at-arms and the rest of the men were gathered around something they had found in the bushes. They all backed away when they saw him and by the looks on their faces he knew that whatever it was, they feared he would hold them responsible.

Renaut.

But Renaut had gone to sleep right there beside him. Why was he out here?

'These two were on sentry duty,' Godfroi said, nodding in the direction of two of his men. 'They said they didn't fall asleep but I say they did. How else could this have happened?'

Renaut lay on his belly, his hands trapped beneath him. Philip rolled him over as gently as he could. He had used Philip's own dagger, taken from his belt while he slept. Expertly done, too, by the look of it; he had held the point just under his ribs so that when he fell it would travel straight upwards, into the heart. He would have died quickly. But still, no easy thing to die quietly, he supposed; die and not even wake the sentries.

'It's not your men's fault. Sooner or later he would have found a way.' He stood up. 'Do we have anything to bury him with?'

Godfroi shook his head.

'Then help me. We'll take him down there to the defile, by the stream. The ground will be softer there. We'll not leave him for the carrion crows. I'll dig his grave with my own hands if I have to.'

'We do not have time! The crusaders, seigneur! They will be hunting for us at first light. The sooner we are out of the Pays d'Oc, the better.'

'We'll leave when I say so,' he said.

It was a shallow grave at best, but they weighted it with large stones from the river to deter the wolves and the foxes, and Philip said a prayer over him.

Godfroi shook his head. 'No good praying, my lord. He's a suicide. You know what happens to suicides up there.' And he glanced to the heavens.

'If God will not allow this good young man entry and opens his gates instead to the men who did this to him, just because they wear a red cross on their tunics, then it's not a heaven that I should wish to go to.'

Godfroi crossed himself when he heard that and exchanged dark looks with the others. Philip did not care that he had spoken a blasphemy. His heart was not on the eternal; all he wanted at that moment was to rip out the heart of the man who had done this to his squire and his friend.

LIV

AFTER THEY HAD buried Renaut, as best they might, the men were eager to be on their way. Philip ignored their entreaties and went instead into the ruins of the church. Such a church it was: a pitiful square box with bare limestone walls, and a floor of beaten earth, save for a few paved stones at the choir and the altar. No windows. There was a smoke-blackened wooden crucifix on the wall. Somehow it had not burned when they had looted it.

He slumped to his knees.

He would never understand God's purpose. Why should He allow victory to torturers and let a boy like Renaut suffer such obscene violation? Where was the reason behind it, the mercy?

'Alezaïs,' he said.

He remembered her standing by the gate the morning he had left for the crusade. She would have never asked him not to go, she understood where his duty lay. Already she was slipping from him. He could no longer conjure the smell of her skin, nor hear her laugh when he closed his eyes, as once he had been able to do. Everything that mattered to him was slipping away, even memory.

Alezaïs, be there in heaven for me. Wait for me.

Wait for me while I do what? he thought. For my wife and for my sickly son and for my squire there is heaven; for me there is a drear castle, full of ghosts and duty. Duty to whom? To the children that Giselle may yet carry in my name? Not to Giselle, surely. If I do not go back she will not be very sad.

The castle and the fief will fall to her brothers, who will be very happy of it. She might cry some false tears, but what might she miss of him? He had been largely indifferent to her and she would be better off without him. She was still young and her family would find her a better husband who might treat her better.

Yet he could not do what Renaut had done. Despite what he had said to Godfroi, he believed as his sergeant did that heaven was shut up to those who took the path of self-destruction. But there were other ways of foreshortening a life; men were hunting him down at this very moment and it would be a simple enough matter just to stop running from them.

And why not? Was he supposed to still have faith in life, and in God, when God Himself had turned His back on him? If God was all powerful, why would He stand aside and let evil have its way like this? This unholy God had taken everything he loved, and everything he believed.

Very well. You may bend me, but I will not break. I shall defy you, God. I shall spit in your eye.

He climbed on to the altar and tore the cross from the wall. He picked it up with both hands and brought it crashing down on the stone slabs. The first time it would not break but the second time it snapped, just below its mid-point, leaving the cross and its victim in two pieces on the floor.

'Damn you, God!'

Godfroi ran in, the men crowding the doorway of the burned church behind him. They stared at this madman and then at the cross that lay at his feet. Their eyes went wide.

'Seigneur, are you all right?'

'Get the horses ready,' he said.

'We are riding back to Vercy?'

'No, we are going to find that devil with the red beard and I am going to settle with him.'

'But, seigneur! We are just five. There are at least four score of them.'

'I only want him. You can kill the rest if you wish.'

He stared them down. They backed out.

After they were gone he sank to his knees and wept for the way the world should be; a world where honour was rewarded and God was merciful; a world where children did not die before they were breeched and wives lived to be mothers and grandmothers and men did not put out other men's eyes and leave them abandoned and in torment. That was what he believed in, but the world was not like that.

He took out his sword and held the hilt against his forehead. 'I swear by my father's soul that I will avenge you, Renaut. I will find the man who did this to you and I will take vengeance for you and for this crime.'

At that moment he heard the door crash shut and something slammed hard against it – a timber wedge, he supposed. Then he heard Godfroi ride away, the last of his men-at-arms with him.

L V

PHILIP THREW HIMSELF against the door. It did not budge. He tried to kick it down though he knew it was wasted effort. Finally he sat down on his haunches, his back against the cold stone wall.

He closed his eyes, imagined Godfroi dismounting in the court-yard at Vercy, he and his ragged band, the stable boys staring wide-eyed. There would be much play over their wounds. Godfroi would go down on one knee when the lady Giselle appeared. *I am sorry, my lady. He was murdered in an ambush by brigands. We scarce got away with our own lives.*

She would howl, for appearance's sake, but life would go fair for her from then on. Godfroi and the others would sleep uneasy in their straw by the fire for a time, starting every time they heard the watchman at the gates, unsure if Philip might yet return. But they would likely think they had gambled well.

But they could not be sure it would turn out this way. Godfroi must know that if it became known what he had done, it would not go well for him.

Yet it must seem a risk worth taking. If they had stayed with him they faced certain doom. If life was more important to them than honour, then he had given them no choice.

He looked around for a way out of this dark little box where they had abandoned him. There was a hole in the roof but he doubted that he could reach it. There was, though, a circular opaque window, set in lead, right above the altar, and he wondered if he might climb through that.

When the crusaders had fired the church, several of the roof beams had fallen in. The blackened timbers were still warm to the touch. He dragged one to the wall and hefted it upright, wedging it just below the window.

He needed something to smash the glass. He supposed the iron upright of the crucifix would do as well as anything. If God wished to save his soul, then He might as well furnish him with some practical help.

Balancing on the beam was difficult. He straddled it and eased his way up and along it until he was within striking distance of the clouded glass. The timber creaked and bent beneath him. A dangerous fall if it gave way, the height of two men to the floor, but there was no choice.

It took three swings of the broken iron cross before the window smashed. But his moment of triumph was short-lived; there was a loud crack and the timber gave way underneath him and he fell.

The floor below the window was beaten earth or perhaps the injury might have been worse. Even so, as he hit the ground, he felt his right ankle turn underneath him. He lay there stunned. God in heaven, please don't let it be broken.

He sat up and felt down his leg for broken or exposed bone. No, it seemed all right. He flexed his knee, gingerly testing it. He climbed back to his feet, supporting himself on the wall; it was painful, but he could stand. He limped over to the corner of the church, hauled another timber from the blackened tangle of beams and dragged it back to the altar. He hefted it against the wall and then worked it higher until it was again under the high window.

He climbed again, holding the iron cross in his right hand, and smashed out the remains of the glass. The hole was small and he was a big man.

He thrust his two arms through it and took a grip on the outside wall. As he pulled himself forward the timber beam slipped and crashed on to the floor of the church. He scrambled for a foothold on the rough wall, working himself forward so that his head and shoulders were through the hole. For a moment he was jammed there, locked by the width of his own shoulders.

He wiggled through, by inches, until first one arm, then the other, were free. He looked down.

It had not seemed so far to the ground when he was standing below. Now it seemed a very long fall indeed. If he had almost broken his ankle falling feet first from the beam, how much more dangerous to fall head first? He twisted himself around in the hole so that he could grip the stone with his knees, tearing his clothes, then his skin, on a stubborn piece of glass that yet remained in the window's frame.

He now hung upside down out of the window. There was a stringy patch of grass below. No hidden rocks, he hoped. All he could do was throw out his arms to break his fall, as best he could. He took a deep breath and braced himself. He relaxed his knees and calves and felt himself fall.

He smashed both his shins on the window frame as he came out, his wrists jarred as they took the fall, his head hit the ground hard and he blacked out.

*

Philip opened his eyes. He was lying face down in the dirt. How long had he been there? He moved his hands, then his arms, first one, then the other; then his feet and his legs, waiting for the pain. Nothing that was too bad. Encouraged, he eased himself over on to his back, spitting the dirt out of his mouth. He felt a loose tooth with his tongue. If that was the worst of it, he could count himself lucky.

He brought up his hands to his face, stared at them. No bones protruding. He could barely move his left wrist, and when he did there was a sharp stabbing pain. He remembered he had extended the left further than the right as he fell, protecting his sword arm.

Now to try and sit up.

His head felt three times its normal size, and once he was upright a wave of nausea made him groan. Instantly his body was bathed in a cold sweat and he retched between his knees. When the spasm had passed he sat quite still for a long time, recovering his strength.

He heard a noise, looked up and saw Leyla. They had tied her to a tree. Her ears pricked up and she strained against the rope to try and reach him.

'Hello, old girl. So they didn't take you as well? Still some honour left in them, then.'

He put a hand to the back of his head. The wound from Redbeard's axe had opened up again. Supporting himself with his good hand against the church wall he got himself to his feet, and rested there until the swimming in his head had stopped.

They had left him his sword and armour. Honour or self-preservation, he wondered? Without armour and a weapon he might forget his vengeance and ride after them. Instead, they had left him fully equipped to go after Redbeard and bring about his own certain death.

He staggered over to Leyla, leaned his forehead against her neck, felt an answering pressure. 'Are you ready for one more fight?' he whispered.

He spent the best part of the next hour sitting under the tree, polishing his armour as best he could, preparing himself for what was to come. He did not want to go to his death looking ragged. When he was satisfied, he eased himself back into the saddle. He took a swift accounting of his readiness; his left arm was in agony and he could not put pressure on his right ankle in the stirrup. He would have to rely on Leyla to know what to do in a close combat, but she had got him through scrapes before.

'One last time,' he whispered to her.

The worst of it was the pounding in his head. He retched twice more before they had left the hamlet. His vision was blurred and just staying in the saddle was a struggle, but he was sure his head would clear when the time came. It always had before.

LVI

THEIR PENNANTS AND shields sported the three blue eagles of Soissons. None of them were really dressed for battle; some only wore half-armour. And there were fewer than two score of them, for Redbeard had split his force to hunt for him. Philip allowed himself a grim smile. From a hundred to one to forty to one: much better odds.

Redbeard rode at the front, his visor up, easy to recognize.

Philip watched from above, through the trees. Redbeard's men followed a narrow path through the forest, riding single file through the Spanish chestnuts and pines. Such arrogance, for this was excellent territory for ambush. Luckily for them this ambush consisted of just one man.

He thought he would feel more afraid than this on his day to die. Other times, with outcomes less certain, he had not felt as steadfast. Perhaps it was just that traitor hope that undid a man. Now that Philip knew what the outcome would be, he felt only a kind of serenity.

Death always won but you did not have to give him the satisfaction of ordering you around. Philip was content that he had chosen his own time and his own place to meet him.

When the column had passed he walked his horse down through the trees and as he reached the path he draw his sword. The sound of steel on steel was unmistakable in the hush of the forest and the last man whirled around in his saddle, startled.

'Was it me you were looking for?' Philip said.

The man drew his sword, and shouted a warning to the others, expecting a trap.

'Don't concern yourself, soldier, you face an army of one,' Philip said. 'Now tell that bitch with the red beard to hook up his skirts and run because I am going to fillet him like a rabbit.'

A rider galloped back through the ranks, his horse pushing the other chevaliers and their mounts aside. Redbeard rode at the vanguard with a handful of fellow knights. 'There you are, you pig-ugly bitch,' Philip said.

Redbeard grinned. He could not believe his luck. He must have thought Philip had fled back to Burgundy by now, and perhaps that was why he was wearing only a leather jerkin and no mail. He drew his sword. Philip noted that he was left-handed.

Redbeard glanced up at the trees on either side. 'You have set a trap for us?'

'If it was a trap, would I tell you?'

'Where's the rest of them? Do not tell me they have run off like frightened rabbits. Are these the sort of men they breed in Burgundy?'

'I am about to show you the sort of men they breed in Burgundy, if you will stand still long enough.'

'You think you can defeat two score men?'

'I do not aim to defeat two score men. Just you. I shall do it for Renaut. Do you remember him? He was the young man whose eyes you put out for having the temerity to fight you.'

'I put out his eyes for being a heretic.'

'He was a Catholic and devout.'

'He fought against men who proudly wear God's cross, so that makes him a heretic. He screamed like a girl. You should have heard him. Enough to wake the dead.'

Philip spurred his horse forward, incensed, but then reined in. That was not the plan. Do not let him goad you, he thought. Fight from anger, his father had once told him, and you will always lose. It takes a clear head to win a combat. 'Well, you'll know how well the dead sleep, soon enough.'

Redbeard grinned, and without further warning galloped straight at him, charging to Philip's left side, as he knew he would, to give himself advantage. Philip was ready for him and took the blow from his sword on his shield. He let him pass, then turned Leyla to face him. Redbeard was now separated from his men, just where he wanted him.

Philip took his bow from his saddle. Redbeard was fifty paces away, sword in his left hand, shield in his right. Philip brought up the bow, hoping his injured wrist would not buckle, and put an arrow through Redbeard's right knee. There was a look of shock on Redbeard's face at this perfidy, before the pain coursed through him and he howled. What did he expect, a fair fight? Were not the odds forty against one?

'The young man you blinded had a good eye. He once hit a boar that was set to kill me at a hundred paces. Where do you think he learned to shoot like that?'

Redbeard tugged at the arrow in his leg, screaming in agony. Philip spurred Leyla forward at the gallop and Redbeard had no time to react, he was mad with pain from the arrow, which was embedded deep in the knee joint. Philip took him on his weak side. Redbeard twisted in the saddle to bring his shield around to his sword arm, but at the last moment Philip changed the direction of the stroke, slashing downwards at his leg. But the blow sliced into horse as well as man, and Redbeard's palfrey shied on to its back legs, lost its footing on the trail and both horse and rider tumbled into the bracken.

Philip jumped down from the saddle. He looked back up the trail. Redbeard's men would kill him, of course, it was only a question of how far they would allow this single combat to continue. He supposed that depended on how popular Redbeard was with his own men.

Redbeard's horse was struggling to stand. Its rider's left leg was crushed beneath it. Redbeard had the arrow still protruding from his knee, the foot below it all but severed by Philip's sword stroke. He had pissed himself and there was saliva in his beard. He called to his men and pointed at Philip. 'Kill him! *Kill him!*'

His soldiers, Philip noted, were slow to react. *Not that popular then.* 'Who did it? You or one of your men?'

'For pity's sake! Look what you have done! You have crippled me!'

One of Redbeard's chevaliers finally broke ranks, and galloped down the trail towards him. Philip wondered if he could finish Redbeard before the rider cut him down.

But there was no time to deliver the coup. Philip swung to face the onrushing rider, parried the sword blow with his shield but went down under the force of the charge. His ankle would not hold him. The others were riding in now. One of the chevaliers jumped down from his horse and Philip scrambled back to his feet to face him.

Redbeard was still screaming.

This first assailant was either too confident or too arrogant; perhaps he wanted to put on a display for his fellows. He came down the slope too fast and Philip let the man's own momentum carry him on to his sword. It was a foolish thing to do, when he was wearing so little armour.

Now the others crowded him, but they were more cautious, having seen the fate of their brother-in-arms. One of them sliced at him with his sword, and Philip parried the blow with his shield and then in one movement struck back with his grip on his sword reversed. The man's hauberk deflected the blow but he supposed he had at least tickled a few of his ribs for the man grunted and went down on one knee.

There was no time to finish him, but it had given the others something to think about. There were three more coming at him now, fanning out, wary. They could take him if they all attacked him at once, but they knew he would kill at least one of them if they did, and none was ready to die. So they feinted and looked to each other, hoping their fellow would make the opening for them and take the risk.

The others were content to watch from their horses, whistling and catcalling and treating it as sport, even over Redbeard's oaths and screams. Finally one of them made a clumsy swing at him with his sword. Philip parried the blow easily and as swiftly moved again to his left so that they could not encircle him. As the man's swing carried him forward and off balance Philip scythed low and took the man at his hams where his half-mail could not protect him. He went down screaming, blood spurting from the back of his legs.

The other two were less certain of themselves now. Perhaps they wished they had not been so eager to claim bragging rights for bringing down a knight; not as easy as you supposed, is it? Philip thought. Redbeard was still shrieking, *'Kill him, kill him!'*

Philip backed away, luring them on, waiting, waiting, and the moment one of the men raised his sword he lunged in, took him with the point just under the armpit where his hauberk offered the least protection. The man dropped his sword and went down writhing like a baited worm. His fellow lost his taste for the fight and backed off.

Redbeard's men had had enough of Philip's heroics. A knight in full armour came at him down the slope, aiming to trample him with his warhorse. Philip jumped aside but had only enough time to raise his shield to protect himself as the force of the charge knocked him off his feet and on to his back. He scrambled to his feet to face his next attacker. Another chevalier, more lightly armed, charged through the bracken and Philip's sword was jarred from his grip, smashing his fingers. He lost balance and a fallen log took his heels from under him.

He lay there, stunned. When he got to his feet his assailant was already on him, and aimed a blow, which Philip did not completely avoid; his mail stopped it from piercing his chest but he felt the elastic snap of his ribs. Philip went down again, felt for his dagger in his belt, then remembered that Renaut had borrowed it the night before for his own grisly purpose.

He was helpless. Now the danger was past the rest of the chevaliers and men-at-arms crowded bravely in; it no longer seemed so urgent to finish this. After all, he was unarmed now.

'Do we kill him now or have a little fun?' someone said.

There was no time to answer. An arrow took the man in the neck and he went down, coughing blood. More bolts hissed through the trees, and several found their mark.

Redbeard's men ran for their horses. Some of them made it, others did not. He saw two of the men heft Redbeard on to a horse and then ride off with their crippled commander through the trees.

Philip had expected the ambush to be followed by a cavalry charge, but instead there was an eerie silence. He lay there listening to the last of Redbeard's men die before finally he heard the rustling of leaves as his rescuers headed down through the trees on foot.

He raised his head and made out the Trencavel device on their shields and tunics. There was only a handful of them, a dozen men at most, but the way the commander had used his archers had made it seem to him – and to Redbeard's men – like a much larger force.

The soldiers went through the forest, finishing off the wounded. One of them stopped by him, a puzzled expression on his face. 'This one's not wearing a cross. What should I do?'

A young knight came over, a boy with scarce a beard. He had one green eye and one blue. 'Spare him. He was the one they were fighting.' He knelt down. 'Who are you?'

Philip tried to answer but then his mouth filled with blood. He coughed and could not breathe. The world turned black.

LVII

H E DID NOT have a cross sewn on his surcoat, so he was not a *crosat.* Yet he wore his hair oiled back from his forehead in the northern style. *He took on an army of them on his own,* the soldiers said. *He had already killed or wounded five of them.*

So: a murderer then, like all these others. Yet he had such a peaceful expression. He looked almost – beautiful.

'Can you do anything for him?'

All this blood in his hair, on his armour and his face. Where to begin? 'I don't know,' she said. The soldiers helped her roll him on his side to remove his hauberk and his tunic. A woman's silver comb fell out on to the ground.

His face and neck were leathered and burned by the sun but underneath his armour his skin was pale as ivory. He smelled of wood smoke and horses and blood. She laid her hands on him and prayed.

She had wondered when he would come into her life and now he was here she wondered – *why?* She did not know who he was but he was no stranger to her. He was the warrior she had seen in the dream, walking beside her horse.

His eyes flickered open. 'Alezaïs,' he said. 'I have missed you.'

*

Philip had been building mud castles in the puddles of rainwater in the courtyard. His grandmother came out in her white coif and told him to come inside. In the kitchen billows of steam rose from the *payrola* that hung over the open fire and brushwood burned red-hot inside the dome-shaped bread oven. His grandmother sat him down to a soup of peas. It was morning and the flagstones were cold and the new rushes on the floor scratched his feet.

He woke: just a dream, then. He called for his squire, Renaut. His wife was leaning over him and his hand moved to her breast and he smiled. She shoved him away, which was rude of her, for his wife's breast was one of his life's great pleasures.

He heard a woman's voice: 'I believe he's feeling better.'

So many people! They had left him lying in the great hall. He looked around for Godfroi or Renaut or the cook. He did not know any of these people. Perhaps Lady Giselle had got rid of his household while he was away. He saw the soldier with no feet and hands. The arrow was still in his chest. 'Rest,' he told him. 'The best thing for it.'

He shouted out: 'What about some quiet in here?' But it came out as just a croak. He thought to try calling out again, but then he forgot. He closed his eyes.

A saint looked up from his ledger. *So what sins have you, Master Philip?*

I have none, they were remitted when I took up the banner of Christ. I am promised paradise. The saint had a little fork beard and black curls. He was wearing a turban. *Not in this heaven,* he laughed.

Redbeard was there, slashing his tail like a lizard. He had Renaut's eyes and rolled them like dice from his hand. Philip gasped and tried to grab him. 'Rest,' someone said to him and then there was a cool cloth on his forehead. Someone else asked him if he wanted to confess.

'No,' he said, 'it will take too long and I am too tired.'

Besides, he was proud of his sins. He would like to discuss them in person with his Maker, man to man. Look, here's my list. Now let's see yours.

He opened his eyes. There was a woman leaning over him. 'I fell on my head trying to get out of a church,' he told her.

'We all do,' she said, which he thought was a curious thing to say, but perhaps he just dreamed it.

He heard the woman say: 'He has taken a blow to the head, perhaps more than one. He has injured his ankle and his left wrist. But the worst is his ribs. Something is broken inside and he is breathing his own blood.'

'Will he die?'

'Perhaps. As God wills.'

She gave him something bitter to drink. He spat it out.

He was tired from keeping count of everyone in his dreams. Thirty-seven. No, three more; forty now. They were sitting in front of the hearth on benches, drying their boots and gaiters before the fire. The smell of wet leather and wool mingled with the stink of dung and clay and rotten straw on the floor.

'Just rest,' Godfroi whispered, disguised as a beautiful woman with red hair.

His squire, Renaut, said: 'It's not your time, seigneur. You have to go back.'

'Back where?' he said, and then his son was there, playing with his sword.

'Put that down,' he said, 'you're not old enough.'

And the knight with the green and the blue eye laughed and said: 'Well, I was old enough to save your miserable skin.'

'He is burning up,' a woman said. He thought of little Renaut, how cold he was. Best to die by ice or by fire? The end was the same. He asked in Latin, and in Arabic, for water and he felt her raise his head and as she trickled the water between his lips her hair tickled his face, and he could smell lavender.

LVIII

'F ABRICIA BÉRENGER,' HE said.

She was tending another of the sick when she heard him say her name. She turned around and found him watching her. He had huge brown eyes and a look so direct that it unsettled her. 'How do you know my name?'

'It is you, isn't it?'

She nodded.

'You are the reason . . . I came to the Pays d'Oc.'

'I do not understand you, seigneur.'

'A wise woman told me you . . . were a great healer. My son was sick. I thought you might save him. But he's . . . but he's dead now. It seems you saved me instead.'

'God saved you. All I did was pray for you.'

'Then God bewilders . . . me. Why would He save me?'

'It is not for us to know God's mind.' She put a hand to his forehead. 'You have lost the fever. Your breathing is better.' She held his head and gave him a sip of water.

'Where am I?' he said.

'This place is called Simoussin.'

'What is it? Is it a castle?'

'A cave. A cave – and a cathedral.'

'How did . . . I get here?'

'The Viscount's soldiers found you. They said you attacked the entire Host single-handed.'

'Is this another dream?' He looked around. There were hundreds of people in the cavern, seated on the ground, lying down, eating, talking. Yet everything seemed orderly. The shouts and laughter of children echoed around the vaulted roof.

As Fabricia had said, a cavern and a cathedral. 'I had chosen my day to die. Why am . . . I here?'

'No one chooses their day to die. It is chosen for them.'

'Did the knight with the red beard escape also?'

'You can ask Trencavel's men yourself when they return. I never ask how you men try to kill each other. It is of no interest to me.'

'Who are all these people?'

'Some are from Béziers, some from Saint-Ybars. They have come to try and get away from the soldiers.'

He caught her wrist. 'Is it true that . . . you can heal? Did . . . you heal me?'

'I gave you herbs and my prayers. Sometimes people get well, and sometimes they don't. It is not up to me.'

'How badly am I wounded?'

'When you came here we thought you were dying.'

'But now I . . . am alive.'

'As God wills it.' She tried to wrench herself free but he held on. 'You are very beautiful,' he said. 'I expected a . . . hag with chicken bones in her hair, smelling of comfrey and cowslip.'

'I bathed this morning. I washed out all the chicken bones. They were starting to itch.'

He smiled. 'I have something important to . . . tell you.' He let her go, exhausted from this small exertion and his hand dropped back to his side.

'Tell me then.'

'I found . . . your mother and father.'

Fabricia caught her breath. 'Where? They are alive and well?'

'They are alive. Thanks to the valour of . . . the men I rode with. They were attacked by crusaders but survived. They are on their way to a place . . . they called Montaillet.'

'You talked to them?'

'Of course. They told me you were at a monastery called Montmercy. It was where we were . . . headed when we were ambushed.'

'It's true. I left the monastery a week ago. I was going to return to the village but then I discovered that the *crosatz* were there, and I came here. I thought my poor parents were dead.'

'I can assure you they are very much . . . alive. They wanted me to tell you this.'

'Thank you for this news. You cannot know what this means to me.'

'It was my pleasure to bring it . . . to you. By the way, my name is Philip, Baron of Vercy.'

'I know who you are,' she said and then moved away to tend to others.

He watched her tend the sick and the injured. There must have been two or three score, lying on the sand near the entrance.

Fabricia Bérenger was long-limbed and green-eyed and flame-haired; she wore a scarf around her hair and a plain brown tunic. There were mittens on her hands, even though it was high summer, and she had a pronounced limp. But this did not detract from her beauty; it made her only more fascinating. There was a serenity about her every small movement he had only ever seen in one other woman, and that was his wife.

'So look at this! It seems some men are impossible to kill!'

Philip looked up; it was the fresh-faced knight with the one green and the one blue eye.

'You should be dead, my friend.' He crouched down and offered his hand. 'My name is Raimon Perella, I am seneschal to the Viscount Trencavel.'

'You were the one who . . . brought me here?' Philip said. 'I owe you a debt of . . . thanks.'

'Not me, that healer woman. I thought you were as good as dead. Once a man coughs up that much blood he is stiff and cold within the hour. Lucky for you she was here.' Raimon pulled up Philip's tunic. 'Look at that! If it wasn't for the hauberk, he would have cut you in half.'

Philip ran a finger gingerly over his ribs. There was a bruise all down his right side, purple and yellow.

'You are either the bravest man I ever met or the maddest. Did you think you were going to defeat them all? Still, I was grateful for the distraction you provided. I doubt our ambush would have been as successful without you.'

'What happened to the knight with . . . the red . . . beard?'

'I saw no such man, at least not among the dead we left there. Was this a personal matter, then?'

Philip nodded. 'Yes, it was.'

'You are an *òme de paratge* then. A man of honour. And a north-erner, too! I did not think the two went together. Why are you not with the *crosatz*?'

'This crusade is the Pope's . . . war, not God's. I came here on my own account. Do you have my . . . horse? Leyla. She's a big Arab mare.'

'Of course we have your horse, we are men of honour too, not horse thieves. There is another cave, further down the mountain-side, where we keep the animals. She is safe there, fed and watered. When you are well, you can take her and ride back to Burgundy, if that's what you wish.'

'And what of the . . . Host?'

'The *crosatz* have invested Carcassonne. Those of us left will fight them here in the Montagne Noir. When winter comes, they will have had enough and go home. And then we will go back to Carcassonne and Béziers and kick the rest of the bastards out.' He clapped Philip on the shoulder, making him wince. 'Good luck, my friend. Till my dying day, I shall never forget the sight of one man riding against two score. I wish you were fighting for us! *Dieu vos benesiga!*' He strode out of the cave.

Philip took stock. His wrist was still stiff and swollen, his ankle too. But he had had enough of lying here like a cripple. He eased himself upright and then slowly climbed to his feet. He looked around. A cave and a cathedral, was that what she had called it? An apt description, for the ceilings were high and arched and every small sound echoed as if he was in a church. But instead of marble or flagstones, the floor of this cathedral was soft white sand. It was bigger than any church he had ever visited. He could not even see the back of the cave, the flickering of torches and cook fires seemed to stretch back hundreds of paces into the dark. The tarred limestone ceilings were supported by heavy timber beams that had been driven deep into the rock walls, in places to the height of half a dozen men or more. This cave must have been here a very long time.

'You should be resting,' a voice said.

'Fabricia,' he said.

She made him sit down again. She was holding an earthenware bowl. 'Here, drink this,' she said. It was a broth of barley and vegetables, the first food he had eaten in days. It took just one sip of it to realize how hungry he was. He brought the bowl up to his lips and thought about nothing else until the last drop of it was gone.

'Thank you,' he said when he had done, and handed her back the bowl. He was suddenly embarrassed for her to have seen his raw hunger.

'How long since you have eaten?'

'A long time. No, wait. I think I had a grasshopper for breakfast two mornings ago.'

Two men, dressed in black robes, ducked their heads as they entered. They looked like starved crows: high cheekbones, pale and bony. 'Who are they?'

'They are *bons òmes.*'

'Heretics?'

'Yes, heretics. The ones the Pope in Rome lives in such terror of.'

'They don't look . . . like much.'

'Well, they are just men. What did you expect?'

'And you . . . are you a heretic, Fabricia Bérenger ?'

'No, I am good Catholic. But I have lived side by side with *bons òmes* and those who follow them all my life and I will tell you this, they are better men than any priest I ever met, and they will certainly be in heaven a thousand years before any bishop.'

'I had expected something . . . more formidable.'

They had dark eyes, long black hair, twisted rope belts. He had heard they were all sodomites and Devil-worshippers, and they certainly looked the part.

They knelt to pray over someone on the other side of the cave. He saw that they each had a scroll of parchment attached to their black robes. The Gospel of John, or so he had been told. Possession of the gospel could get a man burned at the stake in Burgundy. He wondered what might be in God's book that priests did not want him to know.

'Seigneur, did you really come all this way just to find me?'

'I did.'

'And instead you somehow picked a fight with the fifty *crosatz.*'

'By that time I had discovered my son was dead.'

Her face changed, as if a candle had been snuffed out in her eyes. 'I am very sorry. So – does killing assuage your grief?'

'The man I fought put out my squire's eyes and as good as killed him. It was a matter of honour.'

'I have never seen honour in murder, only horror and grief. But you are a knight, seigneur, and I am just the daughter of a church-builder so I am sure you know better.'

He caught hold of the hem of her robe. 'If I had got here soon enough, could you have saved my son?'

She shook her head. 'I am just an ordinary woman. I can save no one.'

'Then why do people think you can?'

'I don't know, seigneur. Perhaps because they want to.' She jumped up.

'Where are you going? Have I offended you somehow? It was not my intention.'

'You are a warrior, seigneur, a man of violence. It is not you that offends me, but your calling. Tell me, what will you do now that God has made you well again, when you should be dead of your wounds?'

'I will find this devil with the red beard and I shall settle my account with him.'

'And then?'

'There is no "and then". He is a knight and he has four score men at his back. Even should I succeed in my vengeance – and I shall – his men will kill me.'

'And when you are both dead, your friend will have his eyes back and come out of the grave? No? Then what is the point?'

'It is a knight's duty to take up arms to protect his family and his property and his king. And most of all – his honour.'

'And his God?'

'Sometimes that.'

'As the *crosatz* fought for God's honour at Béziers and at Saint-Ybars? How can there ever be peace while everyone is fighting for God? In my experience, seigneur, men use God as an excuse to do as they wish. Though I am Catholic, I believe as these *bons òmes* do, that to kill in any circumstance is a sin.'

'Yet you healed me.'

'As I have told you, I did not heal you. I only prayed for you. I am glad you are well.'

'But if you despise me so, why did you pray for me?'

She did a remarkable thing; she crouched down and searched his face with her fingertips, as if she was looking for some small secret that had been written there. Her green eyes locked on his. 'What do you want, Philip?'

'What do I want? I want to know what it all means. I am looking for something that will explain to me what has happened to me and to my life. I was ready to die, eager for it even. God took my wife and my son and my best friend. Yet still He has kept me alive and I do not understand His purpose. None of this makes sense to me. Is there a reason to it or just random good fortune? Is there a God in His black heaven laughing at us or is there truly some sense to my life? That is what I want – I want to know the answer to this before I die.'

She took his hand. 'Come with me,' she said.

LIX

FABRICIA CUPPED HER hand over the candle to shield it from the draughts. 'The caves were cut from the mountains back in the time of the Roman emperors,' she said. 'They were looking for gold.'

The vast cavern tapered along its length to a single narrow tunnel. It was evidently well used for it was reinforced in several places with stout timbers, and torches burned in iron sconces along the walls.

And then: 'By God's holy blood!'

He had experienced something like this, once, when he walked into the new cathedral they were building in Paris. And yet this was a dozen times the size of it. It was as if God Himself had hollowed out the mountain with His fist, like a child scooping the bread out of a loaf and leaving just the crust.

Limestone walls, blackened by centuries of smoke, rose to a ceiling lost to eternal night. Waves of marbled rock were backlit by a thousand candles; rock crystal gleamed like stars. Slick calcite pillars rose from the shadows to form the pews and pillars of a church of living chalk.

A sun and a silver disc of moon had been painted on the marble wall at the far end of the cave. Below it there was a table with a white mantle prepared as an altar. It was silent at first, save for the slow dripping of water, but then he heard the murmur of voices from the tunnel as more people followed them into the cavern; at first a handful, then two score, then a hundred, then a hundred more. None spoke above a whisper but in this perfect cathedral of rock every murmur echoed a dozen times.

Philip paused, clutching his ribs, getting his breath back. 'Who are . . . these people?' he said. 'Are they all . . . heretics?'

'They would not call themselves that, seigneur. They are *crezens* – believers.'

'And what is it they . . . believe?'

'It is what they do not believe that sets them apart, seigneur. They do not believe God made the world. They believe it was the Devil, whom they call Rex Mundi, the King of the World, and that he is God's equal and that the world is *his* creation. Everything we see around us is there to make us forget that we are, in fact, pure spirit and cannot perish. They say there is no hell after we die, that in fact it is this world that is hell. They also believe that everything we touch or see is inherently evil and that the soul's journey is not one of redemption, but of elevation, and that all souls must stay here, migrating from body to body, until the day they learn to yearn once again for the stars.'

'They think . . . this world is hell?'

'They say hell is not a place you go to after you die, it's the place you go to when you're born. That is why God cannot help us here, despite all our prayers, as this is the Devil's realm. All murder is a sin and even eating meat is wrong, because it means the killing of another living thing. But the act of love is the very worst sin of all, for it drags another soul into this world of pain.'

'So all of these people are . . . chaste? They . . . live like monks?'

She shook her head. 'No, only the *bons òmes* live that way. For most people, even the *crezens*, the discipline is too hard. For the believer, all that is required is to perform the act of homage before any *bon òme*. They must bow and say: 'Pray God to make a good Christian of me, and bring me to a good end.' Other than this, the believer can do as they wish; marry, make money, go to war, even attend mass in a Catholic church. It is only at the end that most people take the vows of chastity and poverty and the rest. But then, when you are about to die, I imagine it is not so hard to refuse meat and sexual pleasure.'

'A very practical religion, then.'

'Is it practical that they don't threaten to burn anyone who does not believe in them? To me, it is only human. My own mother is a *crezen*.'

'And you?'

'I love the Madonna, but I respect the *bons òmes*. They are, as their name suggests, good men. And perhaps they are right about the world, I don't know. Perhaps they have the answers you are seeking. It is not God who has punished you in the world this way because God cannot reach you. It is the Devil that has done this. Is that your answer?'

One of the *bons òmes* – Fabricia told him his name was Vital – took his place behind the altar and began to preach. Though he barely spoke above a whisper his voice was distinct even to the back of the cavern, where Fabricia and Philip stood. It was the story of paradise; in the beginning, he said, some spirits fell through a hole in heaven down to earth. God put his foot over the hole but it was too late to stop them falling out. So from that moment until the end of time all the good souls had to work their way back to heaven by becoming *bons òmes* or taking the rites of the *consolamentum*. When there were finally no just men left on the earth then the end of the world would become possible. The sky would fall down to the earth and the sun and the moon would be consumed by fire and the fire would be consumed by the sea. The earth would become a lake of pitch and sulphur.

When the sermon was over the *crezens* knelt as one and said together: 'Pray to God for us sinners so that He will make us good Christians and bring us to a good end.'

And Vital raised his hand in blessing: '*Dieu vos benesiga.* May God bless you, make good Christians of you and bring you to a good end.'

When it was over Fabricia took his hand. 'Come,' she said.

*

He followed her by the flickering light of the candle, deeper into the mountain. He wondered where she was leading him. The tunnel walls closed in on them. He banged his head on an overhang and had to crouch over to walk the rest of the way.

He was conscious of the warmth and closeness of her. Perhaps she wants us to be private, he thought. A long time since he had touched a woman; poor Giselle could have assured her of that.

He struggled to keep up, his ribs aching, his breath short. She stopped and waited for him. 'I am breathless . . . as an . . . old man.'

'Don't worry. Soon you will be yourself again and well enough to start killing again.'

'I do not enjoy . . . killing. The jousts, yes . . . pitting my wits . . . and my arm . . . against another man's for . . . honour or his . . . horse. But taking a life is not something . . . I take pleasure in.'

'Men die whether you take pleasure in it or not. The result is the same.'

'Sometimes there is no choice. To defend his . . . family or his faith or his . . . lands a man must fight. That . . . is the way of it.'

He felt a draught of warm air on his face and knew they were almost at the end of the tunnel. He wondered what new surprise she had in store for him.

'A man can find justification for anything. Words can be twisted. The truth cannot.'

She stepped to the side. He hovered for a moment on the edge of an abyss. He gasped in shock, almost went over, but she grabbed his arm and pulled him back.

'What is . . . this place?' he said, when he had his breath back.

A narrow band of light shot through the ceiling of the cave from a fissure in the earth above, God's finger pointing the way to hell, he thought. Below there was only darkness, all the way down. The light could not penetrate to the bottom of it.

She pointed. He turned around and saw a huge pillar of calcite that had accreted on the very edge of the abyss. Parts of it had fallen away into the pit so that now it formed the shape of a hammer.

'The hammer of God,' she said. 'Only a few have seen it.'

He took the candle from her, held it above his head so that he might see it better. 'Why do they . . . call it that?'

'In the days of the Visigoths they would bring prisoners here and throw them into that hole. I cannot imagine what kind of death that would be. But that is how that rock got its name. The hammer of God, of course, is death. We are all broken by it in the end. It is the only reality there is, the only time in our lives we know the truth, that we are born to die. The rest is the Devil's dream.'

As he turned back to her, she touched his hand lightly with her fingertips. She was so close; through the neck of her robe he glimpsed a pale and ivory shoulder, saw the throb of pulse at her neck. He imagined the scooped hollow below her collarbone and the soft swelling of her breast.

'You are of noble blood, Philip of Vercy?'

'A baron, as I told you.'

'Then forgive me if I have spoken impudently to you. I have only a workman's blood in my veins. I am not of your station.'

'You saved my life. I would allow that you speak to me as you wish.'

'I do not really think that is possible,' she said. 'It is a pity, for I should like to.'

She was so close he could feel her breath on his cheek. She twisted away from him and led the way back down the tunnel, chasing the dying light.

Halfway along she put out a hand and stopped to rest. When she moved on again he saw that she had left a bloody handprint on the limestone.

'You're bleeding,' he said.

'It's nothing.'

'Have you injured . . . yourself?'

She sat down on a rock, wincing with pain. 'I need to stop for a while,' she said. He crouched down beside her. There were ancient figures crudely painted on the walls. A drop of cool water splashed on to his neck.

'What is it? What is wrong?'

'Hold the candle,' she said. He took it from her and she peeled off one of her gloves. It was sticky with blood. She held it out to him. 'Look for yourself.'

Philip had seen such a wound before, in Outremer, when a man had been lanced through the hand by a Saracen spear. But this wound was clean and had a fragrance to it, like fresh-cut lavender. He bent closer to examine it, but at that moment a draught blew out the candle.

'Who did this to you?'

'No one.'

'You should have it properly bound.'

'It will make no difference.' She replaced her glove. 'There is the same wound on my other hand and on both my feet.'

'Then how did you come by them?'

'I don't know. They started as sores and grew bigger each day.'

'These are the wounds of the cross.'

'Yes.'

She stood up and started to limp back towards the main cave. 'Life is mysterious, seigneur. It is why I am not a *crezen*. The *bons òmes* are good men, but they say they know the answers to everything and I do not see how they can.'

'We all have to believe in something.'

'We can believe in whatever we wish, but we don't *have* to. If you will pardon me, seigneur, it seems that what you wish is not something to believe in, but dominion over life, even over God Himself. You want Him to do your bidding, just as you wanted Him to save your son.'

'Was that so unjust?'

'It is neither just nor unjust, it is only the way things are. I see how you loved your boy. You did all you could, perhaps more than any other man might have done to save him. You're a good man. At least, you are when you do not have a sword in your hand.'

They reached the main cave. Fabricia went to tend the sick. Philip slumped down on his haunches, overwhelmed with all he had seen and heard. This cave reminded him of his own life. It seemed to him that there was a world beneath the one of light and air, a subterranean realm waiting for him to explore, the place where his true answers lay.

Sleepless, he watched the stars swing across the heavens through the mouth of the cave. Fabricia moved among the huddled sick by the light of a single candle. The hum of insects rose and fell in the forest outside.

Thoughts of God, thoughts of sex; she had awakened something in him he thought was dead, put a brand again to his flesh. He had thought that when he found her she would give him his answers, but she had instead only posed more questions.

A God helpless to intervene was at least comprehensible, and his life then made a kind of sense. Was that the answer he had been seeking? It surely seemed to be the Devil's world, no matter what the priests said.

LX

THE SKY IN the west was full of red smoke; the *crosatz* at work. But the Montagne Noir was untouched and on a windless evening like this, in the stormlight before the sun disappeared behind the mountains, the air was so clear Philip could make out the leaves on the bushes on the far side of the valley. A tempest was on its way from the north. The afternoon had been oppressively still and as the sun set the first rush of wind was a blessed relief. He heard a roll of thunder.

He followed the path below the smoke-blackened walls that led to the cave. He thought of his son. *I wonder if she could have saved him, had I known about her sooner. I failed him.* He remembered the way little Renaut looked at him that last morning. He trusted me. I told him everything would be all right and I let him down.

A thicket of fig trees and brambles concealed the mouth of the cave. Raimon was there, with some of his soldiers. By the looks on their faces they had just returned from a raid. The flanks of their horses were steaming and streaked with foam.

Raimon grinned when he saw him. 'Are you still here, Northerner? Have you not tired of our company yet?'

'I have almost grown accustomed to your soft southern way of life.'

'Your injuries are healed?'

'My ribs don't hurt any more. My ankle sometimes gives way, but otherwise I am as well as I have ever been. What about you, Raimon? You look like you've been in a fight.'

'We ambushed a party of *crosatz* on the Roman road. They thought they were going home. Well, if they earned a dispensation for heaven by coming here, that's where they are now. We did them a favour. I am told heaven is a better place than France.'

'I certainly hope so.'

'You heard what happened at Carcassonne? The *crosatz* declared

Simon de Montfort the new seigneur in place of Trencavel. Our Viscount was offered safe passage to parlay a truce and instead they took him prisoner. After that nice little business, the people of the town were forced to surrender and had to leave the city with nothing but their shirts and breeches. I tell you, Frenchman, this war is not about heresy, it is about looting. Well, this so-called holy Host will be leaving soon and when they do we will throw this upstart de Montfort out on his arse.'

'When will it be safe for me to go home?'

'In another hundred years. Until then, you will need an escort. The roads are full of mercenaries, bandits and freebooters. A man alone, even a knight, will not get far without a bodyguard.'

'You can provide such an escort?'

'I cannot spare a man to see you safe down to the creek right now. But I'll think on it. For now we have to water these horses before the storm spooks them. God speed, *amic*.'

Inside the cave Philip was assaulted by the smell of dung and animals. His eyes smarted from the smoke of the cook fires. Everywhere he looked he saw vacant stares and silent and unsmiling children. No one here had enough to eat, and none of them knew what tomorrow would bring them.

'A fine seigneur as yourself,' a voice said, 'you must be missing your soft bed and your feather coverlet.'

Philip looked around for whoever had the temerity to speak to him with such disrespect. A man lay on the ground wrapped in a filthy linen sheet. He had the tonsure of a priest. He had an unctuous smile and Philip disliked him immediately.

'You're a priest,' Philip said.

'I am. Do you wish to make confession, my son?' He laughed.

'These people are all heretics. What are you doing here?'

'The *crosatz* would have murdered me with the same enthusiasm they butcher a Cathar, just for being in the way. My name is Father Marty. Yours is Philip, and you are a fine gentleman and knight from Burgundy. You see, I know all about you. We are practically friends. Please, come, sit by me for a while. I should like to talk. It is all I can do these days, talk.'

'What is the matter with you, priest? Are you sick?'

'I am dying, Philip of Vercy.'

'What about the girl? Could she not heal you?'

'See for yourself,' he said.

Philip squatted down on his haunches and lifted the sheet. There was a gross canker on the priest's thigh and it had begun to suppurate. Philip felt his stomach rise.

'It's a pretty thing, isn't it? It will kill me eventually. I can feel it eating me from the inside. She put her hands on me but it didn't do any good. But I told people it had and for a time it added to her reputation.'

'Why would you say such a thing if it were not true?'

Marty shrugged. 'I wanted people to think she was a sorceress. Perhaps that is why she could not heal me. The fault is mine, you see, I am not pure enough to be redeemed. I have the robes of God and the heart of a devil.' He laughed again.

'You find amusement in doing such things?'

'I had my own reasons.'

'How do you know her?'

'I come from the same village as that girl. Well, she and her family had only been there a few years; me, I had lived there all my life. My brother was *bayle* at the castle but I fled before the *crosatz* came. He stayed and they hanged him. Another of life's little jokes. Life has plenty of them for a man with a good sense of humour.'

'Some people laugh to stop themselves weeping.'

'Ah, you have me there. I see you are a student of the human condition. Very good. I think you are right; it is not funny at all. You see that man? His name is Bernart. He says she brought him back to life. Perhaps she did. I see other people getting better all around me – like you; when they brought you in here you had blood spraying out of your mouth and nose with every breath. You were a dead man, too. And she put her hands on you and now look! But not me. Some jest, huh?'

Vital and another of the *bons òmes* passed them. People bowed or prostrated themselves on the ground. Even Father Marty raised a hand to them. 'There they go, the cause of all this trouble. Look like starved crows, don't they? For myself, I don't hold with a single thing they say but they are holier than I will ever be.'

'You don't hate them?'

'I've never minded them if they never minded me. But they don't like the girl. I think she frightens them. She doesn't fit into their perfect picture of how the world is. She has the wounds of Christ and they say that Christ was not crucified. They cannot explain her. I imagine they wish she would just go away.'

'How did she come by those wounds on her hands?'

'Who knows? The *bons òmes* say she made the marks herself.'

'Is that what you believe?'

'It is what I would like to believe. And yet she has had those wounds for months and they do not heal, nor do they weep or discharge anything foul. How do you explain it? Even if they were done by her own hand, how could anyone stand such pain?' Father Marty took a hold of Philip's tunic and drew him closer. Philip winced, his breath was foul. 'Some people say she is a witch, you know? Others call her a saint. Did you know that? I tried to seduce her once. Imagine that! A priest trying to fuck a saint.' He gave a barking laugh. 'I have seen you watching her.'

'What?'

'She is a beauty, isn't she? She is no maid, though. I have it on good authority.'

Philip prised the priest's fingers loose. 'You disgust me,' he said, and walked outside to get some fresh air.

The weather had turned abruptly. The wind rushed through the trees and it was suddenly cold. He felt the first stinging of hard rain on his face.

He closed his eyes, saw his little boy lying in his bed, before he got sick, remembered how he had once pointed in wonder at the tiny splashes as the raindrops fell on the stone sill of his window.

'Can you see the fairies?' Philip said. 'They are the rain fairies and they are dancing just for you.'

The grief hit him like a cramp, so that he almost doubled over where he stood. *Everyone I have loved I have lost.* While he had God to blame for it his anger provided some consolation, but if what the Cathars said was true, there was no one to blame but the Devil.

Then we have no hope, he thought. We are all defenceless in a world of pain. He reached into his tunic, took out the silver comb. What was the use? He could not even remember her smell any more. He drew back and tossed it as far as he could into the darkness.

The rain drove down in sheets. The whole mountain seemed suddenly to tremble with the din of water trying to find passage through the limestone fissures in the rock. He went back inside the cave.

'Too hot in here, too cold out there,' Fabricia said. She flapped a hand to fan herself. The girlish gesture disarmed him. She looked so fragile in the stormlight, all creamy skin and thin bones. 'I see you met Father Marty.'

'He told me that you're a saint.'

'A saint? He tried all he could to desecrate me then. Did he tell you about that?'

'Yes.'

'I think the poor man's conscience weighs heavy on him.'

'He is being reshaped by the hammer of God perhaps?'

She smiled. 'Yes, perhaps that is it.' She put her head to the side. 'Every day I think to find you gone and yet you are still here.'

'I cannot get escort out of these mountains.'

'Is that the reason?'

'Also, I am torn.'

'I can see that.'

'Does it show so plainly?'

'I have never seen a man so tormented.'

He shrugged. 'Well, I have never met a saint before. It has confused me.'

'I am no saint, seigneur.' She moved closer. 'But I will tell you this; I dreamed of you, a long time ago. When they first brought you here, I could not believe it. If I told you that I knew your name before I ever laid eyes on you, you would think me mad. Why wouldn't you? Half the world does. I do not know what it all means, and it terrifies me.'

She turned on her heel and hurried away.

LXI

NUN, OUTCAST, SAINT, witch.

She had been awake since dawn tending to the sick and laying hands on those that asked and cooking broth for those that could not feed themselves. For this short time I belong, she thought. They will adore me and fear me again when the *crosatz* leave. Until then I have found my place.

She left the cave and went into the woods to search for herbs, stopped at the stream to wash linen for wounds. Afterwards she removed the bandages on her own hands and rinsed them in the water. She bit her lip to stop herself crying out from the pain.

She washed the holes in her feet the same way. When it was done she bandaged them again, put the boots back on her feet and limped back up to the caves, where she knew she would find Philip, as always at this time of day, feeding and watering his horse.

She watched him for a while before she let him know she was there. He was rubbing down his big Arab mare, and whispering to her as he worked.

'Why do you do that?' she said, moving out of the shadows. 'Why do you talk to a horse? She can't understand you.'

'She understands well enough. Perhaps not about politics or religion, but she understands the tone of my voice and the touch of my hand.'

'And can she talk back to you?'

'You can laugh at me, as you wish. But she can let me know when she's tired or when she's sick, and she senses trouble before I do. When we ride we ride as one, I feel every little ripple and tension in her muscles and I swear she feels the same from me. If she were a man, she'd be a good friend. If she were a woman, she'd be a wife.'

Fabricia shook her head. He was a complex man: an expert at the arts of war and killing, according to Raimon, yet consumed by a search for meaning in his life and as loving to a brute animal as a father to a child.

'You think she has a soul?'

'I know it. But if you were to ask me about the men who put out my squire's eyes, then I could not be so sure. What brings you down here this fine morning?'

'I need your help.'

'I am at your service.' He threw down the towel, gave the mare a final rub of the muzzle and fed her a handful of hay. 'May I ask what it is you wish of me?'

'Father Marty is dying and wishes to take the *consolamentum*. He needs good Christians as witness.'

'I would not describe myself as a good Christian.'

'Neither would I. But you will just have to do.'

*

As he followed her up the slope he asked her why a priest would take his final consolation from a heretic.

'Because he is dying. He does not wish to die unshriven.'

'But he is a Catholic priest. I know that is just another word for hypocrite, but why would he look to a heretic to save his mortal soul?'

'You call the Cathars heretics, seigneur, but they revere Christ the same as you or I. Because they do not love the Pope does not mean they do not love God. Besides, there is no priest here to give him the final unction, so he has no choice.'

'And these *bons òmes* will do it?'

'They will refuse no one the last consolation. Of course, if Father Marty were in their position, he would do it only if they had the money to pay. That is the difference.'

Father Marty seemed to have shrivelled overnight. As his flesh shrunk, so his eyes appeared to have grown in his skull. He offered them a smile as they knelt down on his left side, with the Cathar priest Guilhèm Vital, and his *socius*, on the other side.

'What about the others?' Philip asked. 'Won't any of the other *crezens* join us?'

She shook her head. 'They hate him,' she whispered. 'They believe this is a sham. In his life he despoiled their women and took their first fruits and charged them for every confession, every birthing. He has no friends here but us, poor man.'

Vital lit several candles around Father Marty's body. 'Brother,' he said. 'Do you wish to embrace our faith?'

'Yes, Father. I have the will; I pray God gives me the strength.'

Vital looked up at Fabricia and at Philip. 'Good Christians, we pray you for the love of God to bestow your blessings upon our friend here present.'

'Father,' Father Marty murmured, 'ask God to lead me, a sinner, to a good end.'

'May God bless you, make a good Christian of you and lead you to a good end.'

'For every sin that I may have committed, by thought, word or action, I beg the forgiveness of God, the Church and all those here present.'

'May God and the Church and all those here present forgive you these sins and we pray God absolve you of them.'

'I promise to dedicate myself to God and his gospel, never to lie, never to take an oath, never to have any contact with a woman, never to kill an animal, never to eat meat and to feed myself only with fruits. In addition I promise never to betray my faith, whatever death awaits me.'

Vital held out the scroll of the Gospel of John and Father Marty brought his lips to it. Then he and his *socius* put their right hands on his head. 'Our Father, Who art in heaven, hallowed be Thy name. Thy will be done on earth as it is in heaven. Give us this day our spiritual sustenance, and deliver us from evil.'

He placed a plaited sash around Father Marty's head and gave his *socius* the kiss of peace. He in turn gave it to Philip, and Philip kissed Fabricia lightly on the cheek. Finally, she bent and kissed Father Marty's forehead.

'The neophyte is to eat nothing but bread and water for the forty days of his *endura*,' Vital said to Fabricia.

Father Marty gave a barking laugh. 'I shall not see another forty hours.'

*

'It seems to me,' Philip said to Fabricia, 'that it is not unreasonable to ask a man to disavow women and meat on his deathbed.'

'That is why so few take the vows until the very end. People admire the *bons òmes*, they may even wish to be like them, but the vows are too hard. Only a few can live their lives that way. Their religion is mild in that it does not condemn our natures.'

'And this *consolamentum*? It will save his soul and send him to heaven?'

'Send him *back* to heaven. Without the vows, his soul will just migrate to another body here on earth and he will suffer, because suffering is inevitable here. If we love, we lose. If we live and are happy, we die. It is the Devil's trap.'

He touched her gloved hand. 'And what is this? Is this the doing of God or the Devil?'

'I don't know what it is.' She winced with pain and stopped to rest, leaning her weight against him. He hesitated, and then put an arm around her shoulders.

'It's not there,' she said, putting her hand lightly on his chest.

'What isn't there?'

'You carried a lady's comb inside your shirt. I found it when they first brought you here.' She patted all around his tunic. 'It's gone.'

'It belonged to Alezaïs. She was my first wife.'

'Where is it now?'

'It's gone, as she is gone.'

'You threw it away? Why?'

He shrugged. 'What is the use?'

'What happened to her, seigneur?'

'She died, this four years now, birthing my boy. I was away, on crusade.'

'And you still miss her?'

'Every day. I loved her very much.'

'I have never loved a man,' Fabricia said. 'I would not know what it is like.'

'Would you like me to describe it to you?'

'Do you think you can?'

He pulled her closer. 'In Outremer, in the desert, they have watering places where travellers can stop and find rest and shade and sustenance and water. Otherwise they would not survive a long desert crossing. It is the kind of place you dream of constantly when you are thirsty. When the heat and the journey have broken you, the promise of such a place keeps you going. When you finally reach there, it is green and cool and you never want to leave it. They call such a place an *oasis*. Alezaïs, she was my oasis.'

Fabricia thought about this for a long time.

Finally: 'One day,' she said, 'I should like to stop for shade and water. But I cannot imagine how this might happen. You are fortunate, seigneur, to have known what an oasis is like.'

She kissed her fingers and placed them on his cheek. 'If only you were a stonemason's apprentice looking for a wife.'

She rose to her feet and left him there.

He sat for a long time, thinking about what she had said. He realized he could not go back now, even if Raimon found him an escort. Yet neither did he wish to die; not tomorrow at least. He would give it one more day and then think again, as he had done every day since they brought him here. When the time was ripe to kill and be killed, he would know it.

LXII

Carcassonne

HUGUES DE BRETON had suffered. For almost a week now he had lain groaning and tossing in the hospital by St Anne's Gate. The nuns prayed by his bed and tended his fever with cool cloths. The palms of his hands and the soles of his feet had been burned by the physician's cautery iron and he had been given sedatives and herbal potions for the pain. But none of it had served, and every day he thrashed and screamed and sweated and raved, red-faced, at the phantoms who came to torment him.

Father Ortiz bent to hear his last confession but could not make out anything that would pass for words. He was babbling, making no sense. He gave him the last unction, and asked God for His mercy.

Gilles watched, one hand on his hip, his face livid.

Simon brushed away a fly. They were persistent and plentiful inside the monastery, attracted by the mountains of bloodied bandages and the putrefying wounds of the knights who had been brought there. The heat was stupefying. Outside, the city seethed. The stink of the bodies that had piled up during the siege pervaded everything even though there had been mass burnings all week. De Montfort and the other barons had returned to their camps on the other side of the river, unable to bear the stench or the heat in the city they had taken such pains to conquer.

'The man who did this is Baron Philip de Vercy,' Gilles hissed. 'We know this by the device on his shield. God rot his eyes and his balls! He attacked my crusaders not once, but twice!'

'We will inform the Pontiff and he will have him excommunicated,' Father Ortiz assured him.

'He will die by degrees. That good man there is my brother-in-law!'

They had joined the Host just as the city had negotiated its surrender. Gilles had been piqued that he had missed the fight. His good humour was not served any better a few days later when his force of knights and their men-at-arms arrived at Carcassonne with a score missing from their original number and Hugues de Breton slumped over his horse with one leg ruined.

The arrow wound had shattered his knee joint but it was the open wound to his lower leg that had become infected. The bonesetter had realigned the ankle only with difficulty and in the heat the wound had become putrid and now the infection had spread to the rest of his body. He was rotting in front of them.

Simon thought it a just punishment but said nothing.

'His soul will fly straight to heaven,' Father Ortiz said to Gilles.

'I hope so, Father, for this last week he has surely tasted enough of purgatory.'

'His sacrifice is for God.'

'Did he make his confession?'

'His soul is pure,' he said diplomatically.

Gilles could not stand to watch this any longer. He went to the window, stared across the roofs of the Saint-Nazaire cathedral and the Bishop's palace to the churning confluence of the Aude.

'You have heard the news? The Count of Nevers is leaving and the Duke of Burgundy won't be far behind him. They say they have served God's army their forty days and it is time to go home.'

'What about you, my lord?' Father Ortiz said. 'You will not abandon our great crusade as well?'

'I shall stay a little longer. To serve God.'

Or is it because you haven't had your share of the loot yet? Simon wondered. Another thought best kept to himself.

'We have orders from de Montfort,' Gilles said. 'While he purges the Toulousain we are to join an advance force that is to strike north into the Montagne Noir. I shall be at the head of this small army. We shall take a trebuchet and twenty knights and take Montaillet and then Cabaret. May God lend favour to all our efforts.'

'I am sure He shall. God has so far blessed us with one miracle after another.'

'I don't think Hugues would share your opinion, Father,' Gilles said and stalked out.

LXIII

PHILIP KNEW BY the comings and goings of Trencavel's soldiers that something had happened. Finally Raimon scrambled on to the rock at the mouth of the cave and called for their attention.

'I have important news for you all,' he said and a hush fell over the cave. 'The *crosatz* have sent an expedition into the mountains against our castles at Montaillet and Cabaret. If we stay here, we risk being discovered by their raiders. Everyone knows of these caves. We may be betrayed.'

'Then where shall we go?' someone called out.

'There is only one place you can go and that is to the fortress at Montaillet. I have been ordered to ride there immediately with my soldiers. Those of you who come with us will have our protection.'

'But how shall we get there?'

'You will have to follow us on foot across the mountains.'

'How far is it?'

'Five leagues. It is a long way but you have no choice. If you have carts you will have to leave them behind. Just take what you can carry.'

When Raimon finished speaking, a sigh passed around the cave. Another march, more of their precious possessions left behind, the future even more uncertain. But, as Raimon said, what choice was there? Besides, it was what they had all been expecting. It had only been a matter of time before the *crosatz* turned north.

*

Father Marty's eyes blinked open. 'Leave me here,' he said to Fabricia. 'I'll be in one heaven or another very soon. You owe me nothing. If you stay, it's just another sin on my head.'

She moved away. A shadow blocked the light from the mouth of the cave. It was Philip.

'What did he say?'

'He wants me to leave him behind.'

'But you won't, will you?'

'There's an old woman over there called Bruna. She was a friend of my mother's. I used to play with her little boy when I was a child. She's too sick to move as well. I cannot leave either of them.'

'I thought that was what you would say.' He sat down beside her. 'If the *crosatz* find you, you know what they will do to you? Would you stay here undefended?'

'I have no choice.'

He shook his head. 'Did Father Marty ever show you kindness? Or anyone? Didn't he try to rape you once? And now you want to help him?'

She shook her head. 'It's not about his conscience, this is about mine.'

Philip shook his head and walked away. Raimon saw him talking to her and, taking him by the arm, led him outside the cave. Father Vital was there, with his *socius*.

'What will you do now, seigneur? You should come with us. It is too dangerous for you to ride alone across the Albigeois until this war has ended. You can winter at Montaillet. Besides, we could do with another good soldier if the *crosatz* come that far.'

Philip shook his head. 'I can't.'

'What will you do then?'

'I intend to stay here with her.'

'Are you mad?'

'If I am, or if I am not, it is no business of yours. Do not presume to question me.'

Raimon squeezed his arm tighter. 'I have seen the way you look at her.'

Philip shook him off. 'You forget yourself. Do not lay a hand on a seigneur unless you wish for another navel.'

'She makes those wounds herself, you know,' Father Vital said. 'Someone saw her. She has a knife and she does it secretly. She is a witch and half-mad. It's in her eyes.'

'Did you see her yourself make these wounds?'

'I trust the man who told me.'

'So you didn't see her.' He turned to Raimon. 'What do you think?'

Raimon shook his head. 'I do not know.'

'You were the one who brought me to her, you were the one who said that she had healed me.'

'Perhaps you would have got better anyway. The father may be right, it could be a trick. I don't know, seigneur, I want to believe.'

'Be careful of her,' Father Vital said.

Philip shook his head in disgust and walked away.

*

Like ghosts, grey and sad, they shuffled towards the mouth of the cave. Some grumbled for leaving, but mostly they were silent. The smaller children whimpered at this early interruption of their sleep. She saw one burgher carring his ledgers under his arm, struggling with his load, a servant behind him carrying scales and some rolls of parchment. Eventually, Fabricia supposed, he would have to surrender his creditors and his old life.

But it seemed he was not ready just yet.

Some of them stopped and knelt down and murmured thanks and left her something: food, a few coins; one merchant left her a ring. Others ignored her, or hissed curses.

They filed out until the last of the refugees were gone, and the cave fell silent. The carts and bundles they had left behind littered the sandy floor of the cave. Now there was just the three of them. Father Marty snored in his sleep. Old Bruna was so silent she thought she was already dead.

As the light grew stronger Fabricia saw a man silhouetted against the mouth of the cave. 'You have come to say goodbye?'

'I should, if I were leaving. But I have decided to stay.'

Fabricia choked a sob of relief. She had hoped that he would have sense enough to leave but prayed that he would not. 'I have wished both my patients dead in the night. Do you still think me a saint?'

'I never thought you a saint.'

'Why do you stay then, seigneur? Why does a man with a castle feel such attachment to a cave?'

'I have asked myself that question every day since I came here. I still don't have an answer.'

'But you will die if you stay here.'

'Perhaps I will die, perhaps I won't. This morning, when I woke, it was clear to me. In the forest, when I rode against the men who killed my young squire – that was when I died. My body survived but it was death just the same, for in that moment I renounced everything I had in this world and with it I bought my freedom. I am a ghost now. I can do as I wish and the world no longer sees me. I am between one life and the next, and quite reconciled to it. What about you?'

Raimon appeared, helmet under his arm, in full armour. 'This is your last chance to change your mind,' he said to Philip.

'I am staying,' Philip said.

'Very well. But if the *crosatz* find you, do the woman a favour and kill her first.' He left.

Philip knelt down beside her. Oh, look at him, she thought. A killer, all long-boned menace with a merry smile that hides his assassin's eyes. What does he want of you – and what do you want of him? Such compassion in him, but look at the sword he carries – paid good money for it from one of Trencavel's soldiers, she had been told, for he could not bear to go unarmed even among refugees in a cave. And yet he is here, this morning, vowing to protect me for no good reason I can think of. If he was so full of violence and self-interest he would have slipped away long ago. I cannot understand this man.

'Would you do it?' she said. 'Would you kill me first if the crusaders find us?'

'Let us pray it does not come to that.'

'Yes, I will pray. Are you a good man, Philip?'

'I have tried to be.'

'Then in the next few days you will see just how good you are.'

He smiled. 'You also.' He stood up. 'I should tend to my horse.' He turned at the mouth of the cave, nodding towards Father Marty. 'How long?'

'A day. Perhaps two.'

'Let us hope it is not longer.'

LXIV

IN THE ABBEY, in the hush of the scriptorium, it had been easier to contemplate the sin of heresy. Here in the mountains, where the *bons òmes* lived and worked and had done so much mischief, it was not as simple to feel the presence of holiness, and the certainty of God's protection.

The geography of the Toulousain was like heaven; it was flat and honest and a man might see where he was headed for there were no shadowed places. But as they headed into the Montagne Noir, and the forests and gullies crowded in and narrowed the way, Simon experienced a chill of doubt. Clusters of pines and oaks threw deep shadows over the morning. The road ahead coiled around vine-clad hills, and above them were rock-strewn gorges and brooding peaks.

He looked back at their ragged army: scarce a dozen knights and two lumbering trebuchets, a bitter remnant of the mighty Host that had collected before Carcassonne a few weeks before. Gilles rode at the vanguard, the three eagles at the forefront of the cluster of gold crosses and gilt-edged pennants of other noble houses; blue wolves and black bears, burgundy-red stripes on virgin white, the yellow of Champagne.

Behind the barons and the knights and the bishops came the host of lesser souls; chevaliers, sergeants and squires, then the foot soldiers and auxiliaries, crossbow-men and longbow archers, sappers and siege engineers.

A pitiful few, or so it seemed to his untrained eye. So few fighting men, so many camp followers! He had never been to war before, had not realized how many men it took to keep even a small army in the field even for a day. Lumbering along behind them there was even a cart with an iron-banded wooden chest containing the holy relics that had been sent to bless the expedition: a finger of John, an ear bone of Paul. Behind this, a finely dressed, long-nosed lady in a wimple with a boy barely able to walk, never mind ride; for one nobleman from Picardy had chosen to bring along his wife and son to the crusade, as if it were a jousting tournament.

And then came the long line of baggage trains: lumbering wagons loaded with weapons and supplies and armour, the rounceys and mules, sway-backed and overloaded, chased by the horse boys and muleteers with their long sticks. And still more to follow: farriers, blacksmiths, butchers, notaries, cooks, carpenters, servants, armourers.

And at the last, following along like ducklings who have toppled carelessly into a drain, a gaggle of malcontents and leeches, the dregs of Europe: first, a tattered band of Gascon mercenaries in ramshackle armour who frightened Simon more than any heretic; some jongleurs; then a small army of pilgrims whose purpose it seemed was to sing hymns as the battle was joined and then strip the bodies for loot afterwards. Even as they marched they sang the *Veni Creator Spiritus*: 'Veni Creator Spiritus, Mentes tuorum visita . . .' He doubted a single one of them knew what the words meant.

And at the very rear, the crowning glory of their holy expedition, a House of Venus on four wheels, the prostitutes running along behind it.

All for the glory of God.

He imagined the cloud of dust raised by their hooves and feet and wheels could be seen in Paris.

And what have we so far achieved? he thought. We have butchered a handful of Trencavel's soldiers and hanged another; we have burned a village and hunted down its inhabitants like dogs; we have lost five knights and two score of men to some minor skirmishes that seemed to serve no apparent purpose. And in all that time he himself had seen not one heretic converted or otherwise despatched to hell.

What am I doing here? Is this really God's intention for me?

LXV

O N A SUMMER morning in the Pays d'Oc it is sometimes possible to see the wind. Looking down from the caves high on the ridge down to the valley floor, Philip could make out the currents and eddies in the breeze from ripples in the dawn haze.

His wife stood beside him, rubbing the gooseflesh on her arms, as if she were still a mortal soul. 'What's done is done,' she said.

'I wish I had not taken up the cross. I wish I had not left you behind.'

'Every knight must go on crusade once in his life. You were doing your duty to God. I understood that.'

'I should have waited. It was too soon to leave you.'

'I would have died birthing our son whether you were there or not. Perhaps better you did not hear my screams. It is not a legacy I would have wanted to leave you. Find peace, darling Philip. And joy, too, if you can. You were faithful to me in my life, more than most noble husbands. I do not expect you to live as a monk now.'

'I would trade everything I have to make things different.'

'Some things are written by fate,' Renaut said. 'You cannot change another man's destiny, any more than you can change your own.' His beautiful dark eyes had been given back to him in heaven. 'Look at you, seigneur. You have given everything you have, but still nothing is different. Your brothers have moved into your castle already, for the Pope has made you excommunicate and anyway they think you are dead. Already they are looking for a new husband for their sister.'

'You are smiling. Why is this amusing to you, Renaut?'

'Because it's what you wanted all along.'

'I only wanted to save my son.'

'And you did your best, Papa,' his little boy said. He looked so plump, and his cheeks were pink; how he had been before he got sick.

'I'm so sorry,' Philip said.

Down in the valley, the fog had begun to clear.

'Who are you talking to?' Fabricia asked him.

He turned around, guiltily; he had not heard her behind him. 'You startled me.'

'What kind of knight lets a girl creep up behind and surprise him?' she said, smiling. 'Is there someone else here?'

'Only ghosts,' he said. 'How are Bruna and Father Marty?'

'Bruna has just this moment made her way to heaven. She made a gentle passing.'

'I have a grave prepared for her. I'll carry her there.'

He made to go back into the cave but she put a hand on his arm and stopped him. 'Do you hear that?' She frowned and scanned the horizon. 'There's a storm on its way.' But the morning promised a fine day, only mare's tails high in a water-blue sky.

'It's not a storm,' Philip said. 'What you can hear is a siege engine. They must be dragging up a trebuchet from Carcassonne. No doubt they are headed for Montaillet.' He pointed to what appeared to be a dust storm, far down the valley. 'There they are.'

'There must be thousands of them,' she said.

'Only a few will be warriors. Still, soon they will send out raiders and scavengers. We should not stay here.'

'We can't move Father Marty.'

'I could build a stretcher from tree limbs and drag it with us, behind Leyla. It will be slow but it will be better than remaining here. It won't be too hard for them to find us.'

'How long will it take to make such a thing?'

'It depends what has been left behind that I can use.' He nodded towards the cave and the litter of poor belongings on the sandy floor. 'I need some blankets, and some rope or twine. And some green branches. I could have it finished by the end of the day.'

'Father Marty might not survive that long.'

'But if he does we will be prepared.'

He carried Bruna to the grave that he had prepared for her, and then went to work. Later that afternoon he dragged the stretcher he had built to the mouth of the cave to show her; he had tied two stout tree limbs together to form a frame, with smaller tree limbs lashed across it to strengthen it. He had used some pieces of rope he had found to secure blankets to it. 'Not a king's feather bed,' he said, 'but I think it will do well enough.'

'So you do not spend all your time in the castle eating lark's tongues and chasing the serving women?'

'I have my uses.'

The distant storm had fallen silent; the *crosatz* must have encamped for the night. In the forest, the hum of the cicadas rose to a crescendo and the sky turned the colour of mulberries.

'You said you dreamed of me.'

'A dream can mean many things.'

'True. But then you saved my life.'

'You might have recovered anyway, seigneur. I certainly did not risk my life for you, as you are doing for me now.'

'Raimon thinks it is madness. But I could not leave you behind.' Without warning he bent to kiss her but she turned her face away.

'I am sure that in the castle the servant girls let the seigneur do as he wishes, but I am no serving girl.'

He had never planned to seduce her. He had surprised himself with his own clumsiness. What was he doing? He could have her if he wanted; yes, just like a serving girl, a strong man alone with a woman like this did not need a by your leave. To be rebuffed in such a manner offended his honour and he drew back. 'My pardon, madam,' he said. 'It won't happen again.'

He turned and walked away.

'Wait.' She ran after him, caught his arm and held it. 'You do not understand my meaning.'

'Do you know who I am, girl? And you, just a workman's daughter.'

'He's a master stonemason.'

'The same thing. I am of noble blood and that I should even think . . .' He shook his arm free. 'We should leave at first light. If someone tells the *crosatz* about these caves there could be a raiding party up here tomorrow.'

And he stalked back inside the cave and left her standing there.

*

That night she lay awake, listening to water dripping somewhere in the cave. A mosquito buzzed about her head, the racket of the insects in the forest outside the cave was almost deafening. Father Marty's breath rattled in his chest. He was taking a long time to die.

A full moon trembled in the sky. She looked for Philip, a dark silhouette on the other side of the cave.

Why should she not hold him for a while? The Church would call her wanton; Father Vital would call it sin. But what did Father Marty say? *It is only a sin if you do not enjoy it.* He said that if you made your confession before you died all your sins were forgiven anyway, so what did it matter what you did? Tomorrow they would leave the shelter of these caves, and she could scarce credit that they would survive the perils between here and Montaillet.

But if they did survive, she did not want just one kiss from him, she wanted a multitude. If she made herself thirsty tonight she would find herself in the desert without . . . what was it he called it? An oasis.

He was right in what he had said; he was a baron and she was common, a nothing. If he really wanted her, he could just take her, she could not stop him. What she had done in rebuffing him was a deadly insult.

She thought about the woman she had seen in the doorway of the sacristy of the great cathedral in Toulouse. I should like to know how that feels before I die, she thought. I should like to know the simple pleasures of having a husband, what it is like to be touched by a man who does not find my bloodied hands repulsive, or backs away from me as if I am bewitched.

She slipped out of her blanket and padded silently across the sand to where Philip lay. He was awake. He heard her and rolled towards her.

It was hot inside the cave. The night was steaming.

She slipped off her tunic. 'Hold me,' she said.

LXVI

A HARD DAY'S journeying; barely a league covered through the thick forest, Philip walking Leyla by the bridle, Father Marty groaning at each bump, each rock, each tree root. They stopped every hundred paces so that he could rest. After noon, they found a small cave to hide in and abandoned their effort.

Philip carried Father Marty inside and laid him on some blankets. Fabricia gave him water. If not for the tumour there would be scarce be anything left of him, she thought.

He had been slipping in and out of consciousness, but the water revived him a little. 'So I shall die a heretic,' he said. 'What a strange life. Hereticated, towed behind a horse, saved by a woman that I slandered.' He glanced up at Philip. 'One grows impatient waiting for death, eh?'

'Take your time.'

'Oh, I shall. A man may only expire at the rate he is allowed. But it is clear I cannot get the flesh off my bones fast enough for some.' His smile seeped into the gloom. 'It smells of wild animals. You are sure there are no bears in here?'

Philip muttered something and went outside. Father Marty looked at Fabricia. 'It is so easy to goad him. What is wrong with him? I am dying. A dying man should be allowed to have a little fun.' His hand clutched hers, bony as a crow's. 'Bear witness that I have led a good and blessed life. A few misdemeanours. I am sure when I sneak into heaven by the back gate God will be too busy kicking out the cardinals and the Jews to notice me.' He gasped at a spasm of pain. 'It is hard to fix your mind on the next world when you are not finished with this one. I wonder if heaven is anything like as good as they say it is? May I have some more water?'

Fabricia held the leather drinking bottle to his lips.

'Do you know the *crosatz* hanged my brother? The *bayle*. Well, you probably didn't like him. But he was family. He told them the secret way into Saint-Ybars and out of gratitude for his good service to them they hanged him. I warned him. I said, the *crosatz* have a churchman giving them counsel; you should never trust a churchman. I should know!' A dry laugh that ended in a fit of coughing. 'A candle, please. Is it me, or does it grow darker?'

Fabricia lit a taper from the small store they had brought with them.

'But my brother said, they are Catholics like us, they will reward me. Well, they rewarded him with heaven, didn't they? Only not quite the way he had hoped.' He closed his eyes. 'I shall be glad to be free of this pain.' He shuddered from head to foot and a tear worked itself from the corner of his eye. 'Here, take this,' he said. There was a crucifix around his neck; it was of an unusual provenance and design, gilded copper inlaid with garnets. 'I want you to have it,' he said and pressed it into her palm.

'Thank you,' Fabricia said, thinking he meant it as payment for her kindnesses.

'I have another brother, in Barcelona. He is a burgher there, and well regarded. Should you need to flee the Pays d'Oc, you should go there. He is not hard to find, just say his name.'

'I don't understand.'

'Give him this crucifix. He will know it came from me. Tell him you did me a great service. He will repay you. He is a good man – it runs in the family.' He gave a dry laugh but this led to another fit of coughing. It went on and on and his face turned purple and he could not breathe. She thought that was the end of him.

But the priest was in no hurry for heaven. He held on another few hours, until just before dawn. Philip and Fabricia were asleep when he died.

*

'What is this business?' Gilles growled. 'Winter will soon be upon us and we have yet to kill all the heretics. And de Montfort says that even if we kill every single one of them here, there are more on the other side of the Toulousain.'

Simon was shocked at his ignorance, even after all these months in the Pays d'Oc. 'Half of the Albigeois is hereticated, seigneur. We may only convert a few at a time.'

They were in the Norman's silk pavilion. They had made only slow progress during the day and the noble lord was growing impatient. 'Convert? Why would we want to convert them? Do we try and convert the Saracens?'

'To kill every heretic would be to kill half of the Pays d'Oc.'

'So be it. But we don't have that much time to do it.'

Simon thought to laugh but then saw the great lord did not intend it as jest. 'Not all these people are converted to the heresy. Some are just misguided.'

'Why do you always contend this point with me, Father Jorda? I am here at the bidding of your own Pontiff. I swear I do not understand churchmen. Is this not a Christian land? Then either these godless wretches are with the Church or they stand against it. Is that not true, Father Ortiz?'

They both turned to the monk for his support.

'Please, Father Ortiz, remind the great lord that we are here to bring the south back to God, not to butcher everyone.'

'Father Jorda, are we not of the one true religion? Do these heretics not despoil our churches and tempt others away from God? Does the Pope himself say it is not a sin if we kill on a crusade?'

'You mean you agree with our noble lord on this? But I thought we came to preach, not to slaughter.'

'The time for preaching is over.'

A wolf howled somewhere in the mountains. Gilles went to the doorway of the tent and peered into the darkness, as if he might see the beast from where he stood. 'I don't like it here,' he said. He had small hands, and was constantly rubbing them together. They said he had a condition which made him sweat more than other men, even in the cold. 'There are caves up there; they say the heretics use them for their orgies and for worshipping the Devil. We shall send some men to find them. What shall we do to the Devil-worshippers when we turn them out, Father Jorda? Would you like to preach to them for a time before I burn them?' When Simon did not answer, he turned to Father Ortiz. 'Father Ortiz, you shall take the head of the column tomorrow. I think I shall go with my chevaliers to the caves, instead of dawdling along with this siege engine and the donkeys. Perhaps I shall bring back a heretic for Father Jorda to convert. It will give him something to pass the time. What do you say, Father?'

LXVII

THE CAW OF a crow startled her.

They were resting in a thicket from the heat of the midday. Fabricia had fallen asleep almost straight away, but for moments, no more. When she woke Philip was sprawled beside her, eyes closed.

She stood up. Something drew her deeper into the forest, through the thick stands of beech and oak. The hum of insects was incessant, a pulsing rhythm that unsettled her. She stumbled on a tree branch.

In front of her, in a burned hollow at the base of a tree, was the tiny black effigy of a woman. Fresh candle grease was smeared down her makeshift altar and the flowers at her shrine were fresh. She reached out to touch her and felt a familiar prickling of her skin, a cold, sticky tide that made her retch. She dropped on to all fours, her vision swimming, her body chill with a cold sweat.

*

Philip could not credit that he had allowed himself to fall asleep in the open. It had never happened before. When he woke Fabricia was gone, though the impression she had left in the grass was still warm. He panicked for a moment, but then heard the sound of her voice, close by. Who was she talking to? He jumped to his feet, his hand on his sword.

He found her kneeling among the bracken. She looked up at him, a dreamy look on her face.

'Who is here?' he said. 'Who were you talking to?'

Someone had carved a small opening at the base of a beech tree. There was a mess of candle wax and flowers around it and inside was a statue, black and squat and ugly. It was clearly female, with flat dugs and an outlandishly fertile belly.

'I saw you dead,' she said.

'What?'

'We were riding together, in the mountains. It was winter. You were hit in the chest with an arrow. I have dreamed it before.'

She was looking at him but her eyes were fixed on something else, behind him and very far away. Her skin was grey as a corpse. He lifted her to her feet and carried her away from the demon in the tree, afraid.

LXVIII

A N ABANDONED SHEPHERD'S hut, a waning three-quarter moon. Fabricia straddling him, kissing his mouth.

'What happened today?' he whispered.

'I don't want to talk about it any more.' She worked the tunic off her shoulders and let it slide to her waist. Her eyes were like moons, her body valleys and shadows. She found a scar on his thigh, tracing the jagged march of it with her fingers.

'That is from Outremer,' he said. 'We were escorting some pilgrims to Akko and we were ambushed by Saracens.'

'Have you killed many men?'

'Until the other day in the forest – only Saracens.'

'Saracens are men.'

'Not as Christians are.'

Her hair tickled his face. 'Their wives and children would tell you different, Philip. Men may be different but widows are the same. I feel like I am about to couple with the Devil.'

'Is that what you think? I have always thought myself a good man.'

She took his hands and put them on her breasts. He brushed his thumbs across her nipples and they stiffened at his touch. She closed her eyes, threw back her head and murmured something he did not hear.

'What is this?' he said fingering the crucifix at her throat.

'Father Marty gave it to me.'

'Is it valuable?'

'I don't know. He says he has a brother across the mountains who will help me if I show this to him.'

'It looks old.'

She bent over him and licked his neck. 'Make me forget about all this.'

He wanted to make her forget; he wanted to forget, too. She took his face in her hands and kissed him again, then she drew back. 'Do my hands disgust you?'

'No,' he said. Part truth, part lie; the wounds themselves did not bother him, he had seen much worse. But wounds they were; the Devil's marks perhaps. He had heard stories about demons taking on female form to ensnare men with their beauty and their sex, and once they had a man in their thrall they would change back into snarling beasts and carry their prize off to hell.

Hadn't he seen her praying to a devil today?

Well then, let her turn into a devil and damn me, for to stop now would be like turning back the sea. Her fingers were around him, teasing. All the ways he had denied himself over these last years came spilling out of him now. 'It's been so long,' he whispered in apology as he felt himself pulsing in her hand. 'Don't stop. I don't want to stop. I never want to stop.'

'I don't want your seed in me, seigneur,' she said. 'I just want your touch, the warmth of you.'

'You do not have to call me seigneur. My name is Philip.'

'I do not know if I could call you that. I would feel I was being too familiar.'

He laughed at that. He rolled her on to her back, delighted in how she sighed and moaned at every little thing he did. Her body exhaled a scent of sweat and violets; her skin tasted of salt.

'This is not my first time,' she whispered.

'You don't have to tell me.'

'I want to tell you. I'm not wanton. It was a priest. He forced himself on me.'

'Even so, I think you would have made a very poor nun.'

'They said I had a very good voice to sing the psalms.' Then she gasped as he entered her. 'Gently,' she murmured.

*

He thought about what she had said; about dying with an arrow in his chest in the snow. At least a little more of life then, for it was not yet autumn. The prospect of his own death had suddenly become fearsome. When did that happen? Somehow everything was easier when he had not cared to live; for a short time all seemed so simple. Now this rebel longing for more life was in him again, and with it came all the old anxieties and uncertainties, as well as that traitor – hope.

He had seen the *crosatz* today, or thought he had, the glint of sunlight on a lance, the flash of colour through the trees. They did not have much time to reach Montaillet.

He kissed the valley between her breasts, ran his hand over her thighs, her belly, her hips. 'You are so lovely,' he said. 'Why are you not married?'

'My father wanted my dowry to go to another mason who might take over his work. But the man he wished me to marry died before he could make the match.'

'There must have been other suitors?'

'Who wants a *faitilhièr* – a witch – with holes in her hands? And a witch who is no longer a maiden, either?'

A wash of moonlight, slight as mercury, slipped on the clouds; dark, then light, then dark again. He explored her with his hands and it seemed to her that he knew her body better than she did. She gasped, her stomach muscles quivering like the fluttering of a small bird. She cried out once, her head thrown back. For the longest time she could not catch her breath.

Finally she gave a boisterous laugh, not like a saint at all. 'Oh, seigneur,' she said. 'You have made a poor stonemason's daughter very happy.'

*

When she woke it was cold and he wasn't there. 'Seigneur?' Then she heard his voice and went outside. She found him on his knees, his hands interlocked in an attitude of prayer. 'What are you doing?' she said.

He got to his feet, abashed. 'I was praying.'

'What were you praying for?'

He hesitated. 'I was asking for a hundred times a hundred more dawns like this one. And that on each one I might find you asleep beside me.'

She smiled and kissed his cheek. Suddenly she thought: so this is what joy feels like? I wonder if I might hold on to this for a while.

LXIX

PHILIP CLIMBED UP through feathered pines, leading Leyla by her bridle. Fabricia swayed in the saddle. Her feet were bleeding again and she could barely stand. He could see Montaillet in the distance, its barbicans rising from the cliffs, silhouetted against a white sky. The heat of the afternoon was draining.

He stopped suddenly and put his finger to his lips. He pointed down the valley. There were a dozen riders, in full armour, their visors up, the red cross emblazoned on their surcoats. The knight at their head had a cross of gold on his right shoulder and his armour looked expensive.

He recognized the three pale blue eagles on their pennants and shields. They were the Normans he had tangled with at Saint-Ybars. Philip swore under his breath. The crusaders were following the path of the river. The rushing of the stream drowned out their voices, though he could see them calling to each other as their horses picked their way through the shallows. Philip held his breath and prayed that they would pass and not see them.

But then one of the chevaliers happened to glance up and he stopped and pointed at them, shouting a warning to his fellows.

'Our luck has run out,' Philip said to Fabricia. He jumped into the saddle behind her and spurred Leyla up the slope. Perhaps they could outride them, for the Normans were yet a hundred paces further down the slope. He looked over his shoulder. The Norman horses were stumbling and sliding on the loose stones of the river-banks, they were not bred for pursuit. One shrieked in panic as it lost its footing.

Two of the chevaliers loosed arrows at them but they fell far short.

He thought they were safe. But the best of men make mistakes; and with horses it was no different. Leyla lurched sideways and he immediately knew something was very wrong. She fought the bridle and shrieked in pain. He leaped down from the saddle, pulling Fabricia after him.

'Leyla!' he shouted, 'what is it, girl, what's wrong?'

She was holding her right foreleg clear of the ground. Philip damned God's eyes. Broken! He could see splintered white bone protruding through her fetlock and there was blood everywhere. He clutched at the bridle to hold her still, whispered to her, his hand at the softest part of her throat. She calmed a little but her eyes were wild with agony. 'Oh, Leyla,' Philip moaned, 'what have you done?' But he knew the answer to that. She had found a rabbit hole while he rode her at full tilt.

'What are we going to do?' Fabricia said.

Philip knelt down. 'Help me get out of this armour! I can't run in this.'

Fabricia fumbled with the ties that held the laces at the back of the hauberk. While she was doing that, he threw off his gauntlets and helmet. A small fortune lying there in the grass; it couldn't be helped. He would keep his sword though.

One of the ties was knotted and she couldn't untangle it. He twisted around and cut it with the edge of his sword.

'Will you kill me now?' she said. 'Isn't that what you promised?'

'For what reason?'

'The captain said you should not let them take me alive.'

'We are not taken yet.'

'I cannot run! I can barely walk.'

'I asked God for a hundred times a hundred mornings. This time he is not going to defy me!' He shrugged off the hauberk and stood up. 'If you cannot run then crawl up to the top of the hill. Go!'

'What about the horse?'

'Just go! I will follow.'

Fabricia did what she thought she could not do; she half-stumbled, half-crawled almost to the crest of the wooded ridge, ignoring the agony in her feet. What good will it do? she thought. They have horses. They will overrun us. Without Leyla, it's hopeless.

She fell to her knees. *Mother Mary, blessed of women, help me now.* She turned and looked back through the trees. She could not see him, but she heard the death shriek of his horse.

She pushed herself to her feet and stumbled on and when she

reached the ridgeline she fell again, rolling over and over down the slope on the far side. Finally she lay on her back, staring up at the sky.

Where was Philip?

She pushed herself to her knees and gasped. She was just two paces from a dizzying drop. She realized she must be on the overhang of a cliff, for the water was directly beneath her, roaring through a narrow defile.

God's breath. It would be like dropping from the top of a cathedral to fall into that.

Something flashed past her face; she felt the draught of it as it passed. She turned around. There was a bowman perhaps two hundred paces further along the cliff, calmly reaching behind his back for another arrow.

She jumped up and cried aloud at the agony in her feet. Her only hope to get away now was to jump, but she couldn't do it. A hundred ways she would rather die, but not that way.

The bowman took careful aim. She closed her eyes and prepared to die.

She felt something slam into her and then she was hurtling forwards, could not stop herself, and she fell shrieking through the air, hitting the water far below.

LXX

FABRICIA CAME UP choking and would have drowned but the current carried her swiftly towards the far bank. She stuck out an arm and caught an overhanging branch. There were black spots in front of her eyes. *I have to hold on.* She felt her grip loosen but she summoned the strength to throw out her other arm and cling on.

She realized it must have been Philip who had pushed her over the edge. With her first clean breath she called out his name. She could not see him anywhere. She worked her way arm over arm along the tree limb, and dragged herself up the bank, and lay there, coughing water through her mouth and nose.

'Philip!'

Now she could see what had saved her; a tree had toppled over near the bank, falling half into the water. Perhaps it came down during the same storm that had flooded the cave.

'Seigneur!' Finally she saw him, clinging to the bank further upriver. The flimsy branch he was holding could not bear his weight and the current picked him up and tossed him downstream towards her.

Fabricia clambered back along the tree limb on her belly. She wrapped one arm around the fallen trunk, stretched out her other hand and screamed his name.

He twisted around in the water when he heard her and threw out his hand. She reached him but he was too heavy; she nearly lost him. Somehow she managed to slow him enough so that he could hold on with his other hand. He pulled himself along the fallen tree, just as she had done, until he was free of the current and safe in the shallows.

He fell face first on the bank, coughing up water. He still held his sword in one hand. How had he done that? she wondered.

She knelt down beside him. 'Are you all right, seigneur?'

'Why didn't you jump?'

'I am afraid of heights.'

He started to laugh, but his laughter became another spasm of coughing. Finally: 'You are less afraid of being raped and butchered?'

'I can't swim.'

'Neither can I.'

'Why did you not leave your sword behind?' she said.

'In case I have to do away with you, as I promised the captain. Or did you forget?'

*

He built a fire to get warm, for it was late in the afternoon and the gorge was already in shadow. There was plenty of tinder for it had been a very hot summer. 'Won't the *crosatz* see the smoke and know where we are?' she said.

'They already know where we are, but they'll only be able to get us if they jump off the cliff into the river like we did.'

He went to the water's edge, washed the linen bandages wrapped around her hands and feet, and dried them in front of the fire. He examined her wounds. They were small and round but very deep; he imagined they went right through the flesh. Those in her feet looked even worse. The flesh around them was pale and puckered from contact with the water. How could someone do such things to herself?

'What happened to your horse?' she said.

'She broke her leg. She must have stepped in a rabbit burrow.'

'You killed her?'

'I did what I had to do.'

'Yet you seemed very fond of that horse.'

'I loved her. Do not think that I am so hardened by wars that I can do what I did and sleep easy. But I could not bear to see her in pain and there was nothing I could do to save her. I asked her forgiveness and then I gave her mercy. It was clean and it was quick. Even if God does not know the meaning of mercy, I like to think that I do.'

'Are you not frightened to say such things? Do you not fear God?'

The bandages were dry. He started to bind her feet. 'Perhaps the heretics are right and the God of this world is the Devil and I do not know the real God. You see, that makes sense to me. This is a heresy I can understand.'

'And what about this,' she said, holding up her hands. 'How does this fit what the heretics say?'

He shook his head. 'As you say, we cannot know everything. Some things are just meant to remain a mystery.'

*

They had no blankets. He fetched as much wood as he could from the forest, and they spooned into each other, using each other's bodies to keep warm.

I never imagined this, she thought. When you are born in a stonemason's house in Toulouse the walls of the city are the world and I thought my life would be like my mother's, as her mother's was before her. And it had not seemed such a very bad life: a good and strong husband who did not beat her, a house with a *solier*, hams hanging above the hearth, good neighbours and a promise of a warm corner in heaven at the end of it.

What she had never imagined was that one day she might be sleeping wild with a French nobleman, hunted like an animal and cursed with a gift that set her apart from everyone else. 'You said you saw my mother and father, that they are heading for Montaillet.'

'It is the only refuge from the *crosatz* in these mountains.'

'So you think they will be there when we arrive?'

'If they survive the journey. I hope it will be less eventful than ours.'

'What did they tell you of me? Do you think they believe me to be a witch or a madwoman, like everyone else?'

'They said that they pray for you every day, and they looked as frantic about you as any mother and father would be. If they knew you were not safe in the monastery tonight they would die of worry. Why did you leave?'

'Because the nuns thought I was a witch, too. They thought I made these wounds myself, either because I am mad, or because I like all the attention. Can you imagine that someone is so needy for the world's gaze that they drive a knife into their hands and feet every day? But that is what people think. You think so too some-times, don't you?'

He did not answer her.

'Will you still want me when we reach Montaillet, seigneur? I am just a stonemason's daughter. You are a lord. Is this just for now? I can endure it if you tell me the truth. But a girl like myself can some-times have ideas above her station.'

'You forget, I am no longer a seigneur, I am landless, penniless and excommunicate. There is no future for me. Is this just for now? Everything in my life is just for now.'

A wolf howled, startling her. Then another.

She gripped Philip's arm. 'They sound very close.'

'It's all right,' he said. 'They won't come near the fire.' But he sat up and drew his sword from its sheath.

A half-moon drifted against high white clouds, throwing quick shadows. The river slipped and shivered and the light slid like mercury. He threw more logs on the fire. Something moved in the bushes.

'What was that?'

He took a brand from the fire and held it high above his head. Somewhere out there a pair of eyes glittered orange; four of them, perhaps more. 'As long as we stay by the fire they won't venture closer,' he said.

'Do we have enough wood to keep it fed?'

'I don't know.' She heard the bell sound for matins at the chapel at Montaillet; still half the night to get through then.

Philip stood watch, fuelling the fire, occasionally walking forward a few paces swinging the brand so that the animals retreated further into the darkness. She could hear them yowling in frustration, padding up and down along the edges of the wood.

'They are hungry,' he said.

The moon sank behind the cliffs. And then, without warning, she heard a rush as one of them took its chance. Philip slashed at it with his sword and then wheeled in a circle slashing again. Sparks from the brand he held in his other hand flickered into the grass.

She heard a yelp as one of the beasts tumbled away and another scampered back up the bank into the wood. He roared and ran at them, swinging the torch in a wide arc. They snarled and retreated, eyes glittering.

Philip kicked more wood into the fire. 'It's all right,' he said. 'They won't come back now.'

Fabricia shivered and drew closer to the flames. 'Can you stand the night?' she said.

'I have done it before. Besides, there are enough things I have done that help to keep me awake on the most serene of nights.'

'What things?'

'I have killed my horse. I have failed my wife and my son.'

'Does calling your grief a failure make it easier to bear?'

'Why do you say that?'

'You blame yourself for so many things that are beyond your power to change. Perhaps you should weep for your boy rather than hurl insults at the Invisible – or at yourself.'

He did not answer her for a long time. But finally he murmured: 'Perhaps you're right.'

*

The wolf pack did not retreat too far. They stayed until the sun inched over the cliffs and then they vanished into the forest, leaving their dead comrade behind.

As the sun rose Philip sank to his haunches in exhaustion, leaning on his sword, his head resting against the hilt. She put her hand on his shoulder. Like the Cathars she believed it was wrong to kill anything. But then it was easier to think that on your knees, in a church. In the dark, surrounded by hungry wolves, it was harder to keep the faith.

LXXI

MONTAILLET SAT ATOP a lonely knuckle of blackened lime-stone. Beneath the fortress walls, the ochre roofs of the town slumbered in a yellow sun. The people who lived there would shortly have a rude awakening, he thought.

Vertiginous cliffs fell away to plummeting ravines on the north and east sides. The southern and western walls were protected by tall barbicans. It could be approached only by the road that led up from the valley.

Philip studied it first with the eyes of a warrior, estimating its weaknesses, where he would place his catapults if he were an enemy, how he might deprive the garrison of water. The red walls that encircled the town might keep out the bandits and the wolves but they would not withstand a determined assault by an army with siege engines. He imagined Trencavel's men would concede that soon enough. But the fortress itself looked formidable.

It was a long, hot climb up to the town, past deserted vineyards and olive groves. Fabricia was walking better today; she said her feet pained her less. Still, it had taken all that morning for her to hobble the remaining half a league from the gorge.

The sides of the road were a riot of thyme and wild buttercups. Some gaiety at last. They passed a mill and a watchtower. A hanged man, or the little that remained of him, swung in the wind.

There were just two watchmen at the gate, lounging on their pikes. One of them stepped forward and barred the way with his weapon. 'Where do you think you're going?'

Philip drew his sword and had it at the man's throat in an instant. He grabbed his hair and brought him to his knees. Then he turned to the man's comrade. 'If you move even your little finger I shall cut out his gizzard and jam it up your arse, you impudent pair of turnips!'

Neither of the men moved. One could not; the other was just too terrified. Philip controlled his temper with difficulty. 'My name is

Philip, Baron de Vercy. I have lost my horse, my armour, my faith and almost my life in your accursed country when I came here in peace, looking for succour. I will not tolerate further bad manners from anyone. If you ever talk to me or this young woman like that again I will cut out your liver and feed it back to you whole. Do I make myself clear?'

The watchmen had no further questions as to their business in Montaillet.

'You have a temper, seigneur,' Fabricia said.

'One of my many faults, my lady. I pray you will excuse it. I have not yet broken the fast and I am insulted by a third-rate bully with a pikestaff and bad teeth. I was raised in noble fashion and it offends me to be so used.'

The town was crowded with sheep, pigs, goats and people. It smelled like a barn. 'Seigneur, in defence of those men at the gate, you do not look like a lord and I do not look like a lady. We blend into the common herd, in our present straits.'

'Sadly, you are right,' he said. 'Do you see your parents yet?'

'Not yet.'

'The refugees may all be inside the fortress. Come on.'

A stone bridge led across a dry moat, and then to a wooden walkway that could be lowered and raised from the gatehouse. The courtyard of the castle was in chaos. Montaillet was preparing for war. Some knights rushed to the forge for last-minute adjustments to armour or the sharpening of a sword. Lacquered helms and shields glittered in the sunlight.

There were refugees camped inside and outside the church. Already it stank and the siege had not yet begun. Fabricia searched the terrified faces for her mother and father.

'Perhaps they did not survive the journey,' she said. She took hold of a stranger, asked if he had seen them; a giant, she said, with fists like hams; his wife, red hair turning to grey and a proud way of walking. The man shook his head and walked away. She saw someone she knew from her village and asked again. He pointed vaguely towards the other side of the courtyard. Yes, he thought he had seen Anselm; look over there.

A ragged tramp sitting on the steps of the church stood up and shouted her name; the tangle-haired woman beside him dropped to her knees and sobbed. Fabricia threw herself at them. The crowd around them stared cold-eyed. So little joy in this place, perhaps they resented it.

'My little rabbit!' the man yelled and picked her up and threw her in the air like a doll. Fabricia burst into tears, as did her mother. Philip hovered, thinking for a moment to join the celebration, but instead turned away. He was not a part of this; he would rejoin her later.

A troop of Trencavel soldiers, their shields emblazoned with the Viscount's mustard and black ensign, went past him at the double, headed for the southern wall. Someone shouted his name. Philip saw Raimon peel away from the squadron and head towards him. 'So, you made it! I would never have believed it. But, seigneur, you look more like a bandit than a lord. Are you well?'

'Well enough for a man who has been chased around the country by fanatics, near drowned and set upon by wild animals.'

'Well, you made it here, that is triumph enough! Come along with me, let me find you a glass of wine.' He put an arm around his shoulders and led him inside the *donjon*.

LXXII

SUCH A CONTRAST in fortunes, Philip thought. One day eating wild figs and berries and lying in the river mud to scoop up water to drink; the next, reclining at his ease drinking Rhenish and gorging from a trencher of rye bread and sheep's cheese.

While he dined Raimon stood at the window watching the preparations for the siege. 'You can stay here in the *donjon*,' he was saying, 'but I'm afraid you won't have a private bed with velvet curtains. But you shall share the straw with fine company, for there will be two barons and much of the minor nobility of the Minervois with you.'

'I've known worse.'

'The straw or the company?' He shook his head. 'What happened to that fine horse of yours?'

Philip shook his head.

'A pity. One of the finest Arabs I ever saw. And your armour?'

'I had to swim a river. It is a task made more difficult with a suit of iron mail, even one made in Toledo. So there was no choice but to leave it as a parting gift to the men who chased me.'

'How quickly a man's luck can change. My circumstances have altered somewhat also since we last met at the caves. One day I was captain of a score of chevaliers harassing the *crosatz*, the next I am seneschal of a castle and charged with stopping the crusader invasion of the Pays d'Oc.'

'A day is a long time in any war. How did you come by such a rapid promotion?'

'The previous seneschal fled after they told him what had happened at Béziers. They caught him and hanged him from the tower – you may have noticed him on your way here. His good looks are not what they were. But tell me, you are a seasoned warrior, what do you think of Montaillet? Can we withstand an assault from the *crosatz*' army, do you think?'

'You have two weak points,' Philip said. 'You draw your water from a well on the southern side. Is that your only source?'

'That is a military secret, seigneur, which I should be foolish to divulge to a man whose loyalty is suspect.'

'You do not have to answer. But you asked my soldier's opinion.'

'What is the other weakness?'

'It is not the fortress itself; it is what is inside it. You will have to surrender the suburbs, probably on the first day, and then you will have even more people and animals inside these walls. If the siege is prolonged you cannot feed them all. And they bring with them the prospect of disease.'

'You are right, but it will not be a prolonged siege. Autumn is coming. These *crosatz* will serve out their forty days of war for the Pope, get their dispensation to heaven and go home. They will not wish to spend the winter here. If they don't have a quick victory as they did at Béziers and Carcassonne, they will soon tire of us. Besides, these people need not be a burden. We'll eat their sheep and their cows and teach the women and children to work the mangonels.'

He heard angry voices from below. He joined Raimon at the window. A tonsured priest stood on the church steps haranguing the crowd. It seemed the people were not happy with his sermon. 'Who is that?'

'The priest from the village. He has been beseeching them all to return to God's good favour by throwing open the gates to the *crosatz* to prove there is no heresy here. But no one believes that; they all know what happened at Béziers. Besides, this is not about religion. These *crosatz* have insulted our honour and taken our land. Even the Catholics hate them now. They could have Moses himself leading the army and we would still slam the doors on him.'

'How do you intend to stop them?'

'This won't be like Béziers or Carcassonne. For one thing, they have only a small part of their army here. And besides, storming a castle on a plain is one thing, but we have mountains and cliffs at our back. See those fellows?' He pointed to a band of routiers, Spanish by the look of them, on the south wall. They were well armed for mercenaries, with good French coats of mail, but the bright red or green scarves around their throats and the gold rings in their ears marked them out as for-hire professionals. Their leader, a handsome brute with tight black curls and a tattered leather jerkin, was laughing as he greased the strings of his bow. Philip had fought with such men before. They would cut out a man's tongue and that same night burst into tears when they talked about their mothers. Mad or godless, the lot of them.

'The leader's name is Martín Navarese. They are well paid and they are not going to surrender because they know what will happen to them if they do. The rest of the garrison are all liegemen of the Trencavels or barons who have been dispossessed by the war and have nothing left to lose. Believe me, Montaillet will not be another Béziers.'

He stopped and listened. Even over the shouts of the preacher and the hecklers from below, they both heard what sounded like distant thunder. The *crosatz* were getting closer. 'I should persuade you to stay if I could. We could use a seasoned warrior like you.'

'What good is a knight without armour?'

'I can provide you with hauberk and helm easily enough.'

'Good armour is expensive.'

'The seneschal will not be needing his any more. Think of it as your wages for your good service to us.'

'And I'll need a good horse to ride out on at the end.'

'You strike a hard bargain. Very well, but it won't be a fine Arab like the one you had before.'

'As long as it has four legs.'

'Before you make up your mind, think about what you're doing, seigneur. You could still get out of this.'

'How?'

'This is not your fight.'

'I may be a northerner, but I am excommunicate. I cannot go back.'

'What red-blooded fellow has not upset the Church from time to time? You could make your peace with the Archbishop. Besides, until now you have been fighting on your own account. Explain the circumstances of your little misunderstanding, promise to make a pilgrimage and donate a little land to the see and they will forgive you soon enough. But once they've witnessed you on these walls standing against them, you become a heretic and they will give you no quarter.'

'So be it. It is a matter of honour now.'

'Ah. *Paratge*. Well, that I understand. But remember, it is not easy to be *faidit* – dispossessed. Ask the men who share your straw tonight; they had castles once too.'

'I am decided. Show me this armour; I may have to take it to the forge to have it buffed and polished. I should not make my final stand looking worn or shabby.'

Raimon grinned. 'Well, I have done my duty and given you fair warning, seigneur. I did not think a man who would ride alone against forty would be easily dissuaded from a fight. I am glad you have decided to stay. I would rather have you on my side than theirs.'

*

It was a large family, five or six small children, all squatted on the ground under the eaves. An urchin, hovering close by, snatched half a loaf of bread from one of the children and ran. Philip put out an arm and caught him by the ear. He took the bread from him and handed it back to its owner while the little wretch squirmed and fought him.

The man drew his knife. 'I'll cut off his fucking nose!'

'If you do I shall have to cut off yours. Now address me as lord, thank me and go back to your family. I will take care of this.'

Scowling, the man touched his forelock, mumbled, 'Yes, seigneur,' and walked away.

Philip turned to the urchin. 'Why do you do this, Loup? You must be the worst thief in the world, you're always getting caught.'

The boy aimed a kick at him. 'What do you care? You abandoned me!'

'I did not abandon you. I helped you from charity, you ingrate. I am not your father and I am not your kinsman.'

'I fucking hate you!'

Philip shook his head. There was nothing to be done with the lad. 'Where is the woman, Guilhemeta?'

The boy nodded towards the church.

'Is she all right?'

'She's sick.'

'Let me see her.'

He released the lad, who led him grudgingly up the steps and into the church. Guilhemeta lay against the wall in the nave, pale and sweating. People stepped over her as if she wasn't there, just another bundle of rags without hope.

'How long has she been like this?'

'Since yesterday.'

'Wait here, I'll get you food and I'll get you help. And don't go stealing anything. You should try and keep your nose. It's the only thing on you that knows how to run.'

LXXII

'GOOD PEOPLE OF Montaillet. The crusaders are coming to rid us of foul heresy! We should throw our gates open to them, or we will burn as they did in Béziers! It is our moment of Judgement! If we fail in our duty to God we shall know His holy wrath! Stay inside these walls and we ally ourselves with the Devil. But if we open the gates and let God's Host in, we will have nothing to fear! They only wish us to give up to them those who worship the Devil and scorn the one and true Holy Church!'

Someone threw a cabbage. There was a scuffle at the front between an onlooker and one of the priest's bully boys. Soldiers waded into the crowd. It was no time for a riot when they were all preparing for war.

'My brother-in-law is a *crezen* and so is my cousin! I'll not let some Frenchman come here and butcher them!'

'They've come here to loot us. They'll rape our women and take our money no matter what we do!'

Fabricia stood with her father at the back of the crowd. He put his hand on her shoulder. 'They're right,' he said. 'If we let a wolf into our house we are the fools, not the wolf. I don't want to listen to this idiot any more.'

He had changed so much since she had last seen him. His skin was loose around his arms where once he had been all muscle; his eyes looked sad and tired; his beard had turned grey and he had grown jowls. He seemed timeworn.

'Where's this fine nobleman of yours?' he asked her.

'I don't know,' Fabricia said.

'I don't want to be the one to say it, girl, but *faidit* or not, he's still noble and he won't think twice about you now he's here among his kind again.'

'He still saved my life, so I won't think badly of him.'

'Well, he saved mine as well, me and your mother. Did he tell you that?'

She shook her head.

'The *crosatz* would have slaughtered us all if not for him. So we should light a candle for him. But he is what he is, so you should not expect to see too much more of him.' They stopped inside the nave and he put his hand on her arm. 'I should never have sent you away to the monastery. It was a cowardly thing to do.'

'You had no choice.'

'I am sorry. It was a mistake. You are my daughter and I shall answer for it to God one day.'

They went back inside the church. It was in an uproar. Hundreds of men and women were crammed in, quarrelling over food and places to camp. There was a stench of sweat and sores and rancid incense; the heat was like a wall. She involuntarily took a step back.

Trencavel's soldiers were at work taking down the cross from the high altar; one even carried away the statue of the Queen of Heaven on his shoulder like the spoils of war. The long-winged angels that had been painted in the high vault watched in shocked confusion.

Elionor sat against the wall with their few belongings, but she was not alone. There was a crowd gathered around her on the flagstones. 'Who are those people?' Fabricia said.

'They have come looking for you,' Anselm said. 'Someone here recognized you and they all know who you are now. This one has a sick child; this man, his mother is dying. They say they want you to help them.'

'What should I do?' she said.

'Well, you can't send them away. If you can end one person's misery then it's what you have to do.'

'I thought you did not believe any of that.'

'I don't know what I believe any more.'

Someone shouted out Fabricia's name and the crowd surged towards her. A murmur went through the church. *There she is, the saint of Saint-Ybars.* Fabricia wanted to run away. *Just leave me alone, please!*

But how could she? So she took the baby that was thrust into her arms, knelt down and started to pray. Soon more came.

And when she thought she was finally done, she heard a familiar voice in her ear. 'When you're finished here,' Philip said, 'will you come with me? There's a woman over here, her name is Guilhemeta. She is very sick.'

'Seigneur, I thought I should not see you again.'

'Well, you were wrong. Now will you come with me, please?'

Fabricia said yes, she would come. She looked down at her gloved hands. They did not ache so much today, and there was no blood crusted into the wool. She wondered what it meant.

*

The people of Montaillet watched them leave: the priest on his mule, his mistress walking beside him, and a few supporters behind, those Catholics too pious or too terrified to remain. Someone shouted out: 'This is the first time I've seen a jackass riding a donkey!' and there was jeering and laughter.

A woman, bolder than her neighbours, hawked in her throat, shot her head back and spat right in the priest's face. Her saliva dribbled down his cowl.

The gates swung open, affording a fine view of the ridge below the town and the bright pennants and pavilions of the crusader encampment. They were already setting up their siege engines.

'You are all damned!' the priest shouted as his final blessing.

The gates swung closed behind him.

Anselm shook his head. 'These priests make me ashamed,' he said to Fabricia.

They walked back to the church. Elionor was sitting between Father Vital and his *socius*, speaking in whispers. Anselm did not seem surprised to see them there. 'What do they want?' Fabricia asked him.

'Your mother has asked to take the *consolamentum*,' he said. 'She wishes to be ordained as a *bona femna*.'

'But why?'

He shook his head. 'She has told me she wants to die in the faith she believes in and I have said I will not to stand in her way. How the world has turned for us, my little rabbit!' She imagined she knew what he was thinking: three years ago he was a member of the guild in Toulouse with a fine house and a marriageable daughter.

Now look.

'She does not care to wait for the moment of death to be perfected,' he went on. 'She says she wishes to purify her soul and live by the Rule. Your mother has been a heretic for many years, Fabricia, you know this. She has always been an honest woman and now she wishes to be more so.' He looked around the church. He had devoted his life to building houses for God, such as this. Now the saints he had lived by all his life were gone, the cross too, loaded on to the cart that followed the priest out of the gates. Even his wife was preparing herself to become a heretic.

'I think it is the end of the world,' he said.

LXXIV

FABRICIA AND ELIONOR sat with their backs to the wall of the nave, staring at the saints painted on the walls of the pillars, the vermilion and gilt peeling away. They were all that was left of the old icons now. On the high altar a small crowd had gathered about Father Vital and were on their knees, praying the Our Father.

'Papa loves you,' Fabricia said.

Elionor reached out and took her hand. 'I do not mean to hurt him with this – or you. I should have taken the *consolamentum* long ago, but for my family. But I have done my duty to you both, and now I have to follow my conscience.'

'But why now?'

'I am tired of the world, Fabricia. Once I thought I should take the *consolamentum* only as I die. But what if it is sudden, what if there is not the time? I do not wish to come back to this world again, despite all the joy you and your father have given me.'

'Will you become a priest, like him, then?'

'Should we somehow survive this – yes, I shall be a priest and preach, as Father Vital does.'

Fabricia hung her head.

'I do not understand why you and your father persist with the Roman Church, the ridiculous nonsense they believe. Babies born to virgins and the dead coming back to life! Does anyone really believe these old bones will creak back into living once they are buried in the earth?'

'I don't know, perhaps you're right. But leaving Papa on his own after all these years doesn't seem like such a good and holy thing either, Mama.'

Elionor squeezed her hand. 'Please, Fabricia. Let me go. My soul yearns for heaven.'

Fabricia winced and withdrew her hand.

'I'm sorry,' Elionor said. 'I forgot myself. How are your wounds?'

'They are a little better.' She took off her mittens. She was surprised to find the bandages clean for the first time in months. The blood had stopped seeping.

'Will you tell me something? The truth?' Elionor asked her.

Fabricia nodded. She knew what she was going to ask her.

'These wounds. Did you . . . did you make them . . . did you do it yourself?'

Fabricia stripped the linen bandage off her right hand. She held it to the light so that her mother could see. 'Look, Mama. The puncture goes straight through. Do you think I could stand the pain of making even one such wound? I have them on both hands and both feet. Why would I do it? How could I?'

'The crucifixion is a lie,' Elionor said. 'Every right-thinking person knows it.'

'Because you do not understand something does not mean it cannot be. Even in the convent they said I was lying, and to them the cross is everything. "Why would Christ's wounds appear on a woman?" they said. As if I would know the answer!'

Elionor touched her daughter's cheek with her fingers. 'I am sorry for everything. I love you.' And she put her head on Fabricia's shoulder and wept.

But there was no time for consolation. Fabricia felt a familiar tugging at her sleeve, a woman kneeling there, with her child. 'Please,' she said, holding out her infant. 'Touch her. Make her well again . . .'

LXXV

THEY SENT IN the bandits and *hoi polloi* first. Philip stood next to Raimon on the barbican and watched them stream up the narrow isthmus towards the *bourg*. 'The walls are not strong enough,' he said. 'You cannot hold your position there.'

'I do not intend to. I have told them merely to hold on for as long as they can, let the archers go about their work, and then to withdraw when things get too hot. If we can frustrate them for a few hours they may lose their stomach for it.'

They were singing a Latin hymn in the crusader camp. They must be going at it with gusto to be able to hear them this far off. Down in the *bourg* Raimon's plan had gone awry. He could see fighting on the walls already.

'God's holy balls,' Raimon muttered and turned to his trumpeter to give the signal for his men to fall back.

'You may not need to do that,' Philip said. 'It seems they have made up their own minds.'

The inhabitants were already streaming through the streets, a panicked wave of men, women and children, the old and the slow falling under the crush. Raimon's soldiers were not far behind them.

Raimon went down the ladder to the gatehouse. Philip heard him bawling at the watchmen to open the gates.

He readied himself for a fight. The old seneschal's armour was a tight fit, but it was well made and would serve well enough; good Toledo steel laced with copper studs, steel gauntlets and thigh pieces, a shield polished smooth as glass. He would not go down easily.

The archers that Raimon had kept in reserve came crowding up the ladders from the court and took their positions along the gatehouse battlements. Philip took his new helm from under his arm and put it on.

As the iron-barred doors creaked open a wave of refugees

streamed through, their panicked screams echoing from the walls of the gatehouse. Raimon waited as long as he dared to close them again. This was not the orderly retreat he had planned and not all were on the right side of the gates when the drawbridge was raised.

Those left behind were butchered right there beneath the walls, some killed by their own archers.

Raimon reappeared on the barbican, his helm still under his arm. His face was the colour of chalk. 'What is wrong with them? My archers are cutting them into windrows and still they keep coming.'

'They think they have God on their side,' Philip said.

When those most urgently seeking heaven had died, their comrades finally left off the attack on the south-east wall and retreated, setting fire to the *bourg* as they went. The town burned slowly at first but by the middle of the afternoon it was well alight. Choking black smoke, driven by the wind, blocked out the sun. Not a good start.

LXXVI

THE CHURCH BELLS were ringing; horns at the south-east gate joined the alarm. Raimon screamed at his archers to follow him and ran along the battlements through the smoke. Philip followed.

They were already fighting hand to hand on the barbican. Men with scarlet crosses emblazoned on their tunics were clambering up ladders they had set against the walls.

A cat – a siege tower – loomed through the smoke, ablaze from the flaming arrows that Raimon's archers had fired into it. Phillp felt a grudging admiration for whoever commanded the crusader army. He had judged the wind, and deliberately sent the bulk of his force against the *bourg* so he could burn it and use the smoke as cover for an attack on the other wall.

The Spanish mercenaries were in the thick of it. He saw their captain, Navarese, heft back a ladder single-handed, sending the men on it screaming into the moat, then urge his men against the handful of crusaders who had gained foothold on one of the towers. Raimon ordered more fire arrows into the cat.

Hard to breathe or even see their enemy through the red smoke. How many of them were already inside the citadel? There was no time to help Raimon reorganize the defences now, it was just strike and parry and run, get to the south-east barbican and the looming threat of the cat as soon as he could.

Philip saw a man-at-arms with the three Norman eagles on his shield and went straight for him. The man fell back, trying to parry his blows, but as he reached the wall Philip put all his weight behind his shield and hit him front on. He had advantage of height and bulk and better armour. The man toppled back and fell.

But in his eagerness to claim a Norman he had left his back exposed. As he turned he saw two others come at him, one with an axe, the other with a broadsword. He took the blow from the axe on his shield; the sword gave him a glancing blow to his helm. His opponents were not knights but, though poorly armoured, they were brave enough. He cut one down with his sword but the man with the axe was determined and a second blow this time glanced off his shield and would have taken off his head if it were not for the good Toledo steel of the helmet Raimon had furnished him. Stunned, he went down.

The soldier raised the axe above his head a third time. Philip could not roll to the right, for there was another man fallen beside him. To his left was the wall. Neither could he bring up his shield to deflect the blow in time.

Suddenly the man gasped and dropped the axe. Martín Navarese used the heel of his boot to prise the man free of his sword, and then kicked him over the edge. He gave Philip his hand and pulled him to his feet. 'You owe me,' he said.

The barbican had been cleared. The cat was fully alight now; men were jumping from the upper works with clothing alight. Horses, their bellies ripped open, were writhing in the ditch. Ladders tilted back all along the wall, crashing into the chaos of struggling and bleeding bodies below.

Through the smoke Philip saw a knight with a gold helm spur his horse close to the walls to snatch one of his men from under a mass of tangled bodies. His coat of mail bristled with arrows.

As if he wished to remove any doubt of his identity, the knight removed his helm and stood in the stirrups of his destrier, pointing up at the battlements. It was an unspeakably reckless thing to do and for a moment Philip almost admired him for it. 'Every one of you shall burn. I will have your filthy castle within the week!'

For a moment their eyes met. They were close enough that Philip saw his face clearly and remembered him from that day in the forest when Leyla had broken her foreleg. They had seen each other then, and he knew that the knight had seen him now. There was a moment of surprise, then recognition. Philip turned to the archer beside him and grabbed his bow. This is my chance to square our ledger, he thought. But when he turned back the knight was gone, lost in the drifting pall of smoke.

LXXVII

THE GREAT HALL had been made into a hospital for the injured. The wounded and dying were carried in and dumped on the floors, to lie there groaning and bleeding. A monk who knew something of herbs had been pressed into service, and the *bons òmes*, who had some reputation for medicine, did what they could. Fabricia and a handful of other women had rolled up their sleeves and joined them, unable to stand the pitiful screams that came from the *donjon*.

Every time she knelt to help some shockingly injured young man she prayed it would not be Philip.

Smoke from the burning siege towers drifted in all through the afternoon, so that the great arches and high windows of the hall seemed to be shrouded in mist. The heat was oppressive, the air putrid and choked with smoke, and there were flies everywhere. A priest wandered between the rows of injured men, stopping to offer the final unction to any who asked for it. She wondered why he had not left. Perhaps, like her, he was more southerner than Catholic.

Tapers were lit. Father Vital mumbled the *consolamentum* over some dying routier and sent him direct to heaven even after a lifetime of rape and murder.

She bent over a longbow-man; he fought for every breath, the arrow that had pierced his leather jerkin still in him. She took a vial of valerian from her tunic and put a drop on his lips to help with his pain.

She felt a warm hand on her shoulder. She looked up; it was Philip.

'I thank God you are unharmed,' she said. She barely recognized him; his face was blackened from smoke, his hair plastered to his skull with sweat. His eyes had a faraway look, as if he were focused on something in the distance. There was blood all over his hands.

'What is happening out there?' she said.

'They burned the *bourg* and attacked the south-east wall. We have beaten them back, for now.'

'Now what will happen?'

'They have lost a lot of men. I doubt they will try another assault very soon. If they cannot scale the walls they will try and bring them down instead.'

Suddenly the ground shook under their feet. It sounded as if the *donjon* had crashed into the square. She gasped and put out a hand to steady herself against one of the pillars. 'What was that?'

'They waste no time. It has started already.'

'It sounded as if the whole castle just came down.'

'It is the trebuchet.'

'What is that?'

'Remember when we were in the caves, you thought you heard thunder? It is a siege engine, it looks like an immense sling; they hauled it up here with a team of oxen. It is the first time I have seen one, though I had lately heard of them. It seems one of the King's engineers thought to use counterweights and pivots on his siege machines instead of the old way of twisted ropes. I am told it is so complex, they employ specialist carpenters to work it. It hurls boulders the size of Paris. So for now we are done with honour and courage, our survival is down to men in aprons and pulley systems.'

'What chance do we have, seigneur?'

'Summer is nearly over,' he said, wiping a lather of sweat from his face and smearing the soot across his cheeks. 'They have only an army of volunteers. As soon as the weather turns they will want to go home. We do not need to win this battle, we just have to hold on for a few weeks.'

LXXVIII

THE CRUSADERS HAULED the trebuchet as close as they dared to the fortress, just out of range of Raimon's crossbow-men. They could see them from the ramparts, forty or fifty men beetling over the infernal machine, finally hurling a massive boulder over the walls. At first the missiles shattered in the courtyard or into the stables or the church, killing or injuring a handful of townspeople or refugees each time. It took them long enough to gauge the height and range, Philip thought, but once they did, the rocks smashed consistently into the upper works of the south-west wall. The bombardment continued day and night.

The archers in the barbican towers wasted many of their bolts trying to pick off the engineers but finally Raimon ordered them to stop and save their ammunition.

Clouds of dust rose at each strike on the walls. But they held, for now.

The *crosat* commander put the rest of his engineers to work building petraries, small wooden catapults built on a trestle frame. They cut down all the holm oaks that grew in the hollows, and used gangs of pilgrims to pull them over the rocks and up the tongues of the spurs to the high ground. They even sent their children scurrying through the *garrigue* to fetch small limestone and granite rocks to hurl down at them.

The long summer dragged on. The stink of the crowded citadel was unbearable. The flies drove them mad and the levels in the water cistern dropped alarmingly.

Anselm found employment once more, trying to repair the damage done to the wall by the trebuchet. He hardly slept. Suddenly he had fire in him again; he stood taller and had a purpose about him. When he was not building stone barricades or reinforcing walls he carried rocks for the mangonels, large slingshots that had been built on the towers under Raimon's orders so that they might give the *crosatz* a taste of what it was like to have their own dinners interrupted by falling masonry.

'You should go up there and help,' Anselm said to Fabricia. 'There are women, even children, carrying rocks up to the towers. Some of the women even work the slings themselves.'

She shook her head. 'I won't kill, Papa.'

'Have you gone soft in the head, like your mother? Why should we show these northerners any mercy? They will butcher us all if we do not defeat them. Will you not even defend yourself?'

But she was resolute. 'I will have no hand in killing,' she said. 'Not ever.'

*

That night Elionor finally took her leave of them.

Anselm had churched her the year Jerusalem fell to the Saracen, perhaps a poor omen, but they had been happy enough over the intervening years. But after that night, she said, she could no longer be his wife; she could not sleep with him, or live under his roof, should he ever find one again. She would take the robes of a *bona femna*, and live a holy life.

They whispered their goodbyes in the candlelight, sitting on the floor of the church. It might be better, Fabricia thought, if she were going away, instead of merely crossing the nave of the church to sleep with the rest of the heretic priests. Seeing her every day would only make it harder for him to accept her decision.

When they had done Anselm walked out of the church, tears in his beard, his face creased in anguish. Once outside he wept aloud, something she had never seen him do, and the sound he made was more like the keening of an injured bird. He would accept no consolation, from her or from anyone. But when he was done he went back up to the ramparts to fetch more rocks for the mangonel, working like a man possessed with devils.

*

Fabricia watched while Father Vital murmured his prayers over her mother in the company of several of his fellow priests and deacons.

He placed the Gospel of John upon her head. 'May God bring you to a good end,' he said. He recited the Benedictus, then the Adoremus three times, and said the paternoster seven times. Elionor spoke her vows and it was done.

She said goodbye to her daughter, embracing her stiffly, and followed Father Vital and the other *bons òmes* out of the church.

*

She woke to find a small boy shaking her by the shoulder. 'Fabricia,' he said. 'She's gone.' It was the urchin, Loup.

Fabricia had been all day at the great hall, mixing herbs and medicines for the wounded soldiers. Exhausted, she had fallen asleep in a quiet corner. She could no longer sleep in the church, for always there was someone wanting her to lay hands.

'Who has gone?' she said.

Loup did not answer, only beckoned her to follow. She stumbled to her feet and went after him. He led her across the cobbled court-yard, now littered with rocks and bodies, to the church. Guilhemeta lay in the nave, cold and blue. Her eyes were open. Fabricia could not close them so she laid her scarf over her face.

'You said you could heal her,' Loup said.

'I never say that to anyone,' she told him. 'People ask me to do things but I have never promised anything, ever. Now go and fetch the Baron de Vercy. Quickly!'

*

Philip bent down to examine her, looking for the tell-tale signs of pestilence. If she had the plague then we are all done for, he thought. He called over two of Raimon's soldiers. 'Get her out of here,' he said. Perhaps too little, too late. Foul humours could spread quickly in conditions like this.

Loup sat slumped against the wall, his head between his knees.

A crowd had gathered. One of the women hissed at Fabricia and an old man spat at her feet. 'What's wrong with them?' Philip said.

'They say I am a fraud, that I said I could heal their children when I could not. I never said I could heal. They believed it, I didn't.'

Another man ventured closer, shouting at her. Philip pushed him back. He took Fabricia's hand and led her outside, and they found a quiet corner in the stables. Fabricia peeled off her gloves and unwrapped one of the bindings on her hands. 'Look,' she said. There were fresh scabs on the wounds; they had crusted almost dry.

'What does it mean?' he asked her.

'Whatever this thing is, it's leaving me.'

'Isn't that what you wanted?'

'Yes, it's what I wanted. But it was selfish of me.'

'I don't understand.'

'It was *you*. Ever since that night, something has been different. You brought me back to my body, to this earth. I do not regret it, but . . . it feels like it cut the thread that led to heaven.'

'But you said yourself you don't understand how this thing happened to you. By your own reasoning how can you know why it has stopped?'

She shrugged and put the bandages back on her hands. 'What will you do,' she asked him 'if we survive this?'

'I don't know. Even if I live out this siege, I will have to face tomorrow without my lands and my castle and my good name as Baron of Vercy. What might I do then?'

'Yet you have thought about it.'

She was right, he had thought about it, and he felt ashamed that she could read him so easily. 'I suppose I might go to Aragon and pledge my services to the King there, though it is unlikely he will accept an excommunicate. Or perhaps the Count of Foix will employ me; I can join all the other southern *faidits* in his court.'

'Have you forgotten asking God for a hundred times a hundred nights with me?'

'How might I keep a wife when I do not know if I can keep myself?'

'I will not press you on the promises you made in the forest,' she said. 'I knew then that you did not mean what you said. You are a good man, seigneur, but I am no foolish girl. You are yet young. If you pay your penance to the Pope, you could find yourself back in your castle before the spring and nothing lost.'

He laughed. 'Yes, I suppose that would be the wise course.'

'Then you should take it.'

He could not answer her. Once he had believed in miracles; it had brought him here to this accursed country, and what good had come of it? And yet from the heart of his own darkness he had met another kind of miracle, a witch with Christ's wounds on her hands and feet who said she had foreseen him in a dream and then saved his life simply with her prayers. Or so some said. What was he to think or believe?

As to the future: it would be easier to die here at Montaillet. He could not imagine a future with his fiefdom and its gloomy castle and fiery wife – or without it.

And what of this woman? How should he reconcile his feelings for a commoner and a witch?

No, easier to die here on the walls. It was living that would make a coward of him.

He saw Raimon striding from the *donjon* with his escort and he walked away, grateful for the intrusion, and crossed the court to meet him.

*

'You should get rid of the body as soon as you can,' Philip said. 'I suspect this woman had some kind of pestilence.'

'If it is plague then it is already too late,' Raimon said. But he turned to his soldiers and gave the order anyway. There was no room to bury the dead inside Montaillet. All they could do was put them into shrouds and pitch them over the north wall into the river.

The ground shuddered as another massive limestone boulder crashed into the walls. Raimon shook his head. 'I have heard de Montfort pays his siege engineers twenty livres a day. Can you imagine? Devil-fuckers! They have no courage and no honour and they grow fat just by throwing rocks at us.' He went to the nave and looked out of the portal towards the barbican. 'I have spoken to the mason – what is his name? Bérenger. He is trying to strengthen the wall but he says that another two or three days of this and it will start to crumble. We have to do something about that infernal machine.'

It was getting on to dusk. Flambeaux bobbed in the streets and ramparts as men toiled at a barricade they were building behind the weakened wall. A horn sounded the alarm at the main gate.

Probably nothing; the sentries were nervous, jumping at shadows.

'Is there a hidden way out of this castle?'

'You wish to leave us?'

'I wish to save you.'

Raimon hesitated. 'Perhaps. On the south-east side, there is a fissure in the rock, just as it falls to the ravine. When the fortress was built an escape tunnel was mined there, just below the cistern.'

'Then we should use it. I have noticed the horses are getting restless, all this time in the stables with no room to gallop. We could give them some exercise tonight.'

Raimon smiled, for the first time in days. 'You think we should try and destroy the trebuchet?'

'That, or our wall comes down. What other choice is there?'

'But who would risk such an expedition?'

'The kind of man, I suppose, who would ride alone against two score.'

'Are you in such a hurry to meet God, Frenchman?'

'More than He is to meet me.'

'I knew fortune brought you to Montaillet for a reason. All right. Let us hurry and make ready.'

LXXIX

SINCE THAT FIRST day the great hall had emptied by natural attrition; men either recovered and went back to the walls, or they died. But there was still a daily influx of injuries, mostly from the bombardment of rocks and stones.

An archer had fallen from the parapet and broken his ankle, but the wound was open and had become infected. Elionor had found a store of dried herbs that the *bons òmes* had led her to, and with it she helped Fabricia mix a concoction of knitbone root and leaves in hot wax and apply it to the poor man's leg as a compress.

When she had done she looked up and found Philip watching her. The candlelight made him look grim, as if he was about to impart bad news. Then suddenly he flashed a smile, and it was like the sun coming out from behind dark clouds.

'I need to talk to you,' he said. He took her hand and led her into a private corner, behind a pillar. 'Fabricia,' he said. 'It's a beautiful name.'

'What is wrong, seigneur?'

He kissed her, without warning.

'You could get this anywhere,' she whispered. 'I am just a girl like any other.'

'No, you're not.' She wondered if he would take her, right there against the pillar. But then he pulled away. He just held her face in his hands, his breathing ragged. 'You are my every hope,' he said, and then he left, leaving her shaken and mystified.

*

So what will happen if you do not come back tonight? he thought. He had gone there, intending to say goodbye, but found he could not. Perhaps there was another way. There was no law that said that only a landed baron might be happy with his lot. He had found joy once with Alezaïs, he might yet find it again.

But first they must do something about the giant siege engine, and if he came back from the raid he might think again about what he would do about the stonemason's daughter.

*

It was chill tonight in the castle keep, autumn not far off. Loup huddled in the straw, his knees to his chest. Some soldiers sat by the hearth talking in low voices, chewing on bread and salted pork.

'Now see you, Loup,' Philip said, crouching beside him. He nodded at two old men lying close by with their cloaks wrapped around themselves. 'You are a fortunate lad, you sleep with royalty tonight. That old man lying on his back and snoring like a hog once had a castle and lands in the Minervois. The man next to him is his cousin. Tonight they sleep with the common round, same as you and I.'

'Will you sleep here tonight, seigneur?'

'Not tonight. There is something I have to do.'

'Can I come with you?'

'Not on this errand.'

Loup tucked his hands inside his jerkin and shivered. 'And when the siege is ended, seigneur? Shall I come with you then?'

There had been a bitch once, in the castle, that had died giving birth to its pups. Only one of the litter had survived. It had attached itself to the tomcat they kept to eat the mice, and followed it faithfully every day even though it showed not the slightest interest in it. Loup is just like that puppy, he thought. 'I could have made you part of my household, if I still had one. Found a job for you in the scullery. But I no longer have a household.'

'Did I not hear you say that you once had servants, seigneur? And a castle? And a horse?

'I had a whole stable of horses.'

'And a wife? And meat to eat every day?'

'Yes. And a feather bed with bolsters and a curtain around it.'

Loup blinked. 'Then if life had given you such fortune, why was it not enough?'

A good question, he supposed, and it would take the rest of the night to answer it. He ruffled the boy's hair, and told him to go to sleep.

*

That night Fabricia risked a return to the church. She did not like the thought of her father sleeping alone in there. By now she had grown accustomed to the stink of so many people crammed inside, and could even sleep through the shock of the rocks hitting the south wall, though it rattled dust from the ceiling and the church shook as if it might crash down around them. No one recognized her in the dark, so there were no curses or entreaties tonight.

She lay down on the flagstones next to him, listened to his slow and even breathing. 'Papa,' she whispered. 'Are you awake?'

'I am awake. What is it, little rabbit?'

'What will we do? When the *crosatz* go home?'

'There will always be work for stonemasons, especially now, with half the country in ruins. I will go back to work and we will see about finding you a husband, I suppose. Though I have not much of a dowry to offer anyone now.'

'Do you think the *crosatz* will go home?'

'What does your fine lord say?'

'He thinks that as soon as the weather turns they will all go back to France.'

'Well then, he would know more about these things than us. All I know is that the Count of Toulouse is vassal to the King of Aragon so sooner or later that fine Spanish gentleman must come with his army and throw these Frenchmen out, if they don't go of their own accord.'

'What will we do without Mama?'

Anselm was silent for a long time. Elionor's defection had affected them more deeply than even the invading *crosatz*, in truth. 'I'll survive. It's you I am worried about. Without dowry, you could end up someone's mistress and never the wife. If only Pèire had watched where he was stepping that day!'

A woman in a black hood and robe knelt down behind him. She leaned over and kissed his cheek, then she did the same to Fabricia.

'Goodnight, sweet ones,' she whispered. '*Dieu vos benesiga* – God bless you!'

Anselm did not move and did not answer. The dark-robed figure moved away again, into the shadows. 'I have never understood that woman,' he said and rolled over towards the wall.

LXXX

THERE WAS A natural fissure in the rock, facing the gorge, just below the east wall. It led to a limestone cavern beneath the fortress and the engineer, when it had been built, had cut a tunnel directly to it from a chamber under the barbican. Philip had been spared a troop of thirty of Trencavel's best chevaliers for the expedition against the trebuchet and now they led their horses down the steep cobblestoned passage and gathered together in the cave. Some of them had baskets of straw and flasks of oil strapped to their saddles.

Philip had ordered sacking tied around the horses' hooves to muffle them. Surprise was their only advantage. The *crosatz* would expect any sortie to come from the main gate, not from the east.

Raimon had told him that there was a narrow path that led along the side of the gorge, almost invisible beneath the fortress walls. 'Even the goats won't go there,' he had said. 'You won't be able to use torches, but there is a full moon to guide you. Try not to look down.' He held a flambeau high above his head and led the way to the tunnel entrance. 'I still don't understand why you're risking your neck like this,' Raimon said. 'It's not your fight.'

'They made it my fight.'

Raimon wished him God speed. Philip nodded and led the palfrey they had given him out of the cave, looking for the path. It fought the bridle, the flaming torch making it skittish. He kept a firm grip.

It was a clear night; the moon like a new-minted silver coin was reflected in the river far below. The horse slid on a loose stone and scrambled for its footing. He did not even hear the rock hit the bottom. They must be on an overhang, he thought, and despite what Raimon had said to him he chanced one quick look down and could see nothing.

Eventually he reached flatter ground and looked up, saw a sentry on the high barbican, his pikestaff silhouetted against the night sky.

He waited for the rest of his squadron to reach him. No one had fallen into the chasm; so far so good. They mounted their horses and started at a walk towards the crusader camp.

He could see the trebuchet in the moonlight; he could have found it blindfolded anyway, had watched it for days now pounding them with missile after missile while he stood with his fists clenched on the parapets. He knew its size and position as well as he knew his own hand.

But he could have found it anyway; the bastards who worked it laboured by night as well as day and so their post was well lit with torches; they even had a cosy log fire to keep them warm on these first cold nights of autumn. They like making war on others well enough, he thought, because they think themselves safe from all retribution. Let us see now how much they like a war that is brought to *them*.

He wanted to let his horse have its head, but the ground was broken and dangerous and he planned only to come at the gallop for the last hundred paces. Holding back, knowing the right moment, this was the hardest thing.

He hoped their luck would hold.

But it didn't.

*

There were no sentries, not on this side of the camp. But one of the *crosatz* had stumbled out of his blanket to relieve himself and as they crested a small rise they came across him standing right in front of them, swaying sleepily as he directed his stream against a small bush. Philip spurred forward to silence him before he could shout an alarm but he was too late. The man had time to let out one piercing scream before he cut him down.

There was nothing for it but to start their charge. But they were too far away and by the time they reached the trebuchet the engineers had already scattered. They cut a few of them down, but not enough; the rest they lost in the dark.

Some of his men attacked the trebuchet with axes, while those carrying baskets had already dismounted and were stuffing the straw under the machine. Another doused the straw with oil and lit it with one of the *crosatz'* own torches.

'Burn!' one of the chevaliers shouted. 'Burn, burn, burn!'

The alarm had been raised through the camp with trumpets and shouts and drums. Philip knew the fire would make them easy targets so he ordered his men to withdraw and wait for the counterattack from the shadows. They could not make their escape yet. They had to stop the crusaders from dousing the flames before they had properly taken hold.

The first crusaders rushed in, still struggling into their armour, and Philip and his chevaliers wheeled in from the dark and cut them down. But there were too many of them streaming out of the camp now. They were everywhere, in and around and behind them, trying to drag them from their horses.

Philip slashed wildly with his sword. Why did it take dry timber so long to burn at the end of such a long summer?

Someone grabbed his horse's bridle and he slashed down with his sword and the man disappeared screaming under the hooves. But close by he saw another of his chevaliers pulled from the saddle, and then another.

A shower of sparks rose from the trebuchet. Suddenly she was fully ablaze. Just as well, he thought, for we have to get out of here now. He wheeled his horse around and signalled for his men to follow him. Another wave of *crosatz* streamed towards them. There was just one last card to play.

He raised his sword. 'The gates are open!' he screamed at them. 'Follow me! For God and de Montfort!' And the crusaders cheered him and followed as he galloped right through the middle of them towards Montaillet.

*

He spurred his palfrey as hard as he dared across the broken ground and only stopped when he was in the shadow of the fortress walls. He turned in the saddle. Only a pitiful number of riders were still with him. They could not wait. The crusaders were streaming after them, thinking it was an attack on the gates.

He led the surviving cavalry towards the cliffs, losing their pursuers in the dark. Then he ordered them to dismount and they walked their horses the rest of the way down the crumbling path back to the cave. Raimon and his men were waiting for them. 'Did you do it?' Raimon shouted when he saw him.

'We did. With any luck it's still burning.'

'And you? Are you all right?'

'I don't know,' Philip said. He handed over his reins and and sat down on a rock. In the light of Raimon's torch he discovered an ugly sword slash between his greaves and shin. He had not even felt it, but it hurt him now, though, well enough.

'How many men did we lose?' he said.

Raimon counted the heads. 'A dozen and one by my count. It might be worth it, if the trebuchet is destroyed.'

'It's well alight. In the morning we will see if we did damage enough to justify the lives of thirteen good men.'

*

But they did not lose thirteen men; only six. Seven of Philip's men were sent back the next day, without noses, lips and eyes. One they only half-blinded, so he could lead the others.

Raimon cut himself with his sword and swore vengeance with his own blood when he saw them. The rest of the day he spent in silent rage. The trebuchet was at least charred ashes, and was still smoking at first light. Was it worth what was done to those men? Philip wondered. They had saved the fortress, so he supposed it could be counted as success. He hoped they would think so too.

'Thank God we are fighting God's own army,' Raimon said when finally he was calm enough to speak. 'For I should hate to fight the Devil's!'

*

Saints; no saints. Hell; no hell. God loves us; God will destroy us. Jesus was meek and mild so I will murder you if you do not eat his body in this bread. Jesus died on the cross; Jesus did not die on the cross.

He had grown tired of men arguing over it; he had especially grown tired of men dying over it.

Did you not once have a castle? Why was it not enough?

What would be enough, then, if not a castle and a horse and servants and a beautiful wife? This: a narrow bed in a shuttered room with no servants but some bread and cheese on the table and a woman he loved in his bed and a plump and healthy baby in the trundle. *Not much but enough.* Oh, and to be left in peace. To not have friends butchered because of him, not to be haunted by the ghosts of the men he himself had killed.

Enough: to tease from the unsmiling gods some glimmer of grace, some transigence in their unflinching retribution.

The softness of a woman's breast. The cooing of an infant. The rising of the sun.

Enough.

*

Fabricia used two thin strips of linen to bind the lips of the wound together, then brought a poultice of herbs and bound it to his leg. 'I thought that we had run out of medicines for the wounded,' he said, 'that you had used them all.'

'I had one saved, in case you were hurt.'

'That is unjust to these other men. They bleed as I do.'

'Why did you not tell me what you were going to do? I might not have seen you again.'

'I would rather do my duty and leave the rest to my fate than go through long farewells. It unnerves me. As it is, you slept through my moments of danger and now it is done and I am here safe.'

'How many men did you kill?'

'I do not know. It was a bloody fight in the darkness and when all is done, I try not to think too much about it.'

'Do they never disturb your sleep, the heads and the limbs you have hacked off?'

'If I did not kill them, they would kill me.'

'I just know I could never do it, seigneur. I could never kill a man. I would always see his blood on my hands.'

'In times of peace we hunt meat in the forest, or we die. And in times of war we defend ourselves from those who would kill us. It is the way of things.' He stood up, testing his weight on the injured leg. 'The *bons òmes* would disagree with me. They are good and holy men, I allow. But they are not me. That night when the wolves were circling us, would you have rather it was Père Vital with you in the dark?'

She did not answer.

'Because I cannot be like you, it does not mean I do not treasure you. Whatever it was that you did when you laid your hands on people, it gave them hope. I saw it in their faces. Whether you have the gift or not, it makes them think that God has not abandoned them. The possibility of a miracle is a precious thing, for everyone. It is a glimpse of the divine amidst all the suffering. You matter a great deal, and not just to me.' He stood up. 'Thank you again for your kindness,' he said, and limped away.

LXXXI

RAIMON ORDERED HIS men to knock down the stables and a grainhouse to get stones for the mangonels; Anselm supervised repairs to the walls damaged by the trebuchet; they dug ditches and built barricades behind the iron-bound oak doors of the main gate, knowing that this was where the *crosatz* would concentrate their next attack.

The burghers raised blisters on their soft merchants' hands, serving as apprentice masons or carpenters; their wives and daughters ran soup kitchens or repaired chain mail or tended the injured or sick, as Fabricia did, their skirts knotted up above their knees. Everyone had been pressed into service, even the children, carrying armfuls of planks or broken beams up shaky ladders for fuel for the cauldrons.

By now the *crosatz* were desperate. They had lost their main weapon and though they still bombarded them night and day with their smaller catapults, they could no longer hurl stones large enough to weaken the walls.

Philip did not believe a frontal assault on the walls could succeed. But time was running out; Montaillet had only one cistern for the whole citadel and it was almost dry. If the rains did not come soon, they would be forced to parlay on whatever terms they could get. Philip did not hold out much hope of mercy from the butchers camped below.

The other problem would not be remedied by the weather, and that was the legacy left them by Guilhemeta.

*

The great hall was packed with bodies. The stench would fell a horse, Philip thought. Soldiers, children and women lay sprawled together on the flagstones, groaning, retching, dying. *Half the garrison must be down here.*

Fabricia was moving among the sick, rationing the scarce medicine they had. She saw him standing on the steps and picked her way through the chaos towards him.

'Pray God they do not attack us now,' she said. 'We have not even room for all the sick, there would be nowhere to put any wounded.'

'There would be scarce be any left to defend us,' he said. 'This is twice as many as yesterday.'

'My mother found some angelica root in the storehouse. We powdered it and mixed it with wine, for there is hardly any water to give them. It will help them if they can keep it down, but most retch it right up again.'

'It was the woman, Guilhemeta.'

'But Loup never got sick. Nor I, and I laid hands on her.'

He looked at her hands. She still wore her gloves but they no longer had those familiar brown bloodstains. 'A pity you cannot still perform your miracles, Fabricia.'

There was a blast of trumpets from the main gate, followed by the urgent clamour of the bells from the church. 'They are going to storm the walls,' she said.

'It may be a false alarm.'

'I think they can smell the sickness. Somehow they *know*.'

'Or they are as desperate as we are,' he said and ran back up the steps to join the muster.

*

The *crosatz* waited until the setting sun blinded the garrison on the western wall. Raimon's soldiers could barely make them out, with the sun in their faces, but they could hear them well enough, beating the earth with their pikes. The rabble of pilgrims that followed them were singing the *Veni Sancte Spiritus*.

Something smashed into the court below. It was the blackened head of one of the soldiers they had killed during the sally against the trebuchet.

'Only half my soldiers are still standing,' Raimon said.

'Then we will have to fight twice as fiercely,' Philip said.

Martín Navarese stood next to him, legs akimbo, his sword tip resting on the stones. He spat over the wall. 'French bastards.'

Loup stood at Raimon's other shoulder holding a slingshot, a pile of stones at his feet. There were three women at one of the mangonels; Anselm the stonemason waited beside them, bare-chested in the sun, loading boulders into the slings. So it's come to this, Philip thought. Women and children to do the killing now.

The sun hovered just two fingers above the horizon when they attacked, their wooden cats swaying and bumping across the plateau. A wagon, covered with a tough canopy of cowhide, slammed against the wall. The *crosatz* sappers would be under there, Philip knew, trying to dig under the wall. Anselm hurled heavy rocks down on them, single-handed, while the women dropped flaming brands. The canopy soon bristled with wasted arrows and bolts.

A cauldron of blazing oil went over the side and the leather fizzed with pitch and caught fire, sending a plume of black smoke into the air. Men ran shrieking with their clothes alight back to the crusader lines. The archers picked them off as they ran.

Now the rest of the army came on, throwing ladders against the walls for the mercenaries and the foot soldiers. If we can throw them back this one last time, he thought, I think we will be safe.

*

'Don't be angry at me,' Elionor said. She had joined all the other *bons òmes* helping tend the sick in the great hall. She no longer looked like Mama; she had shorn her long salt-and-pepper hair so that it was short like a man's. The black hooded robe they had given her was too large and her thin frame was lost inside it.

'I'm not angry, Mama,' Fabricia lied. *I am furious.* You abandoned me and you abandoned Papa when we needed you most. We all risk dying unshriven, why couldn't you? For us?

'I am following my heart in this. We must all follow our hearts.'

Elionor trailed her around, trying to engage her in private debate, perhaps seeking an absolution. Fabricia stopped and listened to the noise from outside. The battle had been joined; soon the wounded would start arriving. Where would they put them?

The worst of it was not knowing what was happening up there. Any moment she might see those brutes with scarlet crosses on their surcoats advancing down the steps, their swords drawn.

'Please, my Fabricia, my little one. We don't know how much time we have left. Let us not part this way.'

Two men staggered down the steps into the cellar carrying a wounded archer. They slipped on a slick of blood and tumbled. 'Someone help us,' one of them said. 'There's too many for us to bring on our own!'

Fabricia started up the stairs after them, but Elionor caught her wrist. 'Stay here! Don't put yourself in harm's way!'

Fabricia shook herself free. She followed the men up the steps and ran after them to the gatehouse. They clambered up the wooden ladder to the lower floor and urged her to follow. When she got there, she stopped, stunned by the heat and the noise. The framework of planks and beams shook under her feet, and then a man dropped from a hatchway above, an arrow through his neck. He lay at her feet, writhing and gurgling and kicking for a few moments, and then he died.

'Help me,' someone said.

She turned around. A man – she realized she knew him, it was the tinker from Saint-Ybars! – was trying to drag a sled of stones up the wooden ladder. He reached out his hand towards her, then gave a shout of surprise and reached behind him. He twisted around, but could not see the arrow that had lodged in his back. He glared at Fabricia as if she were the one who had fired it, then he let go of the ladder and dropped out of sight.

Philip ran towards her along the parapet with a dozen armed men behind him. He ordered them up the steps. 'Get out of here!' he shouted at her. 'We are overrun! You have to get out!'

Three *crosatz* jumped down the wooden ladder from the upper floor. Philip charged them and they fell back. One on one they were no match for him, she could see, for they were poorly armoured and did not have his imposing height and physique. But after they recovered from the surprise of his rushed assault, their numbers told and they forced him to retreat.

He still had time to grab her and almost bodily hurl her down the ladder.

She started to clamber back down. And what then? she thought. Leave him to face the three of them on his own?

She climbed back up again.

The floor of the gatehouse was slippery with blood. Two of them were down, but Philip had lost his sword in the mêlée, and the other *crosat* was standing over him, beating him repeatedly with his sword. Philip was keeping him at bay with just his shield.

Philip's blade lay on the boards in front of her. She picked it up, testing the weight of it. She knew she could not lift it above her head, as the *crosat* was doing, but if she could swing it into the man's back it should stop him right enough. He had only a thick leather jerkin as armour; the steel blade would go straight through it and slice him open.

The man raised his sword again. Philip watched her, pleading with his eyes.

Do it. *Do it!*

But she couldn't. She dropped the sword and instead jumped on the man's back, one arm around his neck, the other clawing at his sword arm. It might have given Philip time to recover if she had been able to hold on, but the crusader was too strong for her and shrugged her off easily, hurling her against the wall.

Philip threw himself at the soldier to protect her, lost his shield in the struggle and fell. Now he was defenceless as the *crosat* came at him a third time.

Something hit the man in the face, and he howled in pain and staggered back. It gave Philip enough time to grab his sword and make the killing stroke, two-handed, bringing the blade up in a practised arc just below the man's midriff and burying it almost to the hilt in his chest.

Fabricia looked around for their unlikely saviour. Loup stood framed in the doorway of the gatehouse, his slingshot in his right hand. He grinned at Philip. 'I just saved your life,' he said. 'Now you owe me.'

LXXXII

THE CHURCH BELLS pealed across the citadel, announcing the victory. The *crosatz* had retreated; even with only half the garrison standing they had somehow beaten them back. Philip slumped to his haunches and took off his helm. He closed his eyes and rested his head against the wall.

Trencavel's soldiers were already dragging the bodies of the dead crusaders across the courtyard, tossing them over the northern wall into the gorge. *Get them out before they bloat and stink. And damn them all.*

At one point they had had their ladders on the gatehouse and the battering ram at the main gate. He had thought it was over. It was the women and the old men that saved them, pouring pitch and boiling water from the barbican, tipping back the ladders, making up in numbers and enthusiasm what they lacked in archers and crossbows and men-at-arms.

He stumbled as he made his way back to the *donjon*. He had never been so tired.

He saw Navarese's routiers below the south-east wall, a score of them, jeering and kicking. Trencavel's own soldiers watched them, but stood off, wary of them. He suspected he knew what this was about and he unsheathed his sword and went over to stop it.

Their crusader prisoner had been stripped and his hands were tied with hemp behind his back. He was writhing on the cobblestones like an animal, blood and saliva in his beard. The mercenaries were prodding him with their lances, but enough only to make him bleed, and scream.

He pushed them aside. The stink of them! They were like a pack of wild animals.

'What is happening here?' he shouted.

'Stay out of this,' Navarese said. 'He is our prisoner. It is none of your business what we do with him.'

'Where is your honour, man?'

'Honour? What has honour to do with anything here? You pay us to fight for you; we will fight. Don't talk to me about honour, you hypocrite.'

'Just kill him and be done with it.'

'You saw what they did to our prisoners. They gouged out their eyes and cut off their faces. Why should this pig expect any different?'

Philip did not answer. He stared at the desperate, bloody thing on the ground at his feet and wondered what this man would do if the tables were turned. 'Who is your lord?' he said to him. He was still crying, so Philip put his boot on his throat to get his attention. 'Who is your lord?' he repeated.

'Gilles de Soissons of Normandy,' he panted. 'Please, Lord, help me. I –'

'What is his device?'

'We have three blue eagles . . .'

Navarese kicked him into silence. 'What is this? What does it matter?'

So, he *was* one of them, Philip thought, one of the men who had stood around, laughing, just like these routiers, when they had blinded Renaut. And now the tables were turned. Let him know then what it is like to have someone do it to him, let him taste the piercing agony and humiliation to the dregs. It is a kind of justice.

And then you'll become just like them, he heard Renaut say. *Is that what you want? Is that what you think I want?*

Philip took off the man's head with one quick blow and stepped back.

There was a shocked silence. Then Navarese stepped close up, eyes red, every muscle twitching. He stabbed a forefinger into his chest. 'You Devil-fucker! You whoreson piece of God-fucking goat-shit. You Frenchman. You whore!' He stood there, prodding him with his finger as if it were a red-hot fork. But the chain mail and the baron's chest were implacable. The words and the threats bounced off.

'Now you can do what you want to him,' Philip said.

'You have made an enemy here today!'

'You will have to wait your turn, I have too many to count.' Philip said and walked away, daring him to strike at his back. But for all his foul mouth, he did not dare.

*

Fabricia sat on the steps of the church, her head between her knees. Everywhere the smell of death. He sat down beside her.

'I knew your trade before this, seigneur, I have seen other men like you fighting and killing each other. But this is the first time I ever saw *you* do it, with my own eyes. The way you killed that man! Not a moment's hesitation. And so expertly done, like you were slaughtering some barnyard animal.'

'It is what a warrior does. I was trained for it since I was a child. I am a knight, Fabricia, not a baker. Or a stonemason. I kill or I am killed, it is the law I live by, the law that has kept you and all these other women and children from their deaths here today.'

'I am not accusing you, seigneur, it is just I never expected to be so shocked when I finally saw it.'

'Why didn't you use that sword yourself? You had the opportunity. He might have killed us both.'

'I told you, I cannot kill. I cannot have another man's death on my conscience, no matter who he is.'

'You do understand that we are only talking like this, here, now, because you have the luxury of being virtuous while I take it upon myself to sin.'

'Perhaps then we have both seen the worst of each other today.'

'We come from different worlds, Fabricia. I suppose it was inevitable that one day we would.'

LXXXIII

RAIMON WAS A young man grown suddenly old. There were lines on his face where there had been none before. His eyes were sunken into plum-coloured bruises in his head from the strain of command and from lack of sleep.

He stood on the barbican with his eyes closed, letting the rain run down his face. 'Fine weather at last,' he said.

'At last,' Philip said.

Such a storm; it had half filled the cistern in a single night. The weather had turned so quickly; Philip had gone to sleep sunburned and woken up shivering with cold.

Now a chill mist hung above the trees behind the crusader encampment. Below them a vulture stood atop one of the bodies below the walls, occasionally lowering its beak to take a leisurely breakfast.

'Perhaps they will give up and go home now,' Raimon said.

*

But they did not give up and go home. Later that day a sentry at the south barbican shouted the alarm. Raimon and Philip ran up the steps to the parapet and stared down the ridge towards the crusader camp. A column of men was riding up the road from the Toulousain and by the standards and pennants they carried he realized it must be Simon de Montfort himself come from Carcassonne to join the assault on Montaillet. He had twenty knights with him. He had also brought another one of his trebuchets.

*

'One in five of my fighting men is dead,' Raimon said. 'Another one in five has succumbed to, or is yet weak from, the fever that woman brought with her. We have enough water, thanks be to God for last

316

night's storm, but we do not have soldiers to drink it all. If they attack again, this time they will overrun us.' He pointed to the crude map, drawn in chalk on the oak table in the centre of the room. 'They will position the trebuchet once more against the west wall.' He looked at Anselm, who had been invited to participate in the conference. 'How long?' he said.

'It is already badly damaged. If they start another bombardment . . . three days, at most, and then part of it may come down.'

'What are our choices?' Philip said.

'We pray that winter comes quickly, for they may yet tire of the work once the snows come. Winter here is vicious. Our other choice is to seek help.'

'Help?' Philip said.

'From Count Raymond in Toulouse.'

'Do you think he will come to the aid of a Trencavel army?'

'Who knows? He has allowed the priests to flog him in the cathedral in his own city, he even rode with the *crosatz* at Béziers and at Carcassonne for a time. But still the Church wants to bring him down and while he tries to appease them he loses the chance to strike back. This may be his chance. Half de Montfort's army left him after Carcassonne and now our little army has stalled him here for almost six weeks. He is not invincible. If Raymond joined the fight now we could put an end to this crusade for good.'

'You think he would listen to such reasoning?'

'Perhaps, if someone makes the argument forcefully enough. If he were to come now, we could trap de Montfort here in the mountains and destroy this crusade. If not, the *crosatz* could come back next spring with reinforcements. It is Raymond they are after; he must see that. The longer he hesitates, the surer his fate. My master, the Viscount Trencavel, was no threat to them and look what they did to him. Count Raymond thinks he can play politics but he has to understand that they don't play politics in Rome; they play for eternity. You cannot trust someone who has his eyes on God.'

'But what ambassador could you send that he would listen to?'

'You, seigneur.'

'Me?'

'I will give you ten of my best knights and chevaliers as escort. The men who rode with you when you burned the trebuchet would follow you anywhere after you led them in and out of the crusader camp.'

Philip warmed his hands on the fire. It was a meagre hearth, for they did not have much timber to spare; Anselm needed it all for the extra barricades he and his carpenters were building behind the west wall.

'How might it be done?'

'You can slip out of the castle as before, and there are gullies and ridgelines that will hide you at night. Dampen your horse's hooves with sacking again.' He took Philip's arm and led him to the window. 'You see that ridge? They are camped just below it. If you were to follow the defile on the other side they would not see you. Once you were in the forest you could climb the spur and then down into the valley. You would have to avoid the road to Cabaret but you could follow the river. It would be slow progress but the north star will lead you to the Toulousain.'

'As I understand it, you Trencavels have been at war with Raymond for years. Why would he receive me when my men carry your colours?'

'You are right; we were most often enemies. He may not receive a Trencavel but he may heed a northern knight who has fought against the *crosatz*.'

Philip considered: a suicide mission, he suspected, much like the last one. Raimon made it all sound so easy from high in his barbican. But what did he have to lose anyway? If he stayed here, and did nothing, they would have to surrender or die. This way, at least his fate was in his own hands again.

'All right, find me good men and good horses. I'll do it.'

'*Dieu vos benesiga!* May God grant you speed and a safe passage. But . . .'

'But?'

'But if you don't return I shall not blame you. Just do your best to persuade him. It is all I ask.'

'I will return, with or without Raymond.'

Raimon laughed and shook his head. 'Return? If you do then I shall know you are quite mad, seigneur.'

LXXXIV

LOUP HAD MADE a circle on the wall of the church with a piece of chalky rock that he had found on the ground, probably a piece of some stone slung at them during the night by the *crosatz*. He used it now as target, a measured thirty paces, his slingshot finding the very centre each time.

'I cannot find Fabricia,' Philip said to him.

'She's sick.'

'Sick?'

'She has a fever and retches constantly. Like Guilhemeta.'

'When did this happen?'

'During the night.' He put down the slingshot. 'Is it true you are leaving us?'

'What?'

'You are going as embassy to Count Raymond.'

How did he know? But of course: Anselm.

'Weren't you going to tell me?'

'We will talk later,' he said, and hurried back across the square to the infirmary.

It was cold in the great hall and his breath frosted on the air. Two days ago they had been gagging from heat. Now they froze. 'Fabricia!' he shouted.

Elionor hurried towards him through the rows of the sick. 'Where is she?' he said.

'This way.'

This is impossible, he thought. Fabricia is not the one who gets sick; she is the healer. But Loup had not lied, Fabricia lay on the floor at the far end of the hall, beneath the great arch. She looked wretched, and she did not rouse even when he called her name.

'How bad?' he said to Elionor.

She shook her head. 'Who knows when it is our time? I have asked

319

her if she will take the *consolamentum,* but she refuses. I worry for her soul.'

Philip picked up Fabricia's hand; it was limp and hot. Her face was pink, and slick with sweat, burning up while there was still frost on the barbican. 'Fabricia,' he said again.

Finally her eyelids flickered. 'Seigneur?' She pitched to the side and retched, nothing but bile.

Elionor soaked a linen cloth in a basin of water and put it on her forehead. 'Before now,' she said, 'those with the sickness died for lack of water. Now we have plenty.' She held her head and dribbled a few drops of rainwater into her daughter's mouth. Fabricia coughed but gulped it down gratefully.

'Make her well,' he said.

'It is out of my hands. It is the fate of her spirit that concerns me now.' She slipped away, a hundred others groaning and crying for her attention.

'Fabricia, my heart. Can you hear me?'

She squeezed his hand to let him know that she had.

'I have to leave here. I am going to get help for us.' The flagstones trembled and dust and flakes of mortar drifted down from the ceiling. A woman screamed. The *crosatz* had assembled their new trebuchet and recommenced their bombardment of the citadel. That one was close. It sounded as if it had landed in the courtyard; the engineers were still finding their range with their new equipment.

'I won't ever see you again,' she murmured.

'But you will. I am coming back for you, I promise.'

He looked at her hands. It was the first time he had seen her without gloves or linen bindings. Her wounds were healing over.

She reached up to her throat for the crucifix that Father Marty had given her and ripped at the thin chain. It snapped easily. She pressed it into his palm.

'What's this?'

'If you get . . . across the mountains . . . to Barcelona . . . Marty has a brother . . . Show him this . . . he will help you.'

'I do not need this. I am coming back for you.'

'Take it. Goodbye, seigneur. We had one dawn together. It seems God is jealous to keep the rest.'

*

Mist settled in the gorge: they were above it now, in their own peculiar heaven, looking down at the clouds. The evening was still; then a sudden shower of rain like a hail of small stones whipped against the rocks.

Somewhere in the citadel, Fabricia tossed and groaned in a slick of her own sweat; Anselm grunted as he hefted a large stone into the sling of the mangonel – he had taken to firing boulders into the crusader camp day and night, each of them stamped with his mason's mark; in the *donjon* Loup whimpered in the straw, troubled by bad dreams.

There was the faint sound of a hymn, the pilgrims perhaps, or holy Christian soldiers drunk on wine.

He took out the cross Fabricia had given him and knotted the chain where she had broken it. Then he put it over his head and tucked it inside his shirt.

The cold weather made the ancient scar on his leg ache while he waited to lead his horse into the black rain right under the noses of his enemies. Death in a thousand forms, hers, his, tormented him.

LXXXV

So HERE WE sit in the wind and the drenching rain, Simon thought, our skin tanned like leather from this endless summer, wondering where it all went wrong. For myself I am glad there will be no more mutilations and massacres.

The wind tore at the fine silk of the pavilion and threatened to blow them all into the gorge.

Simon de Montfort himself sat at the head of the table. He looked every bit of his forty-nine years, grey-bearded and sombre, with a face you could break walnuts on. They said he was no ordinary Christian knight, the kind of man who would retain his virtue even in a barrel of whores. But as strong as an ox, by all accounts, and with a will to match.

Father Ortiz was explaining to him the vagaries of their campaigning so far, God earning credit for every advance, Gilles de Soissons the blame for their every setback. However the canvas was painted, it was clear to Simon that the crusade was dissolving into a shambles. De Montfort may have been acclaimed the new lord of the Trencavel lands but that did not make him master of them. Now that winter was getting closer and the Duke of Burgundy and the Count of Nevers had gone home with all their soldiers, de Montfort had no more than thirty knights and their retainers to contain and conquer the south of France.

'I intend to invest the Cathar fortress at Cabaret,' de Montfort said. 'I cannot do that unless I am sure I will not suffer an attack from the rear. It means we must have this fortress in our possession.'

'Now we have the trebuchet,' Gilles said, 'I guarantee we shall bring down the west wall before All Souls' Day.'

'If you had not lost the first one, it would be in our possession now,' Father Ortiz said.

Gilles gave him a poisonous stare. 'No commander could have foreseen such an impudent action.'

'Anticipating the enemy's moves is what a good commander *does*.'

'We have no time to bicker,' de Montfort said. 'What's done is done. God is testing us but he will surely grant us ultimate victory if we keep faith.'

'Amen,' Father Ortiz said.

'I need more men if I am to storm the walls,' Gilles said.

'I do not have more men,' de Montfort said. 'Many of those who rode with us from Lyons have hurried home with the first cold wind. Just this last week two more counts and even two bishops abandoned our holy quest on account of rain. I have barely enough men to garrison the castles we have already won. You will gain victory with what you have.'

Simon wondered how Gilles would react to this news. He had served his forty days of crusading, he could return to Normandy with glory and his place in heaven assured if he wished it. But he showed no sign of weariness with the siege. Simon guessed that it had become a matter of personal honour for him, perhaps even vengeance. He would stay until Montaillet was rubble.

'I suggest we negotiate,' de Montfort said.

'There is no need. If you will only be patient.'

De Montfort rose to his feet. 'I do not have the time to be patient. I am about God's work here! The entire Church is praying for me. We need their surrender, now. Get it for me, any way you can.'

Simon knew little about warfare but he knew this: the conventions of war required the besiegers to spare the lives of any garrison that surrendered to them. That would not sit well with Gilles, not now. 'I came here to kill heretics,' Gilles said, 'not negotiate with them.'

'If you let them go now,' de Montfort said, 'it will not matter, for we will catch them again later. Justice will be served in the end. Trust me on this. But for now, I need Montaillet.'

'Besides, only a few of those inside the citadel are heretics,' Simon pointed out, choosing his moment to speak up. 'Many are good Catholics.'

'A good Catholic does not protect heresy!' Gilles shouted. 'They are all Devil-worshippers to me and they should suffer for it.'

De Montfort turned to Father Ortiz. 'What say you about this?'

'I think that offering to massacre everyone inside the fortress is hardly a good basis for negotiation.'

'I agree,' de Montfort said and looked at Gilles. 'Are you listening to this, my lord?'

'So you would let them all go free?'

'Let those who love the Church swear an oath to her and yes, we will set them free. Those who will not do this, we shall burn.'

'That is ridiculous,' Gilles shouted. 'A man will swear an oath to his donkey if it will save his life!'

'If that is what you think,' Father Ortiz said, 'then I think you misjudge these people. The true heretics would rather face the fire than swear against their godless beliefs. That is precisely what makes them so vile and so dangerous.'

Another gust of wind and Gilles's purple-sheeted pavilion almost gave way to the wind. Let us parlay and be done with it, Simon thought. I cannot stand another day in this vile country.

'That is settled then,' de Montfort said. 'Send them a message under flag of truce that we wish to parlay.'

'I shall not talk any kind of peace to these dogs,' Gilles said.

'Then let your priests do it.' He turned to the friar. 'Can you find a way to put Montaillet in my possession, Father Ortiz?'

Diego smiled. 'If it is God's will,' he said.

LXXXVI

'TODAY A RIDER from the crusader camp approached the main gate under a flag of truce. They have asked for parlay.'

'Then we have them!' Anselm said. 'They would not want to bargain unless they were at breaking point!'

Raimon shrugged his shoulders. 'But then – so are we.'

He looked around at the three men he had invited to his chamber for counsel. They would carry the opinions of the rest: Navarese, the commander of the mercenaries; Bérenger, the giant stonemason who had become spokesman for the refugees and who now knew every stone and every brick in the castle; and the burgher Joan Belot, in his silk breeches, who had been agitating for a truce, and had many sympathizers among the townspeople.

'We should hear what they have to say,' Navarese said. 'We do not have the men to repel another assault.'

'They do not have enough men to make one,' Anselm said. 'Anyone can see how their numbers have diminished since the end of the summer.'

'You are a mason, not a soldier. How would you know what their army is capable of?' Navarese turned to Raimon. 'Why do you listen to him?'

'I agree with the captain,' Belot said. 'Let us hear what they have to say. After all, they say this is a war against heresy, not against us.'

'Of course it is a war against us!' Anselm shouted. 'Look what they did at Béziers, at Carcassonne!'

'Why don't we offer them the heretics in return for the peace?' Belot said. 'See what they say to that.'

Anselm lunged at him and Navarese had to step in between them. Raimon jumped to his feet. 'Gentlemen!'

'There are no heretics!' Anselm shouted. 'There are only we Albigeois and the invaders! How can you speak such filth! The

Cathars have been our neighbours all our lives and what harm have they done us? And you would betray them?'

'You are only saying this because your wife herself is a heretic,' Belot sneered.

'There will be no betrayal,' Raimon said. 'Either we are all saved or none of us.'

The *donjon* shook as another rock thundered into the wall. Someone, somewhere, was screaming. 'If that wall comes down, we are lost,' Navarese said.

'What about the Baron de Vercy?' Anselm said. 'Any news?'

Raimon shook his head.

'He is dead,' Belot said. 'Or if he did get through the crusader lines, which I very much doubt, then he is back in Burgundy by now, feasting from his own table and counting himself the luckiest man alive.'

'We have to parlay,' Navarese repeated.

'Very well,' Raimon told them. 'A third of the garrison is dead from sickness or from the battle. Another third is sick with the fever. We have slaughtered all the animals and we are running out of fresh meat. We have little choice in this. Let us hear what the *crosatz* have to say.'

*

The sun was pitched at such a height that it was shining through a high window and straight into Fabricia's face; the light was like nails piercing her eyes. Her mother was calling her to get out of bed and help with the morning cook fire.

At least it sounded like her mother but she was wearing a black hood so it could not be her. Pèire was right there beside her. Don't forget the cross, someone said. It was Father Marty. He had a pronged tail, like the Devil.

She is dying, someone else said.

They gave her water and afterwards she went into the forest to pick herbs. There was a meadow with daisies but people kept standing in her way, giving her things to mend for them: an arm, a liver, a leg. She tried to push through them.

A wolf showed her the deep gash in its neck from a sword slash and asked her to put her hands there. But when she reached out, the wolf turned into a soldier and tried to throttle her. She opened her eyes to get away from him. Dust motes, each of them as large as a rock, floated around her and when they landed the floor shook.

She was so tired. She had to sleep. Philip was holding her hand. He had an arrow in his chest. 'When are you coming back?' she said.

'I am never coming back,' he told her.

'Fabricia,' Anselm said. She felt him stroke her face. 'You've been very sick,' he said.

'Are you here?'

'I am here.'

'Are you a dream?'

'No dream,' he said. She waited for him to turn into a devil or a snake or spikes but he did not. She slept again.

When she woke up she watched a shadow come out of one of the bodies lying beside her. It went to join the others gathered in the corner. They were scratching their heads and wondering where to go. Someone carried out their bodies and they followed. She wanted to go with them but her flesh was too heavy and would not let her.

Her father said: 'She is burning up. It is like sitting next to the hearth.'

When she woke again it was as if she was lying in grease, everything soaked and stinking. She asked for water and a man in a black robe gave her a cup and said: 'You look much better.' She was hungry. She felt for the cross at her throat and remembered it was gone.

'Philip,' she said.

LXXXVII

Simon rode out of the camp with Father Ortiz. De Montfort stood outside his pavilion with his hands on his hips and watched them go. Gilles did not even bother to get out of his bed. He had been sleeping badly. Simon often heard him moaning and shouting things at night. He has troubled dreams, Father Ortiz had told him. If the commander at Montaillet knew the state of our alliance! Simon thought.

There were still corpses lying among the ruins of the *bourg* from the attack on that first day of the siege, many just charred skeletons now. Others, from their more recent assault, had bloated and turned blue, their vitals scattered over the peninsula by scavengers. The vultures watched him with disdain.

The defenders of Montaillet lined the walls and the barbican to watch their approach. The Trencavel standards whipped in the wind atop the blackened gatehouse. The main gate creaked open.

Three men rode out under the Trencavel gold and black ensign. Surely that could not be their leader? He looked so young.

They pulled up a dozen paces from them. The man at their head – no more than a boy, really – raised his hand. He had one blue eye and one green, Simon noticed. Remarkable.

'I am Raimon Perella,' he said. 'I am the seneschal of Montaillet.'

'I am Father Diego Ortiz. This is Father Simon Jorda.'

'Why is de Montfort not here?'

'He sent us to parlay on his behalf, for this is not a military affair, but an ecclesiastical one.'

'Really? We are here to talk religion? Then why do you not throw holy bibles at us from your siege engines, instead of rocks?'

'We wish to offer you mercy.'

'I was going to offer you the same. You look cold in your tents and it will snow soon. If you leave here now I shall promise not to ride after you and cut you down like the dogs you are.'

Father Ortiz smiled. 'Now you know that will not happen. In a few days our trebuchet will bring down your walls and you will surely beg *our* mercy then. We are here for God's holy purpose. Why did you shut your gates against us?'

'If you are here on God's business why did you bring an army with you?'

'We are here to stamp out heresy.'

'Heresy? There are no heretics in Montaillet. We are all good Christians.'

'If that is so, give us entrance to your fortress and we will all say a mass together and then leave you in peace.'

'And if we don't?'

'Simon de Montfort wants this castle. He has more siege engines on the way from Carcassonne in order to secure it. Do not misjudge his determination to have his way. But if you make accommodation with him he will be merciful for he is here on the Pope's business. If you are all good Catholics, as you say you are, what do you have to fear?'

Simon saw the young man's hesitation. You only have to hold out a few more days, he thought. If only you knew!

He looked up at the barbican and saw a woman with red hair.

'What terms do you seek?'

'You will all be allowed to leave with any of those possessions you can carry with you. No one will be harmed. It is the fortress de Montfort desires, not your lives.'

'How can we trust you?'

'I am a man of God.'

'Exactly. There were men of God at Béziers.'

'These men here had nothing to do with Béziers.'

More hesitation. 'Where should we go?' Raimon Perella said, as if thinking aloud. 'Winter is closing in.'

'You might go to Narbonne. They gave their fealty to the Church and all live in peace there. As may have been your happy prospect if you had not closed your gates to us.'

'You swear no one will be harmed?'

'You have my word as a man of God.'

'Very well. I will put your proposition to the good people of Montaillet.'

'You have until dawn tomorrow, but if we have no word by then, de Montfort has vowed that the bombardment shall recommence.'

They rode back to their lines. Simon waited until they were out of earshot, then he threw back his hood and shouted: 'You lied to him! That was not the agreement we were vouchsafed to make!'

'Do not think to harangue me, Brother Jorda. You heard what he said. All inside Montaillet are good Christians, and if this is true, they shall go free.'

'You did not mention the oath that they must take first.'

'Did I not? You must be mistaken, for I am sure that I did.'

He rode on ahead. Simon looked back at Montaillet, and for a moment a voice whispered to him: *Go back and warn them.* But he was sure it must be the voice of the Devil and so he ignored it.

Yet he had no sleep that night. It seemed to him that for all his piety, he was becoming something he did not like.

LXXXVIII

FATHER ORTIZ APPEARED to be in great pain this morning. He dipped a crust of bread in his wine and winced at the ache in his leg. He had the rheumatics, he said. He struggled to shift his position but when Simon tried to help him stand he pushed him away. 'I have a little stiffness in the joints, I am not infirm!'

The winter was close now. The mist rolled down the valley like a malevolent presence. Sleet dripped from the canvas of their pavilion.

Simon was startled by the blast of a trumpet very close. This morning the men were showing their first eagerness for many weeks; they had been assured they had passed their last night huddled in leaking tents. You have won a famous victory for Christ, de Montfort had told them.

'Why are you sombre?' Father Ortiz said. 'This is a day of rejoicing. They are opening the gates to us. God has granted us yet another miracle.'

'Is it a miracle, Father Ortiz, when you lie?'

'What is it you wish to say to me, Brother Jorda?'

'You told their commander, Raimon Perella, that they would not be harmed.'

'Providing they swear an oath of fealty to the Church and creed.'

'You neglected to inform him of that condition. They will not all do that, will they? They are not all faithful to the Church.'

Father Ortiz brought the flat of his hand down hard on the trestle table. 'If they cannot profess allegiance to God's Church, then they are not worthy of your poor tears! Why should you concern yourself over the godless? Should God condemn me if such people are deceived? I do not understand you, Brother Jorda. We are at God's work here, and you talk to me like a lawyer!'

'They made their peace with us because you deceived them.'

'If these people knowingly harbour those who would harm God, then they harm our Church and must be brought to heel by whatever means we can devise! They protect those who spit on the cross, they call sodomites and blasphemers and Devil-worshippers their neighbours! But I shall be merciful to them and grant them their lives though if I were just they should all burn this day with the heretics, who are God's enemies!'

Simon knew it was useless to argue further, he had already said too much. And besides, perhaps Father Ortiz was right; in the battle between good and evil a priest of God could not always observe the niceties. They were, as he had said, at war with Satan and could not afford to be too delicate.

He left the tent. The world was damp and dripping. A spatter of rain stung his face. Men in full armour ran at the double; knights called for their horses; there was the clash of steel as pikes and swords and lances were made ready. The handful of pilgrims who yet remained with them had gathered to sing the *Veni Sancte Spiritus*. What a ragged bunch they were, all huddled dripping beneath a tall wooden cross.

De Montfort had left, at first light, to further his quest to be everywhere in the Pays d'Oc at once. Now the truce was concluded he found he had business elsewhere. Once he was gone Gilles rediscovered his enthusiasm for defending Christ. At his orders ragged boys were sent to gather faggots to start building the bonfire for the ungodly, the very moment the gates swung open.

*

Fabricia stood with her father on the battlements, watching the crusaders break their camp and approach the gates. Raimon, his few ragged knights and chevaliers on horseback beside him, waited in the citadel. The mercenaries and foot soldiers stood rank by rank behind, the gatekeepers awaiting his signal. When they see how few of us there are left, she thought, they will regret the cheap bargain they made.

'Is it really over?' she said.

'Let us hope so,' Anselm said. 'But I have made my confession to the priest, just in case.'

'They have guaranteed us all safe passage.'

'When it is done, I will believe it.'

She looked down at the church steps, at the desolate huddle of burghers and shepherds clutching their miserable bundles, the rich hardly distinguished from the poor after a season in this hell. She saw the *bons òmes* standing a little apart in their black hoods, her mother among them.

Anselm took her hand. Raimon gave the signal. The gates creaked open.

*

Once inside the gates, Simon fell on his knees in thanks, clutching the wooden crucifix at his throat between his fingers. He looked up at the barbican. He saw a woman with startling red hair and vivid green eyes. He heard a voice, his own voice, from long ago: '*Fabricia Bérenger, I think of you day and night. I can think of nothing else. I am on fire.*'

Hell, he thought, need not be stoked with coals and flaming sulphur. It can be chill and rain-soaked; regret and self-loathing can serve as well as any devil's pitchfork and a torn mind can be just as excruciating as torn flesh.

LXXXIX

'HUSBAND.'

Anselm turned, surprised. 'I am no longer your husband,' he said to Elionor.

'Yes, of course, I have no right to call you that.' But she took his hand and held it anyway. '*Dieu vos benesiga*, Anselm. May God bless you and may you come to a good end, in their religion or ours.'

Anselm tried to snatch his hand away but she held on.

'You were a good husband and I thank you for all your kindnesses. I am sorry I disappointed you at the end. But this is goodbye now. We shall never see each other here again. Though in heaven perhaps, for that is where I shall be presently.' She turned to Fabricia, embraced her. 'Goodbye, my heart.' Father Vital was accepting the obeisance of dozens of *crezens*. Fabricia realized what was about to happen. 'No, Mama. Please, don't let them do this to you.'

'I have no choice. It's all right, I am prepared. You don't really think they will let us go, do you?'

Gilles de Soissons galloped into the citadel, his knights and chevaliers with him, his white destrier tossing its head, fighting the reins. The crowd fell back to avoid being trampled. Father Ortiz followed behind, holding aloft a tall copper cross.

The foot soldiers rushed in behind them and pushed through the crowd with their pikes and lances. The *bons òmes* were conspicuous targets and did not resist their arrest. In moments the soldiers had them fettered and were shoving them towards the gates.

The mercenaries and Raimon's knights and men-at-arms were quickly disarmed. Their weapons were tossed into a pile in the middle of the courtyard.

'What are you doing?' Raimon shouted. He pointed at Ortiz. 'You promised us all safe passage!'

'You said all here were Christians!' He pointed towards the *bons òmes*. 'So who are they? You lied to me also!'

'This is treachery!'

'An oath is only allowable between fellow Christians. And these devils ...' He pointed at the manacled Cathars now being ushered through the gates. '... these are not Christians.' Father Ortiz wheeled his horse around. 'I shall make a thorough investigation of all here for the good of your eternal souls. Anyone who has endangered his spirit with heresy should make full and frank confession to me and in return will be welcomed back to the Holy Church and receive lenient treatment. Every one of you will make your oath of fealty to Christ and afterwards we shall be merciful, though you have taken arms against us, and sheltered these godless abominations you call *bons òmes*. On this condition you will be allowed to leave here unmolested!'

Elionor had tripped as she was being shoved through the gate. As she went down one of the soldiers brought his pike down hard between her shoulders. She screamed out in pain. Anselm roared and shoved his way through the crowd. At seeing this giant approach, the soldier took a step back, but Gilles had anticipated him and manoeuvred his horse into his path. He felled him without hesitation with the flat of his sword. Everyone else was herded to the other side of the square, to await interrogation.

*

The *bons òmes* were led away through the gate, guarded by the crusader foot soldiers. Simon led them out on a grey cob. A pyre of faggots, straw and pitch had already been prepared. The Cathars were quickly bound together with iron chains.

When it was done, the heretics were herded into the centre of the bonfire. Simon saw that there was a woman among them. He had not expected to be burning women.

They were given the opportunity to recant and return to Christ, but it was formality only. One of the soldiers set a brand to the straw. Simon started to read aloud from his book of prayers, raising his voice over the crackling of the pitch. The woman started to scream. He swallowed hard, his mouth dry. He realized he would have to shout his prayers over their death agonies. Several tried to escape the flames, despite their heavy chains, and were tossed back into the conflagration by the soldiers with their pikes.

Oh God, forgive me.

A bitter wind caught the fire and for a moment he saw the woman and her companions writhing with their clothes alight. Then the wind gusted in the other direction and they were all blanketed in choking black smoke. Even the soldiers were forced to retreat.

He held his hand in front of his face to protect himself from the heat. His cob was stamping the ground, agitated by the flames. He chanted a few more words to the glory of God and then his resolve failed him.

He wanted to cover his ears against the screams but he knew the soldiers were watching him. He tried to remain composed, but the screaming went on and on and on. He could not believe how long it took for a human being to burn. Why could they not die, why must they shriek like this?

It was the first time he had ever attended a burning, had never smelled scorched flesh or heard human fat sizzle into the fire. He had never watched a man's foot split open with the heat and the bones pop into the fire.

But finally it was done, praise be to our Lord Jesus Christ. He stared at the blackened bodies roasting among the flames and held a cloak over his mouth and nose so that the soldiers would not see him vomit.

Afterwards the men-at-arms raked over the glowing ashes. They dragged the blackened corpses from the pyre with long sticks and broke up the bones with metal bars, for the law said that nothing of the heretic's body could remain behind to pollute the earth. The crumbled ash and bone would later be tossed in the river for their final dispersion.

He closed his book of prayer and turned away. He felt polluted. *I shall never be clean again.*

XC

FATHER ORTIZ SAT on a high-backed chair in the gatehouse. A large wooden table had been carried from the *donjon* for his purpose and his leg rested on a stool. He seemed to be in pain. Beside him, a notary sat with quill and knife and parchment, head bowed, ready to make a record of the interrogation, as regulations required.

A few coals had been transported from the fire in the great hall and set in a brazier close to Father Ortiz's chair: a futile gesture, for it was so cold his breath hung in the air in small white clouds. Some tallow candles had been set on the table, and the melting wax leaked on to the wood, the burning fat giving off a foul smell. Not as foul as the stench that wafted from outside the walls.

He had been content up to this point to routinely accept the oaths of fidelity from the soldiers and the citizens of Montaillet, even though it pained him to do so. But when Anselm Bérenger was shoved in front of him his demeanour changed.

'Do you accept the Holy Church as your means of salvation?' he asked him, as he had asked almost a hundred others that morning.

'I do.'

'Do you believe that God alone made the world?'

'I do.'

'Do you believe that Jesus was incarnate and through his sacrifice you have been saved?'

'Yes, I do.'

'Do you believe the bread and wine consecrated by the priest are his body and blood?'

'As you say.'

He finished the list of prepared questions. Anselm expected now to be allowed to pass through the gate. But Father Ortiz was not yet done with him. 'You have never bowed down to a Cathar priest?'

'I have not.'

'Your wife was hereticated though, was she not?'

'She was.'

'And you tried to save her this morning when she went to proper justice?'

'I am a good Catholic, I go to mass every Sunday and I eat meat and make my confession to the priest. I am no heretic.'

Father Ortiz sighed and nodded. The soldiers shoved Anselm through the gate with the others. A red-haired woman was next.

'Your name?'

'Fabricia Bérenger.'

'Ah, Fabricia Bérenger! You are the heretic's daughter?'

Fabricia saw her father watching from the other side of the gate, a hunted, haunted look in his eyes. I am all he has left now, she thought. He lives for me.

'As you say.'

'I have heard of you. Your reputation reached Toulouse, did you know that? Show me your hands.' Fabricia stepped forward and held out her hands, palms up. Father Ortiz examined the scars.

'You are the sorceress who claims to heal people with the touch of your hands?'

'I have never claimed such a gift,' she said. But then she staggered and fell against the table.

'What is wrong with you?' Father Ortiz said.

There was a crazed look in the woman's eyes. It sent a chill through him. Dear Heaven! She is possessed.

'Diego Ortiz,' she said. 'God knows you, and He knows your mind. You will die surrounded by angels before the feast of Saint John the Apostle. You will pass from this earth screaming in pain and fear and there is nothing that can save you.'

She heard her father shout in anguish from the other side of the gate. Father Ortiz jumped to his feet and summoned two of his guards. 'She is condemned by her own words. Lock her away! We shall examine her later.'

XCI

THE JAIL WHERE they threw her had been carved out of the bedrock; the entrance was through a trapdoor from the main prison above. She had been kept in solitude and darkness.

The gaoler, Ganach, unbarred the trapdoor and Simon went down a rope ladder into the pit. Simon waited at the foot of the steps while his eyes grew accustomed to the darkness.

He held up the candle the gaoler had given him. For three days she had been restricted to stale water and a little mouldy bread and already the effects of this stringent diet were plain. Her skin was as translucent as wet linen, and there were dark bruises around her eyes. Her hair was matted and filthy.

He tried to remember what it had been like to sin with her, but the memory vanished each time he reached for it, like smoke. 'What a place we have come to,' he murmured.

She did not stir, not even to look at him.

'Do you remember? Your father wished me to persuade you against entering the cloister. I could not believe my eyes when I saw you here today.' The fat from the candle sizzled as the wick guttered in a draught. 'I have often thought of you.'

When she spoke her voice seemed to come from far away. 'I saw you singing hymns while they burned my mother.'

'I had no hand in that.'

'You are a devil of the worst kind because you tell yourself you are so good and so holy. The Spanish mercenaries who fought with us I understood, they kill for money and they rape when they can and make no bones about it. They don't pretend to be God's right-hand man. They are not . . . sentimental.'

Simon swayed on his feet. 'It grieves me to hear you say such things.'

'I say it for my own benefit, Father. I do not believe for one moment it will penetrate your own armour of sanctity. I can still smell the smoke of my mother's pyre, but I suppose you, being a priest, have grown accustomed to the taint of charred flesh. It is like incense to you.'

He took a deep breath and recited the speech he had rehearsed before coming here. 'I have come here to ask your forgiveness, Fabricia Bérenger, for what took place in Toulouse. What we once shared was lust, not love, and what I did, what you brought me to, dishonoured us both. It has blighted my soul in the face of God and brought your family to this place. We have wallowed in filth and must spend the rest of our lives cleansing ourselves.'

'I know you would like me to share the blame for what happened, but the truth is, I was powerless to stop it. I believe it is a measure of your own pollution that this one act of lust still disturbs you while you torture other human beings to death without qualm and think yourself pious for it. Please leave me now. They have only fed me a little stale bread and water and it is barely enough. I do not want to bring it up, it is all that sustains me until the morrow.'

There was nothing else to be said. He went back up the ladder and called for Ganach. As he left he heard the trapdoor slam shut behind him.

*

He emerged from the *donjon* into the citadel, grateful for the cold, clean air. He braced himself against a pillar and breathed deeply. The last person he wanted to see was Gilles de Soissons. The great lord collared him as if he was some flunkey.

'I need to talk to you, Father. Can we go some place privately?'

'What is this about, seigneur?'

'I need your spiritual counsel. Not here, people are watching. Fetch your stole and come to my quarters.'

*

Gilles had taken the former seneschal's private quarters for his own. He threw his muddy boots on the silk coverlet on the bed. Simon noted that he had used a fine silver ewer as a chamber pot, possibly to show his contempt for all things Provençal.

But the moment the door closed and they were alone, Gilles fell to knees and held his hands out for the stole. He kissed it and Simon placed it around his neck. 'You wish to make confession?'

'Father Jorda, is it true that by serving this crusade faithfully I have obtained remission for all my sins? I have fought more than the required forty days. This is true, yes?'

'You have been most valiant in the field and His Holiness has said that all who serve the crusade shall obtain remission for their sins.'

'What about future sins?'

'I am not sure these were spoken of.'

'But you are certain that I am hereby absolved of . . . everything?'

'Is there something you wish to tell me? If you unburden yourself you may receive peace in this world as well as the next.'

'My youngest brother is a priest also, did you know that, Father? Like you, my family had too many brothers. He carried the burden for being the last of us. I have not seen him for many years, but they tell me he is devout and godly, like you.'

'Is this what you wanted to tell me? We need not have had such a conversation in private.'

'I only tell you this so you might understand me better. You think me a hard man, do you not? But I am only what you would have been, should you have left the womb before your brothers. You do see that?'

'I should never have been like you.'

'I was right then, you have judged me. But I am not such a bad fellow. Your Holy Father in Rome would think so: I have crusaded in the Holy Land and now I am here doing his bidding once more.'

'What is it that you wish to confess?'

'It is a question I have regarding the great service I have done in God's name. Will you reassure me, then, that if I kill a heretic, it is a good thing? It is not murder because a heretic's soul is worth nothing.' Gilles's face was pink, and he was sweating profusely. 'It is not a sin to kill any unbeliever. That is right, isn't it? No matter what age they are?'

'What troubles you, seigneur?'

'I have such dreams! And no matter how many heretics I torch or strike down, the dream comes back, night after night.'

'What dream?'

'This is not my first crusade, Father. I served under the banner of Christ in the Holy Land, many years ago. We raided a village, one night; there were Saracens, women and children. There was an infant, it still had its birth grease on it. I . . .'

*

'You killed the child?' Simon said.

'It would have grown up to be a Saracen warrior! The hand that reaches for the breast will one day hold a sword. But . . .'

'But?'

'But I can still hear it screaming on still nights. Why is this so, Father? I am innocent of any wrongdoing; I do not need to confess it for it is not a sin. This is what Father Ortiz told me. So why do I still dream of it?'

'Perhaps if I grant you absolution and give you penance, this dream will stop.'

'Why should I do penance for something I did for the love of God?'

Simon did not know how to answer him. He put his hand on Gilles's head. 'I absolve you of all sin, in the name of the Father, the Son and the Holy Ghost.' He made the sign of the cross and hurried from the chamber.

But I am only what you would have been, should you have left the womb before your brothers. You do see that?

No, I am not like him, he thought. That man is a brute and everything he does, he does for himself. He uses piety as an excuse when what he serves is his own craving for aggrandizement. How could he possibly make such a comparison?

Yet he could still smell the pyre. The stink of it had seeped into his skin. It was on his clothes and in his hair, the ash and grease of Elionor Bérenger and the others. Have they not screamed in my sleep these past nights, as the child screams for Gilles de Soissons?

But I am not like him. Everything I do, I do for God. Have I not shown this in the terrible sacrifice that I made to be more holy?

He put his hands over his ears. The heretics were still screaming in the flames. He had to find a way to make them stop.

XCII

THERE WAS AN alcove behind the choir in the church. It had once been the shrine of a saint. The *bons òmes* had whitewashed it during their brief time of possession. Father Ortiz had reconsecrated it, and fixed a plain wooden crucifix there, affording a private place for contemplation of the divine while the church was brought back to its former glory.

Simon went there and fell to his knees, hidden from the stares of the pilgrims and ruffians who had taken shelter in the nave. But their unholy hubbub intruded on his thoughts as he fumbled for the words of prayer.

All he could think of was: *Forgive me.*

He had thought she would no longer have power over him, imagined that he might still admire her beauty but only in the way he found pleasure in contemplation of the angels painted in the vault of the cathedral of Saint-Étienne. He did not think he might still desire her, not as she was, filthy and dispirited and in rags. That was indeed too cruel a joke.

He had been with her for just a few minutes and his heart was black once more.

As the light receded in the chapel, he begged the divine for redemption.

'Look what they have done to our church!' a familiar voice said.

'Father Ortiz!' *In pity's name, was there no peace to be had anywhere?*

'It is a dismal thing to see how tenaciously these lost souls cling to the darkness. If only they would embrace Our Saviour the world would be saved and they would find peace in heaven, rather than be damned to eternal pain and suffering. It is such a simple truth that I wonder why men do not grasp it more readily.' Father Ortiz fell to his knees beside him. 'For what do you pray?'

'I am troubled.'

'Are you still disturbed by the burnings? You do well to under-stand that I do not enter lightly upon any act of violence, but Man must suffer for his sins, for that is the nature of things. And those benighted souls we burned are the greatest sinners of all for they are tools of the Devil. If we have been chosen as the instruments of Almighty God, then we should accept our burden stoically and with humility. If you flinch from your duty, then you are of no account to God.'

'Could we not seek to persuade these heretics rather than do them to death in such a manner?'

'If a wound is septic do you not apply the hot iron before the infection spreads to the rest of the body? This is why the heretic must be rooted out, Brother Jorda, for by refusing to abjure, he imperils everyone. He endangers our institutions and our towns, our King, our Vicar in Rome, everything that stands between us and savagery. Remember, we stand sentinel over men's minds. We must destroy everything that comes from the Devil and delays the glorious moment of Christ's final return.'

'But what would you do in their place, Father? Would you not hope for mercy?'

'Mercy? No! Were I ever taken by the infidel I should beg to be torn limb from limb and have my eyes gouged out. I should wallow in my own blood so that I could wear a martyr's crown in heaven!' He put his hand on Simon's arm. 'Brother Jorda, you must not persist with such thoughts. You have been charged with the task of saving this land from the Devil! As a priest of the Holy Church you will answer one day not only for your own sins but for all those who look to you for their salvation. You have been chosen to be a shep-herd of souls. Will you let wolves run wild in your flock or will you stand your watch over them?'

'I have dedicated my life to Christ, Father Ortiz.'

'Many feign to love the divine but they do not have the stomach for true devotion. Remember how Our Lord threw the money-changers out of the Temple? It is good to spend time on your knees, but to love God, a monk should know when to stand firm as well!' Father Ortiz sighed. 'Look at the crack in the wall up there. I believe it was our own war machines that did that. We shall need to find a stonemason for the repairs.'

'We had one right here, but you let him go.'

'What was his name?'

'Bérenger, Anselm Bérenger. He worked for many years on the restoration of the Église de Saint-Antoine in Toulouse. His wife was hereticated and was among those we burned.'

'I know that name. His daughter is here in our prison, is she not? The hysteric who sees visions and mutilates her own flesh?'

'The same.'

'God works in mysterious ways, Brother Jorda. Take an escort in the morning and fetch him back. We will put him to work. His wage will be his daughter's life.'

XCIII

A CHILL AND drenching rain sapped the spirits and froze the bones. Anselm pulled the hood of his cloak over his face, the bitter deluge dripping from its peak. He shivered uncontrollably.

It was a world so dominated by rain it seemed to him that even the rocks were leaking water, though it was just springs appearing from the base of the cliffs. He heard rocks crashing on to the road, sent toppling from their pinnacles by the movement of the mud beneath.

They passed several dead trees that had been blasted apart by lightning.

He could barely see a hundred paces through the veil of rain. He recited the paternoster over and over in his head.

After the surrender, Trencavel's soldiers had headed to Cabaret. But what was there for an honest stonemason? A winter of starvation and snow and another siege when the *crosatz* moved up the valley. The Spanish routiers had gone their own way, God alone knew where, probably to mate with she-wolves in the mountains. He had joined the burghers and townspeople going back down the mountain. That little rogue Loup had to lead him by the hand, else he would have just stayed there outside the gates of Montaillet, howling for them to let his daughter go.

*

Apparently they were all headed to Narbonne, which was untouched so far by the war, and where the winter would be milder. It was a long and bedraggled line, a few foot-carts, many of the women staggering from exhaustion, some cradling silent children in their arms. The infants just look through you, he thought, as if their souls have already been despatched to heaven, leaving their bodies behind.

He felt affinity with them. His wife was dead, his daughter in

347

prison, his house was rubble. What was the point to survival now? Living was just a habit you got yourself into.

He saw a rock by the side of the path and sat down. He watched his toes sink into the mud. Rain dripped from his nose. He thought about his wife's bread, steaming from the oven, and her hot soup, with beans and mutton and cabbage. He watched the steam curl off the surface, and held his hands around it to warm himself.

'Papa Bérenger,' Loup said. 'What are you doing?' The lad shook him by the shoulder. 'What are you doing?'

'I just want to sit a while,' he said.

'If you stop you'll never get up again. Now come on.' He grabbed his arm.

Anselm pulled away. 'I'll catch up.'

Loup shook his head. 'You know you won't.'

'And what if I don't? I should have taken the *consolamentum* with my wife when I had the chance, then we could have stepped into paradise side by side.'

'Only a priest can send you to heaven.'

'Well, we'd be together in hell, then. I was a coward, I let her die alone. I let them take her. I thought that if I stayed alive I could protect Fabricia, but now look, even she's in prison. I'm useless.'

'We have to keep going.'

'Why? Why do you want to survive so much, boy?'

'Because I have promised myself that one day I will have a soft bed and a great horse. The bed has red velvet curtains and the horse has one white patch over its eye. This I dream of and I will not let this dream go!' He hauled again on Anselm's arm and forced him back on to his feet. 'Come on. By tonight the rain will stop and I will steal some food for us and everything will be all right again. You'll see.'

*

Simon set off as the angelus peeled over the valley from the church at Montaillet. Gilles had given him an escort of men-at-arms, and they had found him a cob to ride barely taller than himself, but tame and compliant enough.

He and his entourage made their way down the valley in the rain, following the road to Saint-Ybars. The forest was black and mostly silent, though from time to time he heard a crashing in the undergrowth, a boar perhaps, or goblins.

At one point they stopped at a thicket deep in the wood and the captain of the guard clambered off his horse to study the tracks.

Simon went into the wood to relieve himself. He saw a shrine carved in the heart of a large tree. There was a small black figure in the shrine, a pagan idol, with dugs like a wolf and a swollen belly. There was a crushed mess of flowers at her feet.

He picked up the idol and thought to smash it on the ground, but it was carved from hard black wood. It would take a fire to destroy it, as did all things evil.

He threw it as far as he could, deep into the woods. He did not hear it land.

*

He found the stonemason among a small group of bedraggled men and women struggling through the forest. They all looked up fearfully at their approach.

Simon reined in his horse. 'Anselm Bérenger. Do you remember me?' He pulled back the cowl of his robe from his face.

Anselm looked up at him, then at his crusader escort. 'Why have you come after us? You said you would let us go if we took the oath.'

'We need a stonemason.'

Anselm fell on his knees in the mud. A small boy at his side tried to drag him to his feet.

'What is wrong with him?' Simon said to the urchin.

'He is just hungry, Father.'

'Why can't you people just leave me alone?' Anselm said.

'I have been charged to bring you back to Montaillet. We have a horse here for you. Tonight you will be snug beside a warm fire and there will be hot broth and wine to revive you.'

'Come on, Papa,' the boy said. 'Get up!'

'I have made a bargain for you with Father Ortiz. Repair the church for him and your daughter goes free.'

The boy hauled Anselm to his feet. One of the soldiers brought up the spare horse.

'Get on the horse,' Simon said

'You mean it? You will not hurt her if I do this for you?'

'You have my word.'

'What about him?' Anselm said pointing to the boy.

'Who is he?'

'He's my . . . nephew. He has to come with me.'

Simon shrugged. 'Very well, put him on the horse with you.'

Anselm clambered into the saddle and hauled Loup up after him. They turned back towards Montaillet. The other refugees watched him go. He could see the look in their faces. How they hated him right then: a warm fire and hot broth!

They continued their long, cold walk down the mountain to Narbonne.

*

Fabricia was too frightened to sleep, whenever she did the rats bit small pieces of flesh from her toes. Besides, there was not enough straw and the rock floor of the cell was cold. There was not even a hole or pail for her bodily functions. They left her in constant darkness, chained to the wall, unable to tell night from day.

It was like being buried alive. She wanted only to die.

Whenever she closed her eyes, if only for a moment, she experienced vivid, restless dreams that sent her limbs twitching in fright, bleeding in and out of her present torment so that she could no longer distinguish reality from dream.

She prayed to the Madonna for mercy.

But the face she saw when she prayed was not the Madonna's; it was Philip's. She even believed she could feel his warm breath on her face. 'I am coming back for you,' he said. 'Don't give up.'

But it was just a dream.

XCIV

Toulouse

I AM COMING back for you, he thought. Don't give up.

It was a cold, bright day, the flag of Toulouse whipping in the north wind. The city had achieved a certain fame. Philip had heard travellers talk of it in Burgundy; finer than Paris, they said, and certainly finer than Troyes. They reckoned there were more than three hundred turrets and towers across its skyline, though he did not know who might think to count them all.

And churches, too: there the round basilica of Saint-Sernin, there the square tower of Saint-Étienne, and over there the Notre-Dame de la Daurade, beside the white walls of the Église Dalbade and the Saint-Romain, all clustered like great ships inside a harbour wall.

Rosy Garonne bricks glowed pink in the sun.

A sight to behold indeed; but once inside the gates the press of corbelled houses and the poles of tattered laundry blotted out the sky and Toulouse became something less than beautiful.

They were delayed in the streets by donkeys with swaying loads and farmers with flocks of grey-backed sheep. Carts had formed deep ruts in the mud and these had filled with all manner of rubbish; the stink was dizzying.

He heard shouts; saw a gang of young men, all dressed in black and waving black banners, armed with swords and staves, clash with another yelling mob with red crosses sewn on their white robes. People fled, pouring from the lane into the main street. More blood on the stones. Even in the Count's own backyard the war still raged.

*

He was escorted through the palace like a leper and, having been kept waiting most of the morning, was finally directed into a panelled chamber, the usher curling a lip at his muddied boots and his torn jerkin. That was the problem with servants; after a while they thought of their house of employment as if it were their own.

He was introduced to the Count's principal secretary, Bernard de Signy, a stolid man whose unremarkable physical appearance was at odds with the clothes that he wore, all rich silks and Rheims linen. His fingers bulged with rings of amber and silver. Raimon had warned him to expect tight clothes and foppish manners; he said the courtiers in the south had never chewed meat off the bone in their life.

Philip had known men like de Signy before and they all sang the same song: *Let us be cautious, we should talk about this, don't rush, think of the consequences, let us send a deputation.* These men did not understand travails, had never seen a rat chewing at a corpse or a piece of brimstone as large as a horse stable coming at them over a castle wall; never witnessed men scalded with boiling water, their skin hanging in strips down their back, being ordered back to their place at a battering ram.

He had soft hands and a mouth that smiled independent of his eyes. 'So, seigneur,' he said, after introductions had been made and Philip had stated his business. 'This is . . . unusual. If I may ask, Baron de Vercy, what is the interest of a nobleman such as yourself in the affairs of a small town in the Pays d'Oc?'

'It is a private crusade, if you will. In the service of a just cause.'

'A true knight? The troubadours should like to make a ballad for you. What is it you wish from us?'

'I am here at the behest of Raimon Perella, second cousin to viscount Roger-Raymond Trencavel. I have brought embassy to Count Raymond.'

'I am afraid that Count Raymond is not presently here in Toulouse.'

Philip's shoulders sagged.

'You had not heard this news?'

'I have ridden night and day under escort from Montaillet.'

'Which is under siege, I am told.'

'We rode through their lines under cover of darkness.'

'That was very . . . bold.'

'The situation is desperate. We needed to be . . . *bold*.'

'Then to better inform you in your boldness: the Church has placed our beloved Count under interdict. They have no grounds for this but it is our belief that they wish to confiscate his lands and are using holy writ to do it. The Count is on his way to Paris to visit the King, then he intends to travel to Rome, to plead his case to the Pope in person.'

'I am here to suggest to him that he would be better advised to make his case in the Montagne Noir.'

'Please talk freely, seigneur.'

'Montaillet has been under siege these last two months and during that time we have held off this supposedly invincible army of de Montfort's. I can tell you this, they are a spent force. The Duke of Burgundy and Count of Nevers have gone home and taken the larger part of the army with them. De Montfort has just thirty knights left and perhaps five hundred men, together with a few godless priests and bishops and a ragged bunch of hangers-on. As we speak some of the castles that surrendered to him in the summer are rebelling. If Raymond would join the house of Trencavel in this fight we can end this military expedition right now, so that these *crozatz* lose their appetite for warring here completely.'

A fat and ponderous finger was placed to the lips. Finally: 'We understand the point you are making, but although I myself sympathize with the plight of the citizens and soldiers of Montaillet, we believe it would be unwise for Count Raymond to get involved in this conflict. It would only inflame the situation further. De Montfort has recently met with the King of Aragon in Montpellier and he refused to recognize him as the new viscount. So why should Raymond take up arms? This is exactly what the bishops want him to do. He need only wait and everything will resolve itself without his intervention.'

The square window behind the courtier was protected by a grille. A pigeon strutted and cooed on the windowsill. It has learned its habits from watching de Signy, Philip thought.

'But you could crush them if you attacked now. You could save Montaillet and resolve things more certainly than you can by doing nothing.'

'We are hardly doing nothing. Diplomacy may be every bit as effective as swordplay, seigneur. I am sorry for the people of

Montaillet, but in the larger purpose they count for nothing. We must be politic.'

'Montaillet counts for nothing? You pompous little fop.' It was out of his mouth before he could stop it.

De Signy's cheeks turned pink. 'Seigneur, I shall not tolerate such insults from a man such as yourself. The whole world knows you are excommunicate, that you have betrayed your own.'

Philip got to his feet and grabbed the secretary by the hair. 'They cut out my squire's eyes, damn you! It rested upon my honour to avenge him!'

De Signy shrieked in fear and moments later the guards burst through the door, but seeing him armed they held back. So much for diplomacy, Philip thought. He showed himself out.

XCV

THERE WERE INNUMERABLE candles burning in the choir; a penitent, dressed in rags and with ulcers on his feet, knelt before the altar. Its black and violet covering was embroidered with pearls and silver. He kissed it, his fingers trembling as they touched the cloth.

With winter drawing on, the great crowds of pilgrims had thinned. The innkeepers and the hawkers and the pickpockets were always as sorry to see them go as the monks and the priests. But there were still enough of them, Philip thought, all weeping and trembling as they filed through the ambulatory, gaping at the relics of the True Cross and the bloodied thorn of Jesus's crown and the blessed toenail of St Peter and whatever else the priests had put there. Just this church alone had fragments of no less than twenty-six such saints.

At Sens they had a fragment of Moses's rod; at Saint-Julien in Anjou they had one of Christ's shoes. He was yet to see either of these marvels, though it was said that a glimpse of just one of these relics might bring a remission of sins amounting to a thousand years in purgatory. If only I had more faith, Philip thought, I might yet save myself a lot of time in the sulphur.

It was right here in this church that she said she saw the Virgin move, he thought, just over there in her little shrine. He lit a taper and approached on his knees, ignoring the ache of the cold stone to concentrate his mind on the divine. He addressed his petition not to God, but to the lady. How much more compelling her image than that of the tortured Christ; she just looked so kind. He idly wondered what the world might be like if more men knelt here like this, instead of shouting their violent demands at the world. Would they as easily watch someone scream and burn for *her*?

He felt too numb to pray. Instead he just hung his head and whispered two words: *Help me.*

'What are you doing here?'

He looked up, startled. 'Étienne?'

'I thought you were dead!'

'Only half-dead.' He scrambled to his feet, shamed that someone he knew had found him on his knees. He felt like a pauper next to his cousin. The last time he had seen him was when they had dined together at Vercy. Look at him, he thought, in his rich velvet cloak trimmed with marten fur, and his doublet of green silk and gloves of soft calf-leather. And here I am in the same clothes I rode, fought and slept in these last two months.

'You look half-starved. You are Philip, not his ghost?'

'If I were Philip's ghost, I should haunt somewhere warmer.' They embraced, but Étienne seemed wary, unsure perhaps if Philip in his straitened circumstances might bring him bad luck, or at least a bad reputation.

'What are you doing here in Toulouse?' Philip asked him.

'I have been on pilgrimage to Santiago de Compostela. I told you I was thinking of it.'

Philip smiled. A gentleman's pilgrimage by the looks of it, retainers hovering to hold his cloak as he prayed and two men-at-arms to ensure his personage was not jostled by less celebrated penitents. *A good horse and good whores*, Étienne had said.

'Let me buy you a cup of wine and some supper. It seems you have need of it.'

*

Étienne shook his head. 'Look at you! I have seen men in better straits chained to a stake waiting for the executioner. What has happened to you?'

The tavern smelled of wood smoke and spilled beer. A boy brought a jug of vinegary wine and a hock of lamb and half a loaf of rye bread to their table. 'I have just this morning arrived from the Montagne Noir. I got caught up in the fighting there.'

'You rode here alone?'

'I had escort, soldiers loyal to Viscount Trencavel. As soon as we reached the city they returned to the south, and the war.'

'But how did this happen? Why are you warring down here

alone? Your own men-at-arms returned to Vercy without you. They said you were dead.'

'They left me for dead. A subtle difference but a significant one, don't you think?'

'Indeed.' Étienne drained his goblet of wine and grimaced as if he had just swallowed ditch water. Étienne's bully boys threw out two ruffians who had ventured too close to their table. This was the way to do pilgrimage, Philip thought. No shuffling bare-legged through the ambulatory and sleeping in fields for Étienne. 'But I must tell you, cousin, that life is more of a problem for me than death. I fear I may be excommunicate.'

'Yes, the whole of Burgundy is alive with rumour. They said you killed a crusader.'

'I may have killed more than one.'

'Well, no point in half measures.' And then, in a whisper: 'Please do not tell me you have been fighting on the side of the heretics?'

'That was not my intention, though it might appear that way to some.'

Étienne wearily rubbed his face with his hands. 'Are you out of your mind?'

'One circumstance led to another. The blood runs hot, cousin.'

Philip could see the play of thoughts on his kinsman's face; he was wondering what this might mean for Philip's prospects, and then, of course, his own. A heretic in the family was a hindrance to social or financial advancement.

'Now I, too, have a confession to make. I lied about my presence here. It was no pilgrimage. I came here looking for you.'

'For me?'

'You are kin. And that sergeant of yours could not lie straight in his own grave. I came down here to make my own enquiries about his story, and I am glad that I did. Now tell me all.'

Philip told him about the skirmish with the crusaders, and how they themselves were ambushed and how Soissons's soldiers had mutilated Renaut. Étienne shook his head and cursed under his breath. 'Godfroi and his men shall be held to account for this, I promise you.'

'What of Giselle?'

'She complains she is a widow, but I have not seen too much grieving on her part. Her brothers have not been slow to dispute with the Crown for your lands and I believe she already has several suitors. You must return there at once to save the situation.'

That, of course, was the real reason for Étienne's presence in Toulouse; his family would dispute the ownership of the Vercy fief with the King's lawyers should he not return.

Étienne leaned in. 'Is it true you came here looking for a wise woman to heal your son?'

'Yes, it's true.'

His cousin frowned. 'Well, no one should slander you for trying to save your boy, by whatever means.' But there was something else on his mind. 'Did you ever think . . . there were rumours, you know. About your boy.'

'What rumours?'

'That Giselle was jealous that you already had a son by another woman and that she poisoned him.'

It had never occurred to Philip before, but he dismissed the idea with a wave of his hand. 'People talk. I cannot believe she has it in her to do such a thing.'

'Are you sure?'

No, now Etienne had raised the suspicion, he was not sure. But what did it matter now? What was done was done. 'It's too late now, anyway,' he said.

Étienne gripped the neck of his goblet as if he was throttling a small bird, his knuckles white. He took another gulp of it and spat it on the floor. 'Dog's piss!' He took hold of Philip's arm. 'Now look, you must act, and act quickly.'

'What would you suggest?'

'Do as the Count of Toulouse did when the Church threatened him. Make a big play of switching sides.'

'To what effect?'

'Wear the cross again, Philip.'

'If I ride alone into the Montagne Noir with a red cross on my surcoat I will not live to see the sun set. The place is alive with bandits and Cathars. I heard fifty of de Montfort's men were ambushed near Cabaret.'

'Then go back at the head of an army.'

Philip considered this strange proposal, picking at a tear in his sleeve. 'You know of one for hire?'

'Did you see the battle today, in the *bourg*? The ones with the white crosses sewn on their tunics are a private Catholic army paid for by the Bishop. He is talking of sending them south to reinforce de Montfort. What if you were to lead them?'

Philip laughed at the audacity of his cousin's suggestion. 'Did you think of that just as we were sitting here?'

'The Bishop and the Count have been at each other's throats for years. Now Raymond has gone to Paris the Bishop has become even more vociferous. All you have to do is convince him that you have seen your error and wish for redemption. When you go back to the war you don't have to fight too hard, just make a big show of it to forestall any interdict against you, then you can come home, put your bitch of a wife in a nunnery, throw her brothers into the moat and resume your life. As God intended!'

'You think it will work?'

'It worked for the Count. They say the Pope is fattening peacocks and having his jeweller make gold rings as presents for Raymond's arrival in Italy. No one loves a prodigal son more than a Catholic.'

Philip laughed again and clapped him on the shoulder. They tossed the wine back at the boy and ordered ale instead. They finished off several jugs and Philip ate a hock of lamb, though he suspected it might be the kind of mutton that once barked and wagged its tail. Then they fell into the street.

Étienne took him to a tailor and bought him a new tunic and hose and a fresh linen shirt, and gave him loan of his favourite fox-lined cloak so that he might make a favourable impression on the Bishop. They spent the night as guests of an acquaintance of Étienne's, a wealthy wool merchant in the *bourg*.

The next morning they bade each other farewell; Philip promised to see him back in Burgundy in the spring. Then he made his way to the Bishop's palace to make his peace with Mother Church.

I am coming back for you. Don't give up.

XCVI

I T WAS SAID that the Bishop of Toulouse was not as debauched as
most; he did not keep pretty boys, or women, he did not hear
matins in bed, or play dice, or try to conceal his tonsure by combing
the hair from the back of his head forward to cover it. At least that
was what they said.

Fulk of Marseilles had been born the son of a rich Genoese
merchant, who had the good grace to die early and leave his fortune
to his son, who then set to the task of squandering it. He became an
itinerant troubadour and practised womanizer, before finally abandoning the good life, and a wife and two sons, for the austerity of life
as a monk at the abbey of Le Thoronet. But Fulk was not cut from
humble cloth. Ten years later he was appointed the new Bishop of
Toulouse after Rome kicked out Count Raymond's own appointee.
By all accounts Fulk had applied himself to the task of becoming the
thorn in Raymond's side with the utmost zeal.

The Bishop received him in a great carved armchair, a lay brother
seated at a writing table beside him as notary. There was a white wall
behind him with a black wooden cross on it. He wore a fur of sable
and the aura of perfumes and burned amber that surrounded him
made Philip light-headed.

'You wished audience with us?' the Bishop said. Philip looked
around the room. There was nowhere to sit. He imagined the insult
was a calculated one, and he had no recourse but to endure it.

'On a spiritual matter,' Philip said.

'I have reports of a certain baron from Vercy in Burgundy who
made war on our holy crusaders in the Montagne Noir. I hear that
his lands may shortly come under interdict because of this. Is this
the spiritual matter for which you seek guidance?'

'I think there has been a misunderstanding, *Grandeur*. It was
never my intent to fight on the side of heresy. It was a personal
matter of honour between myself and another man of rich blood.'

'Did this matter extend to you taking part in the defence of the fortress at Montaillet against God's holy Host?'

'I had lost the men-at-arms who had escorted me from Burgundy; I then almost lost my life. I did not take part in the defence of Montaillet; rather, I found myself trapped there.'

The Bishop waved a hand dismissively in the air. 'These are matters for the ecclesiastical courts.'

'Indeed, *Grandeur*. I did not wish to trouble you with it. I came to you instead hoping to atone for my errors and assist your most holy purpose at the same time.'

'Really? And how might you do that?'

'Simon de Montfort's holy crusade faces serious difficulty, as everyone knows.'

'Nonsense! And it is not de Montfort's crusade. He is merely the Holy Father's elect to replace the Trencavels in their seat in the Minervois.'

'Yet if Count Raymond returns from Rome exonerated, the Holy Father's position in this will not be quite as clear and de Montfort's situation will become tenuous.'

'It is true that the Count of Toulouse thinks that he can play politics with Rome. But His Holiness will see through his game soon enough. This crusade should have been directed against Raymond from the very first, for this is the seat of heresy, not Béziers, and not Carcassonne!'

Good. I have him well exercised now, Philip thought, noting a fleck of foam on the Bishop's lower lip.

But the Bishop had not yet finished his rant. 'Raymond joined the crusade and feigned loyalty to the Church to save his own skin. He plays a double game. Trencavel was his enemy but could never defeat him, and so he let us do the job for him! Now he thinks that he will take over the Trencavel lands when our crusaders return home! But this will not stand. The Church knows where its real enemy lies!'

'Yet there have been setbacks, *Grandeur*. De Montfort is in dire need of reinforcements.'

'It is all part of God's grand design to allow even more northern knights to save their souls by taking the cross.'

'But God cannot always work such miracles alone, am I right?'

'Get to your point. Are you here to goad me or to blaspheme?' He turned to the notary. 'I hope you're writing all this down.'

'Forgive me, *Grandeur*. I meant no disrespect. Let me tell you why I am here. As I rode into the city I saw a number of men with white crosses sewn on their robes; they were in a bloody mêlée with a band of other men, dressed in black.'

'The White Brotherhood defends the laws of God in this city. Those they fought are a rabble paid for by Count Raymond.'

'These Whites, who fought so bravely in the street, would be better employed in Simon de Montfort's service, would they not?'

'It has been suggested before. But the logistics of such a plan are not so easily achieved.'

'Indeed. You would need a knight to organize them and lead them, one who has experience of war and, even better, experience also of the conditions of the war in the south.'

The Bishop frowned and leaned forward. 'You?'

'I wish to go home, *Grandeur*, and claim my life again. I have an interdict from the Church hanging over my head, even though I gave a year of my life in God's service in the Holy Land. If I offer this service, I hope it will again prove my loyalty to the Church and remove this ban. And serve God's holy cause also, of course.'

'It is an interesting proposition. I could spare a hundred men. But how will you get them out of the city? Raymond's troops are under orders to keep them here.'

'We would leave at night, by the unwalled suburb to the west. There are no guards there.'

'I also have victualler's carts and a siege engine ready for de Montfort's employ.'

'They would have to be left behind. I need to ride quickly to avoid the Count's patrols.'

The Bishop shrugged. 'A pity. Still, de Montfort would appreciate a hundred good men right now.'

'And for this I ask only that you write to His Holiness in Rome and ask him to remove the interdict against me. I have been a fool; I see that now. If you will do this for me I will lead your men into the Montagne Noir, as their proud general in the war against the heretics.'

The Bishop put a finger to his lower lip. It made him look

wanton. 'Very well, young man, I graciously accept your offer. Prove yourself to me, and you will live as a free man again, under the beneficent grace of the Church. But one other thing.'

'*Grandeur?*'

'You will need to be scourged, for the good of your soul, you understand. I shall perform the ceremony myself at Saint-Gilles.'

Philip's fingers went to his throat, found the copper and garnet crucifix that Fabricia had given him. It had worked itself loose from his cambric undershirt. He tucked it away again, out of sight.

He went down on one knee and kissed the fat amber ring on the Bishop's finger.

'Whatever you think best, *Grandeur*,' he said.

XCVII

SOME YEARS WINTER came slowly to the mountains, Anselm had discovered; it seeped into cracks, silent as frost. But the night he arrived back at Montaillet it came with a rush, glacial winds howling through the pines, followed by a gale of sleet and snow.

The next morning when he woke the entire valley was blanketed in white and the air was so cold it scarified the throat like a razor. Hardened drifts of snow had even found their way into the south transept of the church, where the wall had been damaged during the siege.

He stared up at the roof. There was a long crack in the vault left by a missile stone. 'Not much I can do to repair it in the winter,' he told Simon. 'But you'll not want that to get worse. I can make a temporary repair with some trusses so that it doesn't come down, but I'll need labourers.'

'You think it might? Come down, I mean.'

'I won't know until I can get up there and have a closer look.'

Simon looked around the church. 'Look what these heretics have done! They even took the saints from the corbels. This is all that is left.' He pointed to the two stone angels standing guard either side of the apse.

'Don't worry, Father. I'll give you a new church.' He turned his attention to the priest. 'How is my daughter?'

'She has not been harmed.'

'Can I see her?'

'I will ask Father Ortiz.'

'She won't last long in that rathole where you put her, not in this weather.'

'Finish your work and she will be released.'

'My work will take months. I cannot even start on the roof until spring. You will let my poor daughter rot in there until then?'

'It is up to Father Ortiz,' Simon told him.

'She is innocent of any wrongdoing.'

'She claims miracles for herself.'

'She says she has seen the Virgin and sometimes she prays for people. Where is the harm in it?'

'It beggars belief that the Virgin would reveal herself to a mason's daughter and not to a man of learning and spiritual understanding who could use such a vision for the betterment of all. Paul suffered his own revelation on the road to Damascus and from this came the enlightenment of a great man and the foundation of our Holy Church; if the Lord had instead revealed himself to a shepherdess what good would have come of it?'

'Let her go, for pity's sake.'

'I promise you I will talk to Father Ortiz for you, Anselm. It is all I can do. Now be about your work. I will make labourers available to you from among the pilgrims.'

Anselm watched him walk away. Once he had considered Father Jorda a good man. But it seemed to him now that the monk's heart was rotting inside him, like an apple going bad from the inside.

*

Simon climbed the worn stone staircase to the barbican. Stray flakes of snow whipped from a crouching sky, dissolving into freezing wetness on his bearskin cloak. The wind moaned over the walls and the frost burned his ears.

Far below him he could make out the intricate patterns in the snow left by a small animal. Long fingers of ice hung from the beech trees.

The heretics said that all the beauty of the world was an illusion, that the Devil had created it for the same purpose that he had created physical beauty, to seduce the soul and tempt it to cling to impermanence.

They had persuaded Gilles to stay and garrison the fortress over the winter but the news from elsewhere in the Pays d'Oc was grim. Many of the castles de Montfort had gained during the summer had rebelled. Fifty of his men had been ambushed on the road to Cabaret and sent back to him without their noses, lips and eyes.

They were an island of Christianity now, surrounded by Cathars and the goblins that lived in these polluted forests. He thought about Fabricia, shivering in her dungeon. What Anselm had said was right; she would not survive down there for long in this weather. Father Ortiz had promised to release her and he had gone back on his word.

He was shaken from his bitter reverie by a trumpet sounding the alarm at the main gate. Hooves rang on the frozen road and he heard the jangle of harness. Simon ran to the barbican, thinking they were under attack, but the men who approached wore white crosses on their shoulders and led rounceys loaded with supplies. Some good news, at last.

Well, not quite. As soon as the riders were in the citadel and dismounted, the trouble began. Gilles marched across the frozen puddles, his sword drawn. 'What is this dog doing in my castle?' he shouted.

Father Ortiz threw himself between the baron and the tall knight who commanded their reinforcements. 'What are you doing?' Father Ortiz said. 'He is one of us!'

'He is a traitor!'

'You should pray for more such traitors,' Philip said. 'I have brought you a hundred men to reinforce your garrison. Or would you rather fight Trencavel's soldiers on your own?'

Gilles turned to Father Ortiz. 'I saw this knight on this very barbican when we laid siege! He fought on the side of the heretics then!'

'I am a northerner, same as you. I was trapped here during the siege but I never fought against you. I escaped through my own daring and made my way back to Toulouse. Do you think the Bishop would have entrusted his men to a heretic?'

Father Ortiz rounded on Gilles. 'Put away your sword!'

'I do not believe him!'

'He wears the holy cross. Should you murder him, you will answer for it. Come to your senses. We are surrounded by the enemy and we need every man we can find. Has he not risked his life riding through these mountains to bring us the reinforcements we sorely need? *Now put away your sword.*'

Gilles's face flushed pink. He sheathed his sword with the reluctance of a man ripping off his own arm. He did not take his eyes from Philip. 'We will settle accounts, you and I,' he said. 'I will not let this stand.'

XCVIII

FATHER ORTIZ WAS surprised at how quickly Anselm had erected his scaffolding. Somehow he had already organized his rabble of martial pilgrims into a viable workforce.

He stood in the nave with Father Jorda and watched him work. 'He is nimble for a man of his age,' he said.

'As I told you, Father, he is one of the best. He enjoyed a great reputation in Toulouse. Now that you have seen that he is in earnest, I take it you will release his daughter, as you promised.'

'I promised to consider it.'

'But, Father . . .'

'You have yet to learn the virtue of obedience, Brother Jorda. Why must you always contend with me?'

'But I have spoken to many people who know her. She has never claimed to work miracles. She poses no threat to the faith. We should let her go.'

'Did you not hear how she spoke to me at the gate? I do not intend to discuss this further with you, Brother Jorda.' He returned his attention to the stonemason. 'What is he doing up there, do you think?' He called to him to come down. Anselm shinned down the scaffolding with the ease of a man half his age.

He wears just fingerless gloves and a tunic, Father Ortiz noticed. He seems impervious to cold.

'There is a problem,' Anselm said, jumping nimbly on to the floor.

'What sort of problem?'

'I have been examining the cracks in the vault and while doing so I found an inscription. It is in Latin, I think. I cannot read it. It may be sacred and therefore to be preserved but I worry that it was left there by Cathars.'

'Why would they do such a thing?'

Anselm shrugged. 'I would like you to see it. I have never seen an inscription in such an unlikely place before.'

A wooden ladder had been propped against the scaffold leading to a platform halfway up the structure, a rope ladder ascending the rest of the way. Father Ortiz hesitated, then hitched his cassock into the cord at his waist, as a woman would do with her skirts. He followed Anselm up the ladder. The frame of the platform swayed under their weight.

Anselm easily reached the timber planks spanning the vault. Father Ortiz finally struggled up the rope ladder and joined him.

Anselm pointed to something carved into the stone, halfway across the walkway. Father Ortiz inched across. He had never been on a scaffold before; he started to sweat, despite the cold.

'See here,' Anselm said.

Father Ortiz saw what Anselm was pointing at, a cross carved into the stone and next to it the words: *Rex Mundi*. Rex Mundi, King of the World! It was the name the Cathars gave to the Devil.

'This is sacrilege,' Father Ortiz said. 'How did it get here?'

'I put it there, Father.'

'You? What do you mean?'

'I wanted you to see it before you died. I wanted you to know what I think of you and all priests like you.'

Father Ortiz stared at him, confused. 'What are you talking about?'

'You'll never let her go. I know you won't. You'll let her rot in the dungeon.'

'Of course I will release her. You have my word. Now let me down from here!'

'It's high, isn't it? We're so high we're almost in heaven. We can go there together if you like.'

Father Ortiz looked back over his shoulder. The rope ladder seemed so very far away. He started to shuffle back along the planks, the way he had come. 'Think of your soul, Anselm. Should you harm a priest you would be damned for all time.'

'Perhaps it would be worth it.'

'If I die, she dies too! We had a bargain, remember?' He saw Simon far below. 'Help me!' he shouted.

'Some bargain. I don't trust any of you bastards any more.'

Father Ortiz turned and scrambled for the ladder but Anselm was too quick for him. He wrapped his arms around him and held him easily.

'You will burn in hell for this, for all eternity!'

'Eternity is worth it, you Devil-fucker.' The scaffolding lurched and swayed. 'I wonder who is right, you or the Cathars? One of you must be wrong. Very soon we will find out for sure. No more wondering, eh?'

Father Ortiz soiled himself. Anselm frowned in disgust.

'Come now, why are you frightened? I'm doing you a favour. I am transporting you to paradise!'

'Don't,' Father Ortiz whimpered.

'We shall go to heaven together. Nothing will hurt us, save when we reach the ground. It will be quick, we shall know nothing of it. Not quite the mercy you showed my poor Elionor, was it? Say goodbye to the world, Father Ortiz. If it truly is the Devil's creation then we are both well out of it.'

*

Father Ortiz screamed, but briefly. He struck one of the stone angels as he fell, snapping off her wing and her head. It seemed to Simon that they bounced a finger's breadth from the earthen floor as they landed.

Once dead, they formed an awful, bleeding tableau on the floor; Father Ortiz lay beneath, Anselm above. One of the broken wings from the statue lay by Father Ortiz's skull. The angel's head lay at his feet.

Simon remembered what Fabricia had said: *You will die surrounded by angels.* He staggered back, and then ran for assistance.

XCIX

THE BODY HAD been washed, dressed in liturgical robes and laid out on a catafalque in the nave. His wrists had been tied together so that his hands lay across his chest in the attitude of prayer, clutching a gold crucifix. Hundreds of candles had been lit around him.

Gilles fell on his knees to pray for the soul of Father Ortiz, and when he was done he stood up and walked up to Father Jorda, who stood vigil in the shadows of the chapel. 'You're next,' he said and walked out.

Philip came in to pay his respects. As he examined the corpse he raised an eyebrow. 'Was he very handsome once?'

'He was devout and cared nothing for the flesh.'

'Just as well when one sees what has become of it. You cannot even be sure he had a beard. Did he have a beard?'

'A slight one.'

'This could be the stonemason. You may have burned the wrong body.' Philip glanced towards the door of the crypt. They were quite alone. He took a dagger from his belt and casually held it at Simon's throat.

'What are you doing?' Simon said.

'Where is she?' he said.

'This is your plan? To slice my throat in the crypt?'

'For want of a better one. Threatening to slice a man's jugular has worked for me before.'

'She is in the jail under the *donjon*, and killing me is not going to help you get her out.'

'You are very calm for someone with a knife at his throat.'

'If you meant to kill me you would have done it. I assume you want something from me. And because we both want the same thing I do not think I have anything to fear from you.'

'We both want the same thing? Is that what you think?'

'We both want the girl safely out of that dungeon and away from here. Don't we, Philip?'

'How do you know my name?'

'I spent some hours in the company of her father when I was ordered to bring him back here to Montaillet. He was cold and grieving and miserable and felt the need to unburden his soul. He told me all about you, how Fabricia had placed great hopes in a certain nobleman from Burgundy. He thought you were dead or had abandoned her. I see he was wrong on both counts.'

Philip put the dagger back in his belt. 'You knew who I was when I arrived here at the castle?'

'Of course.'

'You could have betrayed me to Father Ortiz and that other albino bastard.'

'I had no interest in betraying you.'

'Why do you want to help the girl?'

'Not all priests are like Father Ortiz.'

'Yes they are.'

'Well then, perhaps I am not a very good priest. She is unjustly accused.'

'When has justice ever troubled a cleric? There is more to it than that.'

Simon lowered his eyes. 'Perhaps she will tell you herself when you are away from here.'

Philip raised an eyebrow. 'Surely not, you don't look the type. More of a bum-boy than a lover, if you don't mind me saying so.'

'How do you plan to get her out?'

Philip shrugged.

'You have money?'

'A little.'

Simon held out his hand. 'Give it to me. I shall bribe her gaoler.'

'Why don't you just order her release yourself? Can't you do that now he's dead?'

'The gaoler is the baron's man. He is susceptible to gold, not orders, especially from a priest. Do you know a way out of this place except by the main gate?'

'One way. I doubt if the new owners have discovered it yet.'

'Where?'

'Below the stables. There is an iron grille on the end wall; push against it and it leads to what might be a mistaken for a storeroom. But there is another tunnel that leads off it and it goes down under the castle to a cave.'

'Very well, leave it to me. Spend your time in prayer out of the way of the seigneur. I will find you tonight after compline. Be ready to ride.'

Philip decided to trust him because he had no choice. From habit he made the sign of the cross over Father Ortiz's body and left the crypt.

C

THE DEAD WOMAN was a camp follower and would not be missed.

She lay in a corner of the church like a pile of rags. God alone knew what rot or disease had wasted her, though she must have been comely enough once. She mumbled a last confession though she was so weak he could hardly hear her. He gave her absolution anyway; soon enough she would be the problem of a judge more profound than he.

When her last gurgling breath had stopped he made the sign of the cross and got to his feet. 'What shall we do with her?' one of the soldiers said.

'Bring her to the crypt.'

The two soldiers looked at each other. One smirked, the other shook his head; sad to witness how low the reputation of churchmen must have sunk if they thought he intended to violate the corpse. Still, he no longer cared what such men thought of him.

*

Not far away from him, Philip knelt before the shrine of the Madonna in the transept, staring at the bloodstains on the ground. Some of it had splashed up the pillars. Fabricia had always described her father as a gentle giant; but such gentleness is not a constant thing, he thought. They had pushed the poor man beyond madness. Fear the man who has nothing to lose.

He wondered about Fabricia, what she must be suffering. Just a few more hours, he thought, be patient. Tonight he would get her out of that tomb they had buried her in. He would not contemplate failing her. He had failed too many people in his life. Not this time.

'You came back then?' He looked up. It was Loup. 'The stonemason killed the priest. I was here. I saw the whole thing.'

'He was a brave man.'

'He was crazy. *Fou.* Did you come back for me?'

'For the woman.'

'Are you getting her out of here?'

'Tonight. You want to come with us?'

'You're only saying that because if you don't take me, I could tell Gilles everything I know about you.'

'That's true. But I also owe you my life. I have not forgotten it.'

Loup knelt down beside him. He stared at the picture of the Madonna on the wall. 'You will not leave without me then?'

'Be waiting by the stables tonight after compline. You have my word.'

'And you must keep it, seigneur. You'll be sorry if you don't.'

Philip watched him slip away. Had the boy really threatened him? Perhaps he should have listened to Renaut that night by the side of the road. *Seigneur, this is not a good idea.*

*

Simon took the gaoler, Ganach, aside. The man was not, as he had assumed, a complete brute. His breath reeked of garlic and his teeth were rotten, but he knew the value of a coin or two.

Simon could also see that Ganach was frightened of him, so he fixed him with a stare that let him know he could be every bit as ruthless as his predecessor, Father Ortiz. 'Do not breathe a word of this to anyone or it will go badly for you. I shall make sure of that.'

'Father, I am an honest man,' Ganach said, unable to appreciate the irony of that statement. 'You can rely on me.'

I need only rely on you for a few hours, Simon thought. After that it really won't matter.

*

A few hours later Ganach drew out the bolt of the trapdoor and Simon stepped down into the pit.

He held up the torch and studied the pale skeleton before him in the light of the candle. She was covered in filth and sores.

He felt his spirit tear like vellum.

'Take off your clothes,' he said.

She held up her hands to cover her eyes, the torch blinding her. 'Father Jorda?'

'Take off your clothes,' he repeated. He gave her a woollen tunic and a cloak and some boots. 'Put these on. Get dressed, quickly.'

She fumbled with the rotted rags she wore, but the numbing cold made her fingers clumsy. 'Turn your head,' she said. She put on the new robe and cloak he had brought her. The cloak was of bear fur and it had a hood. It was so warm; she had not felt warm since they put her in here.

'We should hurry,' he said.

'What is happening? Where are you taking me?'

'Away from here.'

'Has Father Ortiz released me?'

How could he answer her question without telling her all of it? Instead he knelt down in front of her. 'Do you often think of what we did that day?'

'Sometimes,' she said.

He lifted his cassock. 'Look,' he said. 'Here. What is it you see?'

He held the torch so that she could see. She gagged and looked away.

'I wanted to live a chaste life, like Christ, but thoughts of you haunted me day and night, even after I made my confession to the prior. I tried to purify myself through pain. I whipped my back until the blood ran but I still thought of you, at prayer, while singing a psalm. Even after what I did, I knew it was wrong, but soon I wanted to do it again. And so I did this. I thought that by removing my vilest member it would set me free to carry out the honourable ministrations of my office. I did it for God, and I did it to be free of *you*.'

He shook his head. 'I almost died. I was months in the infirmary. Even now, the wound gives me pain every day and I cannot pass my water properly. So now you see, of all people, I understand what true penitence is.' He pulled down his robe. 'I thought after this I should be free of thoughts of women. Yet from the moment I saw you again the old longings returned, even though I no longer have the flesh to satisfy them. So tell me, Fabricia, is this the love the troubadours sing of? *Amour courtois?* For even though I can never have you again, I cannot bear to see you suffer and I will stake my life to preserve yours.'

He stood up. 'There is a great abomination of eunuchs in the church and I have had to keep this secret. Only the prior and the infirmarian at Saint-Sernin knew of it. But they kept their silence for my sake and now they are both dead.'

'Is it really such a sin to want a woman, Simon?'

'It takes us from God. Even your *bons òmes* agree with us on that.'

Another monk came down the ladder into the dungeon, a body in a linen shroud over his shoulder. He tossed the corpse on to the floor, and drew back his hood.

'Philip!'

He put his arms around her. 'You see? I am not dead. No one shot arrows at me. Your dreams are just dreams.' He scooped her up. 'Let's get her out of here,' he said to Simon.

Simon went to the body of the camp follower and removed the shroud. Now Gilles would have the corpse of a young woman in his dungeon should he remember he had ever thrown one down here; Ganach had earned two months' wages in a single night and the dead girl had earned her absolution. Everyone's interest was served.

*

A fierce cold set the bones to aching; he smelled wood smoke, night-soil and the strong taint of horse from the stables. Philip kept to the shadows, away from the eyes of the night watch. The stable boy jumped up when he heard them but Simon tossed him some coins and told him to go back to sleep.

Loup was waiting, appearing suddenly out of the darkness, dogging their heels. 'Where are we going?' he said.

'You'll see.'

'What's he doing here?' Simon said. 'I don't have a horse for him.'

'He doesn't need one. He can ride with me.' Philip pushed open the grille.

Simon held up the flare, found the tunnel entrance and started down it. They would have to hurry in case the stable boy decided to raise the alarm.

'Are we going back to your castle in Burgundy?' Loup said.

'No, we can't go back there, lad.'

'Why not?'

'After this, there will be no reprieve from the Church for me, I assure you.'

'Then what will you do?'

'Become a *faidit*, I suppose. Go to Catalonia. I can always find employment as a soldier somewhere.'

'You will really give up your castle and your lands? *For this woman?* Is that what you are offering me? A life like I had before?'

'I won't abandon you, Loup, I gave you my word. I owe you my life. But I did not promise you life in a castle, all I promised was that I would not leave you.'

Loup fell silent. One moment he was there, trotting beside them in the dark, the next moment he was gone.

*

There were two horses waiting in the cave. They were restless, their breath rising in thick clouds.

Philip helped Fabricia on to one of the horses. 'Only two mounts?' he said to Simon. 'Are you not coming with us?'

'I am a priest, I have dedicated my life to the divine. Where would I go?'

'The boy will talk. He will betray you.'

'If I am damned, then this time I shall be damned as a man and not half of one.'

'What are you talking about?'

'She will tell you,' Simon said. 'Now go, before someone raises the alarm.'

Fabricia held out a hand to him; Simon took it, and kissed her fingers. 'Go with God,' he said.

Philip jumped on the other horse and nudged her forward. The wind moaned through the mouth of the cave and brought with it flurries of ice. 'Goodbye, priest,' Philip said.

'*Dieu vos benesiga*,' Simon repeated and disappeared into the dark.

CI

Gilles woke sweating. Another bad dream. One of his stewards was standing over him shaking him by the shoulder. He slapped the man's hand away and sat up.

'What are you doing in here?'

The man backed away. 'Seigneur, I am sorry to wake you. But there is someone to see you.'

'It is the witching hour, by the bowels of God!'

'He says it is vital that he see you now.'

One of the guards threw the interloper into the room. The steward handed Gilles his gown and he got out of bed and stared at the upstart who had dared to come to his chamber at this hour. It was just a runt. 'What is this?'

The boy seemed not the least afraid, damn him. 'I'm Loup, sir.'

'Beat him and throw him out,' he said to the guards.

'No, seigneur! Please, seigneur, you will want to hear what I've got to say. You won't be sorry.'

'What could you know that would possibly interest me?'

'Information, seigneur. Things you would like to hear of.'

Gilles wanted to give him a good kicking but he held his temper. 'What kind of information?'

'About the Frenchman, the one you don't like. The one who came from the Bishop with the new soldiers.'

'What about him?'

'He lied about his name to Father Ortiz. His real name's Philip of Vercy. He's the one that ambushed your men.'

'How do you know this?'

'I was with him. I saw it all.'

Gilles folded his arms. 'Who are you, boy? How did you get into Montaillet? Are you with the pilgrims?'

'I'm a shadow, seigneur. I slip here, I slip there, no one notices me. I have seen things about Philip of Vercy that you would like to know. If I could tell you where he is now, wouldn't you like to hear of it?'

'He's here in the fortress.'

'He was, seigneur, but not any more.'

'What do you mean? He has gone? How?'

'You want to see him cold and dead, don't you? So first we bargain, seigneur. That's the right way.'

'Bargain?' He means it too, Gilles thought. This piece of dirt, this gutter trash wants to deal with me? 'The bargain is this. You will tell me what you know and I won't have you beaten to death in the yard.' He stood over him. The boy Loup did not flinch. Well he had balls, no mistake, and he was no bigger than a poker. Gilles held out his hand and the steward handed him his purse. He gave the boy a silver denier. 'Tell me where he is.'

The boy Loup handed back the coin. 'I don't want money, seigneur.'

'What do you want then?'

'I want a horse with one white patch over its eye. And I want to sleep in a feather bed. I want you to take me to Normandy to your castle and make me a squire.'

Gilles grabbed him by the throat and pushed him against the wall. God's blood, he should squeeze him out like a rag and throw him out of the window. But then he threw back his head and laughed. 'By the Devil, you are an impudent little rogue. Very well, you shall have your wish.' He let him go. 'Tell me what you know and be quick about it.'

'There is a tunnel under the stables; it leads out of the castle by a secret way. He has taken the woman from the prison, and he intends to ride with her to Catalonia.'

'How did he get her out of the prison?'

'The priest helped him.'

'The priest? By the Devil's hairy unholy balls, why would he do that?'

'I don't know, seigneur. But I know that he has done it. Saw it with my own eyes, I did.'

Gilles lifted him by the arms and threw him on the bed. 'There, boy, there's your feather bed. Make him comfortable, steward, for he has earned it. Fetch me my armour and wake my sergeant-at-arms. Tell him he has work to do.'

'What about my horse?' Loup said.

Gilles stared at him. 'I'll take you to Normandy to be my little shadow there. If you do me the same kind of service as you have done me here, then one day you shall have a horse.' He shook his head. 'When your balls drop, lad, they'll hear them clang in Constantinople.' He turned to his steward. 'Hurry! I have work to do!'

CII

A BLIZZARD SWEPT in from the *causses* during the night and threw a white veil over the valley. But the dawn broke cold and blue and the glare of the snow in the bright sunlight hurt her eyes.

They were in the high passes and the way was treacherous. Philip led both horses by their halters. Fabricia, still sick from her ordeal in the prison, had to cling to her horse's withers to keep from fainting. Her body was numb with cold, even inside the bearskin cloak that Simon had given her.

The snow had obscured the path up the mountain. The world up here was silent save for the occasional jarring crash of a branch somewhere in the forest giving way under its burden of snow.

'The monastery of Montmercy is just over the ridge,' she said.

As if on cue, a fox ran across the snow with its prize, a chicken hanging limp in its jaws. 'Only one place to steal chickens from up here,' he said. The bird's blood stained the snow, claret on virgin white.

'I never thought to see you again, seigneur.'

'It would have been so easy to go back. I was tempted. I could not do it.'

'What happened in Toulouse?'

'I persuaded the Bishop I was his man. After he accepted my penance he gave me a hundred men to bring to Simon de Montfort. We parted on the best of terms, though he may not speak quite so well of me after this.'

'Your penance?'

'On my knees, bare-backed, with a penitent's cord around my neck, followed by a hundred lashes of the rod, rather meekly applied, I thought. Afterwards I was welcomed back into the loving embrace of the Church.'

'You let him beat you?'

'It was worth it. The pain was not overmuch.' Well, a slight exag-

geration, the popish bastard beat me like a dog. What it took, grovelling to that sanctimonious bastard!

He stopped, stared across the valley. In the distance he could
make out the far sentinels of the Pyrenees, the gateway to Catalonia
and safety. His horse shivered, its hoof stamping the ground.
Vapour rose from its nostrils. He had to tell her about her father
sometime. She had to know. He wondered how he would find the
words to say it.

'Fabricia,' he began, and he did not have to say more. His face
told her everything.

She put her fingers to his lips. 'Please. Don't say it.'

But he had to tell her, how much Anselm had sacrificed for her.

'He came back for you. Father Ortiz had him –'

He did not finish. He heard a sound in the woods to their left, the
jangling of a horse's bridle. He squinted against the glare of the
snow, saw a troop of riders, watching them, very still, from the treeline. What he did not see was the archer whose arrow took him full
in the middle of his chest and sent him tumbling over the edge of
the cliff into the gorge.

CIII

'Philip!'

Fabricia tumbled from her horse. But as soon as her feet touched the ground she slipped on the ice and almost went over the edge as well.

She lay on her back, stunned. She heard the clip of horses' hooves and a man laughing. They came out of the trees then, a dozen of them, all wearing hoods and cloaks. On their shields were the three blue eagles of the house of Soissons.

One of the men held a crossbow. He grinned at her. He had a broken tooth.

Gilles climbed down from his horse, giving the reins to his sergeant-at-arms. He took off his leather gauntlets and tucked them into his belt.

He crouched down. 'I know you,' he said. 'You're the mason's daughter, aren't you? If I'd had my way I'd have burned you with your damned mother. It might have saved that monk's life, but he never listened to me.'

'What are you talking about?'

'You mean you don't know? Of course, you were shut up in the prison. Didn't he tell you, your noble lover? That Spanish monk ordered your father to repair the church and somehow the old bastard persuaded him to go up the scaffold with him. As soon as Ortiz was up there he grabbed him and threw them both off it. It was an earth floor so they left quite a hollow. We burned your father's body and pounded his bones to dust, as we would with any heretic.'

Fabricia spat in his face. Her mouth was dry so it wasn't much but it pleased her to see him flinch. He slapped her hard before he wiped his face. 'Show me your hands,' he said.

Fabricia did not move. He grabbed her wrists, pulled off her gloves and stared at one hand, then the other, and then turned them over. 'Where are these wounds everyone speaks of?'

'They've gone.'

'So, it was just another story. I thought so. What about your magical healing powers? Or were they just another of your whore's tricks?' He slapped her again and stood up. He nodded towards the cliff. 'He died quicker than I had hoped. I wanted to do it myself at my own leisure. Still, honour is served.'

It was as she had dreamed. Philip was gone and now this pink-eyed monster was going to kill her too. She did not care, everyone she loved and who loved her was dead now. She would rather join them.

'Is it true that you heretics believe that all murder is wrong?'

'No matter what else you say about me, I tell you, I am no heretic.'

'Then prove it to me.' He took a dagger from his belt, held the blade under her nose, turning it in the weak sunlight, then ran it lightly across her thumb so that she could see how easily it sliced through her skin. 'Take it,' he said.

She shook her head, but he grabbed her wrist and forced it into her hand. 'Take it! Now – kill me. Prove to me that you are no heretic. A Cathar would not do it, am I right? It would be a blot on their soul. But you have just told me you are no heretic. Yet you have just cause, I ordered the men to build the fire that burned your mother and I have just killed your lover. You must hate me more than any man alive. It's true; I can see it in your eyes. So kill me and show me you are a good Christian.' He held a finger against his neck. 'Strike here. It is the best spot.'

The sergeant-at-arms fidgeted on his horse. 'Seigneur . . .'

Gilles held up a hand to silence him. 'If you cut the vein,' he said to Fabricia, 'there will be nothing anyone can do. It will be the perfect revenge. You want that, don't you?'

His eyes never left hers. He smiled and pointed again to his neck, goading her.

A part of her really wondered if she could do it. Perhaps he wonders too; that is what he is waiting for, a merest flicker of my eyes as I prepare to strike, and that will be his warning. As soon as I move he will grab my wrist and break it.

'You are thinking my men will kill you if you harm me,' he said, 'and you are right, they will. But with them it will be quick. My way, if you let me live, it will be slow. That is your choice.'

Philip would not hesitate, she thought. *Do it, do it.* Was she weak, or was she strong? It would serve nothing, change nothing, to kill him.

Do it now, she heard Philip whisper.

She dropped the knife into the snow.

'I am disappointed,' he said. 'I thought that you would at least try, if only for your lover's sake. He was your lover, wasn't he? That's why he came back for you. You, a common little slut he could have bought for two pennies anywhere. What a fool he turned out to be.'

He picked up the knife and put it back in his belt. 'You should have done it while you had the chance. Things will go very badly for you now. Very badly indeed.'

CIV

PHILIP OPENED HIS eyes to a sky the colour of grey quartz. He tried to move his head and groaned at the pain in his skull. Snow drifted on to his face. He put out his tongue to catch one or two flakes, felt the ice crystals in his beard. 'Fabricia?' he said. He remembered leading her horse by the bridle. What had happened then?

He tried to sit up and saw the arrow sticking out of his chest. He gasped and grabbed the shaft lodged in the chain mail he wore under his cloak. He snapped off the end of the feathered bolt and threw it aside.

'*Fabricia?*'

He felt his gorge rise and he turned to the side and retched. He found himself staring into an abyss. He struck out a hand to pull himself back.

He lay there, fighting back the bile. He did not dare to move. He was lying on a small ledge in a sheer rock wall. The wind stirred the ice, throwing tiny shards of it into his face.

How long have I been here? How far did I fall? He bent both his legs at the knees, testing them. Then he took a deep breath and felt a sharp pain in his back. He supposed his body was too cold to hurt badly. The real pain would come when he was warm again.

If I live to be warm again.

Well, he could not lie here much longer, he would freeze to death. He had to try and get to his feet, climb back up the cliff. He could not do that wearing his coat of mail. It had saved his life for the last time.

First he took off his heavy leather gauntlets, then he reached down to his belt and felt for his dagger. His fingers closed around the handle; they were almost frozen, he could hardly feel them. He flexed them; they felt numb and he blew on them to try and warm them. They would need to be nimble; if he dropped the knife, there would be no way out.

He moved slowly and deliberately, first cutting open his surcoat so that he could reach the ties to the hauberk. It was hard enough to get it on and off standing in the bedchamber of his castle with his steward and another servant to help him; doing it here, flat on his back, seemed an impossible task.

He sat up slowly, his head spinning, and found a crack in the rock. He hooked the fingers of his left hand into it and clung on till the dizziness had passed.

He reached behind him with the knife, found the bottom strap with his left hand and sawed at it with the blade of the knife.

There was another cord at the nape of the neck and he sliced through it. Now there was just one more tie, in the middle of his back, and he knew that would be the hardest to cut. But as he reached behind his frozen fingers caught on the torn edge of the surcoat and he dropped the knife. Oh, God's blood!

He thought it was over for him. He heard the dagger clatter on to the rock. He fumbled blindly for it, sure that it had slipped over the edge.

No, it was still there.

His fingers closed thankfully around the handle. 'If you drop it this time, you're a dead man,' he told himself.

He found the tie in the middle of his back, sawed through it with exaggerated care.

Now to try and get the hauberk off.

The wind gusted and he waited until it eased. He breathed on his fingers before reaching up again for his handhold in the cliff, closing his eyes against a wave of vertigo. *Keep your eyes on the ledge. Don't look to the side.*

He placed the dagger between his knees next to his sword.

He tried to wriggle out of the hauberk but it was too tight and too heavy. He would have to stand up to do it. He found another handhold on the cliff face and pulled himself forward so that he could turn towards the rock and steady himself on his left knee. Then he hauled himself up to his feet, so that his face was against the rock.

From here he found he could reach up and touch the very lip of the cliff. He must have fallen only a little more than his own height, toppling backwards on to a fracture in the rock; this lip of limestone and the encroachment of *garrigue* must have prevented him rolling further.

He braced his forehead against the frozen stone and lifted his right hand to his left shoulder, tugging at his armour. He could not pull too hard in case he lost his balance. He wrestled with the sleeve, freeing it by inches. If he could get one arm out then the other would be easier.

The wind bit into him.

Once the chain mail was off he would have to act quickly; as heavy and cumbersome as it was, it at least afforded him some protection from the cold.

He pulled his left arm free, then started to work the right shoulder. His fingers slipped on the icy rock and he almost fell. He clawed for another handhold.

Be patient, Philip.

Finally he manoeuvred his other arm free and the coat of mail fell at his feet. Immediately he felt much lighter and much colder. He would have to move quickly now or he would soon freeze to death.

Bracing himself against the rock he hooked his toe into his sword belt, brought it up with his boot to knee height and then grabbed it one-handed. He looped sword and belt over his shoulder.

It was not far to climb but the icy rock and the shivering of his limbs would make it more difficult. He reached up, found a hand-hold and pulled. The world started to spin. No good. He lowered himself down again on to the ledge.

'Fabricia!'

No answer. Was she dead?

He inched along the ledge searching for another handhold. He slid his fingers into a crack in the rock, scooped out the snow and braced himself for another effort. He jammed his boot into the rock and hauled. The fingers of his left hand found another fracture.

He pulled himself upwards, saw the tops of trees, and a skein of smoke from higher up the valley. But then he felt his fingers slipping, and he yelled as his shinbone cracked on the rock. God's bones!

He was going to fall.

CV

WHAT MUST I do? Simon prayed, on his knees. *I can no longer depend upon those things I once believed in. Everything that was solid has melted away.*

He heard shouting from above, the ring of hooves on the cobblestones as a squadron of horsemen galloped into the citadel. He supposed this was Gilles at last returned. He steeled himself.

He heard him running down the stone steps and turned in time to see the baron burst into the crypt, dripping melted snow on to the flagstones, pink eyes aflame. He had the look of a man after sex or after killing. 'On your knees again, priest? Be careful, you'll wear them out.'

'You left very suddenly during the night, seigneur. We all wondered what was amiss.'

'I had important business to attend to.'

'You caused much alarm with your departure.'

'I imagine I caused you more alarm than others.' Gilles sniffed the air. 'It still stinks of that monk down here. But then you churchmen reek every bit as much when you're alive. Is that why you burn so much incense?' He fell on to one knee. 'Father, hear my confession.'

'You insult me, then you ask for my absolution?'

'It's your job. Just get on with it.'

'I do not have my stole.' Buy yourself time, Simon thought. Find out what happened tonight. 'I shall have to fetch it.'

But Gilles sprang up again, putting a hand on Simon's chest to stop him leaving. 'You will not need your stole, Father, it is not that kind of confession. I do not need your absolution for I am sure I have done something of which God would heartily approve. The Pope himself says that killing heretics is no sin, so to what should I confess? But I shall tell you what I have done anyway. You are a priest, and you will like to hear of it.'

'I am listening, seigneur.'

'I accuse myself of killing Philip de Vercy. Not by my hand, you understand, but I gave the order for it to be done. I was in all ways merciful for the end was quicker than he deserved.'

'It is a sin to kill another Christian, both in heaven and on earth.'

'He was no Christian, although he purported to be.'

'He was commander of the crusaders sent us by the Bishop of Toulouse!'

'He was a traitor to the Bishop and to God. I found him helping a heretic to escape. Is that the action of a Christian knight?'

'You have proof of his heresy? Because if you don't, you will be damned before God and before the King of France. Philip de Vercy was not yet excommunicate so you had no right to do such a thing!'

'Your monk did not dwell on such legal niceties at Saint-Ybars. He said for me to kill everyone there and let God decide who was heretic and who was faithful. Do you remember? But I believe you have rushed too quickly to judgement. Let me tell you what else I have done, then you may be better persuaded.'

He pushed Simon back against the altar.

'The Bérenger woman. Did you see the scars on her hands? They say that from time to time she had holes there, like Christ after he was crucified. Do you believe these stories, Father?'

'I do not know what I believe.'

'They even say she made miracles, that she could heal the sick. Do you believe that also?'

'Some said she could perform miracles. She always denied it.'

Gilles's eyes went to the tapers guttering black smoke on the altar, the wax sputtering as they burned down. 'What were you praying for?'

'A man's prayers are for his own conscience.'

'Let me guess. I wonder if you were not praying for your own soul? I know what you did, priest! I know you went to the prison and bribed my guard, I know you released Father Ortiz's prisoner and that you conspired with Philip de Vercy to do it. I know you arranged for two horses to be ready for him to escape. All I do not know is why.'

Simon said nothing. So he had killed Philip; but what he done with Fabricia?

'What kind of a priest are you? I have wondered about you from the beginning. There is something about you that troubles me but I cannot work out what it is. Will you tell me?'

'What did you do to the Bérenger girl?'

'Ah, her! Did you see what her father did to the monk? That was the Devil's work if ever I saw it. A man can be consigned to hell for self-harm, but imagine how it must go for a man who murders another at the same time. And a priest into the bargain! What is the punishment for that, do you think? Is there a worse place than hell, with even sterner tortures, for such a man?'

'What did you do with her?'

'What should a Christian knight do with a sorceress, the spawn of a man like that? She should pay for the sins of the father, do you not think?'

Seeing the look on Simon's face, he leaned forward and whispered in the priest's ear exactly what he had done, to the closest detail.

*

Philip scrambled for a foothold, taking the strain on his arms. His fingers were numb and almost useless. He could not hold on much longer, he felt the strength in his arms failing him.

He looked down, found a crack in the rock, jammed his boot in there. His knee was bent now; it would give him just enough leverage to swing up again.

He hauled himself up, searched for another foothold, felt something solid beneath his other boot, and steeled himself for a final effort. He reached up with his right hand and groped blindly for something to hold on to, anything that was not slippery with ice. He even used his chin.

He felt himself slipping back towards the edge.

His shin scraped down the rock, then his fingertips, his fingernails; he clawed at something solid and kicked out again, got one knee over the edge of the cliff and crawled on his belly over the lip and lay grunting with exhaustion in the snow.

Finally, he opened his eyes and looked at his hands. He had lost almost all the fingernails on his right hand, but he was so cold he could hardly feel anything. He stared at them, fascinated. How could he do so much damage and be ignorant of it? Slow black blood oozed.

He rolled on to his knees. 'Fabricia?'

His vision would not clear and what he could see did not make sense. He tried to get to his feet and stumbled. He went down, got up again.

'Fabricia?'

And then he saw her. He rocked back on his heels and moaned. 'No,' he said.

CVI

'**N**o!' Simon said.

Gilles smiled. 'Do you not think it a perfect retribution?'

Simon reached behind him, and his fingers closed around the heavy copper cross on the altar. He swung it at Gilles's head.

Such unanticipated violence took them both by surprise. The point of the transept hit him in the temple, and the force drove the tip into his skull.

He went down without making a sound. He lay on his back, blood spurting rhythmically on to the flagstones. Then his legs kicked, and he was still. His eyes were still open.

Simon dropped the cross on to the floor.

He stared at the corpse for a long time. 'Well then,' he said aloud, almost to reassure himself. 'That's done then.' His legs felt weak. He sat down hard on the steps. 'I've killed him.' The enormity of it was too much to contemplate. He said it aloud again to convince himself: 'I've killed him.'

He stood up and then sat down again. He picked up the crucifix, took his time cleaning it before setting it on the altar, perfectly centred. His knees gave way. He sat back on the floor.

He had to do something, but his mind was blank. There was blood up the wall in a fine spray. There was more blood on his hands.

'You cannot stay here,' he told himself and ran up the stairs out of the crypt.

*

Gilles had crucified her on a pine tree.

They must have brought the crosspiece with them, Philip realized. No random act, then, Gilles must have planned it before he set out. Philip stumbled across the snow and fell on his knees in front of the cross, staring at the two bright stains of blood in the snow that had dripped from her hands.

She was breathing, but barely. A faint drift of vapour rose from her lips as her chest heaved in her tortured effort to inhale. She was not aware of him, and she did not open her eyes when he called her name.

'Don't die,' he said.

They had driven nails through her hands and lashed ropes around her wrists and under her arms to hold her to the cross. The Roman way to die took as much as three days, but out here in winter she would die of cold long before that.

How am I going to get her down? he thought. The crosspiece had been nailed into the trunk of the tree. He stood behind her and slammed the palm of his right hand into it. She groaned as the wood splintered into her back. Then he stood in front of her, braced his right leg against the tree and pulled as hard as he could. Finally the crosspiece came free and she slumped, whimpering, against the ropes. He felt her weight sag against him. He eased her down to her knees, then on to her back. She cried out in pain.

He slashed through the ropes that held her to the crosspiece.

Her eyes blinked open. 'Philip?'

'Don't talk. I'll get you off this thing.'

As he leaned over her the copper and garnet cross she had given him worked free of his undershirt and hung between them, mocking him. He tore it off, ripping the chain and hurling it as far as he could into the trees. He shouted an oath of murder and vengeance, listened to it echo through the mountains. Then he dropped to his knees beside her again, fighting for control.

There was no easy way. He would never be able to pull out the iron clouts, he could only pull them *through*. But her hands were so frozen he supposed the pain might not be as bad as if she were warm. He did it quickly, pulling off her right hand, then her left. She cried out each time, leaving more bright blood on the virgin snow.

He scooped her up in his arms. There was a smudge of smoke over the trees. He remembered she had told him they were close to Montmercy. He would have to hurry, before the cold killed them or the wolves came.

He carried her through the snow, promising her vengeance and life with every step.

*

Bernadette heard the chapel bell strike for terce. The resinous wood they used on the fire in the chapter house seeped a foul, oily smoke that gave out sparse heat and made her cough.

Heavy snow this early signalled a long winter, a brutal change after the relentless summer. She fretted for her charges now that she was abbess. The fate of the monastery and its little community were entirely her responsibility now; the abbess before her had succumbed to her infirmities on the last hot day of the summer.

She stared out of the window over the slate roof of the monastery, watching snow drift from the sky. She worried constantly about bandits. The war had ravaged the countryside, and now there were refugees and Aragonese outlaws wandering everywhere.

Look there! Something was moving up the valley towards them. She murmured a prayer and watched. It was not a wolf, was too large for that, but too small for a bear or a horse. It must be human then. But whoever it was they were alone and moving strangely. She ran down the stone stairs to the cloister, calling for the porteress.

She hurried to the gate, pushed the shutter aside and peered out.

'What is it?' the porteress said, clutching at the skirt of her habit with her hand as she ran.

'There's something out there. Open up!'

The porteress – Sòrre Marie – put her eye to the grate. 'But we don't know who or what it is. It could be dangerous.'

'Open the gate!' Bernadette repeated.

The snow had piled up in a drift, knee-deep. Bernadette had to clamber over it. She could see now that the stranger was a man and that he was carrying something; and the way he was staggering with his burden, he was not going to make it as far as the gate.

As a precaution Sòrre Marie went back for her stick. She placed great value on prayer and the rod.

*

When the man saw Bernadette running towards him, he fell to his knees.

He was carrying someone, she saw, a young woman. There was

ice in his beard and neither of them had cloaks; they were dressed only in their tunics. The woman's hands were bloody and her face was blue. She was clearly dead.

'Help her,' the man said.

The porteress hurried to join her abbess. She was alarmed to see that the man was carrying a sword slung across his back and she took him for a bandit. She hit him on the back of the head with her stick and he collapsed in the snow.

'Sòrre Marie, what are you doing?'

The dead woman moved. She opened her eyes, reached out a gory hand and touched the man's face. 'Thank you, seigneur,' she whispered.

'Get the others!' Bernadette told the porteress. 'Quickly! Get hot baths ready and stoke up the fire. And throw that stick away!' She bent down to cradle the woman in her arms. She was shocked to realize that she knew her.

'Fabricia,' she said.

CVII

THEY WARMED STONES by the fire and put them in her bed; and though the nuns themselves slept even through the harshest winter with just a thin woollen blanket, they piled the one bearskin they possessed on top of her, along with every spare rug they had, to try and warm her. The infirmarian made a poultice for her hands.

And then they prayed for her.

As for the man: he would only say that his name was Philip and that he believed his own wounds to be of no account. Yet for two days he could not rise from his bed without toppling over. He retched each time he moved. 'You have taken a serious blow to your head,' the infirmarian told him. 'You have a lump there as large as a chicken's egg.' His hands were badly lacerated, and she carefully removed the torn shards of his fingernails. He tolerated this without complaint.

She also discovered a livid bruise in the centre of his chest. He said he had been hit by an arrow and that his coat of mail, now discarded, had saved his life. When he knew the girl was alive, and was being cared for, he fell into a deep stupor.

There was a crucifix on the wall of the cell they put him in. The next morning the infirmarian reported that he had torn it down during the night.

When he found his balance again, he made his way to Fabricia's sickbed. She looked like a corpse, save that she was propped up with pillows. When she saw him she reached out to him with her torn hand, kissed his forehead and then closed her eyes again.

*

The abbess kept vigil by the bed with Philip. The logs on the fire were green and the room was so cold it made his teeth ache. The room was lit with tapers. A flurry of snow whipped against the shutters.

'Who are you, seigneur?' Bernadette asked him. 'You are a knight, this is obvious by your bearing, and your accent is northern. But you are not a *crosat*?'

'You are right, I have a castle and lands in the north, but they are now under interdict by the Church. So I shall leave as soon as I may. If anyone should find me here, it will cause a lot of trouble for you.'

'We have no visitors here in winter so do not disturb yourself on that account. We are forgotten here until spring. But why do you find yourself excommunicate, seigneur?'

'For doing as you are doing; helping a heretic.'

'This girl is no heretic.'

'Her mother took the Cathar rites and her father killed a priest.'

The abbess took a moment to compose herself after hearing this news. She made the sign of the cross.

'Will she be all right, do you think?' he asked her.

'The infirmarian says that the wounds in her hands are infected. It is very strange.'

'Strange?'

'When she was with us, she had sores on her hands and feet the whole time, but the wounds never putrefied then. She has also suffered very badly from her exposure to the cold. And she is skin and bone, poor girl.'

'But she will live?'

'If it is God's will.'

And I know how fickle He can be, Philip thought.

'What is worse is the violence that has been done to her spirit. I fear that even if her hands heal, there will still be a scar, deep inside. I think she will need time, long after the wounds have closed over, to recover from the tortures they have submitted her to. She will need kindness and patience and God's grace. Where will she find such gifts out there in the world?'

'I will look after her.'

'I do not think that would be wise. With respect, seigneur, you are a man of violence. What kind of peace will she ever find with you?'

'What are you saying?'

'I think she should stay here with us. The world is no place for a gentle spirit like hers. She may find true sanctuary here. Of course, this is only the opinion of a poor nun who has spent her entire life in the cloister.'

Philip reached out and placed a hand lightly on Fabricia's forehead, smoothed down a stray lock of her hair. 'I love this woman.'

'You need not convince me of that. You have saved her life. But we may display our devotion not only with our possession, but with our sacrifice. After all, you may crush a flower and keep it between the pages of a book, but then it stops being a flower. And if you are held excommunicate by the Church, where will you go that will be safe for you, let alone Fabricia? Let her go, seigneur. Yours is not the kind of life that she needs.'

She's right, Philip thought. The world I live in is no place for her. I came back for her, as I said I would, but to keep her for my own selfish desires would be wrong.

He hung his head. 'I so wished her to be my wife.'

'She is the daughter of a stonemason, inclined to mysterious wounds and visions. You are a man of war. How could that ever be?'

Philip nodded. 'I cannot leave until I know she is well again.'

'You may stay until the weather breaks. We can give you a donkey and a little food. Where will you go?'

'I have business I should attend to. As you say, sister, I am a man of violence. I have one more score to settle before I can leave the Albigeois.'

*

Take a man from his family, Simon thought, and what is left? Take away his mother, his father and his brothers; take away the right to marry and make a family of his own; what is left?

What is left is the hope of God and of heaven; what is left is the cloister and the prieu-dieu; what is left is knowing the Church is the only place you can ever really belong.

But take away the certainty of faith – what is left then? There has to be certainty. A man has to know; there can be no room for doubt. He cannot dedicate his entire life to a faith that will not finally earn him redemption.

Because if you take away God – what do you have? Two things only: the sound of your own heartbeat and a nameless, black terror.

★

The world was smothered in white. It was as if a blanket had been thrown on the earth to silence it.

He made out the black shadow of a cave at the foot of a cliff. There was no sign of habitation but that did not mean they were not there. He could feel their eyes watching him. They would have seen him coming up the valley long ago.

He hitched his horse to a tree.

He imagined that they would have found Gilles by now. He could hear the bells pealing at Montaillet, the sound carried clearly on the frozen air. The stable boy would be babbling to the soldiers about the priest's hurried departure. They would know who it was that had murdered the great lord.

'Hello!' he called. He stepped inside the cave, found the remains of a fire. He rubbed the ashes between his fingers. They were still warm.

He got down on his knees. *Be careful, you'll wear them out,* he heard Gilles mocking him.

Well, we've seen now who wore out first. The floor of the cave was gritty sand. He heard water dripping somewhere.

He spoke the words of the Our Father. He saw movement in the shadows.

There were at least six of them: men or women, it was impossible to tell as they all wore hoods. They waited until he had finished his prayer.

'What do you want here?' a man's voice growled.

'I want to join you.'

'A trick!' another hissed.

'There is no trick,' he said. He took off his cross and spat on it. Then he tossed it on the ashes of the fire. 'If it were a trick I would have soldiers with me. But as you can see, I am quite alone.'

One of the *bons òmes* came out of the shadows. 'Who are you?'

'My name is Father Simon Jorda. I am a monk of the Cistercian order at Toulouse. Or I was. I am a Christian monk no longer.'

'What do you want with us?'

'I killed a man tonight.'

'Priests kill all the time,' another voice said from the shadows. 'They call it holy.'

'This one was a Christian knight and I did it because he killed a *crezen*. So to whom shall I go to for my absolution now?'

'Because you no longer wish to be a priest does not mean you are ready for the *consolamentum*.'

'I know what you believe. I think, perhaps, that I am ready to believe it also.'

One of the *bons òmes* crouched down on the other side of the cold fire. 'You know what your people do to us when they catch us? No doubt you have witnessed it first hand. Are you ready to die that way? And it will be much worse for you if you convert to our religion. They will hate you even more than they hate us.'

'I am looking for God. Help me.'

One of the other *bons òmes* came over. 'Can we trust him?'

'Of course we can. He is right, if he wanted us dead he would have brought soldiers with him.' He turned back to Simon. 'Do you understand what you are about to do? Are you ready to step into the flames?'

'My brother,' Simon said, 'it feels as if I am about to step out of them.'

CVIII

THE ROOM WAS lit by just a few tallow candles, and the black smoke hung heavy in the air. Fabricia, her hands wrapped in linen bandages, wanted to reach for him but he stood two paces back from her bed, as if he was already gone.

The chapel bell rang for vespers. Philip heard the novices hurry across the cloister below to the chapter house.

'How did they know?' she said. 'Did Father Jorda tell them?'

He shook his head. 'Not the priest. It was the boy, Loup.'

Her eyes blinked slowly. 'So what will we do now?'

'They think we are dead, so we are safe, for now.'

'I don't want to stay here. I want to go to Catalonia. I want to forget this place and everything that has happened. Do you still have the cross?'

The cross! He would never find it now. 'You should stay here, get your strength back.'

There was a silence. He could hear the wax sizzling in the candles. Fabricia closed her eyes.

'You should stay here,' he repeated.

'But what about you?'

'I have business to attend to. There is something I must do before I leave the Pays d'Oc.'

'No, please, seigneur. Let it be.'

'I cannot.'

'You have no horse, no armour, no men. He is in a fortress surrounded by soldiers and by snow.'

'I will find a way. I cannot rest until what he did to you and to my squire is avenged.'

There were tears on her face. Under the bandages her hands were encased in the poultices the infirmarian had put on to draw out the infection, but she was able to wipe them away with her thumb. 'We could have a new life, both of us.'

He thought about what Bernadette had said to him. Yes, but what kind of life would that be for you? he thought.

'If you leave here, seigneur, I will never see you again. We both know this. They will kill you. Do you remember the prayer you made, for us to be together? Well, God has given you your miracle. He has answered you. But He has put a price on His gift, and it is that you must give up your vengeance.'

'Should I just forget what he did to Renaut? How can I ever know happiness when I also know that man is still alive?'

'You will be happy because you are happy. You will be happy because you will just forget about him, knowing he cannot harm you more. If remembering means that it makes you unhappy, then happiness is forgetting. That is what I am asking you to do. Forget, for our sake.'

'I may have given up my title and my lands but I cannot give up the code I live by. I cannot give up my honour. You know what I am. But should you stay with me, you would come to hate what I am.'

She did not say anything for a long time. He heard the fat from the candle sizzle on the cold stone of the windowsill.

'You said to me once that when I laid my hands on people, it gave them hope. You said it was not just the healing, that it showed them God had not abandoned them. You said that what I did mattered a great deal.'

'Yes, and I still believe that.'

'But I surrendered that gift; I did it for you, because I wanted you so badly. But what a cost, seigneur, not just to me, but to all those who came to me looking for hope. When I chose you, I chose against them. I turned my back on Bernart and Father Marty and everyone like them.'

'That was not the choice.'

'Wasn't it? From our first night together my hands and my feet stopped bleeding. What does it mean?'

'I don't know what it means. No one does.'

'What if I said that is God's bargain? That I might help others, but in return I must suffer for it. I gave up the gift not because of the pain in my hands but because I would not give up you. What do you say to that?'

'It is for the best,' he said, choking on the words. She closed her eyes.

'You do not truly believe that and neither do I.' Philip kissed her on the cheek.

'My father took his revenge,' she said. 'But you know, if the priest who murdered my mother was at this very moment eating roast pheasant round a warm fire with all the world's jewels laid at his feet, I would say yes, let him drink the best wines and wear the finest silks. Whatever pleases him, as long as I can have my father back. What good is revenge when you lose everything you love?'

'I have given up everything that made me a knight. If I give up my honour as well, I fear there will be nothing left.'

'If there is nothing left, then start again, be something that you have never been.'

'I am a knight. I do not know how to be anything else. This is the only way. You will never find peace in the world I live in.'

'Then I must bid you farewell and Godspeed, seigneur. Know that I will love you until my dying breath and hope that you shall never regret what you are about to do.'

She turned her face to the wall. Philip hesitated, then turned and went out, shutting the door to the cell softly behind him.

*

There was a sheen of ice on the cobblestones and the cold was so deep it hurt to breathe. He loaded the mule. Bernadette watched him as he tightened the straps.

'What do you plan to do?' she said.

'I'll head for Cabaret. Trencavel's soldiers are still holding out there, and they will help me.'

'Is that how you plan to take your revenge?'

'As Fabricia has pointed out to me, I cannot do it by myself.'

'How do you know they will not butcher you on sight?'

Philip reached into his tunic and took out a Trencavel pennant. 'I will show them this. Besides, there will be soldiers there from Montaillet who will remember me.'

'She says she does not want you to go.'

'But as you said to me, sister, if I take her with me, she will never find any peace. I am a man of war. She would ask me to forego my vengeance on the man who tortured my squire, and knowing that I should never find peace either. You are right, there is nothing to be done.'

'Yes, I believe it is better for her to stay here. The world is not the place for a spirit such as hers.'

He picked up the donkey's reins. The abbess barred the way. 'Don't go back to Montaillet, for the sake of your own soul. Violence will never bring you peace.'

'You hide away from the world up here. It is easier to be charitable when the world is not with you.'

'Will you not put down your sword and fall to your prayers?'

'Prayers will not protect you or me from those who wish to destroy us. When we bow our heads it just makes it easier to chop them off.'

'And if you live as your enemy lives, one day you will not be able to distinguish between him and you.'

'Thank you for your kindness. It is true I do not agree with much that you say but I wish I were more like you. Look after her for me.' He went past her but paused at the stable door. 'Do you think . . . these wounds she had before on her hands and her feet . . . you saw them?'

'Of course. They were a constant trial to her as a novice, and several times I saw them unbound.'

'What did you think? Were they real – or is she afflicted with some kind of madness?'

Bernadette sighed. 'I truly believe Fabricia to be a good soul, as pure from sin as it is possible for a mortal woman to be. But I cannot believe these things, Philip, as much as I might want to. She is not like you or I, but that does not make her a saint.'

Philip nodded and led the mule across the cloister towards the open gate.

CIX

Look at this rabble, Martín Navarese thought. They were good fighting men once. Now they look like vagabonds. The *crosatz* had taken away their armour and their weapons at Montaillet and the next day half the men had slipped away, headed for the lowlands or back to Catalonia.

Soon afterwards they had attacked a crusader patrol in the forest, six well-armed men, and themselves armed only with staves and their bare hands. It was an act born of desperation and most of the men he had left had died that day. But they had won. They took the crusader weapons and ate the crusader horses.

However, the winter had left them hungry and homeless and now he had only seven men left. They would have to wait until spring to find employment again, with the *crosatz* or with the Cathars. Until then they would have to find a way to survive.

They crouched in the treeline watching the smoke rise from the monastery's chapter house. 'That is where we will stay until the snow melts,' Martín said.

'Women and food,' one of them said. 'A long time since I've had either.'

'They'll see us coming,' another protested.

'We could have written them a long salutation on vellum, telling them of our plans and despatched it on All Souls' Day,' Martín said. 'It would have made no difference. There's nothing they can do to stop us. It's just a bunch of women.'

'There's a wall.'

'High enough to keep out wolves and angry dwarves,' Martín said and the others laughed. 'Juan here is the tallest. He'll shin over it and open the gate for us.'

They set off through the snow. The men were all Catholic and some were nervous about pillaging a monastery. But Martín was still their commander and he had got them this far. Besides, they were all in it together. None could back out now.

*

His breath froze on the air. He walked slowly, head bowed to the wind, replaying the conversation with Fabricia over and over in his head.

If you leave here, seigneur, I will never see you again. We both know this. They will kill you. Do you remember the prayer you made, for us to be together? Well, God has given you your miracle, He has answered you. But He has put a price on His gift, and it is that you must give up your vengeance.

Something caught his eye, glinting from the branch of a fir, crusted with ice. It was the cross he had torn from her throat when he took her down from the tree. This was the place where Gilles had crucified her.

It should be lost, buried beneath a drift of snow. Somehow it had tangled here in the branches. He reached out and tore it free. What do you want of me? he thought. I truly cannot divine your purpose.

You said to me once that when I laid my hands on people, it gave them hope. You said it was not just the healing, that it showed them God had not abandoned them.

She had sacrificed all she believed in for him. Why could he not do the same for her? Sòrre Bernadette might think he should give her up, but she had lived all her life in a cloister. What did she really know of men and women? He weighed the cross in his fist. Whatever plan there was to this life, he was sure now that no one truly understood it; not the priests, not even the heretics. He put the chain around his neck and resolved anew. He turned the mule around and headed back the way he had come. Hope then, just not the way he had planned it.

*

Juan leaped the wall, but as he clambered down the other side he surprised the porteress coming the other way. The old nun screamed and ran for the chapter house but Juan grabbed her from behind and put a hand over her mouth to silence her. He hesitated, unsure what to do next. The old lady continued to struggle so he took out his knife and cut her throat.

Then he opened the gate.

When Martín saw what he had done, he cuffed the boy. 'Now we'll have to kill all of them, you idiot,' he said. He knew what the punishment was for killing nuns; they could not afford to leave any of them alive now.

They ran into the cellar to look for food. They were disappointed; there were only some stale loaves of bread, a little honey and scarcely any meat. Then Martín heard screams. Someone had found the porteress's body. He sent two men to deal with it.

He led the rest into the chapel. Was this all the gold they had? One of the nuns was ringing the chapel bell, sounding the alarm. Martín sent two more men to silence her and went out, the rest following. Hardly any food, little gold. He wouldn't mind betting the women were all ugly too.

'There must be one good enough for fucking,' Juan said.

'Don't bet on it,' Martín said. 'Why do you think they're nuns?'

C X

PHILIP WATCHED THE two men leave the chapel. There must be something about killing nuns that makes even a professional nervous, he thought. One of them looked back as if he had forgotten something. 'From what I hear, they are not really nuns,' he said to his comrade. 'Most of them are heretics. Killing heretics is not a sin.'

In Paris you would be hanged, drawn and quartered for killing a nun; in heaven the punishment would be infinitely worse. These two clods had followed orders and now they were racked with guilt.

Well, they wouldn't have to suffer their consciences too much longer. He swung out from behind the pillar and killed the first with a single strike, slicing upwards with the edge of the sword at the man's neck. The other stared at him, so astonished that he did not react, a spectator at his own despatch. When it was done Philip turned and listened. He could hear shouts from the cellar and the stables. How many of them were there?

There had been fifty under Navarese's command at Montaillet. They had lost half their number during the siege. How many had survived outside the fortress, or had deserted?

He dragged the two bodies inside the church. He saw the nun they had murdered, still shocked at the ease with which some men killed defenceless women. 'No one will mourn you,' he told the dead Spaniard before dropping him on the flagstones.

He ran across the courtyard to the cellar.

'There's no fucking fresh meat,' he heard one of the routiers saying. 'Just some salted pork.'

'Is this all they have to get them through winter?'

'There's some honey and goat's cheese. And garlic. We could grow fat on garlic!' The man rummaging among the hessian sacks did not hear him. He looked around only at the last moment, perhaps thinking it was one of his comrades come to help. Philip again went for the neck, one swift downward slash, bloody and quick.

But his accomplice was on the other side of the cellar and could not be despatched so easily. Philip had to leap over the vegetables lying about the floor and by the time he reached him the man had drawn his sword and shouted the alarm.

The routier slashed at him. Philip easily sidestepped the stroke and brought up his own sword in a low swinging arc that lay the man open. He clutched at his belly and Philip slashed again with his sword and moments later the man lay dead on the floor.

He ran up the steps. He could hear screams coming from the stables.

Until now surprise had lent him the advantage. But if there were many more of Martín's mercenaries inside the walls he would be overpowered. He could not let that happen. Where were Fabricia and the others? He supposed they were hiding in the chapter house. He had to stop these bastards before they got there. In almost every battle he had fought he had brought with him some advantage, either in armour or in training. But these men were mercenaries, professionals; he would have to be quick and ruthless if he was to succeed.

＊

They had Bernadette on the floor of the stable, her habit and wimple off, her shift around her hips. They had posted no guard; Martín was taking his pleasure with her and the other three were watching him and shouting encouragement. Philip watched from the doorway. Just four of them, then. With speed and good fortune, he might succeed.

He took off his cloak, as it would hinder his movement. Then he slipped inside the stable.

The first routier did not see him. Philip brought down his sword in a wide arc on top of his head. The man had no helmet to protect him and was dead before he hit the ground. The second routier reacted faster than the others, had his sword out and even managed to parry Philip's first blow.

Phillip's second stroke was low and did not kill the man but it slashed open his belly and put him down.

Martín was still fumbling for his weapons. His companion flew at Philip. He parried his first blow, but was thrown back against one of the stalls. The soldier pressed his advantage; he did not recognize him as a knight, perhaps thought it would be an easy kill. As he swung a second time he left himself unguarded for the counter-stroke and went down.

'You,' Martín said, astonished. 'You were at Montaillet.' He rushed him, swinging again and again. Philip backed away, tripped on one of the fallen soldiers and tumbled backwards. Martín brought his sword down, aiming at his head; Philip parried again but lost his grip on his sword. It bounced across the cobblestones.

Martín slashed again and Philip rolled to the side; the blade missed him by inches, raising sparks from the stone. But he could not find his feet and without his sword he was helpless. Martín had the point of his sword aimed at his chest and was steadying himself for the final blow.

And then Philip saw her, behind him. He knew what she would do and it seemed to him somehow worse than his own dying. Martín might take his life but this would take Fabricia's soul. 'Don't!' he screamed at her.

For a moment the Spaniard hesitated, dared one brief glance over his shoulder. Did he see Fabricia standing behind him with the knife raised? She meant to do it, that was plain.

Philip kicked out with his right leg and brought Martín crashing on to the cobbles. He jumped up and snatched the knife from Fabricia's hand and was set to fight on but there was no need. Martín Navarese died with a look of surprise on his face. His eyes, so full of fire just a moment ago, lost their focus. His sword slipped from his fingers as the blood pooled and spread under his head.

He had shattered his skull on the stones.

A sudden stillness. Bernadette was sobbing in the corner; one of Martín's soldiers was dying but taking a long time about it, kicking and crying. But the killing was over, for now. Fabricia stood quite still, her face white. She did not move, even when he put his arms about her.

'You saved my life,' he said.

'I would have killed him,' she said. It was true. He had seen the look on her face. The strength went out of her and she sagged in his arms.

'I should never have left you,' he said. 'I'm so sorry.' He picked her up and carried her out of the stables.

CXI

IN THE DEVIL's perfect world, he thought, the routiers would have killed me and raped Fabricia, and then put her to death as well, at their leisure; in the Cathar world their souls would have joined God in his faraway heaven while Navarese and his bandits would have returned to the Devil's rancid earth in other bodies, to do it all again.

But this time the Devil did not have his way, because his saint had chosen violence over sanctity. It was a sin to commit murder; was it also wrong to love someone so much that you would kill to save them? Priests and philosophers might argue over what she did until the sun died cold in the sky. He was glad that in the end it had not come to that, for in saving him she would have destroyed herself.

Was he condemned also for what he did at Montmercy? If so, then he should not wish to be God on the Day of Judgement, for the weighing of souls would never find a true balance. For himself, he could no longer fathom the right and the wrong of anything. He had had altogether too much of religion. If only men would forget about God and just try to be kind instead.

'There is no castle waiting for you on the other side of those mountains,' she said.

'You are my castle now. I shall seek my refuge with you and defend you with my last breath.'

He led the mule by inches down the defile. Simon Jorda would have liked to see this, he thought. A perfect vision for a Christian priest: a humble man trudging through the snow, no place to sleep and a woman behind swaying atop a mule.

'And what of you?' he went on. 'You would be better served without me now. There is no one for you to heal where we go.'

'Except you.'

'Yes, except me.' He looked back at her over his shoulder. 'I cannot promise what will happen tomorrow.'

'Then I shall make the most of this moment.' His hand was on the halter and she reached forward and laid hers on top of it. He stopped to study the way ahead, looking for the path, but it had been obliterated by new-fallen snow. She is right, he thought; for the first time there is no fortress awaiting my return. I have nothing.

We have nothing.

Except hope. A man cannot live without hope.

STIGMATA

An Historical Perspective:

THERE ARE FEW phenomena as baffling as the stigmata.
Stigmata are bodily marks corresponding to the crucifixion
wounds of Jesus. It is the plural of the Greek word *stigma*, meaning
a mark or a brand. They are primarily associated with the Roman
Catholic faith; many stigmatics are also members of religious
orders, and over 80 per cent are women.

Stigmatics exhibit some or all of the so-called 'holy wounds': to
the hands, the feet, the side (from the injury by the lance); and the
lacerations to the forehead caused by the crown of thorns. Other
reported forms include tears of blood, sweating blood or scourge
marks to the back.

Some stigmatics have bleeding that stops and starts, and many
also exhibit *inedia*; that is, the ability to live for long periods of time
with minimal food or water. Stigmatics are often also ecstatics; at
the time of receiving their wounds they are overwhelmed by their
emotions.

Some Christian theologians believe that the stigmata result from
exceptional religious devotion and the desire to associate oneself
with the suffering Christ. Indeed, no case of stigmata is known to
have occurred before the thirteenth century when the depiction of
the crucified Christ gained wider currency in Western art.

St Francis of Assisi is the first recorded stigmatic in Christian
history. His first biographer, Thomas of Celano, reported this in his
Life of St Francis in 1228:

> . . . the marks of nails began to appear in his hands and feet,
> just as he had seen them slightly earlier in the crucified man
> above him. His wrists and feet seemed to be pierced by nails,
> with the heads of the nails appearing on his wrists and on the

upper sides of his feet, the points appearing on the other side. The marks were round on the palm of each hand but elongated on the other side, and small pieces of flesh jutting out from the rest took on the appearance of the nail-ends, bent and driven back. In the same way the marks of nails were impressed on his feet and projected beyond the rest of the flesh. Moreover, his right side had a large wound as if it had been pierced with a spear, and it often bled so that his tunic and trousers were soaked with his sacred blood.

Since then, three to four hundred Christians have displayed spontaneous injuries, suggesting one or more of those sustained by Christ during the crucifixion.

One of the best-known contemporary figures is Padre Pio of Pietrelcina. He displayed stigmata on his hands and feet that were studied by several twentieth-century physicians. No diagnosis was ever offered, and no signs of infection were ever found. Two of the doctors, however, commented on the smooth edges of the wounds and the total lack of oedema. They found such a presentation utterly extraordinary, as any physician would.

Padre Pio carried the stigmata for most of his life and despite constant observation was never found to have interfered with the wounds in any way. He is also credited with notable cases of healing and was regarded as a saint by local people long before his official canonization by the Church in 2002, some thirty-five years after his death.

Other notable stigmatics include Catherine of Siena and St Rita of Cascia.

Modern researchers believe that stigmata are of hysterical origin, or are the result of unconscious self-mutilation through an abnormally high auto-suggestibility. In other words, the wounds are created by the power of the mind alone.

Bodily stigmata are not a uniquely Catholic phenomenon, however; they have been reported in the Orinoco among the Warao, in those who spend long periods of time in contemplation of their own guardian spirits.

The phenomenon has never been satisfactorily explained.